THE EMANCIPATING DEATH
OF A BORING ENGINEER

THE EMANCIPATING DEATH
OF A BORING ENGINEER

Michel Bruneau

CePages Press

CePages Press, First Edition, October 2012
2nd Printing, August 2013

Library of Congress Control Number: 2012907756

CePages Press ISBN: 978-0-9824752-6-3

Cover Design by Derek Murphy (bookcovers.creativindie.com)

For life and exquisite wines

When the past is present and the present has no future, am I lost?
If the past is present and the present is not, am I a fool?
If the past is present and the present is past, am I dead?

Zero

"My casket shall be filled to the rim with 2005 Saint-Émilion," read the funeral director, poker face.

Carmina thought he was joking—maybe some grim deadpan humor that comes with the job. She couldn't fathom how the dreary task of working with the living to serve the dead could be a dream job to anyone, so it had to be some clumsy attempt by a closet comedian to console his bereaved clients. If it was, it was in poor taste.

But he didn't budge or blink. And bereaved she wasn't.

"What does that mean?"

He didn't know anymore than her, as he had opened the sealed envelope in her presence and was reading the document for the first time. Careful not to sound arrogant, he answered, "I believe it means that the deceased wishes to have his casket filled with an excellent expensive vintage," refraining from interjecting, "and what a waste that is."

This was impossible. Her ex-husband had never been one inclined towards such exuberance—"he was a boring engineer for Christ's sake," she thought.

"Are you sure this is not a mistake? Are we are talking about Keene Mason here?"

"Indeed we are," he said, showing her the name on the file. It was.

Somehow, her ex-husband had gone nuts, she thought. Whether he busted a screw loose just before dying, or slowly developed dementia over the years, nobody told her. She hadn't heard from him for over a decade—since they separated—when the phone rang two days ago informing her that she had been named as next of kin to oversee execution of the funeral arrangements.

"Shall I continue reading?"

She nodded.

"Assuming a standard casket 84 inches long, 28 inches wide, and 23 inches tall, conservatively neglecting the thickness of the walls and space taken by the bedding, and assuming the lid line to be 6 inches from the top, 22,115 ounces of wine would be needed to fill this volume of 39,984 cubic inches. However, per Archimedes' principle, assuming my body-density to be equal to that of water—a reasonable premise as I just barely float in water—my corpse should occupy 4,272 of those cubic inches, leaving 19,789 ounces to fill. The 761 bottles of Saint-Émilion needed for this purpose are stored in my basement."

"Bloody waste, at over $50 a bottle," the funeral director mumbled to himself. He certainly planned to generously pad the box with layers of cheap bedding, allowing to discretely swipe a couple of cases of the precious nectar—as a sort of amusement tax to compensate for the unorthodox follies of such insane clients.

"Neglecting the fact that the formaldehyde, methanol, and ethanol used in embalming fluids are lighter than water, and using a specific gravity of .995 as a reasonable estimate—in absence of an hydrometer reading straight from the Saint-Émilion—the total weight of the wine and self should be 1435 pounds, to which should be added another 150 pounds for the casket. Unless the casket bearers come in weightlifter sizes, this requires special provisions."

Carmina recognized her former husband in those sentences. It was him after all. Obsessed as ever with planning, sizing, calculating the minutia. "He had to engineer the details of his funeral! Couldn't just die like everybody else," she thought, in disbelief for sure, but without animosity. True eccentrics would have left to others the aggravation of dealing with how to execute their Daliesque last wishes. But engineering and eccentricity aren't even close to being synonyms.

"The casket shall be filled with wine only after having been deposited on the pallet loader described in the attached documentation from the specialized rental agency—it's just like the ones used to load the cargo bays of airplanes, and it's fun to operate."

The otherwise impassive funeral director raised an eyebrow. He had no inclination to turn his establishment into an amusement park; he would operate the machinery with the requisite solemnity and dignity—as much as the noise from a hydraulic contraption would allow.

"To compensate for buoyancy, I have provided a diver's belt and a set of ankle and wrist weights to keep me sunk to the bottom of the coffin."

Carmina couldn't reconcile the different signals. On one hand, the predictable fanaticism about numbers; on the other, all this nonsensical talk about turning caskets into giant cocktails. As if the Keene she knew had collided with another one of mysterious origins—so fierce an impact that their DNA entangled during the crash, spawning a weird mutant, familiar yet foreign.

"Using the U.S. Department of Energy rating of 11,585 British Thermal Units (BTU) per pound for ethanol, and a percentage of alcohol of 13.5% per the Saint-Émilion's label, there will be 1.6×10^6 BTUs of energy in the casket—enough for a formidable flambé. Since computer controls designed to keep a cremation chamber operating at less than 2000°F can't cool a runaway fire, the process should start by igniting the wine surface exposed after the casket cover has been removed, letting it burn as a pool fire until the fuel is expended before starting the gas burners and proceeding with the normal cremation process. This approach will be simpler than injecting massive volumes of cold water into the cremation chamber to control its temperature."

"Why not all sing Kumbaya while roasting marshmallows over this 'pool fire' while we're at it?" wondered the funeral director, as he abhorred being told how to do his job by obnoxious amateurs. By now, he was determined to substitute cheap jug wine "boiled and bottled" in California's Central Valley and hide the crates of Saint-Émilion in his own basement.

There were other precise instructions about hermetic seals (to prevent spilling of the wine) and locks to tie down the casket lid (to resist uplift pressures acting on it due to sloshing of the liquid during moving operations), recited without conviction by the bored funeral director, but Carmina wasn't listening. Her frozen stare, as a polite mechanism to feign interest, had never fooled her ex-husband but worked just fine with the haughty director.

Lost in thought, she was confounded. She had been forced to reconnect with her former lover, against all her expectations and wishes, only to find a changed man—changed by death itself of course, as the ultimate personality alterer, but more importantly changed before death in unknown ways, with the nonsensical last wishes that masqueraded as funeral arrangements providing the only evidence of a shifted mindset. Was this entire circus just a veil of frivolity wrapped around a fundamentally unaltered and still flawed soul? Had the hardcore rational Cartesian man remained unchanged for decades just to fall into a momentary lapse of sanity? Had the boring engineer—the one who always tied his shoelaces in the same order—become an unbridled epicurean on the run? One thing for sure, he hadn't been a fanatic oenophile before—in fact, she couldn't remember ever seeing him holding a glass of wine, far less dunking in a coffin full of it. Yet, this seemed to be more than a superficial wine passion—a dilettante trying to nose-dive into a stem glass or drink straight from a decanter surely wouldn't have called for Saint-Émilion.

She felt like a gawker arriving late at a crash scene, trying to reconstruct the events just from the oil, blood stains and skid marks on the asphalt, the wrecks having already been towed away. Albeit a justified curiosity, as the victim in this case was the man with whom she shared years of marital life. Part of her wanted to find the missing pieces of the puzzle, to know it all: what happened, where did that change come from, was it deep or superficial, can people really change, can *stubborn* people really change—how about *obsessively stubborn* people—and how fast? If a compulsive engineer could find space for other loves, maybe things weren't as bleak as she thought—there might be hope after all. Yet, another side of her wanted to stay at arm's-length, physically and emotionally, and didn't care to solve all the freakish puzzles that assaulted her.

"So how many?"

"Say that again," answered Carmina as she snapped out of her absentmindedness.

"I said, by the way, how many people do you expect at the funeral?" repeated the director, overacting with manifest exasperation.

"None," she said without hesitation.

"What do you mean, none?"

"None, like zero. Nobody."

"How's that?" replied the director, offended that all his efforts would be for a bunch of no-shows.

"If he had remarried, I wouldn't be here now, would I?"

The director bobbed his head, unsure if this was a convincing argument.

"And if the new wife died leaving small children behind, you would hope that their godparents could see to this instead of pulling me from out-of-town."

"No children, no living parents or grand-parents?"

"We didn't have children and his parents died in a car accident when he was eighteen years old. His grand-parents also died young—before we started dating, so I've never met them." It crossed her mind to add that, "at least, it saved them the lethal indignity of seeing their offspring marinate like a giant pickle"—but she didn't, feeling guilty to justify their death so crudely.

"Friends and colleagues?"

"Nope. None."

That last response usually stunned whoever asked Carmina about her ex-husband. Not this time. The director just shook his head, feigning sympathy, but thought that it all made perfect sense: who would want to befriend such a weird control freak afflicted with a pathological fixation on numbers. He had met engineers before, and knew them to be fanatically meticulous, for example reading every line of contracts that others were just as pleased to dispatch—without reading—after having been shown where to sign, but this one was the worse of the bunch. In fact, he wondered how a charming lady such as Carmina could ever have fallen for an obsessed engineer who appeared to see the entire world though digital goggles. He rationalized that if such love once existed, then her former husband hadn't always been deranged; the man she wed couldn't have been the same jerk who wasted time computing the cubic inch capacity of a casket and the number of BTUs per bottle of wine. Might have been just a regular guy who had banged up his head pretty bad, long ago enough to have time to cook up his ludicrous funeral plan. But then, that wouldn't explain the total absence of friends.

"Has your ex-husband always been so... shall I say, passionate about numbers?"

"I'm afraid he has always been a consummate engineer. Very passionate about it."

The benefit of the doubt he had previously afforded her just vanished. She had to be a fool. Besides, planning such an elaborate funeral had to have taken a long time, so it couldn't just be the product of hallucinations from a recently banged head.

"Absolutely no friends? How about engineer friends? He must have had some close colleagues who would likely wish to pay their respects?"

"No."

"That's unacceptable! What's a funeral if not to bid a last farewell to your friends and those you love. A funeral is such a beautiful thing. It's like your last show on earth, with a sold-out audience of your best fans who grieve knowing that they'll never-more enjoy the pleasure of your company. It's a grand extrava-ganza in hues of solemnity and undertones of sadness. It's the last step of a grand journey, our common final destination, the grand harbor between worlds, a majestic terminal for the goodbyes to travelers departing to the unknown, leaving behind all the loved ones bathing in the consoling requiems of an inspiring fanfare."

"That's one point of view," she said, unimpressed by the melodramatic tirade.

"Then again," he thought, sorry that he got carried away, "to plain folks, it's just turning a 200-pound body into 5 pounds of ashes." Regaining his composure, and reminding himself that he should never cross that line with his clients—or expect them to share his vision—he resumed the business at hand, focusing on the platitudes of the process since that was what clients desired.

"How old was the deceased, if I may ask?"

"He had just turned 40."

"That's too young to die, and certainly way too old to leave this earth unnoticed, as if traveling incognito. You're positive that he had no friends?"

"Positive."

Feeling there was no point in beating a dead horse, he added, "Will you be there?"

"I guess I will," she ventured after a pause that betrayed an unsure sense of duty.

"So there will be an audience after all," thought the director, annoyed by the inconsistency of living people.

Even though her words hardly suggested a firm commitment, Carmina already wanted to take back her wimpy promise. She felt like a politician handicapped by an inability to comfortably lie.

What else would that devil of her ex-husband make her do against her wishes?

"Is there anything else on his list of wishes for the funeral?" she inquired.

"Uh, yes, here, one more paragraph," he said, resuming the narrative.

"For my last days on this earth, to celebrate the delightful vintages of this world, to underscore the pleasure of amazing discoveries, to cleanse all remains of a conventional life, I wish to soak in the wine-filled casket for an entire week before being cremated."

"A week?"

"It says a week."

"Why so long?"

"Don't know. The text ends there. There's a stack of penciled notes stapled to the letter," he said, flipping slowly in search of recognizable substance, "but it's just a bunch of sketches and mathematics on a strange paper," holding out the green translucent pages as another incomprehensible gimmick.

"No, sorry. I can't wait that long. I'm from out-of-town. I've got work to do. I can't come back here just for that."

"That's it!" thought the director. "To hell with that nonsense. Why even bother to fill the casket with a horrible grape juice from California's desert—as a color-matched substitute for the Saint-Émilion—if nobody will be there? The fool will just get incinerated in a dry box, like all the others." He would keep him in the fridge for a week, just in case, and then bake him and be done with it.

"I'm sorry that you will not be able to attend the final ceremony, but rest assured that we will honor, to the letter and in spirit, in its most intricate details, the wishes of your late husband for his departure to a better world." Years of training to hide emotions served him well, as he felt this was a thigh-slapper, pleased that there would be no witness to the cremation.

"I'm sorry. It's just that it would be quite a problem to come back—"

"What would you like us to do with the cremains?"

"The what?"

"The ashes."

She felt like answering, "Hell if I care. Why should they come back to me?" but believed a more politically correct response was in order.

"What am I supposed to do with them?"

"Actually, that's what I need to know from you. If you have not received instructions in that regard already, then it will be most likely addressed in the will, as part of the testator's wishes for the disposition of his estate. There are so many options, we cannot just presume. Some people request the remains to be sprinkled in parks or at sea, others want them scattered from an airplane, some want them turned into synthetic diamonds to wear as jewelry, more eccentric individuals have mixed the ashes with paint for a portrait of the deceased or with powdered colors for use into blown glass art—"

Noticing Carmina's baffled look, he had to clarify that all his clients weren't weirdos like Keene.

"—but frequently, the ashes are just kept in an urn." He refrained from adding "and, just for you, that urn could be an empty bottle of Saint-Émilion." He continued, "The attorney will provide you with this information, and then just let us know."

"Isn't the meeting with the attorney usually taking place after the cremation? I can't wait a week—"

"I am sure that he will be accommodating and pleased to meet you at the earliest convenience, understanding that you are very busy—the special circumstances and all," he concluded, as he ripped the typewritten pages apart from the handwritten notes, handing her the weird appendix of scribbling and doodles with the same contemptuous nonchalance as if she was a recycling bin.

She grabbed the manuscript and stormed out, hoping that the attorney would turn out to be a human being for a change.

"One more satisfied customer," snickered the director, obviously referring to the deceased.

LLP

Alone in the attorney's waiting room, she wondered if the firm was running a tight ship—respectful of not packing clients like cattle in noisy rooms—or just starving for business. At least, the peace and quiet was conducive to reflection.

The few hours spent perusing the pages of sketches and calculations by her former husband had left her even more perplexed. The green engineering paper provided reassuring familiarity. Its faintly visible grid lines printed on the back to guide freehand sketches at scale while remaining invisible to photocopy machines and scanners, its vertical right margin for annotations and cited references, its Cartesian layout of guiding lines to help align diagrams and support the clean layout of block letters, all designed to facilitate the uncluttered layout required for clear thinking, shouted out loud that Keene very much remained an engineer up until his last breath. Pages after pages of carefully drafted line drawings, charts, pasted bits of data photocopied from books or printed from the internet—all meticulously and logically organized in support of a final design.

Yet, beyond all the equations and figures stretched over the used and abused pages—some curled and wrinkled by vigorous erasing—the nonsensical content of it all was unsettling.

Engineered nonsense.

The silliness and insolence of engineering one's funeral—as far as a weird technological hubris of gross mortuary humor with bacchanal overtones could count as one.

She wondered what mad mind-altering disease could strike one into undertaking such idiotic planning, into pursuing such ludicrous goals. What virus or pathogen could derail a clockwork mind, desynchronize it, break it, jam it, tilt it into madness, transform it into a deranged mind fixed on the utter pursuit of a final insane design.

It then struck her.

Just a subtle detail. One that could have been forever missed, just as easily as it had been for hours already. A little detail hidden in plain view in the information block of the engineering paper: that top part of each page reserved for project identification. Even though it was formal and not intended to be discrete, she had overlooked that section of the calculation sheets that seemed to be an inconsequential running header disconnected from the technical narrative that flowed from page to page—just like the header on each page of a novel, albeit a boring novel full of equations and sketches. Beyond containing the name of the designer, the date, and a brief title to identify the calculations on the page, the right-most entry of the information block was reserved for page numbering. However, here, the pre-printed label "Page" was crossed-out and replaced by the handwritten "Day." Flipping through the pages, Carmina realized that the numbers decreased. At first, she thought that maybe he had stacked his calculation pages face up, piling each new page on top of the previous one, but she easily verified that this was not the case where long explanations ran across pages; without necessarily understanding the technical jargon, the logic of sentence structure alone provided sufficient proof to invalidate her original hypothesis. Therefore, either Keene re-arranged his pages in reversed chronology at completion of the design project, which would be hard to justify and thus unlikely, or this reversed numbering scheme was in fact a sort of countdown.

"He knew exactly when he was going to die!" flashed into her mind.

She checked. The first three pages were labeled "Day 20," others followed in similar clusters of two to five pages per day, down to "Day 10" on the last page. It all ended with a technical footnote jotted in smaller font that she had missed before; it stated: "These calculations are not covered by my liability insurance as they fall outside of my usual practice. However, sue me all you want, I'm dead."

The legal disclaimer only seemed to reinforce the legitimacy of her Eureka moment. Keene had a death clock running, counting the days before his final breath, and his work plan was set to meet that last deadline, with a typical project management rigor. However, her desire to celebrate the discovery of this piece of the puzzle was killed by the frightening conclusion that imposed itself: her ex-husband had committed suicide. It was the only way to know with certainty the day of an appointment with death.

"Dr. Lawson is ready to see you, Ms. Jewell" said the perky receptionist. "This way please."

The bland standard greeting, in spite of its cheerful delivery, reminded Carmina of the dull business at hand. Forced to shelve her inquisitive thoughts for the time being, she sprang into the attorney's office, determined to wrap things up in the time needed for a few signatures, minimizing the vapid conversations and other bits of unavoidable civilities.

Past the door's threshold, the pretentiousness of the office killed her momentum. The room reeked of what might be termed ostentatious law firm decor, with the obligatory walls of mahogany bookcases filled with dusty reference documents intended to intimidate rather than to be read, fancy wainscoting panels and hardwood floors to add an authoritative echo to all legal pronouncements, kitsch bibelots, gold-plated frames, and silver statues to display a wealth presumed synonymous with success.

"Why don't lawyers park their BMWs *in* their offices while they're at it," she thought.

Behind the monstrous modern ebony executive desk that clashed with the decor, Justin Lawson seemed out-of-place. Last in a long lineage of lawyers going as far back as the nation's birth—a proud tradition that included judges, prosecutors, defense attorneys, and a handful of crooks who more or less successfully evaded serving time—the diminutive lawyer didn't have any burning passion for a profession he would have gladly avoided if not for parental pressure. Dealing with testaments full time was his surefire strategy to escape litigation cases, and thus to keep away from lowlife criminals, cheating spouses, grating partners, aggravating neighbors, mentally disturbed offenders, and other quarreling parties fallen prey to the vicious sides of human nature. Not that he didn't have to do business with conspicuous members of that cast on a regular basis—everybody dies at some point after all—but at least, in executing wills, the "defendant" is absent and oblivious to the infighting left behind; or, at worst, is a trickster delighted to have written a will that threw oil on the fire of hostilities, or sowed discord amongst all of the inheritors. When the heirs wished to empower their fighting with lawsuits, he always gladly referred that business to his brothers, satisfied to remain a somewhat independent party. Justin recognized that the bigger financial rewards were in the bigger fights, but found the remuneration for his professional services quite adequate—certainly more than satisfactory given his frugal lifestyle as a single man.

Justin pretended to be busy writing when Carmina entered, as he always did with all his clients, to fake importance, but threw the pen down and jumped up to welcome her upon eye contact. Justin had no interest in the plastic bombshells and artificial beauties coveted by fashion magazines that his brothers liked to parade as glorified cufflinks for a while and eventually dump for the next year's model. He preferred women who radiated a mature confidence and an aura of peacefulness—in spite of the fact that these gems always ignored him—and he saw that Carmina's eyes emanated those qualities in a powerful way.

Afraid to have somewhat overreacted, Justin stuck to formal greetings, a firm hand shake, and polite business-like formulas, then sat back down and pulled the folder with Keene's will from a neat pile on the side desk—although he would have rather put on sweet music, popped open a bottle of champagne, and offered her a dozen red roses. Yet, the canons of professional ethics—"damn canons," he thought—prevented him from courting his client. To clear his mind, he repeated to himself a few times, "a lawyer should decline employment if the intensity of his personal feelings, as distinguished from a community attitude, may impair his effective representation of a prospective client."

With a presumably cleared mind, he proceeded with the task at hand.

"Ms. Jewell. I have in hand the last will of the deceased, which I have been instructed to read in your presence. Is this something for which you are disposed today?"

Carmina, with emotions and thoughts still in turmoil from having potentially unlocked the mystery of Keene's death, had entered the room in a bit of a daze, in spite of her determination to expedite the process—she didn't notice Justin's surprise and efforts to hide his infatuation.

"Yes, absolutely. That's what I'm here for. As I had mentioned to your secretary when setting up this appointment, I need to do this today. I must return to work tomorrow, and I live quite far from here."

"Sorry to hear of this additional strain on your life. May I ask what you do?" Justin slipped, thinking "Damn fool! Remember the canons. That has nothing to do with the job."

"Uh, yes. I am the Director of Placements at a group home for children with special needs."

"Special needs?"

"In this case, it means children with a generally troubled background, who sometimes require special medical, mental, or psychological assistance. My organization cares for children with problems that run the gamut of what's known to exist—you can imagine how hard we work to find loving homes for these orphans, so if you know of parents who would be willing to adopt, we can always use referrals."

"Wow. That is quite something," said Justin, thinking, "I do not have to decline employment because the intensity of my personal feelings, as distinguished from a community attitude, absolutely does not impair my effective representation of this prospective client."

After what he considered to be a touching testimony from Carmina, Justin stalled, not knowing how to return to the business at hand without sounding discourteous, and let silence fill the void.

Sensing the uncomfortable situation, Carmina suggested, "I would be most pleased to describe the particulars of our organization at some point, but I would like to first dispatch the matters that required my presence here at this time."

"Sure! Sure," snapped back Justin.

Shuffling a few documents, regaining composure, he proceeded with the perfunctory legalese required in his duty.

"I, Keene Mason, of no earthly residential attachment, being of sound and disposing mind and memory, do hereby make, publish and declare this to be my Last Will and Testament, hereby revoking all Wills and Codicils previously made by me."

"What does that mean?"

"A Codicil is a supplement or appendix."

"No, I mean, the 'of no earthly residential attachment' part."

"Oh that. That's at the deceased's request. He was adamant that he considered himself 'a citizen of the earth and of no other artificial geopolitical boundary,' to use his exact words. Who knows, in that mind set, he might have also stopped paying his income taxes... if he had lived longer that is," he added, trying to be funny, but failing miserably.

An ominous start. She wondered if her ex-husband, in extremis, had adhered to some sort of hippiedom, living the idealistic credo of "Imagine," or if he was just being facetious.

"We have taken the necessary provisions to register the will with the appropriate local and state government to ensure—"

"He would make John Lennon proud."

"Who?"

She couldn't believe he had said that. That was impossible. He appeared to be about her age. Maybe, she had just mumbled the name—made it unintelligible. Had to be it. In any event, she was in no mood to expand on that silly thought. The circumstances didn't call for such frivolities.

"Never mind. Sorry for interrupting. Please proceed."

"No problem at all. It's my duty to answer all of your questions. Please feel free to interrupt me at will—no pun intended."

The humor fell flat, and unsure of whether he should be embarrassed for not knowing who that John guy was, he returned to the more gratifying legal jargon to break the awkward silence.

"I direct that all of my legally enforceable debts, funeral expenses and estate administration expenses be paid as soon after my death as may be practicable, except that any debt or expense secured by a mortgage, pledge or similar encumbrance on property owned by me at my death need not be paid by my estate, but such property may pass subject to such mortgage, pledge..."

She couldn't latch onto any of the staccato prose, purposely convoluted to keep the uninitiated at bay. Adrift in hazy thoughts emanating from conflicting feelings that she couldn't quite identify—curiosity, discomfort, maybe charity, definitely not compassion—she debated whether she should just stand up and leave him mid-sentence, as rude as it might have been. In truth, she couldn't care less about the ashes. They might as well mix them into concrete and cast the whole thing into a park bench, a curb, or a sewer pipe—after all, wouldn't it become a grand ending for all engineers if it was discovered that human ashes enhanced the longevity of concrete?

"...hereby appoint Mr. Justin Lawson, of Lawson, Lawson, Lawson, Lawson, LLP, to be the Executor of this my last Will and

Testament. In the event he resigns, is removed from office or for any reason ceases to act as the Executor, I hereby appoint Mr. Damien Lawson as Executor of..."

She cursed the polite upbringing that kept her prisoner in the tastelessly decorated den. Without specific thoughts, she stared at the single-page will on legal-size paper, flat on the wide desk that served as a buffer to ensure deferential distance between the law and commoners. Unable to read the upside-down text, she just counted the lines that remained on the page below the blue transparent plastic ruler that Justin shifted down one line at the time to keep focused on the mundane task at hand. And then, at last, the ruler reached the signatures—apparently, all the witnesses named were hired staff from the law firm.

"So in layman's terms, what does all this mean?" she asked, waking up from the haze.

These eyes! Back from the black-and-white world of the written law, her stunning gray irises with their peppering of yellow and brown struck him like a refreshing spring breeze that again challenged the canons. Oh, he really yearned for cannons instead of canons now—big ones that could sink the outdated and contrarian slavers of the professional ethics guard.

Regaining his footing, he answered, "Frankly, it hasn't really said much up to here. Mostly boilerplate statements, referring to the Codicils for more specific details on how the deceased wishes to dispose of his tangible property and estate."

"What?" she said, softly, disheartened that the proceedings weren't over and that she would need to suffer more inane readings just to figure out where to dispatch the troublesome ashes.

"A Codicil is a supplement or appendix."

She slowly stood up.

Realizing that she wasn't just stretching, afraid of seeing her leave, Justin also stood up in a careful and respectful manner that verged on clumsy gallantry, and tried to sugarcoat the chore.

"Contrary to the legal document, the Codicil... I mean the supplementary document, is entirely written by the deceased, in his own words, without legal cluttering. It's like he's talking to you," realizing after the fact that this wasn't a particularly brilliant argument to convince an ex-wife to stay. Trying to recover, he added, nervously, "The last words to the world of someone you once must have cared for—at some point at least, even though I don't wish to presume anything about your former relationship with the deceased, and I sincerely apologize if you feel that my comments are out of line."

The deceased.

It struck her. Everyone kept using the word as if referring to an abstraction. A vague and fuzzy concept. A former human being, akin to a commodity, being systematically processed—like chemicals turned into a loaf of soap, cut into bars, nicely wrapped, all to be eventually dissolved in water. But now, at least, the bar of soap had something to say.

She wondered if this was really the reason why she had taken time off from work and traveled the distance, why she had endured the pompousness of the funeral director? Was it all a futile attempt to achieve some closure? Yet, it shouldn't really matter by now—what is there to see arriving to a concert hall after the last encore? But then, what about all the nonsense about playing submarine in red wine? Maybe hints were hidden in that other document—if not outright answers.

She sat down, slowly.

Reassured, Justin did so too, in sync. Deferentially, he announced "Lecture of the Codicil," and proceeded.

"There is no equation for death. No differential equation, no matrix manipulations, no linear algebra, no complex variables, no vector analysis, no Fourier Series, no Laplace Transform; no Bessel, Gamma, or Legendre functions. No mathematics, period. All of those tools are just useless. There's just no equation for death, so the problem can't be solved. And it's a bummer."

Justin kept an eye on Carmina, as if checking for vital signs between each sentence, at each comma, or at least checking for emotions—big ones that couldn't be missed, as he usually missed subtle clues and body language that others seem to notice easily. Even though he had read aloud personalized last wishes hundreds of times before, to bereaved audiences as well as to bored and greedy ones, he had never taken time to ponder what it might feel like to hear the last words of a dearly loved kin—or someone you at least once loved—through the voice of a perfect stranger. A stranger with a bland voice and no theatrical training to boot. And not so handsome either—he reflected in a self-deprecating way—in spite of the clean suit and tie.

Continuing.

"Engineering can only solve tangible problems; it is therefore a most unsuitable toolbox to solve death, which is as intangible as it gets. There's a lot to be said about this and many other oddities of life, but I will ramble on those matters on different pages, with a different pen. Now is the time to discuss post-death businesses.

"Contrary to fixing death, disposing of personal estate and all other tangible possessions is a quite readily solvable problem. It turns out that absolutely everything can be liquidated—as if cash could be water. So liquidate I did. It is creepy to realize that all the trinkets and assets stashed left and right over a lifetime can pile-up to quite a stack of paper money that must be dutifully disposed of upon death."

Carmina found the tone of this letter to be quite different than the one read by the funeral director—annoyingly incisive perhaps, but certainly less disjointed. She wondered if this was purposeful, to prevent a legal challenge to the statement that this was the will of a person of "sound and disposing mind and memory," or if this was a consequence of having been written at a different time, before the still-unexplained personality change. Likewise, the introduction wasn't compatible to what a person planning suicide would typically write—unless it was a ploy to dissimulate his true intentions, maybe to avoid invalidating his life insurance policies.

"For sure, there is no shortage of outlets that would be delighted to offer a nurturing home to all those colorful bills, but it would be problematic to funnel everything to any one of those competing organizations that appears on your doorstep at the last-minute—like long-lost friends suddenly cured from an acute stretch of Alzheimer's disease and burning to express their rediscovered warmest love for you. Should I shower bundles of cash onto the Society for the Prevention of Cruelty to Animals, even though I have been bitten by dogs, raccoons, squirrels, muskrats, and fishes (big ones)? Should I donate to medical research when physicians are not contributing themselves to the funding of research foundations but rather are investing their personal income into luxury cars and cruises—a different kind of bite after all? Should I shovel my cash to a university so that in exchange for naming a toilet seat in my honor they'll be able to give the football coach a raise? Should I support the arts, sports, religious organizations, farmers, politicians, used-car salesmen, fully or partly rehabilitated criminals or drug-addicts, youth, seniors, or anyone else that promises to care for humans, animals, plants, microorganisms, water, air, minerals, or rocks? And while one could argue that there can be no more noble goal that creating an endowment to support the work of unknown novelists, how could one play god and arbitrarily decide which vampire story is the most deserving of them all? Hasn't it been forever instilled in the collective mind that the best course of action is to let free market pressures dictate who dies and who survives—at the risk of everyone dying except the strongest one in the end?

"In that perspective, it is totally unambiguous and clear that the best and only possible course of action, in accordance with the rules of supply-side economics, is to reduce the total money supply, which will then directly stimulate the economy and create better conditions for everybody at once. Consequently, to meet this goal, my total liquid assets are to be bundled and burnt in a joyful bonfire."

Justin, professionally poker face, considered this no sillier than bequeathing to a dog, which happened more frequently than most would admit, but he worried about Carmina, who seemed aghast. Concerned that Keene was insensitively blunt, he debated whether to propose a break, to give Carmina a breather, to help her swallow the boldness of Keene's extravagance. However, he couldn't find the right words to make such a proposition, and in fear of offending her with an inappropriate approach, without pause, he continued reading.

"Dollar bills bundled-up into logs, soaked in kerosene, and lit afire. They should all be U.S. currency and all burned, except for $100 set aside to pay the fine prescribed in Title 18, Section 333 of the United States code, which states, 'Whoever mutilates, cuts, disfigures, perforates, unites or cements together, or does any other thing to any bank bill, draft, note, or other evidence of debt issued by any national banking association, Federal Reserve Bank, or Federal Reserve System, with intent to render such item(s) unfit to be reissued, shall be fined not more than $100 or imprisoned not more than six months, or both'—unless the judge prefers that my ashes serve time."

Carmina couldn't stand the lecturing anymore.

"This is ridiculous. Sorry Mr. Lawson, but I think I've had enough of this nonsense for a day," she said, while pushing her chair back and standing up. Justin followed suit, keeping his eyes at the level of hers.

"Nonsense, Ms. Jewell?" refraining from calling her Carmina, having not yet dared to inquire about her willingness to interact at a more casual level, and aware that this wasn't a good time to ask.

"Yes, nonsense. People might light a cigar with dollar bills for show, but nobody would set ablaze a mountain of cash. Knowing my ex-husband, there would be a few hundreds of thousands of dollars in that heap. Trust me. Part of my job is to do fund-raising, and people don't part with money easily. Even a pyromaniac would balk at turning a quarter or half million dollars into ashes. Anyone tasked with burning that dough would just stuff their pockets and run, reporting that the money was destroyed as intended."

"Technically, you are correct, Ms. Jewell. I fully agree with your assessment of human nature. But Mr. Mason has engineered a tamper-proof system to make sure his wishes can be executed. Yet, at the same time, he has also stipulated that this plan would be triggered only if the other provisions of his will are not met."

This was the first time she heard him refer to Keene as a person, rather than "the deceased." He didn't even say "my client" as lawyers often say. It felt eerie, as if death was just a veil, a curtain behind which Keene was hiding like a mischievous kid while listening to the conversation.

"Engineered?"

"Yes, engineered."

She didn't dare ask whether he meant "engineered" as in "planned," or as in "designing a contraption to do the job." Given the zany funeral arrangements, she could easily envision that Keene might have designed an apparatus, hidden at an undisclosed location beyond prying eyes, and conceived a devious scheme that would reward a poor sucker a few thousand dollars for pushing a remote-control button that, unbeknown to him, would ignite the bonfire miles away. She could just imagine him linking the spark ignition system of a barbecue grill to a laptop computer itself hooked to Wi-Fi, as if he had turned into the mad scientist of a ludicrous spy movie. But she didn't care to ask.

Hoping to appease her, without revealing the details of his client's stratagem to dispose of the cash, he re-emphasized an important nuance she seemed to be missing: "It will happen for sure, unless the other provisions stated in the Codicil are met."

"All I'm here for is to know what to do with the dust... the ashes... whatever. Apparently, I've been given responsibility..." she paused, wondering if the funeral director had in fact stated that it was her responsibility or whether she had extrapolated too far from his exact words, "...to dispose of them, in whatever goofy way I don't care to discover at this point."

Justin was puzzled by those remarks, given that a clause from page one of the will clearly bequeathed to her the cremains, to dispose of as she saw fit. He assumed that she might have been distracted when he read that clause, or simply missed that detail amidst the legal terminology, as often happens—he regarded his sliding-ruler reading technique as infallible, so he could not have accidentally skipped that sentence. However, it was best not to focus on the ashes at this time.

"I would sincerely appreciate if you could please allow me to read the other provisions of the Codicil. Here, you don't even have to sit."

Not bothering with the plastic ruler, he grabbed the document and continued reading.

"However, as life always wanes too fast, leaving insufficient time to complete some nagging unfinished business before Death bangs down the door, I too have fallen victim to this predicament. Therefore, I would readily trade all of the stupid dollar bills, herein referred to as my entire liquid assets, against the services of Ms. Jewell for a period of a few weeks to gather a few objects I need to cradle in my coffin before departing this world for good."

"A few weeks! No wait a minute here. I have responsibilities. I have a charity organization to serve, kids who depend on me. And my own problems too! I can't just drop everything to serve whoever's fancy for weeks."

She figured that the trinkets he longed for wouldn't be easy to locate, otherwise he would have gathered them himself before dying. Besides, she didn't have to rationalize this nonsense. It was not her problem. Enough was enough.

She moved towards the door, but came back, as if she needed to drive a stake into Keene's heart, to make double sure he would remain dead.

"He's about to be cremated in a week. A month-long treasure hunt to get his teddy bear or Rosebud or whatever he thinks he needs to travel to the afterlife is a few weeks too late."

"Actually not. I have been mandated to instruct the funeral director to keep the deceased immersed in his coffin for a month. That's if you agree to assist with his last wishes. Otherwise, of course, cremation will proceed in a week."

Obviously, he knew about the wine fantasy. And it was back to "the deceased" now.

"I know it sounds like an insane proposition at the outset, like this," Justin said, badly improvising a legal argument that sounded too much like a plea, "but the deceased is not as crazy at it seems. No, I mean, he's not crazy. Not at all. I, for one, found him to be quite sharp during our meetings... keenly aware of what he wanted—no pun intended."

Compelled to qualify his affirmation, he continued, "As I am sure you know, he's a very methodical person. For example, the Saint-Émilion bottles—hundreds of them; what prevents someone to swap them with a cheaper wine, or heaven forbid, something else altogether? Which is important, you know, as the body would severely decompose if it wasn't in alcohol."

The disturbing image of Keene swimming like the little worm at the bottom of a tequila bottle flashed in Carmina's mind. Justin's comments weren't helping.

"He has put in place inspection and quality control mechanisms to ensure that nobody replaces the fine wine in his coffin by cheap ones, mouth wash, or water; not trusting the funeral director, not even me—a harsh judgment maybe, but prudent measures for sure, as people are so easily bribed nowadays."

Justin wondered if that sounded like a self-inflicted indictment? He for one would not have been bribed that easily. With what? Half of the Saint-Émilion bottles? He wouldn't risk losing his professional license for so little. Money? There are plenty of more lucrative segments of the legal enterprise than rubber-stamping testaments. Anyhow, the point was to rally Carmina, not to defend his integrity.

"And among all this..."—refraining from saying "madness"—"whirlwind of activities and problems to solve, he had the good sense of calling for you to help him accomplish his most important last wishes," he added, confident of having scored a big point.

Carmina still looked skeptical, but wasn't running out of the room. The minute of silence seemed like an eternity to Justin, but he dared not say more, having run out of real arguments; he was not about to reveal his real motive for wanting to see her again.

"Why me? I'm sure someone else would be delighted to be of service."

Clearly pleased that she asked, Justin read the next paragraph: "Ms. Jewell is the only one I am willing to trust with the execution of the delicate tasks at hand. Once the tasks are completed, the money could be donated to the charity of her choice, but not used for personal purposes."

Justin had no idea why someone would so much trust an ex-partner. Couples in divorce court never pleaded that extreme trustworthiness was a cause of irreconcilable differences. Most cases in fact hinged on a breach of trust at some level. Maybe the deceased was a bit crazy after all, but he had no desire to investigate and elucidate the mysteries of their disunion. At this time, he only hoped she would seriously consider the offer—so that he could see her again, against the better judgment of all canons—but he wasn't optimistic.

"If he thinks that I can be bought, he is seriously mistaken. The type of woman he's looking for to serve his wishes walks on a different sidewalk."

"Now, Ms. Jewell, it is difficult for me to do this, but I am instructed to read the following passage of the Codicil," the one in which Justin's pessimism was anchored.

"At this point,"—here Keene departed from the formal narrative and addressed her directly for the first time—"I believe that, offended, Ms. Jewell will tell me that I am mistaken to believe that she can be bought, and that she is not a whore to serve my wishes—in so many words."

"It takes an arrogant son of a bitch to pretend knowing what I think."

Embarrassed, Justin read the following footnote in the Codicil: "Note to Mr. Lawson: Please do not be surprised if Ms. Jewell responds that it takes an arrogant son of a bitch to pretend knowing what she thinks. It should be clear that I would be the intended target of such a remark, not you."

Being caught in the crossfire of a quarreling couple, with one of the partners dead no less, Justin was dumbstruck. Before he could think of appropriate words to assuage the situation, Carmina added, "If 'the deceased' thinks he is so smart, then he can retrieve his sentimental knickknacks himself," as she briskly walked away from the desk.

Justin barely had time to add, "You have a week to think about it, you know, before the cremation takes place. Please feel free to call me should you change your—" before she slammed the door of his office.

Never had he looked so long at that door—or rather towards it, as it was more a shield keeping him at bay than a specific object of contemplation. He had been warned, so there was no point to pursue her. His professional duties were to his client, deceased as he may be, and if that paying customer wanted to enlist his hostile ex-wife to help gather and dump junk in his coffin, it was none of his business to question the judiciousness of this pursuit. If Pharaohs decreed that they'd be buried surrounded by their treasures, food, pets, and loyal servants that they believed might be needed in the afterlife, and if Chinese emperors required that queens and concubines be sacrificed and entombed with them to make the eternal journey more pleasurable, who was he to question the motives, fantasies, or phantasms of his client. He didn't know what mysterious items had to be fetched, or where they were hiding, as the envelopes containing these details were to be unsealed only in Carmina's presence—if she ever was to come back—but he trusted that they weren't the usual rubbish available on the internet that was just a credit card number away.

But would she ever come back?

Justin couldn't believe he had reached the last paragraph of the Codicil—granted it was just a second note, not to be read, it could not be avoided. He hadn't cared much initially about the outcome of the meeting, but after connecting with Carmina's eyes, he had hoped that some improvised good manners, courtesy, and plain dumb luck could avert that ending. Keene was—or had been—more experienced at predicting her behavior, most likely on the strength of a period of conjugal bliss of undetermined length, which, in hindsight, made perfect sense. This left Justin searching for some hope in the remaining numbers as he reread that last paragraph.

"Note to Mr. Lawson: At this point, Ms. Jewell should have left your office. However, please be patient. There is a 75% probability that she will call back your office within a week. After three days, this probability drops to 50%, and 10% after six days. The reliability of this assessment is approximately 95%. If no news after a week, you know what to do. In the meantime, no matter what, stick to the plan."

Group Home Office

Timmy scratched his arms until they bled. More effective than fingernails at drawing blood, he had recently started using sharp knives, wherever he found them. But he wasn't on the agenda.

"I am pleased to report that, with yesterday's signature of our last outstanding contract, all of our government grants, from local to federal agencies, have been renewed," said the vice-president of operations.

Eight-year-old Jasmine barked profanity employing a lexicon that could make a drunken sailor blush. Dispatched with assembly line predictability, her Tourette Syndrome outbursts conveniently marked time, like a perfunctory cuckoo clock with a twisted bend. But she wasn't on the agenda.

"We should all thank Frank for his sustained efforts and excellent grantsmanship for the success we have had in this regard." All hands around the conference table clapped.

Jason had stashed away, throughout the building, the various prize possessions he had temporarily swiped from unsuspecting adults charmed by his cute kid demeanor. Like an indiscriminate squirrel, he was attracted to anything that shone—jewelry or junk—and within grasp of his agile fingers. But he wasn't on the agenda.

"However, receipts from individual and corporate donations are down 25% for the year, as the recession has had a substantial negative impact on philanthropy nationwide. Combined with the fact that our government grants were only renewed at the previous year level of funding, without indexation to account for inflation, this leaves us with an important operation shortfall of nearly half a million dollars for the coming year." A few quiet gulps were heard, anticipating.

Eliza's insinuations of statutory rape tarnished the reputation of over two-dozen respectable citizens. The real biological father of her two aborted children remained unknown. But she wasn't on the agenda.

"We will have to reflect over the next few weeks on how to address this shortfall, either by curtailing operations in proportion to the budget gap, or by finding creative ways to raise the money, before our meeting with the Board five weeks from now," concluded the VP, closing his black notebook.

Anorexic Aymee, runaway Ryan, insomniac Iona, autistic Austin, bi-polar Paula, attention deficit disorder Desmond, hyper-allergic Heather, post-traumatic stress disorder Peter, crack-addict Addison, Crown Royal sponge Bob: none of that jolly bunch of bouncing regulars was on the agenda.

Pyromaniac, suicidal Sigfried was. Indirectly.

"Thanks for this report," said the president. "The last item on our agenda is the report on placements. Carmina."

"Thanks Dick. This has been a long meeting, so I'll keep my comments to a minimum. The latest numbers are in front of you in the spreadsheet I circulated earlier. The important numbers are that 200 of our kids are integrated in foster homes at this time. Average placement time is 18 months, which remains close to our prior numbers—lower than the national average for normal kids, as you know, but expected given a profile like ours."

"I hear Sig bounced back again," interrupted the vice-president of operations, always pleased to be a thorn in her foot.

She had discovered over time that the only way to shut up that annoying idiot was to lecture him, condescendingly without appearing to be.

"As you know Dick,"—both the president and vice-president were Dicks—"foster care can be challenging for foster parents dealing with troubled children. As you know, Dick, most of our kids have suffered psychological damage; many are withdrawn, immature, aggressive, difficult to reach, or outright dangerous. As you know, Dick,"—she loved to repeat those words, to remind the thorny Dick that he should have known better than to prick her—"foster placements sometimes fail in spite of the best intentions because surrogate parents simply cannot handle the demands of those children with severe medical and mental problems. Beyond all of that, Dick, you should know that Sig is quite a handful, even in normal conditions. In fact, it is quite remarkable that he remained for six months trouble-free in this last placement. However, the nice folks who have been amazingly kind and patient with him in this case lost it when Sig set their cat on fire. If you happen to know, Dick, a foster family who'd love to have a few of their cats roasted by a pyromaniacal twelve-year-old, just let me know."

"Well that's your job Carmina, not mine," replied Dick.

"Enough of that sparring lovers routine," said the president. "We're all here to serve, folks."

Carmina laughed at the duplicity of a man claiming service to be his higher motivation, given that he negotiated a salary twice above the industry average, in spite of "serving" only on a part-time basis, thanks to generous wining and dining of the Board's members on his private yacht.

"I'd like to remind you all," added the president, "that Springwell Ranch was founded specifically to help those hard-to-love kids, that it is our first and foremost mission to help the children least served by the foster care system—those kids labeled as unadoptable for all kinds of reasons and who forever languish in search of a final adopting and loving family. I remind you that our Ranch, created by a generous gift of the Richard's family estate, as you know, is here to provide, in a pastoral setting, a soothing oasis of peace for those on the absolute lowest rung of the foster care system, where the most battered and fragile human beings in the country can find the support and professional dedication needed to integrate into society as fully functional and respectful citizens. All in a secular humanistic environment free of dogmatic religious interference, per the wishes of our founding members as enshrined in our charter. Only through the exceptional devotion of our professionals and child-care specialists can we aspire to fulfill the vision of our founding members and our patrons. The challenge of ensuring continuity in the quality of our services while facing drying-up funding streams will require sustained vigilance from all of us—from our staff to our Board of Directors—to steer the ship through hard times. Of the half-million kids in the foster care system, ours deserve only the best, for obvious reasons, and the best we shall provide."

Carmina could tell he was rehearsing his speech for the next board of directors meeting.

Seeing no fawning enthusiasm around the table, Dick slightly pouted while wrapping up his thoughts.

"Bottom line, we have 200 kids in placement, a few tough eggs to place, government funding in place, and a half a million dollar hole to fill with pledges within five weeks. Next meeting in two weeks. You're all professionals, so I expect your brilliant ideas before then," said President Dick as he grabbed his notes while standing up—the usual "end of meeting" cue.

As the last two members of the management team to exit the conference room, Gertrude Frutig accosted Carmina with her usual directness.

"I didn't know Ziggy was back?"

Gertrude, director for training, was in charge of parent groups, teen mentor groups, youth advisory boards, ice cream socials, cooking competitions, holiday parties, and all other such hands-on activities designed to enhance the placement rate—for lack of enhancing the adoption rate—of the Ranch's mostly "unadoptable" children. Part of her role was also to teach them behavior expectations, etiquette rules, and successful integration techniques, to optimize their chance of a placement turning them into adoptees, even though the odds against them spoke louder than the cute tactics.

"Yes, back yesterday evening, late."

"That's upsetting."

Carmina wasn't sure if Gertrude was upset that Sig was back, or that nobody had told her. Most at the Ranch understood Gertrude's role to be a glorified social event planner. Her understanding was quite different. She saw herself as a grunt in the front line trenches where the real war of public relations played out, and at the same time as a five-star general creating stratagems to mold the manners of potential adoptees and the opinions of potential adopters—as if totally in charge of quality control, but grossly underpaid given the criticality of her mission. Worse, she thought of herself as a beacon for the kids, overinflating not only her impact on the organization's success, but her popularity rating with the kids.

"Six month was a good run for Ziggy," added Gertrude. "I thought he had a good chance this time."

"Sig."

"Uh?"

"Just saying, he prefers to be called Sig."

"Oh, come on. Ziggy's a perfect name for a cute kid like him! I'm sure he loves it."

No wonder no kids confided in her, thought Carmina. She should have known that Sigfried punched in the nose any kid who called him Ziggy, because he hated the effeminate goofy cartoon blob who had that name. Calling him Ziggy was a blatant admission that she didn't really know Sig well—or any of the other kids for that matter; that she didn't know they called her "Trudy Frutti" in her back; that, in fact, they treated her like nothing more than a distant yet jovial pep talker and ice cream dispenser.

"Maybe he's a cute kid, but a cute kid that usually attempts suicide within days after setting something on fire. We better keep our eyes open."

Gertrude shook her head, as if approving, but mostly waiting for an idea to change the topic.

"Eh, by the way, how was the funeral?"

A nosy ice cream dispenser she was. Desperate as always to be friendly.

"It wasn't a funeral—not yet at least. It was more like a few meetings to put things in order."

"In order. Hmm."

"It's complicated... Crazy ideas as to how to dispose of his estate, and things like that," she added, feeling guilty for a moment to be so purposely distant with Trudy.

"Your ex is a rich guy?"

"Not really. At least, not a millionaire—I think," remembering why she kept her distance with her. She already had said too much.

"Ooh, an almost-millionaire. Wow. Are you going to inherit all that?"

"I don't think so," Carmina said, almost indignantly. "I'm not a gold digger!"

"Well, you can't be a gold digger, you're his ex. For that matter, donating his fortune to you would be the absolute normal thing to do. The right thing to do—if he were a gentleman that is. Besides, what else is there to do?"

Carmina had decided to let the topic die on its own, right there, in the few seconds of silence that followed, but Gertrude, in excitement, answered her own question.

"He could donate his estate to the Ranch!" Gertrude exclaimed, pleased to have just found a possible solution to the current budget crisis. The veiled threat of potential furlough or layoff made during the management meeting hadn't been lost on her. In spite of her solid belief in the criticality of her work, she suspected that her essential functions weren't appreciated by all, and worried that if one director was expendable in the eyes of management, in a time of crisis, she would be first to be axed.

Carmina wasn't going to let "Trudy Frutti" rock 'n' roll her.

"That is off limits. Period. Don't even think of suggesting that to Dick," she said, remaining calm and poised, but inflecting each word with its full threatening potential.

"OK, OK. Fine. I was just trying to help. You know I wouldn't do anything against your wishes."

Trying to leave on a positive note, Carmina suggested, "We're not the only group home with financial challenges this year. I'm sure things will work out fine in the end. The kids are real. Accountants can't just delete them from their spreadsheets."

"I sure hope you're right."

"I bet so," she concluded, as they parted.

These were just reassuring words she didn't really believe. For sure, the population of abandoned and mistreated kids swelled in difficult financial times. Always had. Misery was not a new reality. Steadfast in their mission, orphanages throughout history managed such crises in their days, surviving decades and centuries of hardships, and, like them, responsible group homes and other organizations in this field nowadays surely built rainy-day funds in anticipations of hard times, to even out the ebbs and flows of the economy. However, history is also littered by irresponsible orphanages stopped in the end by legislation, bureaucracy, and at worst, their own failure to meet ethical standards, and she didn't trust Springwell Ranch's current Board and management leadership to be responsible—or particularly honest, for that matter.

As she reached her office, Carmina found Sig waiting in her executive chair, slowly spinning, kicking the surrounding table legs within reach to ensure continued propulsion. He stopped mid-revolution as soon as he saw her in the door frame, and remained silent, staring, feigning surprise and fear of having been discovered—as if it was the first time.

"Sig," she exclaimed, playing along with a false reprimanding tone.

He raised his arms, as a gangster caught by the police.

"How come you're back," she asked, as if she didn't know.

"I'm damaged goods."

She moved towards her chair. He jumped out to the couch while she settled into her chair.

"Here, the command control pod is all yours," he added.

"Damaged goods my eye."

"That's what the psycholo-chick says."

"She doesn't," she objected with conviction, having seen the file. Not in those words at least.

"I have issues, she says," he summarized, before clarifying "but it's all that girls talk about, issues, so I guess it doesn't mean anything."

"She's not a girl or a chick."

"Really? She's a dude? She's a tranny?"

"She has a graduate degree and is a woman."

"Is she old enough to adopt me then?"

"Very funny. Very very very very—"

"Don't say it! Don't say—"

"—cute!"

"Aargh! I'm dying," he said, rolling on the couch in agony.

Carmina's open door policy, according to Dick, had the drawback of delaying her work, but he tolerated it as she convinced him that it was a good way to get to know the kids, and that better knowing the kids was the secret to finding suitable compatible foster homes, and thus more successful placements. Her placement record was exceptional given the hard cases she dealt with. Yet, many regularly bounced back; it was unavoidable.

"So what's the dumb reason for setting Hello Kitty ablaze?" she asked.

"It was no stupid Kitty."

"Garfield then."

"It was a more of mix of Bucky Katt and Scratchy," argued Sig, asserting his incontestable expertise in comics.

"Sig, I don't care if it's Cat in the Hat, Catbert, Bill the Cat, or Tony the Tiger, what is it that turned you into a cat killer?"

"It's not dead. It just has shorter fur. In fact, it has a warmer personality..."

"Don't change the subject."

"It's because of the granny."

"Whose granny?"

"The lady's mother."

"What about her?"

"She came to live with them a few months ago. With her stupid cat."

"So? That happens sometimes in families. As far as I recall, they were very loving foster parents. Did that change? Wasn't there enough love for everyone to nurture and grow?"

"No, no. They were fine."

"So?"

"The granny... she was a weirdo."

"A weirdo?"

"You know, like a nice little old lady, who would give you candies and chocolates, you know, and you wouldn't think anything's wrong with her except that every chance she had, every minute she would find herself alone with me..."

"What?" asked Carmina, not sure what to expect, having already heard so many kids, stopping at that same suspension moment, complete similar sentences by dropping bombs with the most aberrant conclusions.

"Jesus."

"She'd be swearing?"

"No, she'd talk non-stop about her Jesus dude."

She just listened.

"Jesus this, and Jesus that, and if you touch this or do that, Jesus will send you to hell, and if you do this and don't touch that, Jesus will save you in heaven..."

Carmina went to great trouble to ensure that the foster families with whom she worked understood the secular mission of Springwell Ranch, and to screen out all volunteering families with a religious bent—whatever the denomination—particularly since many of the kids in the Ranch "portfolio" had a history of abuse or neglect traceable to a fanatical religious source. Sig's foster family had been thoroughly screened, but as far as she could remember, there was no grandma in the picture when that happened.

"...and then I started to get these nightmares again."

"What kind of nightmares? The same ones as before?" she asked, knowing that those nightmares had often led Sig to one of his many failed suicide attempts.

"No, no. Crazy stuff. The Jesus dude was there, whopping me up every night with his Bible. All night long. I'd wake up with bumps on my head."

"So, if I understand correctly, the crazy granny was messing up with your head during the day, and Jesus would beat you up solid at night."

"The dude whacked me with his Bible! Nonstop. I had to defend myself. So, I set fire to her Bible."

"Sig, you set fire to her cat," she corrected.

"The dumb cat's name was Bible."

That would certify the grandma as a religious nut, thought Carmina.

"Are you still having those nightmare?"

"Slept like a log yesterday. Best dreams in months. Burning Bibles and all. No nightmares."

Peacefully burning Bibles in his sleep. What more could she ask for?

"You're seeing Nancy today?"

"Yeah, I'm on the psycholo-chick's agenda. Right after the Go-Go Goth."

"She has a name too," said Carmina, knowing it would help the girl hiding in black clothes, black make-up, black everything, and who blasted Goth-metal in her ear-drums all day long, if her peers called her Goldie. Any little bit would help to encourage the shy bud buried in black to bloom into a beautiful, colorful flower.

"Go-Go Goth's cool with it. She doesn't mind."

"Doesn't mind isn't good enough for me. Doesn't mind doesn't mean enjoy."

"You have high standards Miss J."

"Does Goldie call you Ziggy?"

"I wouldn't know. She doesn't talk to anyone."

Carmina, always getting trapped into such zig-zagging discussion, tried to return to the topic.

"So, besides the horror story with the grandma, what worked well with these foster parents? Anything good?"

"I think it was good. Overall. No nightmares. They gave me a really nice cell phone full of gadgets... but I lost that now. I hope I can get the same phone number with the next folks."

"Sig. You're not helping me find you a new foster family by setting people's pets on fire."

"Some families have fishes in aquariums, Miss J. That doesn't burn easy."

"Be serious. That's not funny."

"Or pet snakes. Their skin is all scales. That's got to be fireproof too."

Carmina's desk phone rang.

"Off to your appointments. I have to work," she said, as she lifted the received and waved him off. Sig left, giggling away.

Thankfully, it wasn't president Dick on the phone, but she still worried that Gertrude wouldn't be able to keep her mouth shut.

Countdown and Up

"Day 182.5. By the time you'll read this, I'll be dead. Talk about a spoiler—you already know the end, and it's a downer."

Carmina had received the letter by courier, barely 48 hours after leaving Justin Lawson's office. He had forwarded her Keene's letter, in an executive, laminated, twin pocket portfolio, inserted in a padded legal size envelope, all intended to ensure that the precious pages wouldn't be bent. Lawyers' protocol she presumed. Special touches to justify their outrageous hourly rates, most probably.

Justin's cover letter simply stated that he had been instructed to courier this document to her, without indicating its purpose or why it was delivered at this precise moment. It was very un-lawyer-like to fail to provide clear instructions, so his silence had to be imposed by Keene, as part of some silly game in which Justin was just a proxy. Carmina didn't like to be played.

"If my life was a novel, there would be no market for it. It lacks an attractive protagonist, heroic deeds, an inspirational plot line, a poignant love story, and, worse, a happy ending. No climax, no falling action, no resolution. Just a deadpan ending—in 182.5 days. Completely unsalable. The synopsis would summarize: 'An unattractive and boring engineer, living a cowardly and untroubled life, forever unloved, slowly dies like a lone candle running out of wax.' There's no redeeming, uplifting story to be squeezed from that. A novelist couldn't get worse material to work with. Even the Europeans' *cinéma vérité* with its notoriously slow pace and purposefully horrible endings—intended to display the existential-ist dreadfulness of life—requires some provocative premise to justify its existence. In my case, there's none of that.

"Yet, it's the only life I have—or had—so I probably should spend the remaining fuel in the tank wisely. But, what does one do when told 'You have six months to live'?"

She had left the portfolio on her desk for a few hours while she was away from her office, and a few more ignoring it on purpose. Her rational mind wanted to destroy it. It would have taken an instant to throw it into the shredder, to burn it in the garbage pail, to feed it to goats, or to turn it into fertilizer. Yet it stayed on her desk nearly all day. She left, returned, left, returned, ignored it, debated, wondered. Her emotional mind concluded that she should at least peek at the first page—just in case it contained something important. Unfortunately, when she reached the "six months to live" statement, she became captive.

She didn't care for all of Keene's rambling, but had to know the cause of his death. She wanted to know. Needed to know. "He just died" is never enough. Never. That leaves a thirst unquenched. The end always needs an explanation, a storyline, a reason, a causality. Death, as a lone word, is unsatisfying. The inquisitive mind needs to know if one died mangled in an ugly car crash, or decimated by an exotic virus, or crushed by a piano falling from the third floor window, or executed during a drive-by gang shooting, or flattened on rocks when a parachute failed to open, or drowned in a bathtub, or eaten alive by a shark, or blown to bits next to a suicide bomber, or electrocuted while blow-drying hair in the bathtub, or fallen by their own stupidity in some innovative way deserving of a Darwin Award (granted to commemorate those whose fatal actions contribute to improve the quality of the gene pool)—as if all deathstyles defined all lifestyles. It's death just the same, but feelings about it demand this knowledge—as if a tribunal of common sense could adjudicate that some deaths are well deserved and other unconstitutional.

As such, "six months to live" doesn't answer anything. It's just a teaser. The only thing it validated was that Keene had not committed suicide, which had become clear when he had first alluded to being out of time, and because a suicide isn't on a "six month to live" timetable.

For a moment, Carmina suspected that this letter might have been part of some unprincipled strategy to get her to agree to treasure hunt to fulfill Keene's last wishes. However, 182.5 days being exactly six months, she doubted that he would have schemed such a devious plan on the very day he learned of his fate.

It would take more than lingering doubts about Keene's motives to stop her from reading at this point.

"According to popular culture and conventional wisdom, by now I should have been experiencing the famous five stages of grief, namely: (1) denial; (2) anger; (3) bargaining; (4) depression, and; (5) acceptance. In that order, no less. Like the five stages of a rocket lifting off this earth and propelling me into the unknown of deep space. Yet, I haven't been gripped by any of those emotions.

"Turning to the internet in search of an explanation for the causes of my apparent abnormality, I discovered that that the 'grief cycle' theory was coined by a certain Dr. Elisabeth Kübler-Ross in the 1960s, based on her observations of dying people. Apparently, her concept proved to be so attractive that it was then stretched to be applied to every possible semi-catastrophic loss or mundane bad news, from unwanted pregnancies to job loss, divorces, professional championship losses, growing gambling debts, and soufflés that failed to rise.*"

The asterisk led to the footnote comment: "See Appendix A for details on the Kübler-Ross five stages of grief." As if his letter had to be organized like an engineering report, with supplementary documents attached for completeness. Carmina couldn't care less about a lecture on sociology, and tossed the stapled appendix on the end of her desk. The engineer could review all the literature he wanted; there was no solution to the thorny challenge of death. But she cared to know how her ex-husband had reacted to his anguish, prisoner of his engineering mindset. Perversely curious to know.

"However, like so many theories of the 1960's, this compelling list of grief stages sounded like a lot of mumbo-jumbo pseudo-science and feel-good, groovy new age psychology to the engineer in me. Knowing that the world wide web is a giant uncalibrated tool—as demonstrated by the botched or plain erroneous explanations of engineering principles littering cyberspace—data extracted using such an imperfect tool begs for cross-verification. Thankfully, in its vast reach that also embraces scholarly articles, the web also provides infinite opportunities to document opposing views and destroy rosy platitudes held as truisms.

"It turns out that this theory—as systematic and rigorous as it sounds—was formulated based on casual observations of the behavior of dying people. It was constructed using subjective opinions as building blocks rather than on the strength of rigorous scientific research. Not surprisingly, subsequent social science research has debunked the myth, providing all the incontestable data needed to demonstrate what skeptics knew all along.

"Amazingly though, popular culture clings to the five stages model. Maybe this is because it provides a clear and reassuring roadmap through the grieving process—a map being always so helpful when one feels completely lost, even if it is a map full of errors.

"Nonetheless, popular or not, the model doesn't work for me, because I do not deny that I will die, I have no anger, I have nothing to bargain for, and I am not depressed (at least, not to the point of paralysis). As for acceptance, I guess it depends what one is supposed to accept.

"So I am an extreme outlier point in the model's data set. Or maybe Dr. Kübler-Ross' sample group didn't include engineers."

Carmina interpreted this as bravado, hiding an immense frustration that nothing could be engineered to harness the process and control the outcome, contrary to so many forces of nature that engineers manage to exploit, channel, or ride a bit—more or less successfully. For a moment, she wondered if Keene was lecturing her, like an annoying professor who had a single student to dump on, or if he was really talking to himself, for some therapeutic purposes, searching for answers. Rereading the letter from the beginning, she verified that it was not addressed to anyone, targeted no one—at the time it was written at least. Her ego had assumed too much.

"Is this from your friend that died, Miss J.?"

Carmina jumped, startled. Seeing Sig in the doorway, she closed the portfolio.

"How did your session go?" she asked, catching her breath.

"Aah. The usual psycholo-chick stuff. What do you think about this, what are your feelings about that? You know. I told her. I just kicked a stupid cat's ass. What's the big deal? Everybody kills a dozen cows a year to pig out on burgers. Do they get sessions with the psycholo-chick for that? Nooo. But I rough-up a stupid cat—that's still alive by the way—and I get sessions to talk about my feelings."

Carmina looked at him, waiting for privacy.

"So, is this from your friend that died, Miss J.?"

"Who told you one of my friends died?"

"Everybody knows why you went away a few days ago. There's no secrets at the Ranch, you know. So, is this from him?"

"Yes it is."

"You lost a good friend there, right?"

"Everybody's death is tragic," she said, unsure of what would be the actual answer to that specific question.

"So are you in denial, or angry, or depressed or in one of the other stages?"

Had he read the letter? The portfolio had been on her desk for hours after all, and her door had been ajar all day, as always—thanks to her obsessive open door policy. It just hadn't crossed her mind to secure Keene's letter with all her important and private dossiers in the locked file cabinets.

"How do you know about that stuff?"

"Psycholo-chick."

She doubted they would have had this conversation.

"Sig, sorry to tell you, but research has proven that the five stages of grief is just a popular myth, not science."

"Oh, great. I can't wait to shove that in psycholo-chick's face."

"She has a name too, Sig."

"So are you depressed, angry, in denial? It's your friend..."

She wasn't sure how to answer. She wanted to say, "I'm not. Death is a fact of life," but wasn't sure how that would resonate with a suicidal kid. She didn't want to suggest that life is just dandy after someone you know dies. Actually, she didn't know what message was appropriate at all—that was psycholo-chick's job—but, for sure, she didn't think shoving Sig out and shutting the door would be an appropriate response either at that point.

All this confusion, for being afraid of confusing Sig.

"Can I see?"

"See what?"

"Your friend's letter."

"That's private."

"Well read it out loud then. You just bleep out the private parts."

"Bleep out?"

"You know... just go 'beeeep' over them, like on TV when people say shit or fuck or... shit or..." he stopped, realizing that he was speaking with a potty mouth across the generation gap.

She didn't reprimand him or play the "older folks" role.

"I don't think you'll find it interesting. It's got stuff you won't understand in it, and I really don't want to have to stop all the time to explain things to you."

"You won't have to. Promise."

She looked at the beginning of the next sentence, debating.

"What if I talk about the Kübler-Ross matrix?"

"I'll just close my eyes and pretend it's the noise waves make when they crash—just like when I listen to psycholo-chick."

"What's the point then?"

"It's peaceful."

"It's sleep you need, not me reading."

"It's like a lullaby. Besides, nobody ever reads me stories."

She hesitated some more. Sig could sense she was on the fence and just needed a little push to fall on the right side.

"If I don't understand, or find it boring, I'll leave. On tip-toes. You won't even notice."

She reasoned that Keene's introspection was generic enough to not really be private. The harmless wavering cogitations of an engineer, if anything.

"Fine. But don't interrupt me."

"I won't," as he jumped on the couch and laid down on it, eyes closed, with a victory smile.

A little Viking had conquered her sofa and crowbars couldn't pry him out of his newly invaded territory, but she guessed that Keene's tedious monologue would wear him out in less than a few pages. For sure, he'd either surrender the occupied land and re-treat to the frozen north, or visit Valhalla in deep sleep. Curious to see which would happen first, she resumed reading from where she had stopped before the invasion.

"So, since the existing Kübler-Ross matrix failed me," she read, checking that Sig didn't twitch, "I have developed out of necessity the 'Keene's five stages of grief' theory—even though the stages in my construct are mostly griefless, the catchy name underscores that it is intended as a rebuke to Kübler-Ross. Given that psychobabble in the hands of an engineer can be a dangerous thing, I volunteer up front the important disclaimer that my own tool has been developed based on observation of a single dying subject—an unpleasant one to boot.

"The five steps of this controversial and possibly subversive theory go as follows.

"Keene's theory Stage of Grief Number 1: Verify! Also known as the 'Never trust a single M.D.' stage.

"This is because, first and foremost, a sample of one is the average of nothing. It's an average that can't be trusted.

"Here is an analogy: Imagine a 140,000 pound heavy industrial machine, which can't be disassembled into smaller parts, and that must be moved across a concrete bridge spanning a river, from an old plant to a new one. Thousands of trucks cross that bridge every day, but their weight is limited by federal law to 80,000 pounds total, with no more than 34,000 pounds per tandem axle, and 20,000 pounds per single axle, as controlled by truck scales located along highways. The weight of the heavy machine by far exceeds all those numbers."

Carmina paused. The engineer was back, as if nothing could be understood without numbers. As if she couldn't understand without numbers.

"Why you stopped Miss J.? I didn't say a word."

"You didn't. I was just thinking."

"I understood almost everything, you know. Lots of numbers, but I think I'm with it."

"It was written by an engineer."

"Is that a good or a bad thing?"

"Neither, I guess," she said, wondering why she volunteered that information, given that it meant nothing to Sig. "It's just that engineers like numbers. Some of them, at least."

"It's cool."

This might have just meant that he didn't mind.

The subsequent paragraphs were long and full of equations, and details about loads, material strength, safety factors, probabilities, and other boring things. She browsed diagonally and summarized, pretending to read sentences formulated by Keene.

"The existing bridge may be able to carry the extreme load corresponding to the heavy industrial machine... on its own special truck... but only if multiple concrete samples were taken from the bridge and tested to establish its true strength."

"Why are you reading so slow?" asked Sig.

"To make sure I don't have to bleep anything."

Odd as this sounded, he didn't argue, so she continued. The technical stuff seemed to be over.

"Of course, as in all things in life, the larger the number of samples taken, the larger the confidence in the results—be it concrete samples, or medical diagnostics from physicians just the same. Ignoring that professionals vary in their competence would be delusional and dangerous—irrespective of profession."

Carmina wondered whether she should bleep any criticism of professionals, but concluded that Sig harbored no illusions about the adult world, and that censorship on such a mild matter was unnecessary and would only generate an unwarranted curiosity as to the cause of the bleeping, giving the impression that what followed was an intense cussing session.

"Doctors display framed diplomas on their walls, not their actual grades; they could have graduated at the bottom of the class, maybe with final marks a few notches below the passing grade but 'rounded-up' by professors wishing to avoid wasting time with endless rounds of laments and negotiations; they may have relied on team projects to survive the rigors of the educational program, riding the coattails of more competent and conflict adverse colleagues; they might have earned unofficial bonus points for their work for being good-natured, attractive, or just for sleeping with the grader; they may have graduated from the lowest-ranked program legally permitted to grant degrees, or have purchased their diploma on the internet—and they are free to still think of themselves as gods, dispensing life or death sentences on mere mortals between golf rounds. For those reasons alone—irrespective of statistical inference based on random sampling, sample estimators, confidence intervals, and even Bayesian theory—making major life-altering or life-ending decisions based on the dictates of a single M.D. is, at best, foolish. Therefore, I sought the professional opinion of three physicians, which I consider to be an absolute minimum sample size for a diagnostic of such consequences.

"Unfortunately, possibly because they rely on the same tests and technologies, and have studied the same books, they concurred in their verdict, unanimously decreeing without hesitation that imminently I had to cease to live, and that it was my civic duty to abide by the infallible wisdom and precision of medical science—heretics beware. More surprising, though, was their consistent prediction of my longevity, each one of them systematically stating that I had a grand total of six months to live—no more, no less—which is probabilistically impossible given that I met them at two week intervals from each other. As a result, just by starting the clock on the date that lies at the average time between the three consultations, I cheated death by two weeks over the initial prediction.

"Maybe it is standard procedure when announcing such tragic news to anyone, to grant them six months to live, wholesale and non-negotiable, as an incentive to embrace what's left to enjoy of a hopeless situation, or to provide the illusion that there is time to put things in order—or to leisurely pace through Kübler-Ross' bogus stages.

"Yet, even if the six month decree was an absolute fact rather than a gimmick, it would still be unfair in some ways. If one is told on January 1 that there is six months left live, that corresponds to three months with 31 days, two with 30 days, and the poor February bastard, which can't hold steady at 28 or 29 days. If one is told the same thing on July 1st, that time spans four months with 31 days. Not a huge variation in normal circumstances, but still stealing some precious time when there is none to spare.

"Being unable to squeeze any sensible precision from any of the outrageously well-paid physicians I consulted, I circled the date on the calendar 182.6213 days ahead of the day I consulted the second physician, and penned 11:25 p.m. in that square on the calendar, as the official time of my death, given that each of my three identical medical diagnoses were dispensed at 8:30 a.m. precisely two weeks apart from each other—rounding off the times a bit for good engineering measure, particularly since averaging the dates of the three different diagnoses is an arguable hypothesis without a solid statistical basis.

"So there it is, I have the luxury of knowing exactly when I will die, something few of us can aspire to."

"If your dead friend wrote this letter six months ago, how come you're just reading it now, Miss J.?"

She had forgotten about the Viking sunk deep into the sofa.

"You are a curious kid."

"I'm not a kid, I'm twelve. Why didn't you read it earlier?"

"That's private stuff."

"If my dying friend was sending me letters, I wouldn't wait to read them until after he's dead."

This made sense from a suicidal kid's perspective. She felt compelled to explain.

"He didn't send it to me until today."

"I don't believe that. Dead people don't mail letters."

"Of course not. That letter was part of his estate, and he had asked his lawyer to not send it to me until today."

"That's dumb."

Again, logical from a specific perspective, she thought.

"That's because he wasn't sure I would be receptive to it."

"He's not a good friend then."

"So you're a psycholo-dude now?"

Sig laughed, propping himself up on the couch.

"What you must understand is that the letter is not addressed to me. It's written in a generic sense, to himself, like when someone writes in a journal, and the journal is discovered after his death."

"I get it. It's cool," he stated, lying back, as a signal he was ready for more.

"Can I continue?"

"Yep."

She wondered why Sig cared about hearing this. It was utterly boring. For sure he had been deprived of bedtime reading most of his life—along with all his other misfortunes—but to the point of wanting to hear Keene's drivel?

"Keene's theory Stage of Grief Number 2: Quit non-essential activities.

"Therefore, without any regrets, I quit my job. Called my employer and just informed them of my decision without giving a reason. No 'if, but, and when,' no agreeing to come a few extra days to straighten the dossiers and ensure a smooth transition, no cleaning of my desk. All was left in place, for them to figure out. There's nothing of sentimental value for me to retrieve. That's the end there, just like a sudden death—except that I was the one conveying the news. They'll survive. I won't.

"After all, it's just work. Just work. It's hard for an engineer to say that.

"Work.

"What is it exactly? What is it worth?

"It has been solemnly praised and cursed by the greatest minds—promised to be a great calling, and damned just as well.

"Work.

"The activity by which mankind presumably defines itself. Proclaimed as the key to one's own fate. Defined as 'the object of living' by Henry Ford and other workaholic leaders of the capitalist world. Praised for its value to define character in children. Glorified as the currency of atheist proletarians, and of the elects of Calvinistic mind games alike. Pushed down from encyclicals to pulpits, preached as expressing the essential dignity of every man and woman, their moral quality and virtues—yet, simultaneously lamented as a divine punishment. Denounced as a curse from the gods by ancient philosophers. Disdained as hard, degrading, a painful drudgery, and a corrupt waste of time throughout antiquity. An unavoidable punishment to meet physical needs. Forever blamed for transcending and breaking relationships.

"Work.

"A mysterious obsession of the mind that can turn unsuspecting souls into engineers, who, when herded together, easily fall prey to slave drivers. Engineers who, even when working for themselves, being their own bosses, are at the mercy of tyrants; time ceases to exist and commitments wait at the door begging for a distraction that can resurrect reality for a moment.

"In short, work has a knack for stealing the precious time that is critical for those meditative communions with life—the type of activities in which I will likely invest more time over the next few months. No guilt there; I have already paid my dues to society, contributing barrels of sweat to the betterment of life through various engineered products. In fact, during my life—substantially shortened as it may be—I've already clocked in more hours of work than what most will have accumulated by the time they retire. How dumb is that?

"Keene's theory Stage of Grief Number 2 is a quick one to dispatch."

Carmina glanced at Sig, motionless on the couch. Most of this had to go over his head. She wondered if he was sleeping, or just listening to the words as if they were the soothing melody of a lullaby. For a moment, he was grounded in peaceful childhood again, as a twelve-year-old kid should be, but as he rarely was, hardened too fast by a harsh life that pushed him to be a teenager before his time.

She resumed reading, worried that another round of questions would be fired if she paused for too long. She felt it strange nonetheless that an engineer married to his work for a lifetime, would express doubts on its value near death. If only such doubts had arisen earlier.

"Keene's theory Stage of Grief Number 3: Don't annoy anyone with your booboos."

Sig giggled. He clearly wasn't asleep.

"The title says it all. I hereby solemnly declare that throughout my writings, for as long as they may stretch before abruptly stopping, I will not disclose at any time my specific affliction nor the causes of my predicament. No mention of my disease, its symptoms, its debilitating injuries to the body and soul, or its attempts to steer my mind away from clear thinking, will be made. No hidden clues will be cleverly buried in the text to reveal my degenerating self. I will die, and the metabolic road taking me there will remain secret.

"This will no doubt frustrate curious minds, starve their inquisitive flames burning to know. It will not satisfy the archetypal need to probe, to seek anchorage and establish a judgment, be it only as an instinctive self-protection mechanism. My apologies for this brutal and indiscriminate thwarting of both benevolent intentions and nosy invasions of privacy.

"I am too young to solicit pity or attention by parading my fatal disease on the marketplace of compassion. It would remind me too much of elders in their last resting home, telling stories about their individual health problems for lack of news from their friends and family—loved ones who have curtailed visits to the bare minimum as time for them trades on a different scale. Not so much stories as sad geriatric anecdotes, shared as an informal way to chronicle slowly deteriorating conditions, recounted by captains of many Titanics, each tracking the slow progress of the rising waters, going down with their ship because escape is not an option. These stories are the not domain of a public forum."

Carmina worried that she should have stopped reading to Sig many pages ago. The divagations of a dying man—a loner of all things—weren't exactly suitable pedagogical material for a troubled child, and she was suddenly afraid to have messed up with Sig's mind in unforeseen ways. Yet, how could she have stopped, knowing that he trusted her like a big sister, albeit a much older one—like members of a 28 child family in which the 26 between them had mysteriously disappeared. Sig trusted only a few adults at the group home, and she didn't want to risk jeopardizing that fragile bond. Best was to continue reading.

"To prevent accidental disclosure, I will not use a pen that would reveal a hand growing unsteady, or document a weakening stance in a changing typeface or lazier calligraphy. Hiding behind a keyboard, I will never reveal whether I rambled at 50 words per minute with agile fingers, or typed with my toes, or my nose, or with a stick clenched between my teeth to strike one character per minute. Nor will you ever know if I used a voice recognition system, or dictated all my nonsensical thoughts to a personal secretary whose kindness was commensurate with her salary.

"That's the deal. Nonnegotiable. Take it or leave it; because your contracting party is gone by now anyhow."

Carmina recognized there the engineer who didn't want to share his feelings. At the same time, she discerned a genuine, almost noble, desire to escape being an object of pity.

"So what did he die from?" said Sig, propping himself up.

She had again forgotten about him.

"You weren't paying attention. He just said it's a secret."

"Yeah, but that's when he wrote it. He's dead now, so you should know. Everybody knows that after the fact. That's the whole point."

She wasn't sure what he meant by that "whole point," but dared not explore that line of thinking.

"It's still a secret. Nobody told me."

"He's weird, your friend."

"A little bit, I guess," she said, repressing the image of a wine-filled casket that had just popped-back into her mind.

For a man who had no friends, Carmina wondered why the letter spoke as if addressing the world. This certainly wasn't the intimate style befitting to a diary. Yet, who knows what goes through the mind of a dying person.

"And people think I'm weird," sighed Sig, sinking back in the couch.

Carmina raised an eyebrow, but Sig wasn't paying attention. He knew he was right. Lying still, he was just waiting for the story to resume.

"Keene's theory Stage of Grief Number 4: Survey your options to fill the remaining time.

"How would I know what people do when they learn they have six months to live? It's the first time it happened to me—of course.

"Quick to make a buck, the publishing industry offers tons of books on that topic, most of them quite thin, possibly because authors writing from experience lack time to create an encyclopedia, and their readers are also in a hurry. This is not the stage of a lifetime conducive to procrastination.

"However, following a cookbook recipe on how to prepare to die is the last thing I would ever wish to do at this time. I've spent my life following recipes—national codes, international and local ones, design standards, project specifications, safety rules, regulations, typical examples, contractual requirements. Technical recipes that remove thinking from the equation, trading it for efficiency and infinite engineering boredom. So I'm not about to end my days on this earth studying another cookbook.

"Besides, I can easily imagine the list of things that are customarily done at this juncture, and all the items on that list sort themselves into the categories of going wild and crazy, going faster, going charitable, going down or going spiritual.*"

Another asterisk, another footnote, another appendix that she brushed aside, pushing it towards the one previously tossed on the desk, discretely so that Sig wouldn't notice.

"Considering all those options though, none attracts me. Turns out that, for now, I don't have a list of things to do. I only have one impossible dream: many folks who are in the same pickle have the luxury to spend their remaining time with those they love, until they reach the end-of-the-line. I won't have that chance. The only person I ever loved, and still love, isn't here. I won't disturb her either."

"He's a dumb, boring guy your friend who wants to be a pickle."

"You interrupt a lot."

"You didn't say I couldn't."

"Yes, but it's hard to follow the flow of thoughts with all these interruptions."

"It's in writing! You can just read it over and over after I'm gone."

"It would be nice to figure it out straight upon first read."

"I can't help it. He's a dumb pickle."

"How's that?"

"He loves a girl and he won't tell her 'cause he doesn't want to 'disturb' her."

"He never said anything about a girl."

"He's gay?"

"OK, maybe the girl doesn't want to be disturbed. Maybe she doesn't love him."

"Do you know her?"

"How would I know her?" she said after hesitating.

"Then he's a dumb pickle. If you want to set a dumb cat on fire, you don't ask, you just do it."

"Sig. What are you talking about?" she asked, giving him a reproachful look.

"I'm just saying. He should tell the girl."

"Have you told a girl you loved her yet?"

Sig just pouted, debating how to deflect this line of inquiry.

"There's tons of things he could do, and he can't think of one. He's a dumb pickle. He is. Six months is a long time."

To a twelve-year-old, maybe, but she kept the thought to herself. She ruffled the pages to indicate her intention to resume reading. Yet, she wondered, if the letter wasn't addressed to anyone, and Keene had no intention of disturbing "the one he loved" with it, then to whom was the letter intended?

Reading on.

"However, even though I'm not interested in any of the conventional things that people rush to do before dying, I can't just spend 4383 hours watching TV either. Dying is a once in a lifetime opportunity that must be put to good use.

"Which all leads to Keene's theory Stage of Grief Number 5: Scope out your last project. The whole point of it all. One last project, on a tight deadline—no slip in the schedule allowed.

"Makes plenty of sense.

"I'm certainly not going to sleep until I die—I've missed enough of life as it is. Life's a bitch, that's all there is, and one has to make the most of it."

There was a missed bleeping opportunity. Carmina pretended otherwise and kept going.

"But what project? One's last project can't just be a meaningless, trivial, hollow shell of a pursuit. The objective isn't to kill time, as there is no revenge against the time that slowly kills me. Good planning being at the root of any successful project, it will be worthwhile to invest a few days to decide.

"Maybe this is why I felt compelled to write in the first place. When I started this letter, I didn't know to whom it was addressed. I still don't. By reflex, there was an urge to write. Not doodle, sketch, or design. Write. Be it scribbles and scrawls or neat laser printed pages, that's still writing. And that writing imposed itself, like therapy, as a way to organize my thoughts, to translate them into pseudo-engineering calculations, as if to impose order on this whole mess.

"Having a fairly limited social network—to put it mildly—maybe this letter is intended to serve as the foundations of what could become the plans and specifications of this yet undetermined final project. Maybe this will serve as a necessary set of blueprints in case someone is to help me create a lofty swan song.

"Whatever.

"The final goal is unknown, but the means towards the goal have started to take shape."

Carmina put the pages down.

"That's it. End of letter."

"Can't be!" said Sig, jumping up to the desk before Carmina could close the folder. He stunned her by slamming his hand on the portfolio cover to prevent its closure—by stressful determination rather than aggressiveness—and read the last sentence upside down.

"Ah this sucks. He can't stop there. He was just starting to make sense."

Carmina was afraid to ask what made sense in all that nonsense. Sig didn't always make sense to her to start. Neither did Keene for that matter.

"Well, that's where it stops," she said, stating the obvious as if to underline that it was beyond her control.

She didn't want to play psychologist, but was compelled to assess if there was any return on her time investment.

"What do you think of all that?"

"I'm hungry," said Sig, as he ran out with a mischievous smile, as a savvy ploy to escape interrogation. Or he was just really hungry.

Carmina wondered if Sig would forever remain an untamable spirit, wild to the core, or if his rebellious nature was just a temporary defense mechanism, waiting for a loving adopting family to melt away all of his guarded feelings. Who knew?

A question without an answer.

She reflected instead on the turmoil of the past few days, trying to understand why her well-ordered life was being disturbed for no logical reason. If there was a reason for everything in life, then she has no idea what this all meant. Keene's open letter, its nonsensical lecture, Sig's interest. And Bible, the burning cat—which reeked of crass symbolism. All the ingredients for a bad nightmare.

Food for Thought

Beyond the turmoil of the past few days, the recent events had upset Carmina's routine in small ways too.

By far, she preferred to eat her own lunch, not so much because of the peace and comfort of her office, but rather because the Ranch's cafeteria served horrible meals prepared by cooks instructed to care only about the bottom line. Customers weren't going to walk away anyhow as there was no alternative, so the bottom line was subterraneously low.

Imagining lunches as séances of highbrow food tasting, the captive clientele, conducting mock restaurant reviews, had formulated some culinary descriptions that they fantasized should be printed on the menu for the benefit of visitors—even though the management was diligent in keeping guests away from the cafeteria.

The grilled cheese sandwich—common fare at the Ranch—was described as tasteful cardboard pieces covered by a cheap orange latex paint manufactured in China to mimic gooey cheese. The hamburger with brown gravy—another classic—became dried buns drenched in humid crap hugging a slab of charred cow remnants. The spaghetti with suspect vegetables was identified to be the chef's entrails dumped into a plate. The rice curry was dubbed a bowel movement facilitator. The vegetarian pizza was described as chunky bits of vomit cemented into an asbestos tile. And these were, by far, the best dishes offered by the establishment, all deserving at least two "Yummy Stars" out of five. It was pretty much downhill from there.

Unfortunately, Carmina hadn't brought a lunch bag that day, and although fasting was in some ways a more appealing alternative, she figured that spending time with the kids would keep the

"Keene stuff" off her mind—which she had to do to keep her sanity.

As she always did, but more deliberately this time, she walked pass the table where the Ranch's management was enjoying their own brown-bag lunches, and headed straight to the kids' table. She had rationalized that there was no better way to get to know the kids than by sharing a meal, and that this was key to providing placements with a greater chance of a successful outcome. There was no statistics to prove that placements had been more compatible as a result of her initiative, but it had been an absolutely successful excuse to keep at a distance the Dicks and their lackeys. Besides, conversations at the management table were just an endless recitation of meaningless pseudo-accomplishments by boring egos in search of admiration—an exciting conversation that she was delighted to avoid.

In all her years at the Ranch, she had never shared lunch with her colleagues, but the impetus to avoid them was stronger now that the Dicks suspected that she might have access to easy money—thanks to Gertrude's clumsy suggestion that the organization should provide incentives to encourage members of the management team to pursue special relationships with rich donors.

Around the kids' table were the usual culprits. Scratching Timmy, Tourette Jasmine, clepto Jason, insinuating Eliza, anorexic Aymee, runaway Ryan, insomniac Iona, autistic Austin, bi-polar Paula, attention deficit disorder Desmond, hyper-allergic Heather, post-traumatic stress disorder Peter, crack-addict Addison, Crown Royal sponge Bob, and pyromaniac, suicidal Sig.

"What's for lunch today?"

"Another UFO," replied Aymee, which Carmina knew to mean "Unidentified Food Object."

"Same COFFEE," added Timmy, which meant "Crap Offered Free From Easygoing Elijah." Elijah was the cafeteria's chief cook—as far from being a chef as permissible by the food safety board.

"The usual rat poison," clarified Sig.

"Try the green whatchamacallit. It's almost edible," mumbled Eliza.

Carmina got herself a plate of the green stuff and squeezed herself to sit in the middle of the pack. She didn't have time to grab her fork before Addison launched into conversation.

"I heard your friend died."

Rumors ran on steroids at the Ranch. Understandably.

"It's not her friend, stupid ass, it's just an acquaintance," corrected Jasmine, amazingly polite considering her Tourette affliction.

"What's the difference—"

"Thanks for your consideration," cut in Carmina, to defuse a fight, "but that's not something I wish to talk about."

"Why? Everybody dies someday," mumbled Eliza.

"It's a personal matter. That's all. End of story."

The lunch had already become unproductive as far as tightening her bond with the kids.

"Anything exciting happened at the Ranch while I was away?" she asked, trying to steer the conversation in a different direction.

"Why is it that if we refuse to talk about something, the psycholo-chick wants to stuff us with pills, and you can just say 'I don't want to talk about it'? It's a lie, then, that we always have to talk about the stuff that's bothering us, right?" cracked Peter.

Fifteen against one: this wasn't a fight worth picking, even though she knew he was right.

"So nothing happened while I was away then?"

"You don't want to talk about your friend?" insisted Timmy.

"Some friend he must be," guessed Heather.

"Her friend is a total wacko," said Sig.

"Is this why you built a web page about him?" teased Bob. "Because he's a loony just like you?"

"A lunatic," corrected Paula.

"A loonatic," shouted Jasmine.

"That's not even a word," sneered Sig.

"Hey, stop that," snapped Carmina. "First, I would appreciate it if you could respect my privacy."

"That's a good line. I'll try it with psycholo-chick next time," interjected Peter.

That was psycholo-chick's problem as far as Carmina was concerned.

"Second, what's this about a web page?"

"Sig wrote some weird stuff—"

"The stages of death—"

"Five levels—"

"The five steps to die—"

"Stupid idiots, it's the Keene's Five Stages of Grief," corrected Sig, cutting through the cacophony and sulking.

All the tweens stopped talking and stared at Carmina, eager for her reaction.

"Ah. I see."

She was in a bind.

"It's a web page on Keene's Five Stages of Grief," repeated Sig, as if waiting for Carmina's congratulations.

She didn't know what to do.

Sig was starved for her approval. Evidently, Keene's nutty stages of grief had so impressed him that he had felt compelled to enshrine them as a digital monument for posterity, and given Sig's excellent memory, the five stages were most certainly recounted with reasonable fidelity—she didn't need to visit the web site to be sure of that.

In some ways it was touching that he had taken such initiative, and a few compliments might have been appropriate—and would be certain to warm Sig's heart. The problem, however, was that he had violated her trust. She had shared with him the content of a very private letter and he had violated a sacred rule by posting that information on the internet without her permission. Divulging intimate secrets to the world wasn't a way for Sig to endear himself to Carmina, even though he likely had done it innocently—subconsciously—as a way to honor her.

Hence, she was angry and flattered at the same time.

The thirty eyeballs were still staring.

She felt like an intruder in a marsh, surrounded by fifteen frogs, frozen, not twitching a muscle, waiting to see if the threat could be ignored or if they should dive into the pond. This definitely wasn't going to be a great day for bonding.

She also felt cold stares in her back, like knives thrown from the management table, although this might have just been her imagination—she sure wasn't about to turn around to check. The stabbing might have been imaginary, but the animosity wasn't. She had been working for years at the Ranch, and had never once been invited by a colleague to a purely social gathering. There had been various formal functions, office receptions, and obligatory Christmas parties, for which the invitations were sent to all names in the staff directory, but never a friendly invitation to a private party or to a casual day out shopping. In fairness, given that she considered the entire management to be a bunch of dirty scoundrels not genuinely interested in the kids' well being, she didn't wish for their friendship and it wasn't surprising that they kept their distance. As long as her placement track record remained stellar, they couldn't afford firing her—this had to be the only reason she had been at the Ranch all these years, and it was fine with her. As long as she could be there for the kids—with the kids.

Successful placements.

Bonding with the kids.

Kids that she loved—in spite of the fifteen pairs of eyes still awaiting her response to Sig, in a mess of her own making, while the green stuff was getting cold.

Addressing Sig in front of his friends, be it to praise or reprimand, would have established a privileged relationship that she believed would be unhealthy. She was no psycholo-chick, but she wanted her relationship with the kids to show no favorites or whipping boy. The Ranch's orphans always craved to become somebody's favorite, to emotionally latch onto a staff member as a surrogate mother—especially the older ones sitting around the table—and she had always been overly careful to treat all the kids as equals, to never display any bias or preference.

As much as it hurt her at this very moment, it implied she would have to ignore Sig's mix of appeal and provocation, even though she suspected that her guarded reaction would leave Sig in an even sulkier mood. She would make up for it in private, boosting his morale with some motherly compassion—but after a long lecture about the importance of respecting the sanctity of private conversations. For now, she had to jettison both her desire to lecture him in front of his friends, and her inclination to applaud his initiative, both sacrificed to salvage her harmonious relationship with the broader group.

"Isn't this green whatchamacallit good or what?"

The thirty eyeballs couldn't believe it. She was completely avoiding the topic. They badly needed her to share her feelings, to open up, to be upset, angry, or ecstatic, to cry or laugh, and she completed copped out.

"Yeah, delicious," mumbled Eliza. "A grand two Yummy Stars."

Stamped

It had been four days since her visit to Justin's office, and two since Keene's disjointed letter. She wondered if the new padded courier envelope on her desk could be legally considered as harassment. Anyhow, it remained unopened all day, on the corner of her desk—on the edge just above the trash basket, in which it would tumble if "accidentally" pushed off.

The day went on as usual, with phone calls, paperwork, spreadsheets, meetings, pressure from Dick, sandwiches, more calls, more meetings, more annoying pressure from Dick—"stupid Gertrude," she cursed—and more paperwork. At the end of the day, sitting at her desk, she looked at the envelope, and it stared back. Or so it seemed—as much as a dumb, eyeless, padded plastic container could anyhow. She stood up, rested her hand flat on it for a moment, ready to push it into the wastebasket and thus send it on a return trip to its author in wasteland—as she knew it had to contain a letter from Keene. Rather, she grabbed it, uncharacteristically closed the door of her office, and lounged in the couch holding the enveloped against her chest, arms wrapped around it.

An imaginary psychiatrist asked, "Why didn't you just throw away the envelope?"

"You're the professional. You're the expert. Why don't you tell me, instead of asking stupid questions."

"OK then, I'll tell you why," the psychiatrist said, uncharacteristically violating the sacred rules of the psychotherapeutic game.

"Great! Go ahead smart-ass."

"Gotcha! I'm just messing with your head. Like hell I'd tell you. I'm paid the big bucks to torture you, and you think I'd kill the fun right there?"

"Can't even thrust an imaginary psychiatrist. What has the world come to?"

"To hell, my dear. That's what the world has come to. Hell. And hell it is. If I told you all that's on my mind, you'd become suicidal."

"What a great doctor you are. I feel so much better already."

"My professional recommendation, nonetheless, is that you should open the envelope."

"That doesn't tell me why I should do it."

"I've stuck my neck out too much already. My liability insurance doesn't cover me when I venture into making risky recommendations. If you sue me, I'll deny having ever said that. I'll diagnose you as a sad, delusional patient who talks to an imaginary doctor. You could lose your job for less than that you know."

"My imaginary doctor is an imaginary coward. How much worse could it get?"

"I could have you locked in an asylum."

"Ho hum."

"Electroshock every day."

"Uh huh."

"Beat up by Nazi nurses."

"Yahoo."

"I could go on."

"Yeah, but you're just trying to steer things away and avoid answering the question."

"Which question?"

"Why open the letter?"

"Ah, that. Hmm. Well, it's because you are mortal. A sad mortal, like the rest of us."

"So?"

"And curious. A sad, curious mortal."

"Bullshit!"

"Bleep!"

"Bleep-off yourself."

"Someone you know has decided to document his voyage to the end of his life, and you want to make me believe that you aren't curious? Fat chance. You'd read even if that was written by your worst enemy."

"I wouldn't."

"In fact, you'd be done reading this letter by now if you hadn't been so afraid to open it."

"Afraid? Afraid of what?"

"Of what it could do to you."

"Like what?"

"Whoops, the session is over. We'll have to discuss this during our next session."

"Like what?"

"Make sure to schedule your next appointment with the receptionist on your way out."

"Like what?"

"And leave your check or credit card number with her."

"Hey! Like what?"

Silence.

"Like what?"

Silence.

She ripped open the envelope. "Like hell I'm scared of my dead ex," she thought, propping herself on the couch to be in a more comfortable reading position.

"Keene, I'm telling you, no matter what, this is the last one of your letters that I'll be reading."

Same cover letter as last time, same laminated twin pocket portfolio, same bland statements by Justin explaining that this was done at the behest of his client. Only the dates had changed.

Keene's letter was again unaddressed. It was, however, much shorter, which she thought was a good thing.

"Day 150.

"Although it took me over a month, I have figured out how to deal with 'Keene's theory Stage of Grief Number 5: Scope out your last project.' Actually, I'm not done with the serious soul searching to get there, but I've at least determined a few things.

"First, I'm not going to spend my remaining days becoming a old blogger or a twittering idiot, telling the world about how I'm trying to see one concert a day until I die, or swim in a record number of different beaches, or suntan to death, or spread self-important pseudo-gospel to whomever has time to waste in front of a glowing screen and a willingness to read such nonsense. In other words, no ego-show. I'll die alone, as I've lived.

"Second, I'll spend my remaining days thinking about numbers—"

"How original," derided Carmina.

"—in a spiritual way. For a change.

"Now, that requires some clarification."

She agreed, as it didn't make any sense.

"There are three fundamental mysteries in life: Where do we go after death? Where do we come from? What are we doing here in between? When a person is about to die, the first of these three archetypical questions engraved in our DNA might become the most important one. Yet, all three revolve around the idea of finding the meaning of life, be it in a Monty Pythonesque way, or as part of some spiritual or philosophical pursuit.

"There's a truckload of organized religions that propose answers to these questions, and I respect everyone's freedom to embrace any one of them—Christianity, Islam, Judaism, Buddhism, Hinduism, Sikhism, Confucianism, Taoism, Polytheism, Shinto, Falun Gong, or any other 'ism' or 'neo' I'm unaware of—but it's impossible for me to become a devout believer.

"Impossible, first, because of mathematical logic: given three monotheistic religions that claim in their creed that they worship the only true single god (G), there is no solution to the set of equations $G=a$, $G=b$, $G=c$, and $a \neq b \neq c$. Hence, religious wars are anchored in fishy mathematical skills to eliminate two of the three variables.

"Second, because I'm a pacifist. There is arguably no topic more contentious and hotly debated than religion in our world, and billions of practitioners of various denominations have already immersed themselves in endless passionate debates in which I have absolutely no desire to partake. I do not wish to enter a minefield that too often has led to oddly rationalized religious wars (or one-on-one killings for that matter). In short, I cannot pay dues to any religion that has at any point in time justified or sanctified killing. That pretty much eliminates all of them right there.

"I don't know if that makes me an agnostic, an atheist, an apostate, an aphorist, an anarchist, an anachronism, or just a grouchy skeptic, but keep indoctrination discourses away from me. I am not searching for the big G. I have no intention to embrace a grand philosophical framework that could be held as the absolute, total, undeniable, unchallengeable, eternal, truth—particularly not a truth imposed by threats, fear, guilt or other devilish means. I just need some peace to reflect a bit about death. And life. Nothing fancy. Peaceful and introspective."

Carmina was surprised. Keene had never had any inclination toward the spiritual. Maybe impending death predisposed one to flick that switch. An urgent desire for an internal quest at such a tragic crossroad seemed logical—or at least understandable—in that context. She wondered if she'd do the same if she were in his shoes? Yet, maybe she was jumping to conclusions too fast. That quest was only an embryonic idea—at best, a few words on a piece of paper, maybe accidentally typed. She just couldn't see Keene proceeding down such a road. It seemed so utterly un-engineer-like. She bet the rest of the text would contain hints proving her right.

"I just need to find a simple way to appreciate why a sunset is more appealing and romantic that a sunrise, despite the fact that the beginning of a new day should be more inspiring, bringing a new gift every day. Why a butterfly, after experiencing a dreadful caterpillar life and a catatonic chrysalis stage, when finally freed from these boring and excruciating early stages, can be snapped up by a bird for lunch the instant it soars away from its cocoon? Why life can be so cruel and illogical for one butterfly, yet exhilarating and climaxing for another that is given a full lifespan's ride to suck nectar to the point of inebriety?

"I need to experience soaring ideas, not to live my remaining days on false hopes but to embrace the beauty of inspiring imagery. Just like the Maoris, who believe that their spirits sprint down a 90 miles long beach to spring off Cape Reinga into an afterlife above an infinite ocean, I need to dive into a philosophy that resonates with me.

"I need a non-aggressive New Age strand of something compatible with a wrecked engineer's mind. That shouldn't be threatening to anyone, and should keep the zealots at arm's-length."

Knocking on the door interrupted her reading. A determined knock—not banging, but pressing. She didn't want to answer. She deserved not to be disturbed. The open door, for once, was closed. Locked. She was entitled to it. It was past her regular working hours—whatever that meant. She could very well have been home.

What if it was Sig? That would have been that much more reason not to answer. She certainly didn't want to read another of

Keene's letters to him, like a deluxe babysitter pampering a spoiled kid.

She felt guilty for a moment to think of Sig as spoiled—that was so far from the truth. She had overreacted; emotions were making her think nonsense. It's just that she deserved privacy. Period. She deserved not to be disturbed. She had the right not to be disturbed.

The knocking stopped before she could fully convince herself and decide what to do. Her hesitation bought her enough time for the problem to go away; it allowed her to resume reading. The letter was almost over, anyhow.

"Given the profusion of New Age philosophies that propose different—and sometimes competing—approaches to understanding the grand scheme of things, an all-encompassing study was beyond contemplation.

"Rather, I navigated at the mercy of the winds, searching for hospitable shores. On that course, I saw strange islands—filled with ideas that might hold kernels of truth, but totally askew with a lifetime of engineering logic—even though a relatively short lifetime.

"The world of astrology seemed outright weird—to an engineer. Its heavy antique baggage was too much for me to carry. I prefer to think of the Age of Aquarius as a groovy song.

"The sirens of meditation were alluring, but I doubted that the dysfunctional mind of an engineer could find enough peace to do justice to this holistic discipline—especially if it required pretzel-like flexibility in yoga, or near immobility as in tai-chi, or other things similarly beyond my tolerance or capabilities.

"The island of optimism, with its wells of confidence and outpours of positivity with regards to any future outcomes, seemed cynical from the perspective of a drastically shortened future.

"The exotism of lecanomancy—which is divination practiced by throwing three stones into a water basin while invoking the help of demons—was mesmerizing, but of dubious effectiveness, which was unfortunate as it required substantially less effort than Voodoo.

"Other divination islands went by without appeal, as the random casting of dice, bones, cards, and dominos was prisoner to the power of statistical predictions, while divination by reading palms, soles, handwriting, tea leaves, tree bark, rotten cheese, frog entrails, pig bladders, burning coals, swirling smoke, used lottery tickets, and computer printouts, seemed to be strongly influenced by the eyesight of the reader.

"So went by the islands of teleology and synchronicity, of fairies and ghosts, of magic and alchemy, of the great nothingness of homeopathy that cures by placebo waters, and of the gadget-dependency of radionics that massages by unplugged energy fields.

"I also sailed by the vibration islands of chromotherapy that relied on colors to tune the body's vibration frequencies to the health, welfare and harmony channels; of aromatherapy that did the same with odors; and of the myriad others drawing on the powers of crystals, rocks, lights, music, ultrasounds, magnets, coins, marbles, jelly beans, sex, and banana splits; not to forget dangerously lit candles planted in the ears—or other orifices.

"Until reaching the most obvious and hospitable port of call for an engineer: numerology."

It was almost a letdown. Keene's quest for bits of spiritual meaning had slowly kindled Carmina's interest, but she felt duped that he, in the end, latched onto numbers; that he couldn't get out of his comfort zone. She felt like tossing the letter in the garbage.

After a moment, though, she realized that she had judged and condemned him, even though he was just at the onset of the journey, not knowing where it led him. It might have been a tad bit harsh. No, it was definitely harsh.

She decided to give Keene a chance, and see what happened.

"If something is to make sense to an engineer, it has to be numbers. Hence, why not use numbers to try to make sense of it all, to capture the intangible—a simple extension from a lifetime's experience of using numbers for the mundane, tangible world. At their mercy for years, crunched while crunching them, it seemed fair redress to use them for emancipation.

"Freedom.

"Freedom and simplicity. No more torture through convoluted operators—no more sines, cosines, tangents, natural logarithms. Facing death, a logarithm to the base 'e' doesn't matter. The fact that 'e' is an irrational constant 'almost' equal to 2.718281828 doesn't matter. Complex mathematics becomes irrelevant. If meditative insight exists in numbers, it has to exist in the purest ones.

"Numbers are magic after all, in some wicked engineering ways, providing sanity in consistency, abiding by a soothing predictability—be it calculations done manually or computations performed by punched keystrokes on calculator. A magic that is sadly forgotten."

Carmina remembered Keene's anger at people that forgot the magic tricks that made mathematics simple—his exasperation when seeing a salesperson that needed the crutch of a calculator to add 10% to a price, or a cashier who couldn't mentally add $3.99 to $4.99, or teenagers unable to multiply by ten.

"I'm eager to discover whatever new magic numbers hold in the foreign world I am about to explore."

The letter ended there. Unsigned, just as it was unaddressed.

Carmina rested on the couch, unable to formulate any definitive conclusions. She just had a vague feeling that something had been brewing in Keene. Something undefined yet, like a seed planted with the promise of a harvest, yet not really knowing if the weather will nourish or destroy it. Was he walking along a path of spiritual awakening, esotericism, or insanity, or was this just a futile pursuit by a dying hopeless mind?

The phone rang.

She debated for a moment whether or not to answer. Somewhat guilty to have violated her own open door policy already, and wondering if this had anything to do with the knocking on the door earlier, she answered after more rings than warranted.

"Carmina! There you are."

It was Dick. The president. She regretted to have picked up the phone. She wasn't in the mood for more badgering interrogations to find out if she happened to know of recently deceased individuals who could be rich donors to the Ranch.

"What's up?"

"We've been looking for you everywhere."

"And why is that?" she answered, puzzled as to who "we" would be and why she would be needed in the first place this late in the day.

"Sig has attempted to suicide again."

Closing

Carmina sat across from Dick's desk, a massive black mahogany slab coated in a reflective glossy finish designed to enhance Dick's presidential image, which was already framed by a tall executive chair. Expensive furniture purposefully chosen to showcase his authority, and wide enough to keep visitors at a respectful distance from the seat of power. Nancy, the psycholo-chick, was sitting on a straight secretarial chair at the right side of the desk; the other Dick, the vice-president, was standing, leaning on the back wall, on the left side—like a good soldier. Although this was supposed to be a special meeting of a subset of the management group, it seemed that they all faced her, as in a disciplinary hearing of some sort. Almost a tribunal.

What was her crime? Sig was alive and well, but did he say anything that could have led them to believe she had done something wrong? Were there some unfortunate words in Keene's letter that she should have bleeped, that might have almost fatally disturbed him?

Actually, Sig didn't have to say anything. Everybody knew that she had been quite close to him in the past few days. This had to be some sort of witch-hunt, because they were jealous of her privileged relationship with the Ranch's kids. They didn't want to interrogate her with respect to Sig's recent suicide attempt, they wanted to accuse her. She was ready to fight them.

"Carmina, you know I am not the type of guy who goes beating around the bush. I like to tell it like I see it," said Dick, thinking that blunt decisiveness was a sign of leadership.

"I know your style," said Carmina, meaning that she held Dick to be a blabbermouth incapable of nuances and subtleties, but certain that he would understand those words as a compliment rather than the expression of contempt it was.

"I hear that your ex-husband died last week, and that he could donate his estate to a charitable organization."

The meeting wasn't about Sig! She couldn't believe it.

Damn Gertrude. She had buckled. Maybe under repeated hammering by the double-Dick combo, or likely by the promise of a bonus if the deal was to come to fruition—most likely the latter, as Trudy Frutti came across as a relatively cheap person to buy.

So the greedy bastards were after the money.

"It's not that simple," replied Carmina.

"The way I see it, actually, it is quite simple. He's rich, he's dead, and his estate's going to charity."

"I think your information is incorrect. His primary goal is to burn all of his assets."

"Burn?"

"Literally set fire to it."

The two Dicks looked at each other in disbelief.

"OK, so he's a nutcase. But he's considering giving to charity too," said Dick, almost asking.

She wanted to curse Gertrude, but realized that the leak was entirely her own fault. She should have never shared information that should have remained private. In a moment of weakness, she had believed that her colleague might have been a friendly confidante, but she should have remembered that she had no friends at the Ranch.

Denying the part of the story they already knew would have been childish—even though she couldn't remember sharing with Gertrude the part about donating to charity, and suspected that they might have been bluffing to confuse her. However, they had been misled by Gertrude into thinking that this could be easy money.

"Don't count on it. It's a crazy set-up—as I told you, it's not simple. He's not going to give his money to charity just like that. It's only going to happen if I spend weeks and weeks traveling around to collect a bunch of stuff that he wants to be buried with," she said, realizing that this just confirmed him to be a nutcase. She said, "buried" as she didn't want to go into the ludicrous details of his incineration.

"So what's wrong with that?" said Dick. "Every guy wants to be buried with his toys," leaving it unclear as to whether he was sincere or deriding. "Then what? When he has his toys, he donates the money?"

"It might not even be possible to collect all that stuff. It's likely a lunatic's pursuit, or a wasted mind's attempt to fulfill an impossible dream—or just a roundabout way to aggravate his ex-wife for some sick revenge," she argued, although the last option was only an attempt to get the Dicks off her back, as she knew Keene wouldn't do such a cruel thing.

"So what? That doesn't change anything. There's still a real possibility that if he gets his toys, he will donate the money."

"To me. Big nuance. He doesn't donate the money to a charity. He donates it to me, to give to a charity of my choice."

"Well it's pretty clear to me which charity that would be."

Was Dick really that thick, or was that a veiled threat? She wasn't going to negotiate

"Forget it. I'm not going to spend weeks going around gathering his toys."

"The way I see it, Carmina, you are."

"I don't think so. That's my private decision."

"Of course, Carmina, but forecasted staff reductions to meet our reduced operating budget will affect you," he said, looking at the vice-president of operations, who nodded on cue.

"I'm not concerned about that. My skills are highly marketable."

"And they are. We're not concerned about you either Carmina," he said, using "we" for the first time—a strange departure from tone of the discussion up to now. "We are more concerned about Sig. The kid's grown quite attached to you and Nancy tells me that your departure might affect him in unpredicted ways," he said, looking at the psycholo-chick, who nodded as expected.

Sig's last suicide attempt had come as a surprise to Carmina. She had assumed they had shared some wonderful time at the Ranch since he had been ejected from his last foster family. She particularly remembered what she had thought to be a peaceful and nurturing moment, with her "lullaby" reading of Keene's letter, with the openness and confidence she had displayed by not censoring any part of the letter. But there were the doubts. All the doubts that had followed immediately after that precious moment, as she feared that the mature content of a dying man's letter, with its themes of unethical behaviors of all kinds, spiritual vacuity, and—yes—suicide, might have had unpredictable consequences. What if the letter had pushed him to that latest suicide attempt? What if it had been Sig who had knocked on her door, panicked, looking for a reassuring mother figure in extremis to keep him from committing a foolish act, and whom she ignored by not answering—unaware that it was a distress call? What if it was her closed door, violating her grand claims of having an open door policy, which had led to Sig being rushed to the emergency room for a gastric lavage, an endoscopy, intravenous therapy, and 24-hour observation to make sure that the bleach he swallowed didn't do internal damage? Fortunately, bleach tastes horrible and he hadn't ingested much.

Dick could tell by her silence that she was buckling. He could just close the deal.

"The way I see it, it's a done deal. It's worth a try."

"No it's not. It's totally crazy. I told you."

She couldn't leave. Not until she knew why Sig had tried to commit suicide again. It was more than guilt—she needed to know because it made no sense.

She was searching for excuses, without admitting the obvious.

"I'd be gone for at least three weeks..." she weakly complained, without the conviction necessary to push back Dick.

"You take as many weeks as needed to please your ex and get that charity donation in the bank. These aren't vacation weeks either. You'll be at full salary, since I consider this to be a fundraising activity—like a temporary extension of your job description. You'll save many jobs here, and, most importantly, you'll keep Sig safe."

Yet, Dick tossed in a proviso in the deal, like a necessary incentive to ensure she would be back to work as soon as the task was accomplished, instead of vacationing at the Ranch's expense.

"And you will bring Sig along."

"What?"

That was vile—more than usual for any of the Dicks—and incomprehensible. Why would he do that to Sig?

"That is not the place for a fragile kid. You just called my ex a nutcase. You want to expose Sig to a nutcase?"

"The way I see it, I have to trust my expert psychologist when she tells me that it would be excellent for him to tag along," he said, as a cue for Nancy to chip in, sure that she could forge a credible explanation—fake or not—for his incredible decision.

"In my professional opinion, I believe it would be good for Sig for two specific reasons. Unless something dramatic changes in his life, Sig will just struggle along from one suicide attempt to the next—until he succeeds."

"The dramatic change he needs is good foster parents who could become adoptive parents," objected Carmina.

"How many foster homes has he bounced back from already?" interjected Dick, defending his expert. "That's your job, to find such a home, Carmina, so you should know."

"Carmina," pleaded Nancy, in a more conciliatory tone, "we are talking about a huge need for change here. An urgent one. Besides, Sig is already twelve years old, and he has never lasted very long in foster homes."

"His last stay was six months."

"His record before that was six weeks. He is suicidal and a pyromaniac. He will bounce back from every home if that doesn't change. It's not adoption that will change him; rather he has to change before adoption, if he is ever to be adopted. Let's face it, his situation is precarious. He has said many things in sessions that I would consider to be red flags. For example, his favorite number is zero. That says a lot."

Carmina shook her head in disagreement. That example didn't mean anything. Maybe she had been married to an engineer for too long, but she saw zero as just a number, like any other number—not a red flag. Since when were numbers reflective of personality disorders? Just because a kid liked number zero didn't mean he wished to become nothingness himself. Anyhow, she didn't want to play Nancy's psycholo-games on her psycholo-turf.

"He is a very bright kid. He loves to read—"

"But he is also a very unusual tween who sometimes hides in his room listening to heavy metal music with dark lyrics, which doesn't help.

"All of our kids have problems. I'm not any kid's mother."

"It's more complicated—"

"You're not anyone's mother," cut in Dick. "To most kids, you're just the paper-pusher in charge of placement. But somehow, for reasons I don't understand, this kid has latched onto you, Carmina. The way I see it, you're his surrogate mother—which is not healthy. If we want him to grow and free himself of his dark instincts, he has to grow you out of that role," he added, only for sales-pitch value, as he couldn't care less about that convenient diagnosis that Nancy had shared with him earlier.

Nancy was flustered to have been cut off mid-exposé. She was about to shut up as usual, knowing that it was pointless to try to out-speak her president, but had the presence of mind to add, "And the travel will be good for him."

"And, the way I see it, the travel will be good for him," reinforced Dick, always wanting the last word. Ad-libbing, he added, "It will be therapeutic. He'll get to see a bit of real life and the dedication that it takes to make an organization work. It will develop a bit of maturity in him. It might even make him start caring for others and hopefully stop setting everything he finds on fire."

Nancy cringed but remained silent.

Carmina stood up.

Dick was quite an operator. He had shifted the entire focus of the discussion from the pursuit of Keene's inheritance to the benefit of the whole enterprise for Sig's mental health. From the contemptible task of enriching the Ranch coffers, to the admirable one of saving a kid.

She didn't want to say that Keene's world might be a dark place, or reveal that she had read one of his hard letters to Sig. That unwise admission would only have conjured up a harsh judgment without sympathy from the assembled inquisitors. Not that she feared any of them, but there was no point in giving them extra ammunition to try to manipulate her.

She didn't know what to do.

Should she resign? She had changed jobs before without problems.

It'd be just like a divorce. She'd divorce the Ranch! No problem. She wouldn't shed a tear. Or maybe a few, for the kids. She'd miss the kids—and Sig. They were almost like her kids. Could she divorce Sig? Divorcing Keene had been an upsetting experience, but she had done it, so she probably could just as easily divorce from Sig. Besides, as much as she needed to know the reasons for his last suicide attempt, she wasn't married to Sig—nor was she his mother.

Yet, she wondered how Sig would behave when he learned the reason for her quitting her job—as there were no secrets at the Ranch. What would he assume her motives were for not wanting to bring him along? Would these imaginary explanations lead him to feelings of rejection? To commit suicide? A successful one?

Why did all of this matter to her? Did it matter?

She didn't want to drag a ball and chain while doing Keene's stupid wishes. In fact, she didn't want to do any of Keene's stupid wishes.

All these thoughts had flashed in her mind in seconds. The Dicks and Nancy were silent, waiting, with expectant looks, eager to see if their salesmanship had closed the deal.

"I'm not anyone's mother," she declared, as she walked towards the door. She refused to be anybody's puppet and was sorry she had stopped short of using that exact word instead.

"Think about it," said Dick, trying to get the last word.

"I will," said Carmina, getting the last word, and leaving Dick's office.

One

Justin was ecstatic to see Carmina back in his office. As soon as she announced herself, he had phoned the funeral director and instructed him to postpone Keene's roasting for three more weeks. The director grudgingly complied, but only after grumbling that this was outrageously against standard practice, citing some sacrosanct principles to justify how his fees would be commensurate with the unconventional task at hand.

What Justin had not expected was to see her arrive with a pimply teenager in tow. It had never crossed his mind that she might have a son. That not only caught him off guard in a general sense, but it thwarted his hope to introduce more casual, interested friendliness in his discussions with Carmina, expanding a bit upon the business proceedings as a way to break the ice. He wasn't adept at seducing to start, and the thought of having a spectator for his courtship was enough to neutralize his efforts—at last until he grew more comfortable with the spectator.

He wondered until what age boys, gripped by their Oedipus complex, fended away all potential rivals of their mother's love.

"And who is this fine young man?"

"His name is Sig," she replied, unaware that she was failing to answer all the questions in Justin's mind.

Anyhow. He didn't insist. What mattered was that she was—that they were—sitting in his office, ready to proceed with the peculiar wishes of his deceased client. This was phenomenal. He had almost lost hope of ever seeing her again. He didn't know what Keene's two prior letters to her contained, but didn't dare ask what prompted her volte-face, given the manner in which their prior meeting had adjourned.

Carmina was cordial, yet struggled to conceal a certain measure of displeasure.

Agreeing to play in Keene's silly game had been an agonizing decision to make. In the end, she convinced herself that she could start and see where it led, but only to satisfy her own curiosity; she could drop out of this experiment anytime she pleased, and the Dicks had nothing to do with her decision. As for Sig, he wasn't there because she caved in to the pressure, but because she wanted to have him close, to care for his mental health, to make sure he wouldn't attempt anything foolish—and also, admittedly, to ease some of her guilt and to redeem herself of whatever she might have done wrong, but this was only as a side benefit. To her, it was a rational decision, backed by an opt-out option that she could exercise at anytime, at her discretion.

She trusted Justin would not refer to their prior meeting, gentlemanly enough not to embarrass her.

Justin had indeed decided that making any reference to the prior meeting would be ungentlemanly. Playing it safe, he resumed the conversation as if she hadn't been away for a week, assuming that Keene's general concept was still clear in her mind. If Carmina felt any need to revisit the tense moments of the previous meeting, the request should come from her. Forcing his clients into unpleasant discussion was too confrontational for a non-confrontational lawyer.

"There are two letters to read today. The first one is more a short notice, which goes as follows," said Justin, proceeding to read Keene's instructions:

"Thank you, Carmina, for kindly agreeing to help perform the business that I left unfinished for lack of time and clear thinking."

No more formal "Ms. Jewell" from Keene it seemed. For the first time in of all of his letters, he referred to her by first name, and she felt he was trying to strike an intimate conversation—to the extent that intimacy was possible with a kid in tow and Keene's voice channeled through a lawyer who'd used no more inflection than if he had read from a stock ticker tape. She instantly regretted that harsh judgment; Keene could not have foreseen Sig, and if Justin had gone to drama school, he most likely wouldn't have become a lawyer.

She had to lower her boxing gloves a bit, if she cared to hear any of Keene's message. Lower; but not quite drop. Just taking it all in, silently, restraining hasty judgment—to the extent that this was possible.

"Over a period of many weeks, I have laid on paper a number of loose reflections anchored in some aspects of numerology. Re-reading all of them as the end approached, I realized that each one of these ended with a wish. An unfulfilled wish. As a whole, a series of wishes. Ambiguous in some cases, hidden in the subtext or in the words that failed to reach the paper; loud and clear in other cases, conspicuous like a wart on a nose.

"Then it struck me, a few days ago, but much too late, that it was immensely stupid to die wishing. That I should have acted instead of wished. Acted weeks ago, months ago, years ago, a whole life ago. That I was about to die as record holder of the title 'most stupid man on earth.'

"Life can't be undone, but a river of stupidity can be made to flow backwards—just like a real river, given a major engineering effort. Unfortunately, the reality of time forbade me the luxury to undertake that task. This is why I am relying on the only person that I can trust to help me fulfill these few wishes.

"Each of the letters that Mr. Lawson will read to you ends with a specific wish—a wish to gather objects that I wish to have by my side in departing this world."

"Is he a pharaoh?" asked Sig.

"Sig!" protested Carmina.

"What? That's what pharaohs did."

"It's OK," reassured Justin, faking pedagogical talent. "It's a sharp observation. You are right that pharaohs were entombed with food and jewelry—"

"And people too."

"And people too, but—"

"And sacrificed virgins. Is the dude also looking for virgins?"

Justin was a bit taken aback by that comment, coming from a twelve-year-old.

Carmina shrugged.

"I think the idea here is just to collect items that are of symbolic value," clarified Justin.

"Why?" asked Sig. Carmina was pleased to let him question the sensibility of the entire operation.

"I don't know. It's not unusual for people to wish to make symbolic statements a part of their last wishes."

"So what's the stuff he wants?"

"That, we don't know. It's presumably written in the other letters that are all sealed, and that we will open one at a time."

"That's dumb. Just open them all at once."

Carmina thought Sig served as an excellent advocate, showing that Keene's little illogical game didn't even pass muster with a twelve-year-old. Justin could stand a little badgering. Better the kid's boxing gloves than hers.

"Can't do that," answered Justin. "My client's instructions are firm that I can't open a subsequent letter until the missing item he had wished for has been recovered, as it says here in the rest of the letter," he said, having also previously discussed these instructions when his client was alive.

"So you don't work for us," concluded Sig.

This was technically correct, as Keene had put an amount in escrow to cover all legal fees, but possibly an inconvenient truth.

Embarrassed, Justin clarified, "It's more like I'm working with you, for the common good," hoping that this slippery excuse would be redeeming. He certainly didn't want to antagonize the kid, and thus, by ripple effect, his mother.

"Let's go to the first letter then," said Carmina, all business.

"Uh, there's some stuff left here," he cautioned, hesitating, checking to see if the remaining paragraph contained more than what he had just paraphrased, but finding nothing of substance that couldn't be skipped.

"OK. You are right. Let's get down to business."

Sig looked at Carmina with a radiant smile, as proud as a union leader having scored major concessions from management, while Justin searched for an envelope opener.

Sig didn't quite know why Carmina had brought him along, but he had jumped at the offer of a mysterious extended out-of-town trip—anything would have been fine just to be away from the Ranch and the psycholo-chick—and he was delighted to have proven the value of his presence already. For that matter, he was stunned that Justin didn't ignore him, contrary to what most adults usually did—except when they were paid to pay attention to him. Ever more surprising was that a lawyer was listening to a snotty kid—aren't lawyers supposed to be important, fussy, humorless, arrogant, rich, despicable, workaholic pricks with no patience for youngsters?, Sig thought. And not just listening, but conceding points too!

Justin pulled a few pages from the ripped envelope and, with due protocol, proceeded to read Keene's letter with the solemnity fitting a most official document.

"Day 135.

"One. The start of it all—after zero. First, there is nothing—an abstruse concept—and then something. That something is a unity."

"The start is zero, not one," objected Sig. "Zero is something."

Justin was stunned that he had been interrupted barely three sentences into Keene's letter.

"Uh, I'm not sure we need to get into that here. Let's say that we'll trust the engineer on this one."

"Zero is something," insisted Sig. "Zero is the start. I don't care that he's an engineer, he is wrong. Just like a lie is a lie, even if it is a lawyer that says it."

"I—"

"Check it on math websites if you don't believe me."

"But—"

"Nothingness is real. Zero is the most powerful number. It's like an Uzi. It's like a serial killer. You multiply something by zero and, wham, it's zapped. Hasta la vista, baby. You can't just ignore zero."

Justin had no clue where this was coming from. And Carmina that just remained silent, not calling Sig to order, not giving him any clues on how to handle the situation.

"You are probably right, but we need to get through this letter you know."

"I am right."

"And we need to get through this letter. Good thing it's not as thick as a book. We'd never finish," he joked, looking at Carmina for a reaction—there wasn't any.

"If it was a book, we'd never finish it because we'd never start it. Nobody reads books," said Sig, pleased to volunteer plain truths to correct Justin's misconceptions.

Justin wasn't about to start arguing fine points with a twelve-year-old kid. Besides, it saddened him to no end that kids didn't read books anymore. There was a generation that instead had developed the most muscular thumbs since the dawn of time and that would someday lobby to introduce thumb-typing on minuscule handheld keyboards as an Olympic sport. No wonder kids had a fickle attention span nowadays—they never practiced the discipline of reading real books cover to cover. No wonder kids couldn't listen to more than two sentences before feeling the urge to share their enlightening thoughts.

This wasn't text messaging on a cellphone; this was about the final wishes of his client. So, unwilling to dignify Sig's remark with an answer, he picked up the letter and continued reading.

"One is where my numerology explorations start. Or rather divagations, as my methodology is not rigorous, and dangerously subverted by engineering biases. But it is the prerogative of dead people to flaunt rules and conventions, and willingly accept to be cantankerous dunces.

"At least, one is a number for which there is consensus in the literature. The wizards of astrology say that one is ruled by the Sun. Obviously, no sun, no me. Hence, one is the be-all of everything. The corner stone of mathematics that we are counting on—no pun intended."

Justin added, "engineering deadpan humor; just like you can count on an accountant, or trust a trustee, or 're-lie' on a lawyer," trying to lighten the mood after his earlier stressful exchange with Sig, but eliciting no reaction whatsoever. The failed comedian resumed reading.

"Every known numerical system starts there. In essence, everything boils down to one. No wonder it represents the origin of creation and absolute perfection. No wonder that, as the universal common denominator, it is the most powerful number in the universe, symbolizing the universe itself—the absolute unity of it all. No wonder that, in most civilizations and languages, it is represented either by a sun or a pillar—or a phallic symbol, depending on perspective."

Sig giggled. Justin decided not to go there.

"Many testosterone-driven cultures have claimed one to be masculine, but the Pythagoreans—with good engineering common sense, for their time—considered one to be asexual; in their system, odd and even numbers were respectively male and female, thus adding one had the transsexual power to change one gender into the other. One itself therefore couldn't be a mere number—it was the singular source of all plural numbers, almost a deity.

"One is a magnetic pole of attraction, simultaneously dynamic and charismatic, but also egotistical, selfish and melodramatic. And let's face it, it is an obstinate loner. Independent, pioneering, inventive, driven, individualistic, determined, assertive, aggressive, dominating, good or bad, it is the "me" above all—in all its positive and negative energy.

"Sadly or not.

"But truthfully, in essence, at a very fundamental level, all I have is 'Me.' You can take anything away from me, and I'll survive, but take Me away from me, and I'm gone."

"One minus one is zero! That's what I had said," insisted Sig. "It is the first number. I told you."

Justin wasn't sure how to handle Sig's constant interruptions without offending Carmina, particularly since she didn't seem to mind; she remained silent, without reprimanding him.

"I agree you are making a good point," he said hesitatingly, "but I'm not sure you have to take these letters with great mathematical rigor in this context—even though he is an engineer."

"I'm right. Just admit it."

"Yes you are," conceded Justin for expediency, as he had no intentions of arguing with a twelve-year-old boy. He held the letter up in his right hand with a look that asked, "Can we read on now?"

The polite silence confirmed he could proceed.

"From 35,000 feet, we don't even exist. We can't be seen on the face of the earth. Our infrastructure leaves scars of our existence, but as individuals, we are absolutely invisible. Our insignificance is blatant. Even our infrastructure—the monuments of our passage on the planet, more visible than we are today—will disappear. Once we die, they will follow, in time, and become equally insignificant. Grass will reclaim the roads, mold will eat our homes, rust will attack our long spans and tall buildings, turning everything into dust. Dams will fail, dikes will be overtopped, nuclear matter will leak. The infrastructure will crack, burn, collapse, weather away in reverence to the laws of entropy. No traces will be left after the ravages of time.

"Without its army of engineer custodians, working like ants on its preservation, providing the maintenance, repairs, and rehabilitations needed to make it perform like clockwork, fighting the aggressiveness of nature to achieve reliable performance against all odds, the infrastructure is just as doomed as we are. It, like us, is insignificant.

"Yet, all each one of us has is ourselves.

"All I have is Me."

"That's boring," said Sig.

"Sig, please behave," said Carmina, at last helping Justin, feeling he had been tortured enough.

"But it is boring. Really."

"You don't have to listen then. Just daydream some songs in your head, while we conclude our business here."

"Yo, all I have is me, all I have is me," rapped Sig.

"In your head."

Sig kept bobbing his head and moving his hands, like a silent rapper.

Justin resumed his duties.

"All I have is Me.

"Of course, the dry engineer's mind could argue this one.

"Beyond metaphysical mulling, there is no such thing as true unity. There may be one project, one deliverable, but whatever that is, that single idea is an assembly of infinite complexity. Everything is complex. A raspberry, in all its glorious beauty, as a unity, breaks down into multiple juicy red drupelets clinging in a convex shell to its branch. Even its name is a centuries-old construct entrapping a sweet rose-colored wine into a gorgeous berry that should really have been called a 'potentberry' or a 'divineberry,' no less."

"Whoa, your dude has been smoking," said Sig.

"Are you going to interrupt us all the time?" asked Carmina.

"Can't you just, like, skip the boring parts, or make them more interesting?"

"Sig," said Justin. "Maybe it is a bit wordy and maybe it is a bit boring, but what do you expect? These are the words of a dying man."

"He still has 135 days to live. That's lots of time to edit stuff, you know."

"I'll tell you what. Here's the deal. I'm going to read his letters as they were written, because it is beyond me to be a heartless editor trimming the words of a dying man for entertainment purposes. But after I'm done, if you wish to give it a try and see how you could improve the text, I'll be pleased to give you the letter and see what you can do with it."

Sig mulled this over for a few seconds before replying: "Thanks for the offer. Maybe."

"Can I resume now?"

"Sure. Whatever."

Justin picked up exactly where he left, hoping the interruption wouldn't break the logical flow of his client's argumentation.

"Yet, even though I am a complex physical construct, engineered with defective parts that have inadequate mean-time-before-failure, I am my own entity. In the end, myself, alone, is all I have. Parts fail, and it's the one that disappears—not the parts alone.

"Considering that I have no parents, no child, no kin, no friends, this is more than a figurative reality in my case. It is acutely the case. Parts fail, and I disappear."

Carmina worried that this might hit Sig hard, as it also described him with a scary accuracy. The questioning, the solitude, the abandonment, the difficulty to fit in. Carmina recognized that it was far from a perfectly identical situation, but Sig didn't know that Keene had lost his parents in a tragic car accident. Tragic as it may be, that paled in comparison with Sig's scorched path of violent abuses. At face value though, Keene's words had to echo strongly with Sig.

"All we have is ourselves. An inalterable truth. An inalienable concept. An essential one—possibly one of the most important ones. A concept that took a while to sink in, but that eventually seeped through my skull, slowly, filling its cavities, until it became whole with me—a part of my soul.

"Where do I exist? It's all inside. Parts of me may have been duplicated in various databases and computer systems worldwide, but these as mere duplicates of tiny parts. The original self is all within me—home and safe. With one exception. An exception that is the confidential information kept in a special medical file I wish I had the courage to retrieve."

"That's it," said Justin.

"That's what?"

"That's the wish. Keene's wish. The letter ends here."

"What wish? Did I miss anything?"

"I think it is to go and retrieve his medical file."

"Fetch a medical file?"

"There is an index card appended to the letter here. Let's see," he said quickly scanning its content. "Yes, exactly. Here are the coordinates of Doctor Frederick Godefroy," he said, handing over the index card.

"This is silly. Did I drive all the way here just to walk to the clinic across town and ask them to photocopy a medical record?" she asked without even reading the card.

"Big town. It's a thousand miles from here. And I think it's the original file that Mr. Mason wishes to retrieve, not a photocopy. From the little bit I got to know him from our few professional conversations, I believe he would have specified if that was not the case."

Carmina read the instructions on the card in disbelief. She didn't expect that the treasure hunt would involve traveling.

"Of course, all of your travel expenses will be covered, and the dedicated services of our local travel agency have been retained to fully assist you in all your needs," said Justin.

Her needs? What Carmina really needed right now was to go and kick Keene's coffin; she doubted the usefulness of the travel agency for this purpose.

"That also goes for Sig," he volunteered, even though the will never said anything about Carmina's son; Justin had improvised, taking a minor liberty that would likely survive the scrutiny of an audit—in the highly improbable circumstance that anyone would challenge the will.

Sig grabbed the index card and checked out the destination.

"Awesome. We're flying there," shouted Sig. He was determined not to let Carmina prevent his first airplane flight ever.

Emergency Room

To seasoned frequent flyers, a thousand miles is a commuter flight. A non-event. A puddle hop. An annoying small plane, maybe with a pseudo-first-class that consists of slightly wider seats and free alcoholic beverages, maybe not. A dangerous flight at the mercy of the worst paid airline pilots struggling not to fall asleep.

To Sig, it was a mysterious gravity-defying adventure, in which they climbed halfway to the moon on a sofa, without astronaut suits—but with a free soft drink, free refills, and a handful of tiny pretzel bags. From 35,000 feet up, chewing the minuscule pretzels, face glued to the window, he challenged Keene's assertion, determined to discern individual persons at ground level and prove him wrong—yet couldn't, in spite of laborious squinting and grimaces. He was forced to conclude that Keene was right. It was just inescapable that from the perspective of such great height, humans did not exist, in spite of the unmistakable scars of humanity on the landscape. If humans ceased to exist, fallen by the ultimate virus or sacrificed in a unanimous collective suicide, the scars were all that would remain.

It nearly took a scraper to unglue his face from the window, but even trips to the moon must end at some point—either by safely landing at the target base or by giving birth to a new lunar crater. The former had just happened.

The target base in this case was a tough mining town. Carmina had been unaware that Keene had grown up in such a crappy place. He had never talked much about his youth. In fact, he always avoided the topic. "There's nothing to be done about the past," he would say to deflect questions; when pressed, he would claim to be afflicted by a peculiar strain of selective Alzheimer's disease that made it impossible for him to remember anything before he met her. She could cajole, pout, tease, beg—nothing would make him disclose bits of information about his life before they met.

She would have liked to drop Sig off at the mall or at a multiplex theater for a few hours, while she met with Dr. Godefroy, but the town sorely lacked such luxuries—it had an old-style main street dotted by a few shops devoid of interest to a tween and a single-screen derelict theater only open on weekends for wildly popular triple X movies.

The only state-of-the-art infrastructure in town was its medical center, as a consequence of the daily mining incidents of all kinds, from minor hurts to fatal ones. Miners were covered by the company's blanket health (and death) benefits, the hospital was endowed with all of the latest gadgets, the medical staff raked in obscene billable hours, and the mining companies sucked the ore out of the earth at a maddening pace—all contributing to lubricate the local economy.

"Ms. Jewell," said Dr. Godefroy, welcoming her into his office. "I'm pleased to meet you. And this must be your son."

Carmina wasn't sure how to react to this assumption. She felt dumb to have neither anticipated the question and nor prepared an answer. The obvious answer was "no," but that begged for an explanation that she didn't quite know how to formulate in a truthful way that wouldn't at the same time offend Sig. She couldn't say, "No, it's just a poor orphan that is tagging along," nor could she say, "This is the suicidal kid that keeps bouncing back from foster care and that my boss saddled me with against my will." There was no politically correct simple sentence that she could think of on the spot and that would fit well, so she went for simplicity.

"Yes it is. His name is Sig."

Sig gave her a brief incredulous look, but played along, not knowing quite why.

"Hi doc," said Sig, shaking his hand. "Don't think of hitting on my mom, I'm here to protect her. I'm purple belt in Karate."

"Purple? There is a purple belt in Karate? Must be above the pink one, right?"

"I could break your leg with two fingers," answered Sig by reflex, responding to a threat by a threat.

"Sig!" said Carmina.

"That's fine," laughed Frederick, "We've got all it takes here to fix broken bones, so that would be swell, but instead, why don't we spend our time together seeing how I could be of assistance to you both."

"I'm sorry about that," said Carmina. "Sig is not used to...," she hesitated, not sure what credible excuse to invent.

"I've got Tourette Syndrome," boasted Sig, refraining from adding, "I'm allergic to smart ass rich dudes who flash their gold watches and stuff to rub it in," out of respect for his surprised adoptive mother. He was eager to learn the explanation for her lie, but would not wish to embarrass her in public—as a mother, she had probably suddenly acquired the authority to send him to his room or punish him otherwise if he did anything to disrespect her.

Yet, maybe she had the power to dispense motherly authority, but she couldn't force him to respect medical doctors. He harbored a grudge against doctors. A huge chip on his shoulder, because of a former foster family—a few foster families back—which happened to be half physician and half bored-wife. At first, he thought he had landed in a golden foster home, a rare oasis of opulence in a desert of wrecked shacks. A fully equipped family with fully equipped cars and a fully equipped house, with gadgets to last a lifetime of entertainment. However, the excitement of having landed in Toyland rapidly faded. The swanky pool, the wall-size videogame screen, the menagerie of pets, the private go-kart track, all became meaningless junk when he realized that he had been acquired to sprinkle some purpose into the boring life of a bored wife that needed to be entertained until her death. A sad wife who was fed distractions while her husband slept with whomever was gullible enough to imagine that he would saddle himself with a costly divorce just to get entrapped by a gold-digger from whom he could already get an endless supply of sex for free. Gadgets alone couldn't replace what Sig truly needed, so he had set fire to the office library. The tall bookcases full of dull medical books, which also skillfully hid a collection of pornographic magazines, were set ablaze at a strategically chosen time when the good doctor was busy dispensing care to a young patient in the guest bedroom while his wife was away visiting her sister. After the firemen left, when asked by the doting foster-father why he had done that, he replied, "I wanted to see you run out of the room naked, to see if a dork like you had two penises"—explaining later to the psycholo-chick that he couldn't think of any other reason why medical doctors regarded themselves as superior beings.

Nonetheless, Sig thought he had remained particularly calm up to now, hiding his phobia of hospitals and their kings. At least, he hadn't set fire to anything yet, which he attributed to Carmina's impromptu motherly love.

Frederick, accustomed to dealing with the bravado of the town's tough kids—haranguing like ghetto rappers to hide their hypochondriac weakness—could have ignored Sig's minor league provocations. At the same time, he couldn't resist the opportunity to tease.

"Tourette Syndrome is fine. I respect that. At least, it's not as bad as pneumonoultramicroscopicsilicovolcanoconiosis," he said, as if drawing a line in the sand by making a credible sentence with the longest word in the English language. Sig could only think of four letter words in response, but refrained from doing so, again out of deference to his newly acquired mother.

"I gather you are both here to collect Keene's special medical file," said Frederick to return the discussion to the business at hand.

She hadn't mentioned that over the phone. Seeing her surprise, he added, "Keene notified me by mail that there was a probability that someone might show up eventually to collect that document. How is he doing by the way?"

"He is dead actually," she replied, finding it strange to catch him unaware in spite of the familiarity—having said "Keene" instead of the "Mr. Mason" she had expected.

"Oh," said Frederick, stunned. "My condolences to you and his relatives."

Relatives? He obviously didn't know him all that well, thought Carmina.

"How did it happen?" he asked, in a tone that hinted at more than professional interest.

"I honestly don't know."

"Well, that doesn't quite surprise me. Keene isn't... hasn't been the most talkative person."

She refrained from saying she had had more than an earful of Keene over the past week, when Sig replied, "But the dude writes a lot. Lots and lots of crap."

"Let's not go there," said Carmina. "I'm indeed here on Keene's behalf to collect his medical file. I have a letter here from his lawyer authorizing me—"

"Oh you don't need a letter for that."

"What do you mean? I was told a medical file is a legally protected document."

"The medical file is. I can give you that too if you wish—with your lawyer's letter authorizing me to do so—but that's pretty boring stuff, and there's nothing in it except for a single visit here when he was fifteen. I think Keene wanted you to retrieve his 'special' medical file."

"What's the difference?"

"He didn't tell you?"

"Tell me what?"

"Oh, he did not. Allow me then to go back to square one," said Frederick.

He spent a few moments thinking, eyes closed, as a convict trying to remember the events that led to his downfall.

"The first and only time I met Keene was when he was fifteen. He arrived at the emergency room late one night, in an ambulance, with the paramedics who picked him up off the street. It was my first year on staff, just recently graduated."

Sig searched the wall for the diploma, remembering Keene's earlier letter.

"What were your grades?" he asked.

"What grades?"

"When you graduated. The grades for your diploma."

"That's was long time ago," said Frederick, remaining patient, "and it's not relevant to what we are talking about."

Sig concluded that he had been last of the class and had to sleep with some lady prof to pump up his grades.

"I had spent my time until then dealing with a few broken bones, some inflammatory problems, the odd infection. Nothing major. Then, this teenager arrived. In such bad shape. I'd never seen anything like that before," he said, reliving that day as if it was yesterday, yet remaining professionally calm.

"I didn't know where to start—I don't even know how to start to just describe it. Without any x-rays, one could see that he had six fractured ribs, a fractured arm, multiple fractures on the legs, a cracked skull, a broken jaw, and a punctured lung. His face was blood-soaked; his eyes were swollen shut; his nose was broken; his skull was visible through long cuts; his limbs were bent in directions defying anatomic logic; he had internal bleeding at multiple locations. All that complicated by cardiac arrhythmia as his heart struggled to keep him alive."

There was more, but he felt that this summarized adequately the urgency of the situation.

"Beyond medical verdict, he just looked like he had been run over by a truck and dragged under it for a mile. Nobody knew what had happened to him, but it had to be something that even a purple belt could not have stopped," he said, winking at Sig.

Sig remained calm. Based on his experience, when a medical doctor made ridiculous statements demeaning others, it was followed by boasts of superior accomplishments. Frederick wouldn't crack his shell.

"I spent hours in the operating room fixing him up. I coordinated an entire team working at the same time, around the clock—a great team of highly competent experts.

Just as Sig expected, the thundering of false-gods.

"In the end, the operation turned out extremely well, without any lasting debilitating residual problems, but for a while, I thought that we would lose him. He was very weak."

"Wow," said Carmina, in shock, aghast at how close to death Keene had been, wondering why he never bothered to mention any of this during their years together.

Sig, misreading her, was upset to see his new mom fawn over a damn doctor. Why were all girls the same? Couldn't she see the clues all over that revealed the doctor to be an idiot? The golf shoes under the desk, at the ready to escape the office, a clear sign of devotion to indulge in selfish pursuits rather than caring for his patients; the pack of cigarettes and lighter hidden behind the telephone on the edge of the desk, like an insult testifying that health is just an income generator rather than a philosophy of life; the Porsche key bigger than all others in the key chain purposefully displayed like a sexual appendage celebrating the hedonistic rewards bestowed on his profession by the pain and suffering of those justifying his salary.

"We kept him under observation for four weeks, to monitor his recovery."

Frederick paused a moment, to steady his professional composure and not reveal a hint of indignation.

"All that time, the thing that struck me was that nobody ever came to see him. No one. We tried everything to contact relatives, but found none."

"Wait a minute," interjected Carmina. "That's impossible. He lost his parents when he was eighteen. How come they didn't come to see him?"

"Eighteen? Who told you that?"

"He did."

Frederick paused again, wondering if there was a diplomatic way to sugarcoat the truth.

"I don't think he has been straightforward with you," he said, never skillful at telling bad news. "We learned at the time that he was living in a group home—not a very good one either, in my opinion, as nobody from there bothered to visit him. He had lived there all his life, since the day he had been found in a garbage dumpster, as a newborn abandoned by his mother. Nobody knows who she was—or who his father was for that matter."

Fearing he might have been a bit blunt, Frederick thought that providing some social perspective would help.

"It's not that unusual in this town, you know. It's hard work and long hours for many, which some people have a hard time coping with," he said, alluding to the debilitating work conditions but refraining from any specific criticisms of the town's main employer—and hospital owner. "Sadly, this kind of stuff happens here. At least, abandoned children have a chance to live. We often find dead pregnant teenagers, overdosed on Vicodin or Oxycotin, or Xanax, or even Adderal. Or young adults with hypoxic brain damage because they got loaded on cough medicine and the overdose of dextromethorphan cut the flow of oxygen to the brain. Drug addiction to Demerol and Dexedrine is also a big problem, with consequences being..."

Carmina didn't pay attention to his medical recitation. She was just speechless. For many reasons.

Keene—her own husband for years—had lied to her about his parents. This was a terrible breach of trust. A shocking revelation. Not as shocking as if he had conveniently forgotten to mention he once was a neo-Nazi or an axe murderer, but certainly distressing enough to send a shiver down her spine. As if their love, for better or worse, lacked the strength to unshackle such dark secrets and heal the painful wounds. Waiting until after his death—beyond the sanctity of their marital bonds—to reveal a horrifying part of his life was a cruel insult to their presumed past communion.

At the same time, Keene's indirect confession—through Frederick—of his bruised birth partly explained why Keene never wanted to discuss the past. He must have felt horrible about his miserable childhood. She had been married to a kind of Sig, without ever knowing it.

Sig didn't express anything. It sounded all too familiar to him to be a shock. Pretending that a car crash took away model parents—unsuspecting victims swiped by a despicable drunk driver—could make an orphan acceptable to "normal" people, worthy of pity and deserving a second chance at a happy life. Being the bastard of a destitute drug addicted teenager willing to dump her dead weight kid in the garbage attracted far more contempt than compassion, more harassment than sympathy, if only because the true victim of that tragedy was plagued by the stigma of possibly carrying the same genes of irresponsibility and immorality as the defective mother—guilty without trial simply by DNA association.

Determined not to give into sentimentality, he asked, "So what's the stupid special file? What does it have to do with all this?"

Frederick calmly continued, as if Sig's outburst was the perfect setup line to the climax of his story.

"When Keene regained consciousness, he started to call me 'dad,' which I found to be awkward. He told me, 'You gave me my life back, so you're more like a father to me than my own father,' to which I didn't quite know how to respond."

Frederick opened the front drawer of his desk, from which he pulled a bulging manila folder.

"Intrigued?" he said, handing it over to Carmina.

Opening the file with a bit of hesitation, she revealed a stack of wish cards, all proclaiming "Happy Father's Day" in various ways, relying on the inspiration of professional writers to translate into words deeply felt sentiments that some couldn't muster the courage to express themselves—for fear of lack of originality, or fear of the sentiments themselves.

Twenty-five cards.

"Year after year, every father's day, I received a card from Keene. No explanatory note. No return address. Just a signature."

Sig grabbed a few randomly.

"A special day of celebration for special role models," he read aloud. "That's so corny!"

Another one proclaimed, "Fathers are the forgotten mothers. Not today."

Sig put his finger in his mouth, pretending to throw up. Sig, who had wholeheartedly embraced Keene's earlier disparaging comments on the dubious credibility of the medical profession, was stunned. This troubling reversal of allegiances was unexplainable to him.

"The file is all yours," said Frederick, "for your total enjoyment," he added, looking at Sig, unsure of whether Keene was Sig's father, but judging that it might be inappropriate to ask.

"No return address," emphasized Carmina, realizing that some of those cards had been secretly sent while they were married. The words "All I have is me," from Keene's last letter read in Justin's office, were more meaningful than ever in light of the revelation that he had no family, that his biological parents literally threw him in the garbage, and that no one ever found him adorable enough to adopt. She appreciated the weight of that burden—with greater compassion than what her professional conscience would normally inspire.

Yet, if Sig was immensely more qualified than she to fully understand the pain of such emotional scars, he didn't display any emotion. Waiting for Carmina to return from her thoughts, he scanned the office wondering what would provide good combustion. Maybe setting fire to the framed diploma would be appropriate to commemorate the cynical side of Keene and pay homage to his more clairvoyant posthumous philosophy.

One Plus One

Justin was delighted to see Carmina back. Last time, she had caught him off-guard, partly because of her inexplicable willingness to assist Keene's in his enterprise, but mostly because Sig's appearance had been unexpected and unsettling. Justin had some talents—mostly of the discreet kind—but the ability to improvise when thrown into an uncontrolled situation was not one of them.

This time, he was prepared. He had adorned his desk with a slender and stylish flowerpot designed to emphasize the single red rose standing guard in it, hoping that it would catch her eye. He even cleaned up his office to some extent, although only he would notice that five rows of legal proceedings had been dumped into Bankers Boxes and sent to storage—and that he dusted the shelves of the library. He was eager to see the effect of all of these changes.

Carmina didn't see any of it. She was still too mad at the Ranch for their blindness. After all, it was not a small thing. Frederick had asked her to follow him to get a photocopy of the other medical file—the real one. When the fire alarm started, they rushed back to the room to save Sig, only to find him calmly waiting in his seat, showered by the sprinkler system, the good doctor's lighter in hand, contemplating the burning diploma on the wall. Frederick ruined his jacket, soaking it in water under the sprinkler head and flapping it on the charred wall to extinguish the flames that had already propagated to a broader circle on the wallpaper.

All that the psycholo-chick could say was that it was still in Sig's best interest that he stayed with her—that taking him back to the Ranch would be caving in to his impulsive need to escape any uncomfortable position, and that he had to confront his fears and replace his irrational wishes with realistic goals. What kind of garbage was that? Psycholo-chick didn't deserve a real person's name after all. She was just Dick's puppet, and Dick wanted Sig away from the Ranch mostly to protect his cash cow from a juvenile pyromaniac.

Sig was surprised to still be part of this field trip that had started funny. Normally, life never went back to normal in the days after he set parts of the world ablaze—although he was a lot quieter than usual, unsure if some retribution for his last deed was just being delayed.

"Ready to serve," he said to Justin, as Carmina handed him the folders.

"Had a good trip?" Justin asked Carmina.

"Smashing," replied Sig, jumping on a seat. Like a regular client, he took the same chair as last time, ready for the reading of another story—even though he didn't always get all of it in its intricate details, because that Keene guy was seriously weird.

"OK," replied Justin, upset that Sig answered all of his questions for Carmina. "I hope you didn't encounter any major difficulties," he said, looking at Carmina straight in the eyes.

"Nope," answered Sig. "Got some more stuff for us to go and get for you?"

Justin didn't press. For unknown reasons, Carmina was moody, and seemed perfectly happy to let Sig take care of the small talk. A mini-inquisition wasn't necessarily the best course of action.

"That's for us to read about, now, isn't it?" he replied to Sig.

A bit dispirited that nobody commented on the rose, he reminded himself of his professional duties—the stupid canons—and proceeded to read Keene's letter. Everybody knew the protocol by now, so he didn't waste time in with explanations. It seemed to Justin that Carmina was all about business—more so than last time—and serious, just wanting instructions to bring back as fast as possible the other items on Keene's list.

So he read.

"Day 110.

"Two.

"As a mathematical concept going back to the days when Neanderthals started counting on their fingers, the number two defines the second unity of two identical things—something which, frankly, is a plain lie. At least, it's an illusion. Nothing exists that is a perfect copy of something else in nature.

"No two snowflakes are alike, no two giraffes have the same spot patterns, no two days are identical, no twins—with or without mystical powers—are the same. Manufactured items vary from each other, even if only at the atomic scale. From the days of Neolithic engineers piling rocks into dolmens, to the silicon age of monolithic integrated circuits packing billions of transistors on a chip, engineering tolerances have been accounting for variations in presumably similar objects. One can theoretically calculate with great precision the number of cubic yards of concrete needed to build the Hoover Dam, but either significantly fall short or end up with an oversupply if field variations in volume from one cubic yard poured to the other are not considered, and the dimension tolerances of the formwork in which the concrete is cast are not factored in—however, note that no error would be incurred by forgetting to subtract the volume of the bodies accidentally cast in the Dam during its construction, as there is no truth to that myth.

"The manmade arbitrary constructs of dimensions, weights, and distances—or even time for that matter, as astronomical cycles change and the universe imperceptibly expands—are just convenient illusions. At best, they are absolute ideals that can only be imperfectly measured. A yard only exists as a fictitious distance along an arbitrarily oriented straight axis, which itself only exists within an artificial Cartesian world that is a simplification of an infinite space that is curved. Thirty-six inches a yard that doesn't even agree with a meter. And what's an inch anyhow?

"In the continuum of an infinite world, with an infinite number of decimals, how can 2.0 exist between 1.9999... (with the number of nines being infinite) and 2.00000...1 (with the number of zeros before the one also being infinite)?

"Absolutely divided units and identical things just don't exist. Therefore, in its purest form, two is a fraud."

Carmina almost cracked up. Keene's journey into numerology didn't even make it past number two and he was already thrashing the fundamental tenets of his new adoptive religion, on the grounds that it only focused on whole numbers. Was it really impossible for an engineer—even one about to retire from planet earth—to relax and see simple things the way they are, without looking for the bugs, the errors, the omissions, or the fatal flaws? Tempting at it was, she didn't smirk—didn't even raise an eyebrow. She remained impassive; she didn't want to strike up a conversation with Justin, she just wanted Keene's story to end as fast as possible. She let Justin read uninterrupted.

"Obviously, such hogwash is simply self-gratifying intellectual stimulation designed to make math more complicated than it deserves to be. Just divagations, looking at our strange world through engineering lenses, where absolutes can only be probabilistically estimated, and where probabilities are just another higher level of divagations.

"There lies the problem: engineers sometimes know just enough to be dangerous—and boring—and never enough to make any sense.

"Down to earth, the number two exists as a convenient approximation—after all, no perfectly identical Neanderthal fingers ever existed. Entire economies are based on counting currencies; so arguing with the checkout counter clerk that two individual dollar bills aren't the same won't buy much sympathy from those waiting in line. Lottery winners want absolute payout, not a relativist speech on how numbers lie. Sometimes, it is too convenient to live in a lie than to wish otherwise.

"Fortunately, facing death, reasonable accommodations are possible. Some deviations from the hard absolutes of a lifetime are tolerable. Maybe even desirable—all these nice absolute concepts didn't change a thing in the end anyhow, and I'm still going to die. In 110 days—to use the absolute numeric lies of eminent doctors.

"And so, I've lived long enough to reach number two in pursuing my studies in the field of numerology—a field which can be, in many regards, a lot more interesting that the corrupted engineering view of the mathematical world."

Justin was surprised at the silence. Not a single interruption from Sig. Intent but silent staring from Carmina. They had brought bad vibes into the room the minute they had arrived. He wondered if such a thing as a bad-vibe-o-meter existed. If it did, it would overheat for sure.

It was quite a contrast with the previous session, as he could now read entire sentences—even multiple paragraphs—without a single clowning remark from Sig. He almost missed that riotous atmosphere. For a moment he feared that their silence might have been a consequence of something he had said or done during the last visit, but concluded that it was unlikely because that visit had gone so well—at least, he had respected all the canons. More likely, it had to be the physician's fault—that Frederick guy. That had to be it. For sure. These quacks are just highway bandits who invent false scares for the sake of prescribing massive quantities of pills and collecting free cruise rewards from the big pharmaceutical companies; they're thieves who call for unnecessary blood works and CAT scans just to double-dip billing-wise because they own the lab's equipment. People call lawyers crooks, but at least lawyers don't kill people just to reward themselves with the fees to execute the wills—an inexact analogy, but one that he thought summarized well his aversion to medical doctors.

Justin started to worry that Keene's grand plan might have some negative consequences—not the least being that Carmina could drop out of the whole ridiculous adventure rather quickly. He resumed reading, hoping for some uplifting material that could warm the general mood.

"In numerology, two is the first acknowledgment that something exists beyond one. Something different. A contrast, an opposition, yet united together in a common purpose, in perfect yin yang balance.

"If one is the sun, two is the moon, because there needs to be day and night. If there is male, there is female, or we don't exist. Likewise, there is yes and no, true and false, left and right, on and off, action and reaction.

"There is life and death. What is and what isn't.

"Two symbolizes all the basic dualities of the universe, of our human life.

"It is the number of cooperation and emotion. The number of relationships, and thus of unity, communication, sensitivity, diplomacy, sincerity, adaptability, harmony, as much as rivalry, self-consciousness and depression."

Carmina found it exasperating to be preached at about unity and relationships by a divorced husband with no personal success stories to report in that regard. She thought this would be a good time for Sig to jump in and negotiate skipping all the pompous parts, forcing Justin to only read the end of the letter and the instructions on the index card.

"Interestingly, as in all other human activities, universal agreement didn't last long in numerology either. Disharmonious views start at number two already. While it's understood that the self-important one is supreme, confusion exists as to whether poor old number two is good or bad, male or female, godly or evil, union or division, or—strangely or not—a church. Such feuding isn't surprising, given that two is at the root of duplicity—the attribute of two-faced liars.

"So here, more than ever, two options require that a choice be made—by us or for us. A judgment underlies this choice, willingly or not. Often a difficult decision, which is maybe why the curved shape of the symbol '2' itself looks like a kneeling person bowed in a praying position.

"What is certain though, is that inescapably, for one to exist and be independent, two must exist. Therefore, it is this fundamental interdependence and primal complementarity that is at the root of the couple."

Justin thought it might be an appropriate point to push the flowerpot sideways a bit, to make the rose more conspicuous. He did so, acting naturally as if by reflex, rearranging his desk to shine more light from the desk lamp on the document. It must have been convincingly natural, as Carmina didn't blink and Sig made no comment. He might have left the rose alone if he had known that her silence was hiding an boiling anger, that it irritated her to no end to be sermonized by Keene about the harmony and complementarity of the couple, as a barely veiled roundabout way to idealize love now that it was too late.

Disappointed that the long-stemmed declaration of love remained invisible in spite of being almost waggled in their faces, Justin continued reading.

"Which leads to love.

"It took me 25 days just to understand number 2, to the point where I can explain it a bit in a few paragraphs. Imagine trying to explain love. It is a dangerous pitfall—an impossible task. I have no hope to ever understand love—at least, not any better in 110 days than I have understood it in a few decades."

"At last an honest admission," thought Carmina.

"The unexplained mystery of romantic love. A mystifying riddle I discovered as a spectator sport while a pubescent boy, scratching my head watching pubescent girls falling for the worse jerks on earth, fawning for selfish, manipulative bastards who treated them as nothing more than sexual playgrounds. Jerks whose sole purpose was to score and discard, so as to rake up the largest possible number of sexual conquests.

"There was Virginia, the cute little brunette, who was infatuated with Deltoic Duke, the supra moron with large shoulders who would have been expelled for dismal academic performance if not for rich parents who wrote large checks to the school's endowment. Virginia unknowingly contributed to Duke's private collection of pubic hair plucked from every pair of panties that he had the opportunity to plunge into—an amazing scrapbook, complete with accompanying photos of the silly girls and their body parts, that served as a trophy case proudly displaying Duke's harvest to all the boys at school.

"There was Crystal, a voluptuous beauty, who was smitten with Spiky Mikey, the fathead with a rainbow-colored liberty-spikes hairdo—like a Statue of Liberty on L.S.D.—who quit school to work in an assembly line, shoving mufflers in cars' ass twelve hours per day, six shifts per week, and who used the totality of his weekly paycheck to lease one of the sporty convertibles that came out at the end of the line. A sexmobile that Mikey periodically drove back to school to pick up impressionable feather-brains—and away to another assembly line in another state after Crystal became pregnant.

"There was Holly, with the big eyes and matching breasts, who didn't bother to sweat a cheerleader's life to ensnare Big Willy, the high school quarterback. Holly dreamed about an insanely rich future, but failed miserably in math, not recognizing that 14,445 graduating high school quarterbacks competing for 14 pro-football job openings every year, results in a payoff probability of 0.0998%. Definitely worse than the odds faced by the 125,000 engineering graduates that plan to join a professional family two million strong.

"There was Wendy with the killer mile-long smile, Dawn like morning dew, Melody with the angelic voice, Tanya the multi-talented, and all the others who deserted their brain for the pursuit of Goths, neo-Nazis, goofs, and jocks who made them laugh. Girls gawking in awe at the mural-size homage to the extreme-metal album cover tattooed on that guy's back—which will cost a fortune to remove a decade later when the extreme-metal band members will admit to be pedophiles and end up in jail for having produced child pornography.

"Girls falling for guys who made them forget their low self-esteem. Girls wanting to become chameleons, blending into a different identify. Girls wanting to skip a few years of teenage dread by latching onto an older guy who could elevate them above the other 'kids' their age—for such a small price.

"Girls who would never fall in love with a boy their age who loved math—because that is 'so not cool.' "

"How much more of this misogynic stuff is there?" blasted Carmina. She had remained silent, waiting for the tirade to end, but each silly example just increased her pressure until she blew a gasket. Why was Keene straining her patience on purpose? Was there a point to the badgering—was it supposed to be funny—or was Keene just losing his mind and purging his petty rancor?

"I'm not going to be lectured. Not on anything, and certainly not on crazy garbage like that. How would you like me to waste your time with stories about Stevie the egomaniac, Georgio the womanizer, Ivan the lazy stoner, Jack the wife-beater, Billy the pervert—?"

She interrupted herself, fearing that she had accidentally described the sad loser of a proxy-father in some of Sig's ex-foster families, but she had to continue blowing-off steam.

"—and these are all adults, not pubescent boys. Guys are stupid too, in case you hadn't noticed," she lectured to her captive audience of one pubescent boy and one adult.

"Would you like to hear my views about all the hunks too dumb to notice the sensible, level headed girls? How about all those boneheads drooling about the voluptuous vixens, and the scantily dressed air brains, and the gold-diggers in training, and the skanky bimbos? How about all the hormone-driven boneheads who are blind to all the brilliant women around them?"

Justin waited for the storm to pass. There was no point in responding. He would have loved to side with her, to offer wide-open supportive arms, to show unconditional empathy, but there was something in Keene's comments on this point that hit too close for comfort. Instead, he did his best to assuage Carmina and reconcile her with his client, while subliminally sharing his feelings for her, hoping she would get the subtle message.

"I might be out of order to share this thought, but I guess your ex-husband is maybe saying, in so many words, that sometimes in life women forget to look at the obvious. That maybe true lasting love can be just right there, in front of them, when they are searching for it in some strange places where it doesn't exist."

"You are right."

"You think?" asked Justin, hopes kindled.

"Yes. You are absolutely out of order," she insisted, wondering how he could dare insinuate that she refused to acknowledge her true feelings, dare suggest that a flame still burned for her ex-husband and that she was blind to it. Had he been paid by Keene to make such an outlandish proposition? Or worse, was it something he deducted by himself? Or saw? Was she unknowingly radiating such emotions?

In any event, whether Justin was right or wrong was none of his business. He was a lawyer, not a marriage counselor. Besides, there was no marriage to counsel—there was not even an ex-husband anymore.

"My mistake," he said ruefully. He picked up the document, tapped its edge on the desk to straighten the pages—unsuccessfully—and continued with the job to which he was charging his billable hours.

"The unexplained mystery of romantic love. Amazingly, through all that noise and nonsense, I still found one love in life—the one puzzle piece that made prefect sense. A perfect fit.

"A miracle.

"No less.

"More than a cute, voluptuous, shapely, fashionable girl alluring to the senses.

"A woman.

"A woman I couldn't resist. A gorgeous someone who valued inner beauty over skin-deep hankering. A generous soul that had no interest in superficial addictions. A woman who was worth loving.

"A woman who loved me.

"For a while, at least.

"A woman who left when her penetrating mind resolved that there was no possible satisfying outcome. Hating me, understandably."

Carmina knew exactly whom he was talking about. She knew he was also wrong, somewhat, because that woman never hated him. Often angry, obviously, but never hateful.

"Far from being an illusion put on a pedestal by a forlorn heart, she was an imperfect human, just like me—just like all of us. Yet, even though I knew all of her faults and foibles—better than my own—and even though she abandoned me, I am unable to hate her.

"I tried.

"I failed.

"My connection with her is beyond my control; it is engraved in my DNA, as if some Velcro-coated atoms had latched onto her ethereal signature, preventing me from breaking the bond, keeping me forever glued to her. She left with my heart, and I still love her.

"It's ridiculous.

"So ridiculous that after she left, I spent months listening to that song about our love being an old love, older than all of our years, with familiar tears in strange eyes, surviving all the ages."

"Old souls last forever, never fear a goodbye," remembered Carmina.

"My numerological two being baldy broken, I dusted off the old record, and listened to it again and again, letting the needle erode a Grand Canyon in the vinyl of an archaic technology, seeking solace in the hope that our old souls could never be so shattered—maybe a bit 'yin-ed and yang-ed,' but not irremediably shattered.

"That single song set me adrift.

"Musing, contemplating, forgetting the lyrics, dissolving with the music.

"The music. Just the music.

"The ethereal beauty of the music. Notes hitting the resonant frequency of my undamped atoms, throwing them into unstable vibrations of unbounded magnitude, making them explode like fireworks, in a joyous self-destruction.

"That sparked me to dust off all of my old vinyl LPs, and play them back, one last time—at least a few of them, as there will not be sufficient time. It was exquisite.

"The amazing communion with a soaring symphonic orchestra, a screaming electric guitar, a fluid piano scale, a soothing flute, a grinding bass, a dissonant chord, a note sustained to silence—all ephemeral, like our lives.

"After a few records, not knowing why—maybe subliminally inspired by the lyrics of a song—I poured myself a glass of wine. I hadn't had wine in years, but it felt appropriate, as a proper pairing with the music.

"Music and wine.

"Wine never tasted so good before."

Carmina found that to be a striking remark. Maybe not so unexpected, as there had to be a reason for Keene to be soaking in a casket of fermented grapes, but she had never heard Keene utter a word of praise about wine. Once, she asked him to help her choose between a Chardonnay and a Riesling for a gift, and he replied that she was asking the wrong person as he couldn't tell the difference between wine and water.

Justin noticed her raised eyebrows. He would have loved to drop his professional duties by responding to Carmina's expression, but couldn't figure out an appropriate line to break the ice. Not after his disastrous failure to connect emotionally a few minutes earlier.

He resumed reading instead—that was easier.

"Music and wine.

"Wine had never tasted so good before"

"You said that already," said Sig. "You should use your ruler."

"I just lost my spot for a moment," he admitted, thinking that maybe he should have lied—saying that it was written twice, for poetic flourish—instead of bowing to a kid.

"Like a breeze in a glass, a cajoling perfume, wine and music tasted like an unfulfilled romance.

"Like the unfulfilled number two. The essential part around the one central axis, needed for the wheel to work.

"Wine, like a reflection on a lake, is a meditative elixir, fueled by divine music, to apotheosis. The perfect couple.

"Or is it just more divagations?

"Is wine indeed so sublime, or is my destiny taking over my rationality?

"Am I becoming attuned to a new reality, or living a horrible illusion?

"How would I know?

"The last discussion I ever had about wine was with Didier the Hermit. I wish he didn't live so far."

"That's it," said Justin. He had an uncanny talent for blunt endings.

"That's what?" asked Sig.

"That's the wish. Keene's wish. The letter ends here," like he said last time—days ago.

"I get it. You're going to give us another card with an address on it, right?" said Sig, extending an arm ready to grab the forthcoming index card.

Card in hand, he read a few lines of the address, and jumped in the air with screams of joy. Carmina concluded it meant more traveling.

"Again, all of your travel expenses will be covered—"

"I know," she said, leaving.

"I hope you noticed the special travel arrangements on the card—" he said as she closed his office door. Anyhow, the travel agent had attended to all the details.

Justin was just sad to see his beautiful client leave as abruptly as last time—without a word about the rose.

Stupid rotten life! He had to figure this out.

Col-de-l'Enfer

To Sig, just getting to the *Col-de-l'Enfer* was the adventure of a lifetime. If the commuter flight to Keene's hometown had been a trip to the moon, the jumbo jet cruise across the Atlantic was reaching for the galaxies. In first class! Like riding a flying living room, courtesy of Keene's estate.

The first hour—when not glued to the window—was spent playing with the articulated seat, raising and lowering the footrest, infinitely adjusting the back, turning the massaging lumbar supports on and off, unfolding the seat into a flatbed and back, rearranging the pocket's contents, twisting and bending the reading light in various pretzel shapes, trying every possible positions and arrangements of the high-tech cocoon. All to the snobbish dismay of the other first class passengers who had paid extra to escape the economy cabin, its proletarian mob, and—worse of all—their kids. Like an army of curmudgeons in suits, they expressed their impatience with sighs and growls of little menace so easy to ignore. Besides, Sig could tell that Carmina was equally exhilarated but too much of an adult (and too shy) to toy with all the gadgets, and he assumed that she was pleased to let him enact her fantasies.

The second hour—when not glued to the window—was spent gulping down a five course meal that, mysteriously, in spite of the reputation of airplane food, put to shame all of the Ranch's cafeteria offerings.

The third hour—when not glued to the window—was spent surfing through all of the entertainment channels, trying to decide which of the 182 movies, 54 television programs, 18 music videos, and miscellaneous other goodies, deserved his attention.

The remaining four hours were spent trekking through the aisles, comparing the amenities across the various classes, grabbing snacks in the galleys while evading the probing polite questions of the cute and not-so-cute stewardesses, staring down at the stars through the night, contemplating the bare and infinite ocean after sunrise, studying the unfamiliar infrastructure scars inland of the shores of a different continent, and wondering if those who bragged about making love inside the tiny closet-size toilet facilities were exceptional liars or exceptional contortionists.

Although he had enough curiosity and adrenalin to counter fatigue through the flight, Sig collapsed through the mundane bus, trains, and subways rides that followed, dozing on the luggage cart, benches, and seats, but waking up in time for the fantastic ride on the *Train à Grande Vitesse* (high-speed train), fighting sleep for half the trip, in awe at the exhilarating speed by which the landscape scrolled.

Carmina, in spite of the maddening sequence of transportation modes coupled with the responsibility of dealing with Sig and jet lag, found time to decompress and find some peace with the process. Not that she enjoyed it, but she decided that it was best to accept the current circumstances, view them as a temporary distraction from work, and embrace the opportunity to spend some quality time with Sig. With some luck, she might even treat the whole thing like a vacation and enjoy it—or at least, try to. Being in Europe helped a bit in that sense.

From a mid-country train station, in a rented car whose name neither Carmina or Sig could pronounce, she drove the remaining few hundred miles through valleys, hills, and mountains, along progressively more windy, narrow, and steep roads, to the remote village of *Col-de-l'Enfer*—a village in as much as a few distant homes within sight of each other could constitute a community, by arbitrary political decree more than by blood or shared interests.

Didier's modest adobe, encroaching onto the road on one side, perched on a stone foundation wall that dived into the ravine on the other side, clung to the cliff in defiance of the laws of gravity that Keene had so divinely upheld. Carmina couldn't fathom why one would choose to erect a stone dwelling in such a ludicrous location, teetering on the edge of an impending disaster, struggling to resist the heavy winds that gushed through the valley and tempting fate as an attractive bull's-eye for the odd landslide.

Wedged between the house's front door and a subcompact car that fitted like a whale in the shrimp-size parking available, she swung the rusted steel knocker, for lack of an electric doorbell.

Carmina could hear a faint, *"Foutez nous la paix. Allez vous-en. On n'a besoin de rien,"* yelled from a distance, shooing away any possible itinerant salesman—as if canvassing neighborhoods with less than one house per square kilometer was a remotely viable sales tactic.

"We need to talk to Didier Lemoyne. We are here on behalf of Mr. Keene Mason," yelled back Carmina, hearing her voice echo in the valley.

A shadow filled the peephole.

"Putain de bordel de merde," could be heard through the door, as it was unlatched.

The open door revealed a disheveled, bearded man in sandals, khaki shorts, and an oversized t-shirt covered with psychedelic patterns; he looked like a fallen guru without charisma and followers, in so far as spiritual gurus could go bankrupt and survive collecting unemployment insurance benefits.

"You must be Carrrmilla," said the man with a French accent, rolling his r's in a way that would add pages to a book if all of them were written.

"Carmina," she corrected, puzzled that he knew her. Maybe Keene had warned him too of her impending visit.

"Keene's girlfriend, right?"

"Wife would be more appropriate," she corrected, omitting to mention the divorce, as saying former wife instead would have required too many explanations she wasn't ready to provide.

"Wife? *Merde alors,*" he said with mouth agape.

Didier seemed surprised. She wondered what Keene had said or omitted to say about her visit.

"You smell like goats," said Sig.

"And who is this little punk?"

He hadn't said, "dis" as many Frenchmen would, or "this" either for that matter, but rather something in between. Speckles of an accent here and there, like rust on a stainless international experience.

"I'm her son," he answered before she could even change the story. She'd have to play along, but reminded herself to straighten that matter during the return trip.

"A wife! A son!" he said in disbelief, refraining best he could from saying *putain, bordel,* or any of the other expletives he used all the time when at loss for words, but somewhat inappropriate in the circumstances.

"Please come in," he said, as he ushered them in, across the kitchen, and through a crooked door that led to an uneven wood balcony hung over a 90-degree cliff. The nails weren't rusted and the wood wasn't rotten, but Carmina was nonetheless stressed as the setting was like the perfect leap-off platform for a sure suicide. She sat where she could keep Sig within eyesight and grabbing distance.

Didier pulled out two extra rudimentary stools and two more glasses to honor the bottle of homemade red wine already open and waiting on a wooden table.

Sig was thrilled to be poured a full glass, ready to honor the civil traditions of the old continent—maybe even emigrate there if the tasting met his expectations—daring Carmina to stop him. She tolerated the glass, not wishing to jinx the meeting with a petty argument over such a trifling matter.

Settled around the table, glasses ready for a toast, Didier welcomed them with a solemn "*À votre santé!*"

Sig took a sip and grimaced. He rated the wine as "tasting like goats," not ready to forego his passport, after all.

Carmina found the full bodied-wine flavorful—most surprising, for a bottle without a label.

Didier smiled, as life was good, basking in the Provencal sun, drinking good wine. For him, that's all it took. Simple life, simple pleasures.

"Do you have goats?" asked Sig.

"Sig!"

Didier laughed, without answering.

"How do you know Keene?" asked Carmina, charging into the business at hand. "Actually, how come you know me?" she added, which was the real enigma.

"Aaaah, yes. That's a very good question."

He sipped some wine to let the suspense hang. Wrinkles fanned from the corner of his playful eyes—eyes that smiled.

"Truth is, I don't 'know' you. I mean, not in the sense of who you are, what you do, what you like, what you hate, what you think. But I know of you. That's because I've seen you before."

Carmina couldn't recollect any such meeting.

"Let me explain to you," as he topped-off the glasses—even Sig's glass, which was only missing a drop.

In less than a blink after the bottle landed back on the table, Didier emptied three-quarters of his glass in one shot. Then, like a repentant afterthought, he lifted it, inspected the deformed sun and clouds through it, tilted it, rocked it, put it back on the table, swirled the remaining wine vigorously, smelled it, repeated the entire ritual twice... thrice... as if stalled on how to begin his story.

"You're not a very fast story teller," said Sig.

"That's because it's not a story, it's a memory."

"What's the difference?"

The wrinkled fans re-appeared.

"Huge difference. In the brain, stories live near the surface. They're all fluff, inconsequential, irresponsible. They just sunbathe in the window, or on the balcony, listening to the wind, the noise, the gossips, the nonsense. They are passing time, meaningless and interchangeable, fickle and in constant flux—because, in the end, they're all the same. Free. But memories... ah memories, that's different."

He swirled his wine endlessly while talking.

"Memories have anchors... on very short chains. They like quietness and peace, even if it means darker rooms. Memories... once they're engraved, that's it. They're unique and forever. And it costs every time you call one to duty, so you better get the right one, or it's all meaningless."

He finished his glass.

"Can't just fetch any one of them. It's got to be the right one. But the one I'm looking for is very shy. It lives far, far, far, inside. Some memories like it better that way. That's just how they are. They don't like being dragged out of bed."

He swirled an imaginary wine in his empty glass.

"This memory has no beginning and no end. It is eternal like a flashback lost in time. It is a memory of Keene and I working on a big international construction project miles from civilization—the stuff young people do when they are free to travel, because the paychecks are huge. He was one of those guys with a white hard hat. I had a blue one."

"What does that mean?" asked Sig.

"White is for the engineers and architects, the management, the bigwigs. Blue is for skilled trades—I was an electrician. Yellow is for the general workers, the handymen, the laborers. You get the idea. Anyhow, it's not important."

"So, if it's not important, why do people do it?"

"I guess men like to put people in little boxes," he said without the wrinkled fans. "Hard hat colors are just petty little social classes, like labels that identify to which caste everyone belongs, to make sure that talking to someone of a different status is never done without a legitimate purpose. Just like the logos of political parties, or the symbols of religions, hard hat colors are just convenient artificial barriers for fools. It's an attempt to force people of shared specific privileges only to associate among themselves, and rarely—or never—with others."

"So how come Keene was your friend then?" insisted Sig.

"Friend? I didn't say we were friends. I don't even know what's a friend. I'm not a very social guy."

That wasn't much of a revelation coming from the owner of a cliff-side shack in a one-horse town, thought Carmina, again perfectly happy to let Sig drive the conversation.

"Keene wasn't a very social guy either, you know, but he didn't care which hat you wore. He was comfortable talking across the color barrier. A decent man. So we talked a lot, like two young guys away from home would do. Talked about being misfits in the outland of a backward society, of being tourists in a land of medieval intellect, of the absurdity of too many things. Maybe a bit of youthful anger and existential angst too, I don't remember...

"What I will always remember is the day when a rogue and extremely well armed militia stormed the construction site. Fifty jeeps. AK-47s and bazookas. The looks of blazing hatred.

"It was mayhem."

Sig was silent, as a kid mesmerized watching *Apocalypse Now*. Carmina didn't know if she should censor—or how. They couldn't leave. All she could do now is hope that Didier would spare the gory details—while cursing the psycholo-chick for putting Sig in this situation and making her feel like a terrible mother.

"They were only after those under the yellow hard hats: the recognizable locals who couldn't be mistaken for foreigners. It was not the color of their hats that gave them away; it was the tattoos of their religious allegiance. These symbols, etched on their skin, branded their faith and shouted their difference, loud and clear.

"It was that horrible."

The "dragged-out-of-bed" memory was emerging from the darkness, not pretty, disheveled, displeased to have been disturbed from a peaceful slumber that allowed it to be forgotten.

"The screams. Screams of excitement, like tourists on a wild safari, and screams of terror from those being slaughtered. The reeving engines, the machine gun rattle, the bullets ricocheting off steel and concrete, slicing through air too close. The sound of blazing hatred.

"Then, the butchery. Slices of bodies, like cheap cold cuts. Organs dug out their bloody shells, like oysters pulled from the mud. Intestines ripped out, resisting like rotten roots pulled from the soil. All tortures happening on live, wrenching bodies until silenced by the excruciating pain. The sight of blazing hatred."

Still swirling the empty glass.

"The foreigners were then pushed together in a huddle, circled by jeeps and weapons, away from the genocide that continued. Squeezed tight in a country that abounds with virgin space, we waited a possibly hopeless fate. After an hour, the maddening noise ceased. Shortly thereafter, a ruthless militia member approached us. Acting with authority, drenched in blood as a sign of leadership by example, arms crossed in defiance, he barked his orders. 'You have not seen anything. You don't know anything. You weren't here.'

"One of the white hats asked, 'Why did you do this?'

"The bloody leader shot him in the head.

"That created some commotion among the militia. They argued for a while, then dragged the body from the huddle and dumped it into a jeep. They obviously didn't want it to be found.

"The bloody leader came back, yelling at us this time. 'Arrogant imbeciles! You know nothing of this place. Tell your bosses to hire the right people if they want to come back here. No more of these tattooed monkeys that hassle us with their dumb god, no more of these infidels that reproduce faster than rabbits to take over our land. They are nothing! You send more, we'll swat them like flies, because they are less than flies. They are a pollution. Even your arrogant governments don't care for a few tattooed monkeys. Nobody cares. We'll clean the place, get rid of some garbage, and the world won't notice.'

"He motioned to his cohort of murderers and they drove away. As one jeep picked him up, he shouted, 'You have seen nothing!'

"But it was all there to be seen. The red earth, the bodies shoved into machinery, the men crushed like cockroaches, the icky fluids oozing out of dismembered carcasses, the horror, and the smell. The smell of blazing hatred."

Didier stopped swirling the glass.

"The aftermath, the disgust, the nausea, the pangs. The feel of blazing hatred. It was overwhelming."

There was a long pause that neither Sig nor Carmina dared break. The words had drawn horrible pictures, which they knew to be merely repugnant pencil sketches compared to the living fresco of monstrosities that he had survived.

"I spent days in bed. Near catatonic."

"What's catatonic," asked Sig, a bit afraid to interrupt, but even more afraid to lose the thread of the story—of the memory.

"It's being in a coma," answered Carmina.

"No, not a coma," clarified Didier. "I could hear everything, I remember everything. I wasn't a vegetable. I was just completely shocked. Like terminally depressed. It was like an existential crisis: I had lost all interest in living; I couldn't see the point of investing myself emotionally in life when all of it could end abruptly, without warning. One second you're alive, and, boom, one second later you're gone."

"It's just a boundary, like all other boundaries," said Sig, to Carmina's astonishment.

"Exactly!" said Didier. "Like jumping across the frontier from France to Germany. It's that easy. Except that it's a special border crossing, because once you emigrate, you can't come back—like emigrating to a communist country."

Didier tried to down some more wine, putting the glass to his lips and lifting the elbow, but nothing came out of its emptiness. He refilled his glass—the only one that wasn't full at that time—as if it was essential fuel for his sermon.

"Yeah, death is like a *putain de* communist country. If communist countries were the paradises on earth that their propaganda proclaims, they wouldn't need a guarded border. Nobody would ever want to leave. Nobody.

"Now, of course, if people were free to travel back and forth across the border at will, some would be curious to venture out of paradise once in a while, if only to see what hell looks like. In fact, those tourists abroad would be like accidental missionaries, spreading the gospel simply by exhibiting their joyful attitude and their passionate determination to return home—to return to the best place on earth. Obviously, that's not the case. When you can't cross a guarded border at will, it becomes a prison wall.

"So death is like a communist country. It's a prison from which nobody escapes.

"Nobody.

"No dead friends ever come back to tell us, 'Hey buddy, quit this stupid life, the fun is all on the other side!' No hordes of tourists come back down memory lane to recollect how horrible life was on earth, to be overheard saying 'I can't believe we suffered all this nonsense for so many years; we should have moved on years ago.'

"No. When you die, it's boring and gray. Life becomes really dull after you die. There's no paradise there."

Didier downed another glass of wine, and Carmina feared they were about to become captives of the rants of a drunk. Sig was also scarily enthralled by these divagations.

"So how did the catatonic state end?" asked Carmina, to speed the story from its somber passage, hopefully to jump straight to its uplifting resolution, which had to be there in the end since Didier obviously survived.

"I died."

Poker face, he savored the moment. Carmina's quizzical look was about as much entertainment one could get in *Col-de-l'Enfer*.

"On my own terms, that is."

Didier refilled his glass, and tried to top the other glasses, to be a good host, pushing the liquid over their rims.

"Let me explain. Keene came to visit me every day. He would talk to me, read the newspapers aloud, put some music on. None of it changed anything. I was still caught in my catatonic state, having lost interest in living.

"Then, one day, he showed up quite late and stayed quiet. No talking, no reading, no music. He just looked at me, for what seemed like an hour. Then, he sat on the edge of the bed, and told me that he had met a wonderful woman a few months before. I was startled, but my body didn't twitch, and I realized that, even though I hadn't known Keene for a long time, this was the first time that he ever talked about someone close to him.

"He said just a few more words. Basically, he declared that she was the only person he had ever loved, that she was the only person who had ever loved him, and that he hoped that, someday, he would find the courage to ask her for her hand in marriage. He said that if she refused to marry him, he would probably lie in bed all day and sever all contacts with the world; there would be no point in talking to him, reading to him, or playing music to him either.

"He opened his wallet, took out a small photo, softly laid it in my hand like a leaf that fell from a tree, and left. I never saw Keene again."

Didier didn't bother refilling the glass. He grabbed the bottle and sucked it dry without guilt, as the other glasses were still red to the rim.

"It was like an electroshock in slow motion, stretching over a day. Within an hour, my hand had lifted the photo. A few hours later, my eyes reached the peaceful image of a young woman. Spellbound, I could just think of her with Keene, married, finding love and happiness, carving a precious piece of life and rushing to enjoy it before death came to ruin everything—like kids stealing a watermelon from a psychopathic farmer. I saw them at peace, defying the ravages of time, banking a few years of bliss, fleeing the absurdity of life, trying to cheat death for as long as they could."

Didier pulled his wallet out of his back pocket and painstakingly flipped through its contents. A few euros flew out in the wind and twirled down the ravine but this did not affect his determined search.

With a huge smile that declared his search a success, he flicked a photo to Carmina. It showed a young woman laughing, eyes sparkling with joy, embracing life with the abandon and freedom of youth, arms wide open ready to hug the hidden photographer—presumably Keene.

She recognized the pretty lady. And her smile. And her dress. And the shores of the lake along which they had strolled during that beautiful summer day she remembered almost as yesterday. Her hand shook; she almost dropped the photo. The gorge's wind failed to steal it, but taking advantage of her weakened grip, flipped it around her hand. On the back was written "Carmina."

She knew that this was the memento of Keene's life that she had been sent to recover. It made perfect sense. All of his discourse about the number two, all that mumbo jumbo numerology. She hoped she'd be able to bring the photo back without having to explain to Didier the purpose of her visit, or having to disclose the unusual details of Keene's last wishes. Didier would have been one to enjoy the story of the wine-filled coffin, but she didn't dare reveal that folly in front of Sig.

"Same eyes," said Didier. "Eyes never age. That's how I recognized you."

Sig wondered if another dirty old man was trying to hit on his newly minted mother. Before he could threaten some purple belt magic, Didier clarified the situation.

"As I withdrew from my catatonic state and tried to reintegrate into life, I realized that things would never be the same. Human interactions would be difficult. Petty arguments would annoy me endlessly. Social niceties would repulse me. Urban noise would irritate me. All that time wasted on meaningless pursuits and futile labors, filling the week with ego-stroking activities, power plays, and emptiness—too many people killing time, when it is the only precious resource we have.

"To find peace and happiness, to regain sanity, I had to die. Not a stupid death that is nothing but a portal to some communist afterlife prison. Rather, a convenient death that would free me from the shackles of society while allowing me to enjoy paradise on earth.

"So, while at the hospital, nosing around in my last few hours there, I found out where they kept their official 'certificate of death' forms, and snatched a few. Joking around with the staff about all the paperwork I saved them from filling and filing by not dying—social engineering as some call it—I gathered all the information I needed to forge the document. After emptying all of my bank accounts, I submitted the death certificate along with the other necessary paperwork, so that I could officially die.

"No more address, no more driver's license, no more credit cards, no more social security, no more income tax.

"No more of me.

"Thus, I moved here, where I could enjoy some pastoral peace while raising a few crops and livestock on a small piece of borrowed land atop the cliff. I withdrew from the craziness that some call life, just like I withdrew from my catatonic state. All the same.

"Officially dead, to find a real life.

"The only person to whom I ever wrote since moving here was Keene, just to thank him for having given me a new life—without explaining how it happened, and conveniently skipping the details about my legal nonexistence.

"Here alone, at last, I have lived. In full communion with nature and without regrets. And whenever I got depressed by my self-imposed solitude, I pulled out that photo, remembering that another loner I knew found true love, or that maybe true love somehow found him."

Carmina couldn't bring herself to tell him that they were divorced. She hoped Sig wouldn't commit a faux pas.

Sig!

Her heart stopped, realizing that, captivated by Didier's story, she hadn't kept an eye riveted on Sig as she had intended. Instead of being right next to her, within grabbing distance, he had sneaked out of her range. How could she have trusted a wine-guzzling hermit that officially killed himself to warn her if Sig was doing something silly?

As she swung around, she saw Sig lying on his belly along the balcony's wooden railing, sliced in half by it, one leg dangling over the balcony's platform, another over the abyss, holding to wooden posts with both hands, an arm on each side of the railing, face flat towards the story teller.

He didn't see Carmina's terrified face, or that she was frozen by the fear that screaming or moving abruptly would make him lose his grip on life.

"Why do they call you a hermit?" asked Sig.

Didier laughed, as if Sig had missed the punch line of an elaborate joke tedious in its details. The little fans were back.

"Do you want to see my goats?"

Sig jumped on the balcony, eager as a kid.

Three

Justin was more thrilled than ever to see Carmina return. He had come to realize that the single rose of their prior meeting was a serious mistake. What was he thinking?

This time, a large pot hugging a dozen roses sat on the corner of his desk—the corner closest to her. It couldn't possibly be missed. A single flower could escape attention when the senses are blurred by a heartbreaking loss, but even the most bereaved woman couldn't be blind to the assault of a dozen roses displayed within arm's reach—almost in her face. Besides, a dozen roses screamed passion like a burning shrubbery, immensely more effective than a skinny stem crested by a sad lonely bud—just like revealing one's feelings through a love song was immensely more effective than declaring them using Morse code.

So he thought.

Carmina sat in the customary client chair, unbothered by the partially obstructed view. Like a convict talking to a lawyer through a glass, accustomed to the unnatural setting, she was all about the business at hand. Again.

Justin felt like an idiot trying to play hide-and-seek in a bamboo forest. Stabbed through the heart by the utter failure of his plan, he felt like walking to the window, opening it wide, and leaping off to his death—and although very few ever die jumping off a ground-floor window, the symbolic suicidal exit dominated his thoughts, as an irrational escape from the torture of an enthralling siren beyond reach.

Carmina was captive to her own tortures. For the entire return trip, she agonized over Sig's escape from her guardianship, blaming herself for the moment of negligent inattention that allowed him to climb onto the balcony railing, and to hang nonchalantly at the edge of suicide. Was it a defiant act meant to undermine her authority, a teenage prank to torment her, or a genuine cry for help from a suicidal kid? Would calling the psycholo-chick make things worse and break his trust in her?

"Can we go to Japan next?" quipped Sig, popping all those merry suicidal bubbles.

"What?"

"Yeah, yeah, Japan. Let's go see sushi-men, and samurai, and ninjas—real ones, not turtles—and earthquakes, and Godzilla—"

"Whoa, whoa. Where do you get these crazy ideas?" asked Carmina.

"That would be way cool," said Sig, not answering a question that could only lead to a comment like, "You watch way too much television."

"Way cool to you maybe, but I have a life you know."

"Sure. Like what? Slaving for two stupid Dicks?"

Justin didn't dare ask what that meant.

Carmina ignored Sig and addressed Justin.

"Dear lawyer, can we get down to business?"

The "lawyer" epithet felt like a dagger.

"Please, call me Justin," he said, thinking, "Aaarrrggghhh, please, please, please, call me Justin, please."

"Sure. Mr. Justin, can we get down to business, then?"

The "Mr." qualifier was barely better. It was like wiggling the dagger's handle while the blade was still in the wound.

Summoning whatever he had left of morale, he unsealed the manila envelope, pulled out Keene's letter, took two deep breaths, and started to read.

"Day 85.

"Whereas number one fakes obviousness to never be fully revealed, and number two at best complicates things, number three is where problems really start.

"Three is a magic number. Mathematically, physically, metaphysically, and so much more. It is pervasive; it is everywhere, in everything.

"Physically, our entire tangible world is three dimensional, and shapes must have at least three sides to fill that space. Plato believed that triangles were the fundamental building blocks of the world, and he was right as far as protons, neutrons, and electrons are the sides of those triangles that fill all solids, liquids, and gases.

"Mathematically, it is a cornerstone. As a consequence of being the first odd prime number, heir to the only even prime number, it gives birth to endless bizarre theorems and trivialities. For example, if three dollar bills existed, it would be really helpful to know that a number is divisible by three if the sum of its digits is divisible by three—because five plus four equals nine, which is divisible by three, I could pay a $54 purchase only using three dollar bills. Whoopee.

"More pragmatically, to an engineer, the world boils down to Newton's three laws of motion, three equations of static equilibrium, and three equations of dynamic equilibrium—a world where the sum of forces and sum of moments both equal zero with respect to each of the three orthogonal principal axes that define space in Newtonian physics.

"Like a tripod, three is where stability starts, but like a three-legged table, it can be precarious. Naturally, no creature in this world walks on three legs (unless accidentally amputated). Nobody has three arms."

Carmina wondered why Keene had taken time to put to paper his contrived thoughts on numerology. There was nothing wrong with being passionate about the topic, or becoming fascinated by some of the implications of his new philosophical hobby, but he didn't need to be a missionary for it. Was obsession the only mode of operation known to engineers? At least, he retained a bit of his critical judgment and wasn't becoming fanatic about the whole thing—yet.

"Life is a three ring circus parading an endless string of triads. Three blind mice, three little pigs, three musketeers, three stooges, three wise monkeys. The three witches of Macbeth, the three sisters of Chekhov, the three Furies of Greek and Roman mythology. Three ghosts for Christmas, three bears for Goldilocks, three rings for Neptune, three Great Pyramids for Giza, and the Niña, the Pinta, and the Santa Maria.

"Like three course meals, from the times of the Oresteia Trilogy to our era of Star War trilogies, art has been served in triptychs and three act plays.

"Three is a magic number.

"On this third planet from the sun where we have a past, present, and future, which we don't understand and can't comprehend, three is a steroid boost to mysticism, spawning the three pillars of Zen, the three jewels of Buddhism, the three pure ones of Taoism, and all the triple gods and trinities—crucifixion also coming in threesomes, with prerequisite three days before resurrections.

"Three is a magic number.

"There is good, better, or best.

"Gold, silver, and bronze medals, beyond which one doesn't exist.

"Three strikes and you're out, a hat trick and you're a hero. A triathlon and you're superhuman.

"There is good, better, or worse—like earth, some kind of heaven, and some kind of abyss.

"There is certainly yes, certainly no, and maybe—like green, red, and yellow lights.

"There is a beginning, a middle, and an end—like sunrise, midday, and sunset—like life.

"There is a unity created beyond the discordant polarity of two—like mind, body, and spirit, that combine to create a whole.

"There is good luck, bad luck, and contradictions. Third time's a charm, but three times a bridesmaid, never a bride.

"There is the id, the ego, the superego, three branches of government, and all other dysfunctions.

"No wonder the Morse code for SOS is three short bars, three long bars, three short bars.

"Three is when a repetition becomes a pattern.

"Three is when a repetition becomes a pattern.

"Three is when a repetition becomes a pattern.

"And a pattern become the truth, the whole truth, and nothing but the truth. Just like life, liberty, and the pursuit of happiness. Just like Reading, 'Riting, and 'Rithmetic; Respect, Responsibility, and Remorse; Risk, Reward, and Responsibility; Recycle, Reuse, and Reduce; and all the other three R's.

"Tic-Tac-Toe."

That was it: At that instant, Carmina believed she had figured it out. All his dithyrambic reflections, all his disconnected ideas, all his rambling thoughts, betrayed his secret. It had to be dementia. Keene had gone nuts. Not figuratively, but factually. Not asylum-bound cuckoo, but some strain of dementia for sure. Everybody had told her he was a nutcase, but somehow it was just now that it seemed to suddenly make sense, in his disjointed prose and aimless descriptions.

It was a certainty.

Actually, in fairness, more of a highly probable explanation. Or a reasonable guess.

At least, a possibility.

Although, maybe a doubtful one, she debated.

The flaw in her theory was that the symptoms of insanity—if it really had been that—would transpire in Keene's letters, irrespectively of how they would be written. Yet, he had claimed to be hiding behind a computer keyboard in order to prevent revealing the nature of his fatal disease—apparently because his handwriting could divulge too much information on the cause of his degenerating health. So much for her Sherlock Holmes moment. At least, it was worthwhile to consider this theory, if only to be able to rationally discard it. Keene would eventually slip though, and tell it all. These are the kinds of secrets that never die with their host; such burdens have to be unloaded into compassionate listeners. She remained convinced he would eventually disclose it. She just had to continue listening for clues.

"From the nothingness of zero arose the independent one, whose essential relationship with two led to the need to express our understanding or misunderstanding of the universe. In character, three embodies a free flow of energy, our innate desire to verbalize, to imagine, to paint, to sculpt, to sing and shout our love of life. It can be insightful, magically intuitive, versatile, joyful—perfect. It can be life. It is a symbol of fecundity, rewards, and success.

"Yet, like all free flows of energy, it can be a turbulent flow of scattered energies, leading to a pile of unfinished projects, victims to a lack of direction and moodiness. It can be imperfect and self-centered, pessimist and foolhardy, and a risk taker against its more positive attributes of wisdom and knowledge.

"While three notes create a chord, chords are not necessarily harmonious."

"I get it," said Sig, jumping. "This is about kids!"

Carmina and Justin, surprised by the sudden outburst, didn't answer. Not knowing Sig as well as Carmina, Justin had assumed that Keene's ramblings would have gone over the head of a twelve-year-old kid, or at least bored him senseless. After all, Sig hadn't said much in the previous meeting—at least, compared to the first one.

"Come on," Sig added, as if he alone had solved the riddle. "One plus two equals three, you know," he explained, flabbergasted that adults were so thick.

Justin, hesitant to respond and afraid to appear condescending, was relieved when Carmina said, "I think we had figured it out too."

Justin didn't say a word, as the whole three little pigs to tic-tac-toe think had been gibberish to him. He hadn't figured anything out. Numerology wasn't his bag.

"Easy to say, now that I've told everybody."

"Sig, I think it was obvious."

"Can you prove it?"

Carmina frowned, not about to enter into such a silly argument.

"I guess we can't," replied Justin, playing along.

Justin pushed the big flower vase to the desk side, to clear the line of sight between Sig and himself.

"You can't."

"Impossible. That's a fundamental legal principle. Once the cat is out of the bag, nobody can prove they knew what was in the bag before hand."

"Ha! Justin agrees. I'm right," he said, raising his arms triumphantly.

Justin cringed, as his plea to do business on a first name basis had been directed at Carmina. "Mr. Lawyer" would have been perfectly suitable coming from Sig.

"OK, then. Can we listen now to what the rest of the letter says about kids?" asked Carmina.

"Why bother? That dude's crazy," answered Sig. "All I want to know is where we're going next. Just give us the little card," he said to Justin, with more enthusiasm than insolence, hoping that the card would send him on an expedition to the largest theme park on earth.

Carmina wouldn't have minded that approach.

"I'm afraid we have to read the whole letter. That's part of the covenant—I mean the deal. No letter, no card, no deal."

Sig straightened up in the chair and crossed his arms.

"Can you read it like super fast? A thousand words a minutes, like at the ends of the ads on TV when they tell you the part of the deal that is a rip-off. You know, blablablablabla."

"I'm afraid that wouldn't be very respectful to my client."

"No, that would be fine with us," replied Sig, assuming Carmina could only concur.

"No. My client. The one who pays the bill. Mr. Keene—"

"The dead dude is dead. What does he care?"

"Sig," scolded Carmina

"It's true."

"Sig!" she repeated, more firmly.

"It's OK. He's just full of inquisitive sheen."

"You're full of sheen yourself."

"It was a compliment, Sig."

"Yeah, you bet. What I said too."

"Can I resume the reading now?"

"As fast as you can, please."

"Please do, and take your time," corrected Carmina.

Pleased that she endorsed his professionalism, he resumed Keene's letter, at a normal pace—in fact, a bit slower, in hope of not missing those things that were presumably so clear to Carmina and Sig, but that seemed like hopeless irrational rambles to him.

"Yet, in spite of these glorified triads, I never reached three. It's been me, then Carmina and me, and, in the end, just me again. There's a reason for everything, of course. And a time for everything.

"We are all thrown into this world and left alone to fend for ourselves—in spite of well-intentioned parents or not. There are no shelters against predators in our man-made jungles, so while I'm shocked to die now, I'm in fact surprised that I've lived so long. It's true that I'm too young to die per the statistical expectations of our contemporary world; it's also true that in other civilizations I'd be an old geezer beating the odds. The miracle, however, is that I've made it this far.

"In fact, it's a miracle that anyone makes it past their teens, escaping the claws of the ravening wolves hiding their malevolence under the guise of friendship and compassion. It's a miracle to survive the rapacious thieves who dispatch violence and destruction, either openly or deceitfully. It's a miracle that one makes it to adulthood, not bruised enough to recognize the duplicity in a business partner's back-slapping praises, not broken enough to discern the fake smiles and good-natured encouragements of fat liars.

"It's a miracle we don't end up like terrified cats, hunched at the back of our cages, staying away from the open door, bearing battle-scars as reminders that freedom is a trap. That love and friendship can both harbor terrorists conniving to blow up one's peacefulness and sanity. It's a miracle given that each human being is designed like a system without any safeguard against misuse and without any mechanism to protect himself in case of failure.

"A fundamental engineering principle is to create fail-safe mechanisms, to ensure that devices will not cause intolerable harm to other devices or humans in the event of their failure. For example, elevator cabins have a braking mechanism that automatically deploys during free fall accelerations if their cable fails, and a lawnmower's blade rotation automatically stops if one loses grip on its handle bar. Critical buildings can be designed to survive even if one of their columns is blown out, and aircrafts can fly with only half of their engines operating.

"Yet, without taking any fail-safe measure, we fall prey to sweet talkers and seducer like peons dying to stand up and be counted in the survey of suckers born every minute. And sure enough, failure of these fickle relationships leads to intolerable hurt and pain.

"It is amazing that we can simultaneously succeed at engineering highly reliable gadgets, and miserably fail at detecting untrustworthy relationships. At least, just like experience makes for better engineering, time is an ally allowing one to hone the necessary skills to detect the phonies and other pirates that swarm us. Unfortunately, that experience is often the cumulated sum of one's stupid mistakes. More tragic still, new lives are born devoid of any such experience, in pure innocence and ignorance, and history forever repeats itself.

"Think of how wise we'll be the day we die. Too bad life is engineered in such a way that this wisdom isn't there when we needed it. Too bad life can't be lived backwards. Bad engineering. Although, sometimes, it's just a matter of perspective."

Sig didn't dare interrupt anymore after Carmina's reprimand. It just was a tiny admonition for sure—it wouldn't turn into a cold war—but that was the first time during their travels that she had disapproved one of his interruptions, and he couldn't figure out why. Why would she suddenly care about these demented letters?

Carmina had decided to minimize the interruptions. Not that it would be easy with Sig, but she was trying to figure out if Keene really believed he was writing a diary that nobody would ever find—presuming that he had decided to ensnare her in his crackpot venture only after having written it. Except for the engineering examples that sprung up here and there, as if offering explanations to the uninitiated, the tone of the letters, the narrative, the vagueness of the structure, all suggested an abstract audience that could have been only himself. Yet, doing something for no purpose other than to satisfy a selfish need seemed incredibly counter to the engineering mindset. She would continue searching for clues.

"There's always more than two ways to look at things. To an optimist, a glass can be half full, while for a pessimist it is half empty. To an engineer, it just is twice as big than it needs to be. In that perspective, our lives are twice as short as what they should be.

"Or death comes too soon, unexpectedly, like an alarm clock in a hotel room set too early by the previous occupant and that somebody forgot to turn off, in which case, one dies with a lot less wisdom, or has to do some last minute cramming. Dying with so little accumulated wisdom, it's virtually impossible to fill my skull with anything of significance, just like I'm not making any inroads in my study of numerology—hell, I'm still stuck on number three after a hundred days.

"At least, I've settled on one profound thought regarding number three. To geeks, the most important colors are red, green, and blue, because they can be blended four billion different ways to paint a computer screen. To me, today, white, red and rose, are the only three colors that matter as these paint the light of life in wines.

"I'm getting better at recognizing wines, and am still amazed at the variety and richness of that world. After so many years lost in meaningless numbers, slaving to serve ingrate masters, I have finally found beauty in the world. I feel like a prisoner, born in an isolation unit, totally disconnected from the essence of life, locked within bland walls and behind a steel door, without even a keyhole to peek through for glimpses of the real world, who is suddenly released, thrown outside the prison walls, without warning, onto railroad tracks, finding himself staring at the sun, the blue sky, the blue world, the blue sun, whatever, in awe and puzzlement, mesmerized by the beauty of it all, standing on a railroad, immobile—until a train will pass through.

"And at that moment, I will make peace with the past, hugging a few mementos of my years here."

"Is it over? Can we get the address?" asked Sig, as if he deserved a reward for having remained silent so long.

"Yes it's over."

Keene's abrupt finishes always left Carmina unsettled, as if he assumed she would continue to serve as his glorified courier, that she was willing to religiously follow his instructions, without questioning. It was her right to be insubordinate. How did he know she wouldn't? Or was he just gambling she wouldn't, at the risk of his letters remaining unread and his dollars fueling a wasteful bonfire.

"Give me the card," begged Sig.

Justin handed it to him without saying a word, assuming Carmina implicitly acquiesced. Then, he gave Carmina a small letter.

"It's a personalized note to your attention that Keene has attached to the index card," he clarified.

She opened it and read it silently.

"Thanks to you for the photo," wrote Keene, given that if she was to read this letter, she had made it that far and had the photo in hand.

"At first, I wished I could have returned the favor. I looked for a picture of me—one taken before I learned I was going to die—but such a thing doesn't seem to exist. I found one in which I'm 25 years old. In some ways, it could have been suitable, because in my head that's the age I'll always be—the clock in my brain has stopped, even though the biological one refuses to honor that brilliant idea. In truth though, such a photo would serve no purpose, as you already know what I looked like then. So I have no photo for you. Maybe it's better that way. The ravages of time are invisible to lovers navigating together, but less kind to broken relationships.

"Thanks again, Carmina, for continuing to repatriate a few precious mementoes of my insignificant passage through this world."

This was the first time he had addressed Carmina directly.

"What does it say?" asked Sig.

"Where do we go now," she replied. "Another exciting place?"

"Pfff. That's not Japan for sure," said Sig, disappointed to not repeat the plane experience.

"Where then?" asked Carmina.

"Boring! Just a boring car ride away."

Carmina was delighted to avoid another tiresome trip, but kept her feelings to herself to not sadden Sig. She left it to Justin to try to cheer him up—but he said nothing.

His silence was heavy. In fact, if anything, she thought he looked a bit gloomy.

"Is everything fine?"

"Yeah, sure, I'm OK."

"Good to hear. It's just that you looked worried."

Justin wished he had something clever to offer, if only just reassuring cautions. A bright and beautiful woman like Carmina wouldn't come back once her business was over unless he could win her with some wit or brilliance—anything to be deemed worthy of a possible relationship.

"Damn roses didn't work," was all he could think. Maybe something else would? Would brighter curtains help, lifting the flowers out of the shadow? There had to be professionals knowledgeable about such things.

"Nope. Just tired. Professional wear and tear," he said, upset that such a bland response was all he could muster, thinking that this was just as effective as bashing his own head with a hammer.

Enforcement

In this day and age of widespread obesity, Sig was used to being surrounded by adults who stood to benefit from shedding a few dozen pounds—or more. He recognized obesity to be both the trademark of a successful football lineman, and the calamity that awaits soda-guzzling folks with sedentary careers that sit on their ass all evening watching television. He knew that fat computer scientists and beer-bellied policemen were favorite Hollywood clichés—and, at times, real-life characters too.

Yet, there was something about a 500-pound policeman that fascinated Sig in a less than courteous manner. More than siphoning beer kegs, more than unbridled calorie intake, more than an idle lifestyle, this had to be suicide in slow motion. The policeman, while of grumpy demeanor—like all policemen Sig ever met, it seemed—gave no hints of a self-destructive bent; nor did he show signs of a depressive personality. Yet, to Sig, he was a fat, grumpy, pig that had found a lousy way to attempt suicide.

Carmina was grateful that Captain Dalton Rock had agreed to meet them on such a short notice. Given that the previous meetings had been problematic in unexpected ways, she was apprehensive of Sig's behavior in a police station. Her nervousness showed, which the policeman interpreted as either a sort of uneasiness toward his weight problem, or as a consequence of the impact that the mighty law enforcement enterprise can have on impressionable minds. He preferred to not dwell on this topic.

"Flogging crappy news," he said repeatedly, like a mantra, when he learned of Keene's death.

In spite of being used to dealing with bums and lowlifes, Dalton attempted to be considerate enough in the presence of a lady and her kid to adapt his professional lexicon, substituting his favorite custom profanities with "flogging" and "crap." That unnatural old fashion sensibility made him feel like a ridiculous hick about to say "dagnabbit" every two sentences, so a few translation omissions slipped by during the mantra, grating Carmina's ears.

"I apologize ma'am for that, but I deal with bums all day. Those words, ma'am, they're my working clothes. They're glued to my skin, I can't take them off easily."

Sig was amused that a mountain of a man had to apologize for the same cusswords that all kids at the Ranch had been saying since birth, albeit not in the presence of Ranch staff, and certainly not while in the care of potential adopting parents—unless things got ugly and specific events created an unredeemable parental mismatch, at which point all censorship was lifted.

Clearly, given his reaction to the news, Dalton hadn't been in contact with Keene, nor had he been warned of their upcoming visit. She explained the purpose of the visit, sticking to the business at hand, not going into the details of the treasure hunt, and certainly not mentioning the wine-filled coffin awaiting her return.

"It is strange that we are here to get something from you, not knowing exactly what that is, but Keene indicated that you were an old friend and that you would know exactly what he's looking for," she explained, paraphrasing the information on the index card—which might have used the word "acquaintance" instead.

"Embarrassing" would likely have been more appropriate than "strange" in most circumstances, but she wasn't about to apologize for Keene's folly.

"An old friend? That's interesting."

"That's not the case?" she replied, half annoyed, half disappointed. So much for paraphrasing.

Dalton might have twitched a bit, but nobody could tell as his wrapping made him look impassive.

"It depends really on what you call a friend, doesn't it?"

Carmina wondered what kind of crazy nutcase Keene had again rubbed elbows with.

"I don't know. Friend, as in a person attached to another by friendship I guess," she suggested, realizing that this was a circular definition, and that this was a moot point since Keene had no friends anyhow. "Some kind of personal regard... like the bonding between guys who watch football together, maybe?"

She was in slippery territory, and knew it. Dalton remained impassive.

"I don't know... Whatever you want to call that relationship. I'm just a messenger here," she added, taking some distance to hide her frustration.

Unsure of whether she was impatient or just nervous, Dalton decided to clarify his views on the topic, for the record.

"In my opinion, ma'am, whether you want it or not, a gang of guys is never a gang of friends."

His poetic soul would have said, "Men together are like a pack of blood-thirsty wolves. They can't live in harmony with the rest of nature, unless harmony means finding new prey, day after day. It's in their nature to terrorize, destroy, and chew up 'harmony' that lies across their path. And when their hunt is unsuccessful, they'll ostracize the weakest of their lot and turn to cannibalism without hesitation."

It came out as, "Gangs are like flogging wolves."

His soul would have said, "Except that men are more vicious than wolves. Wolves are prisoners of their genetic heritage, carnivores for their survival, in a brutal world ruled by the cruel laws of the jungle. Men have options. Yet these vanish at once when the peace of solitude is broken."

It came out as, "But worse."

His soul would have said, "Men can't treat each other as equals. They just can't. They can preach eternally whatever gospel of solidarity or equality they wish; their actions speak a different language. Their allegiance is only to themselves. Their egos are the only driver. Like little kids starved for attention, kicking and hitting the walls or anybody around to be noticed, they are sad little brats. The smaller and more insignificant they are, the more they crave power, the more they need to bully their way to the top."

It came out as, "Guys will crap on each other's heads and crush anyone to get ahead."

His soul would have said, "The world is a cruel jungle where charm exists to lull the naive souls into the claws of predators, where individuals willingly sacrifice others to ensure not only their survival, but their mere advancement in status and other petty ambitions. Kindness is an illusion for fools about to be crushed, as too many humans plainly lack humanity. Kindness is like offering your neck to vampires about to suck you dry in hope of immortalizing a few fleeting friendships. Kindness is a dangerous proposition when it blinds to the mask of lies that friends wear to steal your ideas, your time, your possessions, your life, until they are ready to move to leech off of another host who has more to offer, leaving your empty carcass to rot. Friends will abandon you, leave you to fend for yourself in threatening situations—when they are not outright the most dangerous threat themselves."

It came out as, "Don't ever trust anyone. A guy will pretend to be your friend only when he can use you to his benefit. He'll pretend to respect you, slap you on the back, joke around with you, be buddy buddy all he can. But once there's nothing else he can suck out of you, he'll backstab you, have you gunned down, or—if he's not a flogging coward—just plain shoot you in the face himself."

His soul would have said, "The insanity of it all is that most arrogant charmers do their dirty deeds convinced that they are being good mates, great friends, helpful colleagues, considerate and attentive confidants. That they are absolutely great human beings who would never imagine for a moment that their feeling of superiority, their so-called stronger vision, deeper values, better something over everybody else, is just wrong. If anything, they could only feel misunderstood and take by force or by stratagems what they believe to justly deserve."

It came out as, "Whether it's gangs in the street, or co-workers in the office, doesn't matter. Whether the bastards are on asphalt or in glass towers, it's just the same crap, except that the kills are more in your face on the street."

His soul would have said, "They'll scheme to get what they long for, subconsciously knowing that this requires intense dishonesty, hypocrisy, duplicity, rapacity, and treason; consciously unaware that they are ignoble individuals."

It came out as, "Don't ever get fooled. Friends will lie to you. They'll betray you. They'll abandon you. Friends are crap in a gang of guys."

His soul would have said, "Face it. Friends just don't exist."

It came out as, "Face it. Friends just don't exist."

His soul would have said, "Covetous crooks and despicable liars that pretend to be friends will never change. Whether they are drug dealers or stock brokers, whether they dropped out of sixth grade or have Ph.D.s, whether they operate in strip joints or universities, it doesn't matter. They'll never change. Never. Unless struck by the lightning of a life-changing dramatic event."

It came out at, "Scumbags will remain scumbags—until they snap out of it."

He paused, playing with his pen, hesitating for a moment, sighing, before re-emphasizing, "Until they just flogging snap out of it."

Carmina was upset. She should have known better. Why did she believe that Keene could possibly have had a friend? For a moment, she almost imagined that he was sending her to meet more than mere acquaintances. Frederick and Didier were odd, but appeared to be decent human beings—at least, on the surface. Dalton, on the other hand, was without a doubt a grumpy, bitter, grating, appalling jerk—and most likely with low self-esteem to boot.

There it was, in front of her, a mountain of evidence that Keene had remained the same guy she had known, even during the days leading to his death—because, for some cynical reason, he had sent her to meet a most horrible person. She had to chase from her mind all those asinine hopes of late-life spiritual metamorphosis—these melodramatic fantasies of exuberant optimism triumphing over dark cynicism. She had to stop imagining Keene as a born-again human being, or a mysterious angel trapped by the curse of an oddball personality—or anything else than the boring engineer he had always been for that matter—and focus instead on completing her mission, which, simply enough, consisted of fetching a few meaningless baubles as fast as possible to be able to resume her normal life after this ordeal. She couldn't care less to make small talk with members of Keene's club of crazies.

"Are you a detective?" asked Sig.

Stunned by the question out of the blue, it took him a moment to respond.

"No. Why? Is this what you want to be when you grow up?"

"I'm already grown up," said Sig. Looking at the 500 pound mass of flesh behind the desk, he added, "Not as much as you maybe, but I'm grown up."

Sig felt anyone could be a detective. He could tell from the condensation on the half-empty soda bottle on the desk that it had been opened just before they arrived. The fact that the policemen had already downed half of the two-liter bottle by 9 a.m. provided evidence suggesting that the full-sized fridge—not a mini as found in many offices—was filled solid with similar bottles; and maybe chocolates too. Sig the sleuth also imagined half a dozen hypotheses to explain Dalton's morbid obesity—psycholo-chick would be proud.

Dalton sensed Carmina's hostility. Prickly urbanites who disliked cops, but enjoyed a freedom that was never free after all—what else was new? He would have much preferred to be left alone, for sure, but Keene had sent her. He had no choice. He maybe couldn't chitchat with a puritan, bourgeois lady without being rude—at least to some degree—but he thought that a sassy kid was within his reach.

"So you're grown up, eh?" he said, taking a good look. "I guess you are. But there's grown up, and 'grown up.' That's two different things, kid."

He called him kid on purpose.

"Says who?"

"I don't know. I'll tell you what. Why don't you decide? I'll tell you a story, then you decide."

"What do I get out of it?"

"There's no prize, kid. You just get one more story."

"For what?"

"For nothing. Just to compare. In the end, there's no gift in life. Two crappy lives aren't better than one. But, it's always nice to compare. You've had a rough run at it? Fine. But if your life's not as crappy as the other guy, you won't win a stuffed bear, but you'll sleep good at night, I promise."

"I'm too old for fairy tales."

"This one's real. There's no pink skies, no purple animals, no magic, no fake good ending. Just the real deal."

Dalton paused a moment, just in case there were other objections to extinguish. Carmina didn't look happy, or particularly approving, but didn't seem scandalized either—at least, not yet. Satisfied by the silence, he started his story.

"It happened years ago. Decades ago. Not here. Another small town—far enough from here. It doesn't matter where. A crappy town greased by one giant ore-sucking company that plays God and Devil, like a half-mad sheriff that nobody can stand, but that nobody dares stand up to."

Sig faked a yawn, not impressed by the policeman's story telling abilities, but to no effect—the yawning looked too real and nobody was paying attention to him anyhow. Or so it seemed.

"A rough place, like many others, with too little respect and too much back-breaking labor; too few cops and too much crime, too little freedom and too much booze; too little love and too much anger. The worse school of life with the worst teachers, letting too many ignorant teenagers be fooled by all kind of bull, leading them to think that gangs of scumbags are like cozy little families."

Dalton paused. Like a front row witness to a senseless butchery, forever trying—in vain—to suppress the horrific memories as if nothing ever happened, he wasn't eager to return to the past. This was a story that would have remained untold to his death, if not for Keene's dying first.

"One can 'make a living' in that town for sure. Most of the time, the average Joe will marry the average Jane, have a few kids, buy a bungalow, a car, a TV, some toys, and enough crap to find some measure of happiness. But there are no guarantees. So many things can go wrong—as they often do. Life happens, and things can get ugly. Someone can upset the mad sheriff, someone else can be crushed by fear—even if only the fear of a claustrophobic life—another one can drown the pain in rubbing alcohol for the muscles and non-rubbing alcohol for the rest. It all adds to the jungle."

Sig had stopped yawning. This was too familiar a decor, in a country foreign to fairy tales.

"There was a poor kid in that town. A high school kid I knew. He didn't get many lucky breaks in life, but he was a hard worker that kid, I tell you. One summer, he took all the odd jobs he could find—day jobs, night jobs, pushing papers, cleaning toilets, anything—trying to fit into the system it seemed, scraping by and saving all of his money because somebody somehow had planted in his head the idea that he might be able to go to some college. So all his paychecks went straight to the bank. All piled up there in case his dream ever came true. He saved it all. Never spending a dime, except once. By the end of the summer, to reward himself for three months of punishing labor, he bought himself one gift. One stupid gift, for three months of eighty hour work weeks: a pair of 'Flubex Air' sneakers."

"I remember those," said Carmina. "Trendy and expensive. They were the rage when I was young. They were everywhere."

"Yes ma'am, they were. But they're 'everywhere' only on TV when you live in a crappy town. They had to be special ordered. That was a stupid thing to do, but kids do stupid things. Like walking on the wrong street, at the wrong time, taking a short cut through a usually deserted area and running into a gang of scumbags."

"They stole his shoes?" asked Sig.

"Yes son, but it's—"

"That's dumb! Why didn't they just steal his money and buy themselves some shoes?"

"It's because—"

"Why didn't they just break into a store and steal shoes there?"

Tired of being interrupted, Dalton just waited for Sig to cool off.

"So?" added Sig, as if it should have been obvious that he was done, patiently silent, and eager to know why criminals were so dumb in that moronic village that Dalton kept talking about.

"It had nothing to do with the sneakers, and everything to do with the crab bucket syndrome."

"The what?" asked Sig.

"Here's a fishing tip for you son: If you put crabs in a bucket, don't bother putting a lid on it, even if it is a shallow bucket from which a single crab could manage to escape, because if any crab tries to climb the bucket wall, the other crabs will pull him back. Nobody escapes the crab bucket. Everybody's fate is to be the same. Anyone who can succeed where the others can't will be pulled back down by his peers."

"How is stealing stupid running shoes going to prevent him from going to college?"

"It won't. The shoes were just an excuse. When the leader of the scumbags asked for the shoes, it wouldn't have mattered one bit if he had given them the shoes or had swallowed them whole in one gulp instead. He would still have punched him in the face with brass knuckles, opening gashes and breaking his nose. He would still have grabbed him by the hair, dragged him around like a puppet, and thrown him on the pavement. He would still have kicked him in the ribs with his steel-toed boots and heard the sharp sound of a bone fracture. He would still have called him a faggot for not fighting back while kicking him five more times in the ribs, with more bones snapping like broken twigs. He would still have lifted him and told two of his thugs to pin him against a dumpster while he swung a baseball bat at his arms and legs, as if trying to hit home runs over the fenced street, fracturing bones into fragments inside the folded limbs. He would still have taken the masonry block that kept a garbage lid shut tighter than what rats could push, and thrown it at him, missing bull's-eye but bouncing on the side of his head with a cracking noise. He would still have pulled his jackknife, ready to ram it through multiple times, and probably could have killed the kid if not disturbed in his crabby anger by the sound and headlights of an approaching car. He would still have run away leaving the broken body in a pool of blood."

Carmina was shocked by the gory play-by-play description of the horrible beating.

Undeserved.

Unjustifiable.

Unjust.

Petty jealousy hidden behind the lame pretext of a robbery—the stealing of dumb running shoes having an overblown and artificial prestige, courtesy of the crushing blow of devious marketing on impressionable minds.

"What does the story have to do with friends?" asked Sig, nowhere near as shocked as Carmina, and waiting for the whole thing to make sense.

"Ah, yeah. Friends. I forgot. Yeah, that kid had a friend. Quite a friend. A friend that considered himself to be his best friend. Indeed, being such good friends, they were together on that fateful day, but he didn't have trendy running shoes and it was well known that he'd never go college, so he was of no interest to them. The leader of the scumbags gave him a simple choice: To be punched in the face until his nose popped up behind his head, or to himself kick his best friend in the balls. He didn't hesitate one bit, and after a few vigorous kicks, they let him run away—making it clear that he hadn't seen anything, and that they'd come for him if he ever said otherwise to anyone. So much for friendship in this dog-eat-dog world."

"Did you ever catch that criminal? Was he ever brought to justice?"

"Uh, no ma'am. But he caught himself, in some ways. I mean, some things caught up to him. It's one thing for a bum to kill a bum. It can be quite a vicious fight with slashing blows exchanged both ways. Or it can be a swift bullet dispensing an expedient kill. But it's quite something else for a bum to nearly pummel to near death a defenseless human being who's clueless as to what caused such a crazy assault. I'm not a philosopher, and I wasn't in school long, but I think that there are still some kids that weren't born with an urge to kill—especially not to kill those who haven't done anything wrong. There maybe is a point of no return in a criminal's life, but long before jumping off that cliff, there are opportunities to turn one's life around. These appear, like beacons of hope, showing where the roads taken and not taken will lead. Well, to be honest, 'beacons of hope' is a cute image, but it's a lie. It's actually more like emotional numbness, sweaty nightmares, shaking hands, and an overall inability to function. Anyhow, this was one such unique chance to redeem oneself, to put back on track a life gone astray, and that criminal decided to turn his life around. Overnight, he moved to a different town, far away—had to be another town, 'cause snitches would otherwise have brought him back into the crab bucket. There, he wrote and mailed a long and sincere apology letter to his last victim, joined the local police force, and spent his life trying to turn some scumbags into human beings—fighting a good fight, but not always winning."

"There's no 'growing up' in that stupid story," said Sig. "That guy should be rotting in jail."

"In some ways, a part of him is in a jail he'll never escape, but I agree with you, that this may not be sufficient. But, as a cop, I'd rather have him outside helping put scumbags inside, than inside just waiting to continue being a scumbag when he gets out."

As far as Sig was concerned, this was pure hogwash. That kind of clemency was impossible—unbelievable. This had to be a total lie or some false and wishful outcome, fit for feel-good Hollywood movies with syrupy endings, but bearing no relationship to what really happened. Yet, he didn't say it. He believed it was pointless to argue with a policeman, as cops too easily confused truth with power. Besides—purple belt or not—he wasn't about to pick a fight with such an intimidating mountain of a policeman.

"Did he get a reply to his letter?" asked Carmina.

"Unreplied, ma'am. Goes without saying. Who would have replied after such a beating? Would you?"

"An apology letter is a weak way to amend—"

"Right. A stupid letter. Bad English too, you can bet—bums can't write anything but flogging crap anyhow. What was he thinking, right? Even Jesus wouldn't have flogging forgiven him. A stupid letter..."

"I didn't mean—"

"We're dealing with bums here, ma'am. That's probably all he could think of, or all he could do."

"That's a great fairy tale, Jabba," said Sig, "but we're here for business."

"Sig!" said Carmina.

She feigned outrage at the deliberate provocation—she had to—but only measuredly, as she was also eager to leave.

"I'm sorry, we've had a long trip, and it's still a long drive back—"

"I know, ma'am. I shouldn't bother you with all this nonsense."

"We're only here to pick—"

"Yeah, I got that. You said it already."

Carmina resented being interrupted constantly. Maybe she shouldn't have stopped Sig after all.

"I know exactly what Keene is looking for," he said. "It can be only one thing."

Sig, thinking that Dalton was about to stand up, was curious to see how that would happen, but the Captain just swiveled his chair to reach the bottom drawer of a file cabinet from which he pulled a wrinkled paper bag. He slammed the bag on his desk—maybe it was just normal for a heavy arm—and rested cross-armed on it, trying to think of appropriate parting words. Crushed down to a few inches thick under his weight, the bag clearly didn't contain anything fragile.

After a sigh, handing the bag over to Carmina, he said, "I sincerely hope that Keene didn't die because of complications from a debilitating injury that never fully healed."

She grabbed the bag.

They exchanged polite thanks and other formalities.

They were pleased to leave; he was relieved they left.

Their encounter ended abruptly, like a bad amateur movie shot before the digital era and whose script was truncated when the last foot of film that the producer could afford spun through the camera's sprockets. End of budget, end of film, end of story—whether or not there was time to shoot a happy ending.

Carmina threw the bag on the back seat and drove off. Windows down, no radio, she needed to let the wind cleanse the weirdness of that nonsense.

Easier said than done.

Her mind wandered, trying to make sense of the nonsense. It couldn't just be nonsense. Not with Keene. Yet, it wasn't the Keene she knew, so maybe it was just nonsense and nothing more. Or maybe not.

At least, the tumult in her mind thwarted the risk of falling asleep at the wheel while driving on the dull, dark road. It reminded her of a magazine article that described how people who survived horrible car accidents often recalled seeing their entire life flash before their eyes an instant before the crash. Images from childhood to their last memory just rushing in a burst, like a movie fast-forwarding at warp speed. Some theorized that this phenomenon was due to the brain frantically scanning all memories in search of a solution to escape the collision. Others conjecture religious explanations of various kinds.

So maybe this was what Keene was doing—replaying his life before dying. Except that, in this case, the instant before the final collision had slowed down into a crawling six months, affording him the luxury of replaying in real time some defining moments of his life. Not necessarily in order.

The thought was interesting, but it didn't answer why Keene would wish to do that. It was an explanation that just replaced a question with another one, without really solving the problem—just like science keeps finding more about the origin of the world while never explaining how something got created out of nothingness.

She drove distracted, bored by the highway, unable to read Keene's mind, not paying attention to anything, not paying attention to Sig... Until he unbuckled and jumped over to the back seat. It stunned her, but the car didn't swerve a bit. She knew this moment would come.

Sig opened the bag, stared into it, and pulled out something he had never seen before, but correctly guessed to be a brand new pair of Flubex Air sneakers.

Four

Justin had scattered bouquets of red roses throughout the office. On his desks, on the coffee tables, on the windowsill, on the floor, on the computer, on the file cabinets, as well as on the library shelves—sacrificing more books to storage for the occasion. He would have even wrapped some around the dog's collar and dunked a bunch in the aquarium if he had owned pets. A dozen dozens, in plain vases not competing for attention.

Not bunches of fancy flower arrangements, because it could have reminded her of a funeral, and he would not have known how to react if she had commented on it. The embarrassment would have literally killed him, and with funeral flowers at the ready like an awkward farewell note, it would have left others wondering in disbelief how he had managed to commit suicide by a self-induced heart attack—in full ignorance of that extremely rare phenomenon called a broken-heart attack.

Not any kind of flowers either. It had to be the perfect expression of his true sentiments. He had spent hours on the internet reading about the meaning of flowers; on how Chrysanthemums and Irises shyly proclaim "You are a wonderful friend" (delivering a grossly inadequate message); on how a red carnation bled, "My heart aches for you," while a striped one replied, "No, Sorry, I cannot be with you" (risking a dangerous petal dialogue); on how Orchids are too sensually seductive (almost pornographically explicit when viewed straight-on); and concluding that the whole flower world is rife with conniving double and triple meanings that could benefit from the expert advice of a legal clean up team well versed in contract law.

Hours of internet browsing, to end up back at the starting point. At least, red roses seemed a safe bet—almost an archetype—to unequivocally express a precious love and passion, although it never occurred to him that 144 of them shouted it a bit loud.

"Wow. You've made nice changes to your office," Carmina said as she entered.

It worked!

"How did you end up with all these flowers?"

Silence.

He had worked so hard on getting the flowers noticed, he didn't have time to hatch a well-thought-out follow-up plan to start the courtship.

Panic.

"I bought them for you," he thought of saying, but pleased he didn't, fearing that putting all his cards on the table was not an advisable strategy. It would have been like trying to attract squirrels by shouting, "Peanuts!" in a megaphone.

"I thought, like, well, that it would enliven things a bit; the office that is, you know."

He felt like a bumbling idiot.

"It certainly does, doesn't it," she said looking at Sig.

Sig pouted and shrugged.

"Well I think it does. And it smells great too," she added. "It will definitely make it more pleasant to work."

"Work?" thought Justin.

"Of course, let's work," he said—without rolling his eyes or banging his head on the wall or jumping off the window.

He sat at his desk, shuffled papers distractedly, trying to find a way to put the courtship back on track, but couldn't think of anything clever—or even just effective without being clever. "What kid of miserable lawyer can't make a decent opening statement?" he thought. "A stupid one," was the only answer that came to mind. Stupid, stupid, stupid. This was his case to solve, and he wasn't about to demean himself to ask his brothers or his colleagues to help. The shame it would have been; he'd be a laughing stock. But how, by all means, how was he to crack this case?

Stupid, stupid, stupid, stupid, stupid...

"Is this what you're looking for?" said Sig, pointing to a folder under twelve roses and a vase.

"Ha! Yes, yes, yes. There it is."

Sig wondered why adults never could see what's in front of them. Had to be stupidity—or that they needed glasses but were too proud to admit it.

"Did your last visit go well at least?"

"Got old smelly sneakers out of it," said Sig, trying to sound cool. He had tried on the Flubex Airs, to see what the commotion of times bygone was all about, and concluded that they were nothing more than uncomfortable, cheaply made clown shoes—although being three sizes too big didn't help. Nothing to kill for.

"No problem otherwise?" asked Justin, still stalling for time, unable to think of anything.

"It... It went fine. As far as the trip is concerned," she said.

Justin wasn't a friend, far less a confidant, but a lawyer living in a field of roses who happened to care for his clients beyond duty and invoicing, so Carmina shared her burden, if only a bit.

"It's just, in some strange way, demanding."

"They're weirdos," volunteered Sig.

"No they're not."

"Freaks."

"Stop that. You can't understand."

Sig waited, raising one eyebrow, daring a logical explanation better than his.

She had none.

"I should quit this," she sighed.

"That's not even an explanation," shouted Sig.

Justin feared the worst, and this wasn't about loss of billable hours.

"Ms. Jewell. I'm so sorry to hear this. Is there anything I could do to help? I'd love to be of any assistance if you wish—"

"There's nothing you can do. It's just me. Please understand. These visits... My ex-husband... These people he knew and I didn't. These letters... It's surreal."

"You are certainly free to stop at anytime," he said, out of duty, but feeling even more stupid for jeopardizing his chances of ever seeing her again. He rectified his mistake by adding, "Or maybe just a little break of a few days, or few hours—"

"No, I'm fine," she said, shaking her head quickly.

"Freaks, that's all," clarified Sig.

"That's right, Sig," she said, giving up, smiling eyes closed.

Justin melted. The most beautiful smile he had seen since the day she had walked into his life. The most gorgeous smile of his entire life. The canons were forever shot!

"May I suggest we proceed then?" he said, gambling that time was the best ally to counter the futility of his total lack of strategy. Now that the flowers had broken the ice, he needed to figure out how to stay afloat, and sail. There would be another session; there would be time before then.

He unsealed the enveloped and started to read.

"Day 55.

"Four has to be the engineer's number in numerology. It reveals itself as the most practical. It is like a contractor hired by Number Three to built a bridge from the conceptual idealism of Number Three, to the practical world of Number Four, because even though we live in a 3-D world, the simplest solid object that can be created with straight lines is a tetrahedron—built with four triangles."

"He missed a number," shouted Sig.

"What do you mean?"

"I'm telling you, he missed a number."

"The last letter was about number three, Sig," corrected Justin.

"No, there's that other number," searching for his words.

"Well, let's continue to read for now, and just tell us later if you remember," concluded Justin.

"Four is the first number that can be created from others, the first that can result from the multiplication of numbers other than one and itself. It is the number of the tangible creation, of structure and organization. It's the boring engineer of numerology. It defines our physical world, with its four classical elements of earth, air, fire, and water, its four cardinal points, and its four seasons. It is the number of invention and ingenuity, symbol of the struggle to break down limits and create value, armed with a scientific mind and a practical attention to details. The organization and management foundation on which rest the genie of achievement. It is used to define the four phases of the moon, and force-fit roughly four weeks per month.

"It was coopted by various faiths to structure their beliefs, with four noble Buddhist truths, four gospels, four types of Sioux gods, and the four letters of the Jewish Tetragrammaton. It was even interwoven into the tetractys of the Pythagoreans, with its pyramidal row of 1, 2, 3, and 4 entries, which has served as the oath of allegiance for Greek philosophers, as the basis for brain-twisters of mathematical curiosity, and as a map to arrange pins in a bowling alley."

Keene was back into his quest for truth in numerology, which bored Justin to no end. It puzzled him that Carmina had once married such a guy, but couldn't see his flowers until today. He had hoped to find the key to Carmina's heart in some of Keene's letters, but it was becoming clear that this was most unlikely to happen.

"Being the product of other numbers, it can be an eccentric personality driven by the conflicting drives of its original impulses, as if suffering a multiple personality disorder, like all the strikingly innovative creators do—shocking their audience, like some English four letter words do."

Sig flashed a mischievous smile, but Carmina's stern look stopped him before he could demonstrate his ability to shock.

"Except for the dissidence of Oriental numerology, because the Chinese word for four is an homonym of the one for death; except for the four humors of Hippocratic medicine that led to appalling treatments to rebalance the levels of black bile, yellow bile, phlegm, and blood in sick people—before telling patients they were left with six months to live; and except for the Four Horsemen of the Apocalypse whose purpose is to destroy the world, four is a number of stability and solid grounding. It is the roots and the foundation.

"And then, thinking about all of these soaring numerology images, reading about how projects formulated at the higher ideal stage of number three often fail to materialize because of the constraints and limitations that must be satisfied to embody that ideal at the stage of number four—and all that jazz—it struck me that numerologists, in their grand but far from infinite wisdom, skipped over one of the most important numbers, and casually remained silent about one of the universe's rules. They conveniently forgot about the mystery of pi."

"That's the one, that's the one!" shouted Sig.

"What pi?" asked Justin.

"Lawyers don't know pi?" he asked, looking at Carmina, pointing his thumb towards Justin, eyes wide open, as if lawyers went to school on a different planet.

"I'm sure he knows. It's just not something they use every day in court."

"There you go," said Justin, with a gleam of hope that Carmina's protective excuse revealed that she harbored at least a fondness towards him—possibly other endearing feelings too.

"Pfff! That's fifth grade stuff."

"Fifth grade is a long time ago for us you know," she said, as if one was allowed to empty one's brain of the older curricular material to make room for newer stuff.

More gleaming hope.

"Let's continue, if we may," said Justin. "Where were we? There: 'conveniently forgot about the mystery of pi.'"

"Numerologists were clearly counting on their fingers, where there is obviously no pi.

"Yet, while they can wax at length about how pyramids that consist of four triangles (i.e. each three-sided) resting on a four-sided square—like the Pyramid of Cheops—are links between abstract ideals and their embodiment, they completely missed the infinite number wedged in between three and four. That's a crucial omission, especially given that the length of any side of Cheops' pyramid is equal to half its height times pi—the infinite number that starts with 3.141592653 and extends to infinity without ever using an infinitely repeating pattern of numbers in the process. Supercomputers number crunching around the clock in the search for the end of pi, have not yet found it after trillions of digits, and may never—which is fine.

"After all, it would be a bummer if somebody ever found the last digit of pi. All of those grand concepts of infinite and infinity would be thrown out the window if the gazillionth and final decimal of pi was to be found. The books would be closed on the topic, thousands of nerds would move on to something else to do, a definitive website could be compiled, and one more mystery would just become a mundane entry in the annals of mathematics. The ratio of a circle's circumference to its diameter would be heralded to be a finite constant value, stored on an official international repository, and life would move on, as it always does.

"Maybe numerologists aren't interested by the infinite. Or maybe they tried to capture infinite intangibles with finite numbers, letting three and four conveniently straddle pi. Or maybe it's just that the theories of numerologists, like too many other human constructs, sadly sin by absolutism.

"That major oversight is significant enough to cool any engineer's enthusiasm for numerology. Maybe this is the inescapable crisis of faith that ardent believers reach at some point. However, in my case it won't change much. First, I have already invested nearly three quarters of my new life to that study, so a change of course at this stage would be futile. Second, numerology is more of a curiosity than a faith to me, so the crisis isn't acute. Actually, even the crisis is a curiosity in itself, as I wonder which number I'll reach before losing interest or losing my breath—whichever comes first. Third, I found another passion, growing in intensity everyday, surpassing all other interests, as it embraces life better than any abstract numerical mind game. It even is fully compatible with the concept of infinity and non-whole numbers, which is essential to blend varieties into a sublime continuum of possible flavors, colors, and smells.

"For that matter, if numerologists had been wine masters, Cabernet Sauvignon, Merlot, Cabernet Franc, and Malbec would have never met in the divine Saint-Émilions, Margaux, and Pomerols, because they would have been unable to rationalize the infinite variety of Bordeaux that can be created by blending three or four different types of grapes. Such is the curse of stuck-up absolutists.

"As such, my decision to investigate numerology, while still an interesting pursuit, now pales to my passion to discover new wines. If this constitutes unfaithfulness to the dogma of numbers, then I confess my sins since I can't renounce my addiction to wine.

"I'll never become an oenophile—fleeting time being the obstacle—but at the current sampling rate, I am powerless to resist the seduction. Just like orchids in their delicate mystery, wines are like women and I'm in love."

For a brief moment, Carmina wondered if that was a generic—possibly inebriated—statement intended to be inclusive of all of womankind, or if he was in love with another woman. Then, she realized her confusion.

"I am in love with the velvety smoothness of Chardonnays that caress like voluptuous encounters, the freshness of Rieslings that kiss like angels, the fragrant romance of Gewurztraminers that entrap like devilish perfumes, the soothing tenderness of Merlots that fell like gratifying massages of goddesses, the devious corruption of the White Zinfandels whose pink nectar hides behind their misleading name.

"In silence, the wines that surround me play their own music—like alluring ballads for lonely souls and romantic concertos with deadly endings.

"It is a courtship in moderation, always, as I do not have the luxury to squander my remaining hours. Each and every minute is one of my most precious possessions. Seconds are the only things left that matter.

"So, I don't want number four. I don't want anymore the practical, rational, organized, structured, engineered four that is servant to all the wishes and fancies of the idealist threes.

"I want to rip that straightjacket and reject the shackles of servitude. I want to renounce the engineering vow and the ridiculous idea of Rudyard Kipling that engineers are the 'Sons of Martha,' forever condemned to toil for long hours for the benefit of everyone else without any recognition for their service, and his assertion that the Sons of Martha 'have inherited that good part.' What was Rudyard smoking when he wrote that? And how could engineers think it a good idea to anchor that silly poem into a 'Ritual of the Calling of an Engineer' for graduates preparing to enter the profession? How dumb is that?

"A poem inspired by the Biblical story of Jesus stopping at Martha's home, which describes her sister Mary sitting at his feet, fawning at his preaching, while Martha was toiling like mad to make all the preparations and be a good hostess. A story that turns for the worse when the busy bee asks Jesus to tell her sister to help her, and he apparently replies: 'Martha, Martha, you are worried and upset about many things, but Mary has chosen what is better, and it will not be taken away from her.' Isn't it so? Martha, the transcendental engineer, chided for her mundane concerns? Engineers must be masochistic fools who like a good spanking to glorify their role.

"History must be rewritten once and for all: Martha opens the door, greets her guests, sits on the sofa, feet on the table, and enjoys the master storyteller. After two hours, her shallow sister asks: 'What's for dinner?' Martha, not even looking at her, replies: 'Not my problem, girl!' The little brat starts whining and bitching, but Martha doesn't raise a finger. 'I'm not your slave,' she says. 'If you want little hors-d'oeuvres and cocktails, go make some. The engineers are on strike forever. They've blown a fuse. They're tired of cooking, and cleaning, and wiping the ass of lazy imbeciles, and they're planning to have a good time instead. The world may go to hell (sorry Jesus buddy), but I don't give a damn. See, I'm choosing the better life. I really am.'

"Jesus, who's a cool dude, laughed hard and ordered pizza for everybody. End of story. [Excerpt from 'Bible Re-engineered,' by an unknown bummed out engineer.]

"Right then and there, like Mary, we all choose the better life and enjoy our pizza slice; engineers worldwide turn into philosophy or theology students. The Roman aqueducts or the Roman roads never get built. The profession disappears and the future is rewritten. No more running water or flushing toilets and all roads remain impassable muddy tracks. No printing press, no gas engine, no electricity, no concrete, no steel, no bridges. No trains, planes, or automobiles. In a medieval-like 21st century, water—and maybe dysentery—will still come from the well two miles down on the dirt path, while the flock of never-been engineers reaps the rewards of a pizza-fueled metaphysical bliss cogitating on the meaning of life.

"An utopian world devoid of engineering servitude. A low-tech paradise free of scorn and derision.

"No more slaving.

"No more nonsense.

"Enough is enough.

"This is my turn to enjoy life.

"All I want is peace.

"Peace and life.

"And divine wines.

"And a postcard from Hannelore."

Sig was laughing at thought of pizza delivered by camel, or donkey, but Carmina was somber. She never thought she'd hear again about Hannelore.

Beliefs

Sig hadn't been sure if Carmina had mumbled "the beach" or "the bitch" while reading the address on Keene's index card, but didn't dare ask and the road signs getting there provided no clues—the city name didn't include "beach," as if ditching the appendage could have kept unwelcome guests away from the pedantic neighborhood. So when the azure horizon was revealed as the road reached the top of the hill before diving into the valley, he jumped in excitement.

"We're going to the ocean! We're going to swim!" he repeated in a loop.

"There's no time for that," snapped Carmina after a few loops.

"What? No way."

"There's no time."

"There's always time."

"Not to play."

"It's the ocean!"

He wondered what kind of crotchety virus had invaded Carmina.

"There's just no time, that's all. Besides, the water's too cold."

"You don't have to swim with me."

"You don't have a swim suit."

"I'll swim in my underwear. I'll swim naked. I don't care. It's the beach!"

"President Dick said no."

Just as the words left her lips, she felt like a coward to hide behind such a lame excuse. How could she possibly think that this would have stopped Sig?

"When did he say that?"

"You already forgot that he called when we were at the rest area?"

"I didn't hear you ask him about any beach."

"I did. When you were in the restroom."

"Why would he care? He's just an idiot."

No, she was being an idiot. Why was she lying? She had no grounds to kill his exuberant desire for a joyful communion with the infinite beauty of the ocean. The beach had cast a spell on him, as if the baptismal immersion into the salty waters could liberate him from a dreadful life, and nothing could break that spell. It occurred to her that Sig might have never seen the ocean before; there was no point asking, as he would be too embarrassed to admit it.

"OK, then. Just a very quick dip," she conceded. "After the meeting, not before," she forcefully clarified.

Ashamed, she wished she could have blamed President Dick for her mood. True, she was upset that he had called. While he had mostly dispensed polite statements, expressing best wishes and caring intentions, enquiring about the well-being of Sig, and professing vague assurances that he was ready to be of assistance if needed, it was clear to her that he wanted a progress report—to know if she was getting closer to the money that would flow into the Ranch's coffers. How people fall for the charm of consummate liars was beyond her. She knew Dick to be a careerist who only cared about himself, who would offer the utmost kindness to someone for as long as there was juice to be squeezed out of the lemon, but ready to instantly abandon all courtesies as soon as it was more profitable to move on to leech from another host—lavishing praises and other lies on the new host until sucked dry.

It was a long walk from the parking lot to the staircase leading to Hannelore's office, and hundreds of steps up before they landed on the porch of the house clinging to the face of a steep hill—almost a cliff—with a million dollar view of the ocean. Every parcel of land on the flats wedged between two cliffs leading to the sandy beach was prime real estate not to be wasted, so the parking lot was half a mile out.

Sig had noticed that the phone call had turned Carmina's already concerned mood into a gloomier one. He had guessed from some of Carmina's answers that the phone call had been an unpleasant drudgery and tried to cheer her up a bit.

"Don't let the PODWO bother you. They're just idiots," he said.

"The what?"

"The PODWO"

"What are you talking about?"

"You don't know PODWO? I can't believe it. Come on. Everyone at the Ranch knows what PODWO means."

"My Ranch office is a very small soundproof cocoon with a 'Do Not Disturb' sign on the door."

"No it's not. There's no sign. The door's always open."

"Just feels like it. Nobody ever visits."

"I do."

"Almost nobody. Anyhow, not enough people for me to know what is a POADWA."

"Not POADWA. PODWO. It's the Dicks. We call them "Pair of Dicks Without One: PODWO. That's all."

"Eek! That's mean," she said, refusing to acknowledge that she found the acronym fitting.

"No. They're mean. PODWO's just a friendly, umm..."

"Insult?"

"No, a friendly nickname."

"Nickname?"

"Yes, like psycholo-chick. You know, everybody has a nick-name."

"So what's my nickname?"

Sig refused to respond, and continued walking as if he hadn't heard.

"So what's mine?"

"You don't have one."

"I don't believe you. You said everybody has one."

"Except you."

"I still don't believe you."

They walked some more before he concluded that there was no point lying to her. She wouldn't be able to make sense of it anyhow.

"It's SOMUNOM."

"What does that mean?"

"Nothing."

"It's bad, isn't it?"

"No it's not."

"What does it mean?"

He had already said too much. He determined that the best way to not lie was to remain silent for the rest of the walk up to the cliff-hanging house.

"Does it mean 'Super Out-of-this-world Miss Universe Needs Overdose of Magic?' she guessed, pinning random words to each of the letters.

He smiled, but remained silent.

"Does it mean 'Sexy Oo la la Mama mia Unbelievable Nothing-like-it Oh-my-god Maneater?"

Still silent.

"Someone Outstandingly Mind-blowing-ly Uppity Not Objectively Magnificent?"

Silent.

"Stupid Off-putting Miserable Ugly Nitwit Overweight Moron?"

Nothing.

"Superfragilisticexpialidocious Ob-la-di-ob-la-da Mambo-jumbo Humpty Dumpty Nabucodonosor Otolaryngologist Yankeedoodle Jackassification Sasquatch."

"That doesn't even match the letters."

At least he was paying attention.

"Scary Ogre Monster of the Underworld Nibbling Ordinary Minions"

Sig giggled as if saying, "You're thinking way too much."

She tried a few more times to pry it out of him but nothing worked. She spent the rest of the walk and climb thinking about the possible meaning of that nickname, hoping it was benign—some childish ditty of no defaming character—but nothing was sacred to the kids at the Ranch. They had been too battered to care about not hurting feelings.

Once on the porch of the house, her thoughts were back on Hannelore. This was going to be a dreadful visit.

The sign on the door announced "The Conviction Fortress."

The Hannelore that greeted them at the door looked like a former model, slender and attractive in spite of the cruel bruises of time—just like a rose still glorious when wilted and dried. Carmina had wished her to be short and round, deteriorated by years of munching chips, dunking in the ice-cream pail, and slurping soft-drinks—no luck.

A warm smile suggesting a warm personality invited them to her office. Strike two, as Carmina had hoped her to be a rude witch. As she handed over her business card, she dreaded strike three.

"So what can I do for you, Ms. Jewell?"

She didn't know. Carmina could breathe a little.

They were there to talk business.

The office was Spartan: Full-height windows the length of the office, a diving view of the beach, a glass table, and three modern chairs—the two facing the director's seat curvy and elegant in design but deliberately of hardwood finish to ensure that meetings remained short. In spite of the perks of her executive chair, Hannelore sat without a curve in her spine, not touching the padded back of the seat.

"What's a conviction fortress?" asked Sig, as he took the chair closer to the window—staring at the beach, almost drooling in anticipation.

"That's a very good question, young man."

Of course.

"How can I explain?" she said, trying to translate the official spiel into a simpler message comprehensible to a twelve-year-old kid, unintentionally deflating Sig's illusion of having been promoted to manhood.

"It's an organization, you know, that brings together many different groups, you know, that have serious beliefs about certain things."

Carmina was pleased to hear Hannelore pepper her sentences with "you know's"—the annoying verbal tic was a welcome imperfection.

"A congregation," he affirmed to assert maturity, reading the word on a poster behind her describing one of the member organizations.

"Exactly!"

"Of course," he thought. "I'm not a bright kid; I'm a bright young man."

"So many groups have contracted us, you know, hired us, to help them get organized, set-up their operations, you know, meetings, websites, you know, non-profit tax status, things like that."

"Like which groups?" he said, realizing in hindsight that it would have looked more mature to drop the "like."

Carmina didn't mind letting the discussion go astray. She was not eager to talk to Hannelore.

"There's many, you know. There's various holocaust denial organizations, a group of Aids denialists, you know, the moon-landing disbelievers, the International Flat Earth Society, the—"

"Flat earth?"

"Yes, International Flat Earth Society."

"Like as if the earth is flat."

"Exactly."

"There's a bunch of people who think the earth is flat?"

"There are."

"Did they all skip fifth grade?"

"Don't be smart, young man. That's one of our high profile member organizations. Founded in the 1800s."

No more "you know's" it seemed. Maybe they vanished in confrontations.

"Miss. Look out the window. You see the ocean and boats disappearing on the horizon. Where do they go?"

"It's not for me to answer every kid's question."

No more young man. He had been demoted back to kid.

"You know, I'll be pleased to provide you with their literature if you are interested and, you know, can approach things with an open mind."

An open mind?

"No thanks ma'am. I'm just a kid. Not sure I would get all of that."

Silence hung for a minute.

"Again, what can I do for you?" she asked Carmina.

Carmina pulled out the envelope that Justin had given her. Addressed to Hannelore, in Keene's handwriting. Nothing but her address on the envelope.

"I was tasked to deliver this."

She felt like throwing it on her desk, but rather extended her arm in a dignified way.

"Thanks, said Hannelore putting it on the desk, as if intent on reading later, in privacy.

That wouldn't do.

"Do you know why I'm here?"

"To give me a letter, as you just said," she answered, puzzled by the question.

"Keene did not warn you of my visit?"

"Keene who?"

"What do you mean, Keene who? Keene Mason," she snapped.

"Keene Mason. Wow." Breathless. "I haven't heard from Keene in a long, long time. What is he up to?"

"He's dead," she said, deadpan, to see her reaction, upset that she had called him Keene, instead of Mr. Mason. She had been tempted to reply instead, "He's, you know, dead, you know," but that would have been a blatant provocation—unwarranted at this point.

"Oh. How did that happen?"

"I don't know. I mean, nobody knows."

"Nobody knows?"

She thought about it for a few seconds.

"It doesn't surprise me after all. That's much like him."

Carmina wasn't here for small talk. She had to pick up a postcard, and this meeting was not going anywhere.

"So you have no idea why I'm here."

"The letter?" she said, lifting it up as evidence.

The damn letter.

Carmina had wanted to read it, had tried to read it. Tried to read it through light. Fifty-watt bulb, 100-watt bulb, halogen lamp, the sun. Nothing worked. The letter inside had been wrapped in cardboard. Steaming the envelope would have warped it, making hand delivery embarrassing.

"Not really. I'm here to pick up a postcard. Keene asked me to pick-up a postcard."

"Oh. When was that?"

Carmina wanted to answer, "Before he died, you know, dum-dum," but then realized he actually asked her after his death, which would call for awkward explanations she didn't wish to provide.

"I'm just here to pick up a postcard."

"Hmm. And what postcard would that be?"

"That I don't know. I suspect it is mentioned in the letter."

Hannelore paused. She wanted to kick the rude woman out of her office, yet wondered why Carmina stayed, given that she clearly wasn't enjoying any of this.

"Ms. Jewell," she said looking at her business card. "How did you know Mr. Mason?"

Carmina didn't want to answer that question. Not yet. She paused, thinking about how to frame her answer.

"She was married to him," said Sig, pleased to contribute in moving along what had become a boring meeting, stalled in small talk.

So much for taking time to think things through.

"Oh. I'm sorry to hear."

She hated these "Oh's" repeated with snobbish conviction. They were worse than the "you know's."

"He was my ex-husband," she clarified, watching for her reaction.

"I see."

Hannelore was calm. Thinking.

She pulled a letter opener with a golden blade and fine wood handle, and ripped the envelope in a slow deliberate motion; the sound of each tiny paper tear pounded Carmina like the drops of a Chinese water torture that seemed to last forever.

Hannelore took an eternity to read. A few sparse "Hmm hmm's" and "Oh's" were all that she shared with Carmina.

After the eternity, she folded the letter and inserted it back into the envelope.

"Ms. Jewell. I understand how difficult it must be for you to be here." Hannelore was solemn and deliberate, carefully choosing her words; no more flippant "you know's."

"You have no idea. I know who you are," thought Carmina.

"I'm sorry that at some point during your marriage, you believed he became involved with an improper extra-marital relationship."

"She knows," thought Carmina. "How can she know? It must have been in Keene's letter."

"I can only imagine how terrible it can be for a woman to harbor such suspicions."

"No you can't. You can't," thought Carmina. "Don't be condescending."

"But I wouldn't know. I never enjoyed the joy of a tender and blissful relationship that led to marriage. I never met a man who loved me, and whom I loved, enough for such a commitment. In some ways, I envy you. Even though your relationship ended in a divorce—tragically, as it can't be otherwise—you have enjoyed such a pleasure. It had to be a pleasure. At least for a period. A pleasure I have never known, and will never know."

What did Keene tell her? How could he? This was none of her business.

"For a date, for the hope of a night, men would shower me with gifts, take me out—all the time. Men would line up for the opportunity to parade me, showing off the trophy date like a prestigious lapel pin. But where were the real men? The serious ones, the ones who can see a life that doesn't end when the skin-deep interests have been consumed. Were they scared by the hordes of clowns, buffoons, bozos, and creeps that circled around me?"

Carmina felt a shiver run down her spine. The room felt stuffy, too hot. She didn't like where it led.

"Keene was different. How can I say? There was a sparkle in his eyes; a presence of mind; an inquisitive mindset. Like a tormented curiosity to always know the 'why' of everything, a pained soul that burned because so many things remained without answers. There was such a strong interest."

This was too much. Too much to bear. The shiver had spread. Alarm bells were going off. She had to leave. Keene could get his postcard mailed. She didn't have to hear anymore. She didn't want to hear the rest.

"I found him to be very attractive. I would have loved to marry this man—"

Carmina burst into tears. She knew exactly where this was going. She curled up on the uncomfortable chair, shaking, unable to run away.

"Oh."

Sig was frozen. He had seen plenty of horrors and cries, but this was the first time someone dear to him—a proxy mother no less—collapsed. He didn't care about the beach anymore. How could he enjoy waves when she was drowning? No need to rush. He was still young. Time was on his side. There would be other days for swimming in the ocean.

Hannelore stood and tried to put her arm around her.

She reacted in spasms—she wasn't to be touched. Not by her.

It was pain. That pain. The one more tearing than physical hurt. The realization that a sacred trust had been broken, that the one intimate soul mate in whom all trust could be invested went bankrupt. The shame of having been lied to.

Part of her tried to rationalize that all this didn't matter. That it didn't matter that Keene had cheated on her. That it didn't matter that he had lied to her. That it didn't matter that he had broken her trust. That they were separated anyhow, and that this would have been the logical outcome anyhow. Forget separated: "Keene's dead for Christ's sake. Come on Carmina, get a grip," she told herself.

But he had broken her trust. He had slept with the she-devil and lied about it. He had turned her into a fool. A clown. A cheap date—used. Her humanity, her feelings, her blind devotion, her honesty: trampled. Crushed under the boot of a liar in whom she crazily invested her faith.

Worse, when she had shared her suspicions, her fears that there was another woman stealing him, he had denied it all. Denied it all! So convincingly. Said that he loved her—loved her with all the tenderness and passion that he had not imagined possible in this world before meeting her. Sworn that she was the person with whom he wanted to spend his life—all of it. Reassuring her. Calming her. Holding her tight in a warm embrace, testifying that his unbounded and unconditional love for her was his most precious reason to live and that he would carry that unbreakable love for her up to his last breath.

As much as she wanted to believe him—she did want to, how she did—the suspicions she harbored ate her alive, destroyed her. It became the straw that broke the camel's back.

Now she knew they were all lies.

How could Keene be so cruel as to dare throw her in Hannelore's den? Couldn't he just die with his dark secret? Why did he have to scar her?

Hannelore didn't know how to soothe away anybody's sorrows. She believed life hadn't equipped her well for that task. However, realizing that being more direct might have averted this awkward moment, she went straight to the point.

"I would have loved to be his mistress..."

That's not helping. Focus. Straight to the point.

"We never had an affair."

"Liar. You, conniving bitch," thought Carmina.

She stood up to leave, but unable to see the door through her watery eyes, sat back to wipe her eyes.

"It never happened. Oh, I desired him for sure. I wanted to be his mistress, even if never his wife—which shows how little I was willing to settle for. Of course, I would have married him in a heartbeat if it had become possible. But none of these things ever happened."

"You're just a liar. You're just a marriage-breaking monster."

"I don't deserve the insult—"

"I don't have anything to explain—" said Carmina, with a second attempt to leave, now that she could see the door—blurry, but right there.

"Here, read for yourself," said Hannelore, handing over Keene's letter.

Keene had been nothing but letters to her in recent days. She wasn't starved of letters from him. Right then, she couldn't care less about reading another dithyramb—by a boring engineer—on the beauty of life and wine. But this was a letter to "the other woman."

She snatched the letter from Hannelore's hand, and paced nervously, until she could see clearly enough to read. In the corner of the room, she leaned her forehead against the wall, her shoulder on the window, to hide her feelings, and braced herself.

"Dear Hannelore."

Dear. A term of endearment, or just a formal greeting? Her first name.

"Carmina, Carmina. You'll never be able to read the stupid letter if you analyze every word as it emerges along the way," she thought. "Just dive to the bottom, holding your breath."

"Dear Hannelore.

"I apologize for surprising you today, like a ghost, after all these years of silence. I wasn't dead—until recently at least—and should have found the courage to contact you earlier. Although it didn't happen, I sincerely hope you will find the peace to grace this letter with your reading to its very end.

"I apologize for so suddenly disappearing from your life. Maybe not like a thief, as I did leave some footprints behind, but certainly like a boor, without leaving a note or explanation. It was a loss for me, as I truly enjoyed your wit, your insightful opinions, your humanity (socialistic as it might be), and your many other talents. I even forgave the lack of engineering rigor you displayed by helping lost souls perpetuate their arcane beliefs and medieval predispositions, as your warmth and kindness towards all living beings compensated for that Cartesian-deficiency. I loved your passionate taste for wacky humor, secretly hidden by your business rigor. All in all, I dearly valued your friendship.

"However, when I noticed deep in your distressed eyes a readiness and desire to become attached in a way that transcended friendship, it became clear to me that I had to disappear from your life, as my continued presence could only hurt you. I deeply loved my wife and cherished every moment of our married life together. That romantic relationship took all of the available real estate in my heart, leaving no room, no needs, no thoughts, for an affair.

"Short-circuiting so abruptly such a beautiful friendship was not a very tactful thing to do, but I couldn't find a satisfactory equation to resolve this particular problem, and, like all thorny problems I couldn't find words to solve then, I left it on the heap of baffling mysteries that I hoped to find time to address someday. Just like one of those boring engineers who are too blunt for their own good. If there is wisdom in never saying no, like a Japanese leaving to ambiguity and time the task of laying a path for the true meaning of a 'maybe' to be discovered, then clearly I'm not a sage. I take the blame for saying no, when a longing pregnant with deception may have left my audience less bruised.

"I'm not asking for forgiveness, as it is unforgivable to break a heart. I can only assure you, with my very best intentions, that I never meant to hurt your feelings, and sincerely hope that time—if certainly not ambiguity—has healed your scars.

"I purposely exiled myself from your life, by fear of reopening old wounds. Sadly, my wife eventually left me. But despite my loss, my sadness, and my hurt, she remained the sole resident of all that real estate in my heart, and the property never became vacant. Unknowingly, she still has full ownership and the keys to it.

"Today, now that I'm dead, I'd love to rest in peace with one of your zany postcards; something profound and yet utterly silly that underscores the folly of the human experience. Those outrageous postcards that you collected and sometimes pulled in the middle of a business meeting or a conversation to make a point, immediately sinking someone's pompous philosophical argument or preposterous grandstanding.

"My ex-wife, who hand-delivered this note, is helping me fulfill my last wishes—a kindest messenger for sure, as there may be no point to my insane divagations. Please be kind to her as I'm sure this has been an ordeal for her. In spite of my bad behavior, I hope you'll be willing to forever part with one of your postcards. Give her a good one.

"Keene (former friend, former living human)."

Carmina stayed leaning on the wall for a few minutes—instants that lasted an eternity—trying to get a grip on her emotions.

She returned to the punishing wooden chair.

Hannelore, unsure how else she could ease Carmina's pain, felt compelled to re-emphasize the plain facts.

"Keene had no intention of entering into an affair, and no intention of making me suffer by lingering with the thought that it might happen—with time, or a bit of persistence, as I would have likely made myself believe. He was a gentle men—in the truest sense."

He was.

Had been.

Carmina was most embarrassed for it was she all along who had doubted his integrity. Blind.

She felt like saying, "I'm sorry," but not to Hannelore. She would have stolen Keene at the first chance—by her very own admission. She felt sorry nonetheless.

Likewise, Hannelore couldn't offer much in terms of sympathy to the woman who had the man she desired and who eventually dumped him.

They sat face to face, in the absurdity of it all, in silence.

Hannelore went to the desk along the wall, flipped through files for a moment. She returned with a postcard that she laid on the table, facing Carmina.

"I believe Keene would have found this one to his taste."

It was a one page comic, shrunken postcard-size, signed "Don Martin." In the first panels, an electrician sets up to install a light fixture. Standing on a stepladder, he drills a hole into the ceiling, when the drill suddenly starts to shake and make loud creaky noises. Without stopping, he presses on, drilling on in spite of the weird noises. In the last panel, in a cut-through view revealing two stories of the building, the electrician on the lower floor inspects the damaged drill bit, wondering what happened, while on the upper floor, in a yoga academy full of customers doing head stands, the path of the drilled hole reaches deep into the head of one dazed customer who says: "Gosh! I think I just reached Nirvana!"

"Yes. I believe, he will enjoy it very much," said Carmina.

Five

Enough with the roses. This time, Justin had decided to invite them to lunch. For lack of other resources or a trustworthy confidant, he had spent hours browsing the web for advice on how to pick a good date restaurant.

A lot—too much—was written about watching the budget, stressing that the perfect romantic evening could be ruined if the prices on the menu exceeded expectations, sending one of the dining party into cardiac arrest, or having to pawn the car to pay for the hors-d'oeuvres. But money was no issue in this case.

Lots of advice could be found too on choosing the right type of food—avoid bringing a vegetarian to the joint whose star menu item is its five-pound hamburger, and stay away from Indian restaurants if your partner travels with bottles of antacids. Justin had no idea what kind of food would please Carmina. And the kid! He could just see him poking the sashimi with chopsticks, wondering when the waiter would come to cook the meal, or spitting out the raw fish in the sushi roll.

A fancy Italian restaurant? Too stereotypically romantic. And the hazards of flopping pasta, splashing red sauce stains on his tie and shirt, shifting focus to laundry concerns rather than the business at hand.

A theme restaurant? Too kiddish. An amusement park of food for family outings, sure to be noisy and crowded. He wasn't about to bring a bullhorn to have a conversation.

A chain restaurant? No romance there. Bright lights and tables crammed together in a cafeteria ambiance, elbowing the guy at the neighboring table when cutting your food, with waiters throwing plates on the table as a reminder that there are others piled in the lobby waiting for your seat.

No.

It had to be a place with a good atmosphere, classy yet not snobbish, Zen in decor, but not nakedly sober, and—more importantly—quiet enough to keep a business discussion away from the prying ears of those bored couples who eat out in the hopes of finding entertainment in the conversations of others.

That kind of classy, Zen, quiet restaurant would have been perfect, except that there was no such place in town. Only giant-burger joints, ethnic restaurants, kid eateries, and an endless string of franchises with their ho-hum menus of pre-packaged frozen items trucked across the country; for sure, none of those options would impress a date past her teenage years.

After desperate hours—non billable hours—Justin had found the perfect score: a winery half-an-hour out of town, serving gourmet cuisine, but including continental food on the menu to accommodate accompanying persons having less daring tastes.

He had lugged his big briefcase along, underscoring that this was a business meeting even though he had pre-ordered roses for the table. Maybe this was a strategic mistake, but he needed the ambiguity—she was still his client.

Yet, in spite of his intensifying attempts to give her more glimpses of his true feelings, from meeting to meeting, she was becoming gloomier.

"Thanks for dinner at such a nice restaurant, Justin. It's very kind of you."

Carmina hesitated, wanting to tell him more, to declare that this silly treasure hunt had to stop, that it was pointless, and cruel to her. But he would then ask her why, and she wouldn't be able to provide an answer. She didn't have to explain herself to him, but it bothered her that she was unable to articulate her reasons. In her debate on whether or not to continue, she felt there had to be a coherent reason to stop—one at least stronger than the pressure to continue, based on more than emotions.

This entire undertaking could not—should not—be sustained by an obsessive curiosity. That's what rediscovering Keene had to be. Just a curiosity. An unhealthy one. The greater her exhaustion, the more spellbound she was. The deeper her desire to terminate the adventure, the more enslaved to it she became. As if hypnotized to act against her will, subjugated by a subconscious desire to understand.

Totally unhealthy.

Sig didn't answer.

"Makes no sense. A nice kid like you wouldn't do that."

"I'm not a kid."

"A nice person like you wouldn't do that."

"I'm not nice."

"You are. Stop that nonsense."

"Is this a lawyer-type of argument?"

"No. You're not under trial here."

"If I had set your office on fire, you would have had me arrested."

Justin pretended to reflect deeply on the case, as if Sig's mischief was a complex legal matter.

"No. Probably not."

"You're lying. I'm not your son, so you can't beat me, you can't ground me, and you can't punish me, so you'd have me arrested."

"Absolutely not. You're Carmina's buddy, so you're my friend, no matter what."

"I would have burned your office. You would be steaming mad."

"Mad? No. Sad? Yes. I would be really sad."

"Because I turned out different than you expected."

"No. People are who they are. I accept that. I'm a lawyer. I make a living from imperfection. I'd be sad because all my books would have burned."

"Your books?"

"I know, it's materialistically stupid, but books matter to me."

"It's just stupid books—"

"Enough, Sig," snapped Carmina. "I think you've made your point clear. We're at a nice restaurant, in good company. There's no need for your grumpiness."

"It's stupid books just the same. Nobody reads books."

"You're allowed to like what you want, Sig, but I like books," replied Justin. "And I read them. What can I say? They're like friends to me. Long lost friends, taking time to share with me their thoughts, their fears, their hopes, their vision of what the world is and could be. People who steal time from the whirlwind of life to commit soundly articulated thoughts to paper. People who invest an inordinate amount of time to communicate, create, imagine, describe what life is or should be, instead of pursuing ventures that could be more financially rewarding—many times over. People who choose ideas over money. People who find a way to work alone, yet reach many. Yes, Sig, I like books. A lot. In my opinion, there is nothing comparable on the littered highways or dark alleys of the noisy internet."

Carmina was surprised to hear Justin talk about himself, revealing one of his passions. Must have been the relaxed setting of the restaurant. Or the wine. It had to be the wine.

It just struck her that, in spite of all their dealings, she didn't know a thing about Justin. For sure, Keene had not just thrown a dart on an open phone book page—especially given that he hated "legal liars" that never produced anything concrete—but his motives for picking Justin were forever sealed. He likely never told Justin either. They had to share something in common, but there was no point speculating.

"If you like boring books, you must really enjoy Keene's boring letters then," concluded Sig.

"I had never stopped to think about it in those terms, but I guess you're right Sig. I like Keene's writing because he does some of what I've just said—except that he wrote those letters only for your... for your friend, Carmina."

"It's a good thing. Nobody else would ever want to read that," said Sig.

"Ha! Maybe you're right on that. I can't imagine a book publisher making money with that kind of book."

"Why is that?" asked Carmina.

"Because Keene's a boring engineer," replied Sig.

"That's not what I meant," said Justin. "It's just that it seems like nearly all books published today are sweet uplifting stories—if not teenage vampire stories. Light sugarcoated escapism must sell well, because it seems to fill all the display shelves at the bookstore—I never can find new releases I like there. Keene's letters, like existential novels of the 1950s, wouldn't appeal to book publishers nowadays."

"Meaning?" asked Sig, to whom 1950 was prehistoric.

"Meaning Keene's letters are a bit on the depressive side."

"They're not depressing," argued Carmina.

"He's dying," said Sig. "You know the end, and it's a bummer."

"You're just repeating what he wrote in his first letter, kid."
She called him kid and could get away with it. "There's a lot of
uplifting stuff in there. You don't even have to read between the
lines to see it."

"He'll die at the end, just the same."

"We are all correct, you know," said Justin. "He dies, it's
depressing, and yet there's more to it than that."

"Is this the lawyer trying to find the terms of settlement,"
asked Carmina, "or do you really believe this?"

"I believe it," he affirmed, pulling one of Keene's numbered
envelopes from the manila folder to make his point—one marked
by a number five on it. Its reading wouldn't wait for the main
course.

Nobody complained, which vindicated Carmina's opinion.

"I hope you ordered a good wine with that," she added.

"Perfect pairing. I've taken cues from a budding oenophile."

As a sort of experiment, Sig decided to imagine that instead
of Justin's flat tone, he would hear the letter being read by a deep
voice narrator, to determine if it had the stature of a real
book—whatever a real book is, since, like most of his contempo-
raries, he hadn't read any himself.

"Day 29.

"Still alive. Have reached number 5.

"The five senses. It's all anchored right in there. It's too
obvious.

"Five is the number of exploration, which leads to awareness,
action, restlessness, new experiences, new ideas. This sensual
awareness is our natural drug to push life to its limits, hardwired
into our brain. It serves and protects our physical and mental
health, and can destroy it as well.

"Five is our analytical and critical self, the feeder of our intellect, our curiosity, our visionary thinking. It is expansive, constructive, versatile, resourceful, and unfortunately edgy, in need of
hasty decisions that can ruin everything. Hence, it is at the root of
unpredictability, instability, chaos. For that reason, it begs us to
marvel at the wonders of life—which could disappear so soon.
And marveling, I do. It's my full time job.

"I used to marvel at amazing feats of engineering: buildings
that tickle the clouds and aims for the stratosphere; bridges that
leapfrog obstacles and attempt to cross oceans; dams that interrupt

the flow of life, sending it on a redirected journey; guardians of safe harbors that welcome vessels in search of hospitable landings; parabolic valleys searching for galactic islands of intelligence; all those manmade landmarks that harness the laws of physics, forever stacking steel pieces, concrete forms, and composite matrices into more daring functional sculptures, creating sand castles where flat beaches laid before. For a long time, these were my wonders.

"Now, from a simpler perspective, I only marvel at the easily overlooked miracles of life—those that happened without design or human intervention, that emerged from a chaotic bang into amazing orders of functional complexity.

"Where I was once compelled to channel my awe of manmade wonders into constructive actions, I'm now fully satisfied by a purely contemplative curiosity of a world order that existed long before us. That's one decision made and not regretted.

"From our five fingers to the five-pointed stars, from the Babylonians' Ishtar to Islam's five Pillars and five prayers per day, from the pentagram of occultism to the pentagon that connects the five extended extremities of the human body (head, arms and legs), from the Maya's center point of the compass to the quintessence of humanity, five is the intersection at which decisions must be made. So I'm at that point; I made some decisions, and I have a few more to make.

"The dying engineer in me is delighted that, if I were to trust fate to make my decisions, there exist only five types of dices that have regular polygon faces of equal size; these Platonic solids are the tetrahedron, the cube, the octahedron, the dodecahedron, and the icosahedron. Mysterious, yet maybe boring—I apologize."

"Dodecamoron, octamoron, tetramoron," muttered Sig, pretending to snore, as if he had fallen asleep out of sheer boredom. Justin and Carmina didn't pay attention.

"Marvel and decide. Marvel and decide.

"Did I marvel enough today?

"I've seen five ducks cross the street walking—not flying—up to a little island of grass. Walking. Why? They can fly. A thousand times that distance. Why walk? They hobbled along, clumsily, in and off balance, comically awkward compared to their graceful flight. Why? Maybe it was the pleasure of the expedition, like a little vacation to Europe—a pilgrimage to the patch of grass, just because it was there. Maybe it was a critical exercise to lose weight. Ducks. It reminded me of Wynn, and some unfinished business.

"Marvel.

"Writing is a marvel. The marvel of ideas that refuse to die. Ideas that escape the viciousness of mortality to be engraved for eternity. Ideas that find a way to escape the brutality of loud-mouths that monopolize all the space and all the air pushing their vacuous words down the throats of all within reach—self-righteous loudmouths who perceive opposing views as insults to their gospel, as personal attacks no less."

Justin gloated, "Here's another one of us who likes books."

"Pfff," countered Sig. He wasn't about to enrich the debate. It was clear enough that Keene and Justin were just about equally boring.

Carmina's smile reinforced Justin's, who continued reading.

"Writing is a marvel. An endangered one.

"I went to the book fair, yesterday. My last one. What bliss. Who needs a paradise tomorrow when there's a book fair today? Yet, I couldn't help notice the odd ladies at the stands that picked up books, flipped a few pages, looked at the back covers, and said 'That's too expensive!' Inevitably. From stand to stand, book to book, always the same complaint—obviously not buying.

"Too expensive? Compared to what? A fast food meal that will end up in the toilet? The dollar given to the squeegee man who dirtied up her windshield at the traffic light outside the fair? Should we, then, encourage citizens to grab a squeegee and sponge on odd ladies' cars rather than grab a pen and use their brain? Not only can little actions have big consequences, but—most importantly—there are priorities in life, and in that list of priorities, books are sacred."

Justin was starting to like Keene.

"Odd grumpy ladies: not marvels. Books: Marvels."

Carmina wondered if this was Keene's sentence, or Justin editorializing or trying to be funny again.

"I bet he'll say 'wine' soon," said Sig.

"Colors are a marvel," read Justin.

"He will. Just wait."

"Colors are a marvel," repeated Justin.

"The deep blue of the sky. I had forgotten what a contemplative pleasure it was to stare at it for hours—a mistake now corrected. The pacifying vitality of green that wraps our lives. The striking joy of orange. The soothing blend of crazy light bouncing from all surfaces with their unique signatures, owing its existence to the paintbrushes of our minds.

"Fragrances are a marvel."

"What's wrong with the guy? Look further down on the page. It's got to be there."

"Honor the process, Sig."

Sig pushed his back against the chair, arms crossed.

"The infinite palette of mesmerizing aromas; the flowery bouquet, the sweetly jolts, the spicy fixes, the chocolaty caresses.

"Wines are a marvel."

"I knew it! Ha! I knew it," said Sig, vindicated.

"Congratulations," said Justin, playing along, as if all had forgotten that the letter's author was soaking in Saint-Émilion—like a giant worm in a small tequila bottle. He resumed.

"They wrap color, perfume, and poetry into one.

"The signature of oak barrels diffused with this divine blend of nature recreates flavors of fruits, nuts, and flowers foreign to the mixture. The scents and flavors of life, distilled through raw solar energy, filtered through billion years of stardust, to yield unique nectars, never the same, wrapped in velvety robes waiting for their ceremonial celebration. The foreboding pleasures, hinted at by the lyricism of the labels, the chateaux, the courtship before the taste.

"Colors, aromas, flavor. All actors on the grand stage, determined to confuse us, to confound our perception of reality.

"The marvel.

"This is what marvelous is.

"This is life.

"On the sacred strength of that marvelousness, and because I'm running out of life and death is pointlessness, I have now decided that since I can't plan my life beyond the next 29 days, I might as well plan my funeral."

Carmina guessed that this might have been the D-day in Keene's reversed chronology; the point from which he started formulating his crazy incineration plans. She didn't remember the exact countdown numbers on his engineering papers, but it had to match. She would check that later.

Justin folded the letter, as it ended there.

"If wine is so marvelous, how come I can't have any?"

Carmina and Justin looked at each other.

Good question.

Carmina reminded him, "You tasted some of Didier's wine and hated it, remember?"

"That was goat piss. Keene's always talking about fantastic wines made by gods. Why can't I taste that stuff? You said you took Keene's advice to order an excellent wine. So, if that's the real deal, then I want some."

Should they? There was indeed a potent Cabernet Sauvignon on the table that had waited all of its life to be savored.

Why not?

There were the laws of nature and the laws of man; inescapable laws and fabricated ones; both rational and irrational at the same time, as rationality commands a subjective assessment anchored in the beliefs of self-righteous dictators, or in the dictatorship of the majority.

"Taste it then," said Carmina, shrugging off governmental decrees with parental authority, yet pretending to look away in order to plead accidental oversight should the restaurant staff spot the dangerous violation of their liquor license.

Sig discretely took a good gulp from Carmina's glass, not to miss this once in a lifetime opportunity—followed not so discretely by four large glasses of water to wash off the horrible taste. Sig now knew for sure that Keene was crazy as a bat.

Justin and Carmina acted oblivious to Sig's reaction, hiding their amusement, wondering if he would comment on the experience—which he didn't.

Justin handed Carmina the index card with instructions for the next stage of the treasure hunt.

"I'm tired of this, Justin. Part of me wants to stop."

"No, no, no, we go. We go now," said Sig, which sounded as if he had declared, "Stop whining and give me the car keys—no time to waste."

Carmina was stunned—Justin delighted. In his assessment, it had been a glorious meeting. First, she'd be back again; to ensure that, Sig was an amazing ally. Second, she had called him Justin, which was like an exalting sunrise—thanks maybe to the mysterious magic of wine.

"Let's go. No quitting," repeated Sig. "We're on a mission for your crazy-bat ex-husband. If you quit now, I'll set fire to the table with the candle," he said, as a matter-of-fact, not as a threat.

doesn't matter. Doing the job or not, doesn't matter. Big or small, doesn't matter. Titles impress. Nobody's going to check if any real creative work or input was required in any of the titled positions listed in a person's CV. What matters are the titles! Board member of an international organization? Oooh, impressive! Director of some agency or division? Wow, serious stuff! President of anything? That's a wild card!

"Nobody will ever check whether or not Joe missed all the board meetings—he can miss half of them and people will only remember the ones he attended, during which he made a few grand statements that basically restated what everybody else had already agreed on. Nobody's going to know that the Director of Strategic Planning shot from the hip without much planning—decisions are decisions, and all that matters is that he was decisive without wasting time, which is called 'time management,' because being an efficient time manager is highly regarded. Nobody cares that Mr. Big Cheese President delegated everything to a huge staff and only called up staff meeting once in a while to pretend making the decisions that had already been made. What matters are the titles.

"Once promoted, a successful leech must immediately start working on achieving the next promotion. Every job is just a trampoline, providing a higher plateau to pad the CV in ways to make it easier to climb to the next level.

"As for errors and bad decisions, they're always because of somebody else. A leader is never wrong. Nowadays, the captain of the Titanic would blame the iceberg. It's the iceberg's fault! And the engineers' fault too. Everybody knows that!

"It doesn't matter whether Joe the Leech is right or wrong. What matters is that he confidently says what he says. That makes him right, automatically. To insecure humans, knowledge lies in certainty, and power is in the hand of those who demonstrate this certainty. Hence, the image. Fokaduk! Look at the best examples on this earth: religions. Religions are so absolutely confident, no wonder they are so powerful! Yet, what else is there in this world that is founded on less evidence—in fact, entirely founded on beliefs so utterly impossible to prove that their entire structures entirely rely on faith for their survival? These guys are the masters of image. Create everything out of nothing! That's something.

"What? You're afraid Keene's going to sue you?"

Afraid? Was he really always afraid of something?

"Two after this one," declared Justin, with courage.

"Can't we just open them all at the same time?"

"Now you're pushing the envelope—no pun intended." Another bad joke. "Stop that, idiot lawyer; you're not funny," he reminded himself.

Sig giggled.

"Come on, Carmina. Only three left," said Sig. "One at the time. That's the rule of the game."

Carmina looked at him tenderly.

"We're on a mission. You can't rush a mission," he added, with religious conviction.

He kept pushing. His enthusiasm melted some of her despair, bringing back a smile.

Their eyes were locked, like mother and son. Justin realized his fatal mistake. He had invited the women—never mentioning Sig. She couldn't just park him off somewhere in an arcade or dump him in a theater for a few hours. They were one. Like a wine paired with the right dish—or vice-versa. It was just a big misunderstanding, a simple failure of communication. Carmina hadn't dumped him. She had been cautious. It just wasn't clear enough that Sig had also been invited.

Justin would get another chance. The gray clouds vanished and spring was back. There was hope.

"So are we going to read that letter or not?" insisted Sig.

Carmina imagined Sig as her own son—a real son. The wonderfully passionate kid that seemed to bloom through their journey—trying as the journey may be for her. She crushed him in a powerful embrace.

"Are you going to cry again?"

"No I'm not," she replied, barely releasing the grip, just enough for him to escape the teenage embarrassment of a motherly hug—in front of Justin, of all things.

"Please, start reading before my mom starts crying again."

"Day 13.

"It is so amazing that wine and chocolate are so hard to pair. Some say it can't be done. Fine wines and fine chocolates, each sublime on their own, yet sour companions.

"Yet, it can't be impossible. The engineer in me rejects that notion. Engineers make the impossible possible every day. And miracles too—except that those take a little bit longer to execute. Experimental validation being at the root of sound theories, I splurged at the local wine store, rounding up a palette of reds, from Beaujolais to Cabernet Sauvignon, from Zinfandel to Merlot, from Chianti to Pinot Noir, from Barbera to Shiraz, like an invincible armada in bottles, setting course upon an impossible conquest.

"Like all experiments crippled at the onset by the lack of an underlying theory making it possible to predict their outcomes, the randomness of the approach led to some unpredictable and often catastrophic pairings. Combinations of bitterness and sweetness, swirls of unmixable fruits and coffee flavors, disturbing attacks of dryness and spiciness, sinking the enthusiasm of the experimentalist with each taste, against best hopes and expectations.

"Horrible pairings, bad ones, dubious ones, abounded. Yet, beyond the frustration of failed attempts—and slight weight gain—emerged a few winners. Like rays of hope after floods—or in this case, red torrents. I'm pleased to have established that elegant chocolates could be happily married to light-body wines. Darker chocolates, on the other hand, better espoused the sharp tannins of full-body reds, the more bittersweet ones passionately embracing the stouter tannins. Incompatibilities were at last resolved, improbable loves reconciled, conflicting desires reconnected. Awesome discoveries, made too late."

"He's drunk," said Sig.

"I don't think so," said Carmina. "He knows exactly what he means."

"What? What?"

"Keep on reading, Justin," added Carmina, disregarding Sig's curiosity. She wasn't ready to disclose Keene's coded message.

Justin complied.

"Why is wine so divine? Like chocolate. Like music. Like love. Why are we so strangely wired and unwired, so pathetically broken in our combined perfection and imperfection?

"Strangely, six is the number of perfection.

"First, it is so in a mathematical sense, because a 'perfect' number is defined as one equal to the sum of its divisors (excluding itself), and $(1 + 2 + 3)$ makes six the first perfect number (the next one is $1 + 2 + 4 + 7 + 14 = 28$); as a mathematical coincidence, (1 × 2 × 3) also equals six (which thus makes it more of a curiosity than 28). This I understand.

"Second, to the engineer who refuses to die, one of the universe's fundamental laws is defined by the six equations of static equilibrium in space: the sum of forces equals zero along each of three arbitrary orthogonal directions, and the sum of moments equals zero about the same axes. This, I understand too. But that's just a rehash of three—times two.

"Third, in a numerological sense, it is perfection, because numerologists say so—which I don't understand. Maybe it is because there is no such thing as perfection to engineers, only the constant challenge to balance imperfections of all kinds to achieve some tangible and usable result. More or less successfully. With more or less durable outcomes. Just like my engineered funeral plans, maybe not perfect, but definitely usable and possibly enjoyable—although I would have preferred to enjoy the whole thing from outside the box if there had been such an option.

"Maybe numerologists are nuts too—in a different way than engineers, but possibly worse—for glorifying the ideal of perfection. Either there is no such thing as perfection, or else it's the boring engineer that refuses to die. Who knows?

"So perfection it is for loopy number six.

"It is therefore said to be artistic and musical, at the root of tact, beauty, harmony, balance, sincerity, truth, calm, love, enlightenment, balance, compassion, forgiveness, charm, grace, and nurturing.

"It is the number of parents—ideal parents. Nurturing love, family, and social responsibility, on the strength of insights, perspectives, and meaningful experiences.

"Parents and perfection together! Either numerologists have a sick, twisted sense of humor, or they are all another bunch of childless gurus preaching disconnected lies from atop ivory towers.

"Or maybe they're just trying to pair wine and chocolate."

Sig saw a tear slide on Carmina's cheek.

"What? What? You have to tell," said Sig. "We're on the same team you know. You can't continue keeping secrets."

"We can take a moment if you wish—"

"We're not divorced," said Carmina. "We're separated."

Sig wondered what this had to do with chocolate and wine. Besides, divorced, separated, what's the difference?

Justin panicked. He didn't know what prompted this sudden disclosure, but feared it might threaten his courtship of Carmina. The thought that he might never get the chance to showcase his famous bouillabaisse was unbearable. He had to probe.

"Would you like a tissue?"

"What a wimpy, inane, stupid, ineffective, imbecile, moronic, witless thing to say," he thought. He handed her a paper napkin from a drawer, silently chastising himself. More guts, more guts.

"Please tell me how I can help you."

The desk between them was an ocean he couldn't figure how to cross, while he debated whether a hug would be a major faux pas at this time—or whether not hugging would be the fatal mistake.

"The chocolate, the wine," she lamented. "It's us. He never agreed to divorce, you know. He's trying to pair us, again, against all odds."

Justin gambled. Although he felt like jumping across the desk like Superman over a tall building, the odds of tripping and falling flat face on the ground were too high. Nonetheless, he came from behind his desk and comforted her in his arms. Sig also hugged her.

She welcomed the compassion and abandoned her sorrows in their arms for a moment.

Justin felt a million things. Like a hero for having vanquished the Atlantic, as this embrace was definitely beyond mere service to a client—an item clearly not covered by the profession's recommended fee schedule. Like a man for holding in his arms the object of his desire. Like an explorer for discovering that her hair smelled like a breeze and her firm and warm body like volcanic rocks lashed by crisp waves from an abating gale. Like a saint for holding a broken angel in his arms. Like a lousy lawyer for not knowing what to say beyond this point.

"Are you thinking of going back to him," asked Justin.

"He's dead, stupid!" answered Sig, stepping back from the group hug.

"Figuratively, I meant. Figuratively."

Carmina slowly broke free of the embrace, and looked Justin straight in the eyes.

"I've always loved him. That has never been the issue. The problem—our only problem—was that he refused to have kids.

Never. He claimed life to be too cruel and unfair to punish a small kid with it."

Keene had a point, thought Sig.

"You would have been wonderful parents, I'm sure," said Justin, with sincere empathy.

"Keene didn't believe in perfect parents. You've just read it."

"Nobody's perfect. Parents aren't perfect, but neither are singles. Do you think I'm perfect?" he said, to underscore his eligibility more than his defects. "I'm shy, I'm indecisive, insecure, not particularly in shape, a bad communicator, unattractive—"

"Don't be so hard on yourself."

Justin prayed that it implied she disagreed with the "unattractive" part.

"So what?" said Sig, trying to put the treasure hunt back on track. "He's not the only one who doesn't want kids. At least the dude didn't father kids he didn't want. That's better than most."

"Sometimes people change, you know," said Carmina.

"Yeah. Happens a lot, I'm sure. Best if they change their mind before having kids, if you ask me."

"If you wish, Carmina, we could resume reading another day."

"What? No, no, no," said Sig. "There's no time to waste here. Keene needs his stuff. He won't wait forever."

"I asked Carmina's opinion."

"I'm fine. I'm sorry," she almost whispered, eyes closed and pushing her hair up, hands like five-finger combs.

"You have nothing to be sorry about."

"I don't know why I broke down. There's no reason."

"I fully understand that these are painful moments. I'm sure Keene loved you," Justin, said, emphasizing the past tense to put some distance between himself and his competitor, "but he is not making it easy on you."

"Please continue reading," she replied, as if she had fully recovered her grip—even though it was painfully clear to Justin she hadn't.

Observing her for a moment, making sure she indeed looked strong enough to continue, he navigated back to his chair without losing sight of her. He picked up the letter and looked sorry to resume reading, as if about to inflict pain in ways that partly escaped his comprehension.

"Sorry, but I see no perfection in six. I see perfection in wine and nature—or universal laws if need be—but not in number six. If six was such a perfect number, then why is 666 linked to Satan, no better worshiped by heavy metal band than feared by hexakosioihexekontahexaphobics (amazing as it is that a word actually exists for those afraid of the number 666).

"If there is a hell, it is that we work six days to rest on the seventh, which is completely asinine. To live—fully live—each single day of work should be followed by a six-day long sabbatical. Work is not life. With great sadness, I confess I have wasted a life working. Our entire societal structures with respect to work have been dictated by flawed project management in a creationist genesis that dramatically curtailed vacation time, creating in the process generations of workaholics burning the candle from both ends, dying too young before they have had a chance to live.

"The world has bred generations of worker bees gambling that more time will appear later—always later, as there is none today—rolling six-sided dices as building blocks for a future that may never happen, as luck so happens. Workers finding solace in a six-pack as a meager panacea for the burning wounds of exhaustion.

"Number six is number sick!

"I apologize for being so violently paranoid about number six. I know why and it goes beyond numerology. It has to do with a certain sixth sense that makes me grumpy.

"Besides, I must have got up on the wrong foot. Who in their right mind wouldn't be upset to have only less than two weeks left to live?"

The letter abruptly ended there.

Sig had already jumped out of his chair, ready to lead the next charge, to ascent the next summit.

Carmina and Justin wondered where he found all that energy.

Locked

Spike Leonhardt's humid basement studio looked like a cluttered dorm room—one that was inexplicably invaded by a hirsute middle-aged man. Specks of gray in his beard and drooping eyebrows worsened the sadness emanating from the disheveled room and scruffy man. First impressions hardly came worse.

Spike strived to sound hospitable, but his inviting words poorly concealed an ingrained discomfort in social circumstances. In spite of his imposing size—square shoulders, no neck, trunk-size arms, refrigerator-like stature—he appeared to be incredibly timid. Intimidating, but timid just the same. The kind of timidity one wouldn't dare tease though.

Carmina had pushed Sig forward, as his feet refused to cross the threshold. Sitting on wooden chairs—grabbed to avoid a damp-looking sofa—they browsed the posters and frames hung on the walls while Spike wiped some glasses clean.

"Ice with your juice?"

"Yes."

"No, no, not me," insisted Sig, afraid that terrifying water bugs had to bunk in the pipes, as Spike's logical roommates.

Fancy cars, funny cars, fantasy cars of all vintages, with or without fire-blasting engines—on the walls, bookshelves, tables, glasses, carpet—set the interior decoration's obsessive recurring theme. Engines, engines, engines. And a set of pumping iron gear tucked in a corner, between the sofa and the wall.

Sig stared deep into his glass, wondering if the car freak had mixed in 10W-40 to add flavor to the unidentifiable juice. His own taste-test was on hold, waiting to see if Carmina would develop odd side effects after her few polite sips.

Spike pulled a stool uncomfortably close—given that they didn't know if the giant was a dangerous psychopath—and sat, starring at his own glass for a minute. He raised his head and flashed a smile. Only an instant. A feeble attempt to put his guests at ease. Sig and Carmina didn't dare break the silence, waiting for the human steamroller to play his cards first. After all, he knew why they were there.

Unaware of what could have been Spike's relationship with Keene, Carmina wondered why their visit felt so awkward. Sig would have too if he hadn't been so busy watching her, studying her, trying to discern side effects from the smelly water—possibly rapid hair growth turning her into a werewolf, or radioactivity making her skin glow purple.

"Keene's letter was a surprise," he said haltingly, cutting the silence, weighing each word. "He has asked me to give you something. There's a story to it. It's been a secret for a long time."

Sig wondered if that meant they were gay lovers, but didn't dare ask. For sure, if Spike pulled up a dildo, he would run out, leaving it to Carmina to collect the slimy used tool. Sig's eyes begged her to say: "Just give us the stuff we're here to pick; we really don't need the story that goes with it."

"I must honor his request. He says you are trustworthy."

"We are only here at his bequest," said Carmina.

"He was an honorable man." The past tense revealed his knowledge of Keene's death.

"He was," she added by reflex, possibly with empathy more than conviction.

"He trusted you," he added, with a pause that confirmed he didn't know Keene's motives. "He must have had good reasons."

He stood up and walked towards the dumbbell rack. Images of skulls crushed by an iron weight in the hands of a psychopath flashed in Sig's mind before the giant opened a drawer in the desk next to the training gear, pulling a dirty brown envelope out of it. It reassured him. To the best of his knowledge, no lunatic had ever hammered anyone to death using a brown envelope.

Back to his stool, he pulled an old discolored photo out of the envelope and handed it to Carmina. It was a team picture—a wrestling team, in competition singlet, posing with arms wide open under the club banner of the "Sixth Sense Wrestling Gym." Standard memorabilia of a bunch of skinny school kids trying to look intimidating; members of a club whose name bragged of future victories presumably bolstered by special powers.

"We were twelve years old on that photo."

She thought she recognized someone, and pointed.

"Yes, that's Keene. I'm just next to him—like his right arm."

Sig, gazing over Carmina's arm, was stunned that the refrigerator holding the envelope had once been as skinny as him. Tall,
but skinny. It had to be steroids! Only extensive use of steroids
could have turned a wimpy tween into a monster. Massive dangerous doses injected on a hourly basis—needle marks being so nu-
merous that his butt checks must have looked afflicted by a local-
ized eruption of permanent measles.

"Wrestling was a way out of the streets. A way for us to gain
some respect, to escape the gratuitous violence of daily life, to
scare away packs of dirty kids that had fallen into thuggery to erase
the pain and shame of poverty."

"It could have been a martial art. It could have been boxing.
Just the same. Our neighborhood only had a wrestling program.
Although it was privately run, the wrestling coach who ran the
club had convinced a few charity organizations of the noble purposes of wrestling—learning fair play and respect of others, valu-
ing honor and discipline, developing healthy bodies as temples for
healthy minds and morals. He skillfully maintained a stream of
donations to fully fund his operations so that all willing kids could
enroll for free. Board members of those charity organizations
didn't care for his fancy words and glorified ideals, but they understood that kids locked in a wrestling studio didn't have time to
steal and vandalize their property, and funded the whole enterprise, just like some people buy one more insurance policy or a
burglar alarm. Many of those board members, having stolen their
way into wealth one way or another, saw this as an investment that
would maybe produce a few honorable citizens down the line, but,
as a more tangible return for the money, would definitely keep kids
busy with a respectable activity sure to consume a fair chuck of
their free time—idle time in the hands of poverty being at the root
of criminality."

Spike was slow to find words, but once started, he delivered
his monologue at steady pace, as if it had been rehearsed. Sig
imagined Spike as an old lawn mower: painful to crank-start, and
a nonstop annoying sputtering once fired up. He wondered how
much longer before the engine would shut off and they could
leave.

Carmina quietly listened, discovering more of Keene's youth—learning more about his secret history in the past few days than during all her years of marriage. Although, by now, she had become accustomed to the notion that she had been married to only half of Keene, as the rest of him had remained a stranger.

Spike's eyes were all that moved, either staring at his glass, or Carmina irises, pensive or confiding, back and forth.

He re-emphasized: "For me—and Keene—this started as a possible haven from the streets. We were both eight years old when we started there. It was an attractive way to forget the harshness of our gray lives, to escape the ugliness of poverty. A brightly lit studio, nice uniforms, a team spirit, refereed fairness, an honor code. What was there not to like?"

Spike stopped talking. As if silence could start abruptly. Without explanations. He stood up, pushing away the stool, and left the room.

Carmina and Sig looked at each other. This couldn't be the end of the story, as it didn't mean anything. What kind of prize possession could Spike bring back that was so dear to Keene? Only a madman would wish to be cremated with the sweaty singlet of an old wrestling buddy—or worse, his old jock strap. Then again, in some ways, Keene had gone completely mad after all.

Spike came back with a small brown bag, dirty but not wrinkled—presumably handled with care, but by dirty fingers. Back on the stool, bag on his lap, he carefully weighted his every word.

"Keene assured me that I could trust you. So I trust you to never reveal to anyone else what I am about to tell you," he said, pulling a gun out of the bag. The same type of black handheld piece Sig remembered seeing in cop flicks—but it was right here, within his arm's reach, on the lap of what had to be for sure a deranged wrestler; or, for sure, a dangerous psychopath; or, for sure, a serial killer. All three were sure bets—or worse. An old jock strap would have not been so bad after all.

"Or you'll have to kill us?" asked Carmina, surprised of how calmly she sounded while her mind was racing in a million directions under the rush of adrenalin.

"Or I'll have to kill myself," answered Spike, emotionless.

Carmina was speechless.

Sig was shocked that the opportunity of witnessing some-one's suicide freaked him out. Wasn't there anything more unre-markable than a suicide? Yet, at the mere thought of someone blowing up a hole in his head while looking him in the eye, an uncontrollable chill traveled up his spine and shook him. Couldn't he just wait till they were gone? Or swallow a handful of pills, or put his head in the gas oven, or walk on a railroad in the middle of the night, or dive into a pool holding a plugged hair dryer, or jump feet-first into a wood shredder, or hold a ten foot steel rod in a strawberry field during a thunderstorm, or swim a rocky shore during a hurricane, or stand behind a horse's kicking legs while poking a screwdriver in its butt, or run naked kicking beehives, or whatever other less messy time-proven technique that doesn't splash brains on guests? Yet, even the thought of a clean suicide, after they would have left, freaked him out. Something was wrong. Definitely wrong. Suicide had never been a bothersome matter before, but he never considered it as a spectator sport.

Carmina was upset that Keene had put her in harm's way—Sig and her, although he couldn't have known about Sig. She wanted to leave, but feared the consequence could be fatal somehow, one way or another. "What would the psycholo-chick do?" she thought.

"So, are you going to tell us your story or not?" blasted Sig as a nervous reaction, without thinking. As if threatening him was the sensible thing to do.

Carmina's heart stopped, dreading what insolence could trigger.

Spike, unfazed, took her silence for acquiescence.

"I was your age, buddy..." he said, answering Sig. He stop-ped, as if rewinding the story a few scenes back such that it would all make sense.

"The wrestling coach... I'm sure you've seen people like that, kid. They're everywhere. So full of themselves."

Sig immediately thought of the Dicks. Carmina too.

"That coach was living a superstar fantasy in his mind. He was loved by the parents: he kept their kids out of their hair and off the streets; he drilled some discipline into them; he preached the virtues of wrestling better than seasoned snake-oil salesmen. At the start and end of each training session, he forced all the kids, who were lined up like soldiers, to recite the club's tenets: 'We will

honor the art of wrestling through the respect of our opponents
with whom we will spar with honor and dignity, and through
fairness and discipline in all our actions within and outside of the
competition arena, in the spirit of a sound mind in a healthy body.'
Like the silly ditty of a stupid jerk playing god—a god dictating the
prayers that he wanted to hear. As if this propaganda for obedi-
ence meant anything.

"He loved to display his skills—clawholds, cobra clutch,
hammerlock, armbars, dragon sleeper, guillotine chokes, Indian
deathlock, gorilla press, kneebar, whatever. On kids half his size.
Pretending to be a superhuman fighting machine, an indestructible
weapon. He relished his image of mentor, grand master, know-it-
all guru. A god that knew better than anybody else and deigned
share his immense knowledge with his flock of impressionable
minds.

"Showboating to impress kids... what a pathetic life! Absolutely pathetic."

Sig had to agree, but there was nothing there to justify blowing up anyone's brains.

"But this guy was no hero!" shouted Spike, becoming more
agitated. "He was a miserable imbecile that never achieved anything of value in his entire life; a scumbag whose only talent was
conning adults; a foul mind in a disgusting body; a disrespectful
liar who didn't know the meaning of honor, dignity, and discipline."

Realizing he scared his guests, Spike took a few deep breaths
to cool down and regain his composure. To put them at ease, he
laid the gun on the table right next to him—with limited benefit,
as Carmina felt that if it came to reflexes, the gun was closer to
him than her.

"He had favorites; one after another. He lavished with praises the student whom he deemed to be more talented than all
others, showering him with more attention, using him to give
demos to the class, giving him private lessons to help him excel at
the sport—at the art. Until the day the kid left the club, because
he had nothing else to teach them, as he told all those that remained; because there comes a time when the student surpasses
the master and must fly with his own wings towards greater challenges. What a bunch of crock! Everyone in the class could tell
that the favorites were no more talented than others, that this

whole glorification was bogus—nothing more than the unfair judgment of a biased teacher who, like all teachers in fields where grading is nothing but subjective, believed his own judgment to be supreme, infallible, and beyond reproach. Just like the literature professor who praises the silly rhymes of the gorgeous blonde with the deep blue eyes and mesmerizing bosom, and criticizes the ugly kid whose creative prose goes over his head.

"Then, one day, I understood. I started to receive the increased attention, I was showered by subtle unexpected praises, I heard unbelievable claims that I performed better than my peers. And like a stupid kid starved for love in a little tough town, I believed it. I was on my way to become the favorite. How amazing was that? A unique stoke of luck in one's lifetime. Unable to say no, and unsure if I should, I gave the demos when asked, I took all the praise, I wallowed in the limelight, I crossed the threshold when the door of private lessons swung wide open."

Carmen noticed Spike's watery eyes, but he wouldn't shed a tear. The time for tears was long past.

"The confusion that happened then is unexplainable. There are no words to describe the disgust, the violated trust, the shame... The damned private lessons. Lessons they were. Lessons on the ignominy of some men who stop at nothing to stroke their ego, who put their own satisfaction above anything else, for whom nothing is sacred. Nothing is sacred."

He took the gun back in his hands.

Sig had seen too much nonsense in his life, and heard too many horror stories from his friends at the Ranch to be a naive kid who did not know what this was all about. Nonetheless, because he was twelve after all, this was no less a horror story that left him almost speechless. Spike had his blessing to blow out his mind, right here, on the spot, if he so wanted; it was a suitable remedy.

"The coach was a slimy rat," said Sig, as an acknowledgment—like the handshake of a scarred brotherhood—that twelve-year-old kids are easy marks in this world.

"Worse. Much worse," signed Spike.

"A slimy rat turd then," corrected Sig.

"Not even close."

"A slimy bacteria in a stinky rat turd."

Spike just looked at Sig, shaking his head, as no words were vile enough to describe a man less honorable than a lousy E. coli.

"There are shames that even grown men can't describe in words.

"Then one day, waking along the river, I found a gun," he said, unclenching the metal in his hand. "Was it thrown off a car window, landing short of the river, or was it a gift from the gods dropped from heaven to help a lost kid? I didn't care. It became mine. With its three remaining bullets. I spent one rehearsing on a trunk as target in the middle of the wood. The other two were an open question."

Carmina understood that the object of the treasure hunt in this case was cursed. She couldn't tell if her sadness welling up was for Spike, for having been subjected to this ordeal, or for Sig, for being the consummate victim of a world that fails its kids, or for her disappointment that Keene's twisted wishes made her brush with this tragedy.

"When I was finally sure that I had garnered enough courage, confident that my resolve was unwavering, certain that I had found the only solution, the right time had come. I purposely missed one class and waited outside. After all the other kids left, after the coach did his evening paperwork, after he closed the indoor and outdoor lights, as he turned around after locking the door, there I was, six feet from him, gun pointed at his head. That's the advantage of a gun. A sniper hides far away, swiping lives away with the precision of laser surgery, completely detached from the cancerous cells that are exterminated for the greater good. With a gun, like a dentist about to pull teeth without anesthesia, you're facing head-on the pain you are about to inflict; it's so personal, so feral, so... therapeutic.

"Veins pumped red by anger on my forehead, I wanted to shout at him, to scream: 'So you think you're so smart? You think you're a killing machine? You think you're untouchable; that you can defeat anyone? Go ahead, show me! Show me how a big jock with big muscles will stop me from blowing his brains out. Go ahead. Brag! Try to impress me. Just tell me how wrestling is going to stop this bullet.'

"But I didn't make it that far.

"The minute he saw the gun, the powerful, boasting, cocky coach—the poseur who thought of himself above everybody else—became a coward.

"A damn coward.

"Six feet away from a gun, all of his mighty wrestling skills were useless. Completely useless. He was no more powerful, no more boasting, no more cocky; he was just a little kid about to be abused. As if the roles had been reversed.

" 'Beg for your life,' I shouted. 'Beg! Bastard. Say you're a bastard. Louder!' I trashed him like a criminal about to beat a sad dog.

"I had him beg, admit that he was a scumbag, an idiot, a coward. I told him to cry like a little girl if he wanted to save his life, and he did—large tears streaming on his ugly face—and it didn't faze me one bit. Like a scared puppet, he did everything a little twelve-year-old kid told him to do, because he knew I could pull the trigger after what he had done to me and so many others. He knew I could exterminate him right there, in the middle of the night, on the doorstep of his disgusting wrestling studio, without any remorse.

"And I did."

Carmina and Sig would have gasped, but didn't—maybe out of fear, maybe out of sadness that their hopes for a better ending had vanished right there.

"I wished his head had exploded like a water balloon—like in Hollywood's gory movies. The bullet just left a small hole between his eyes; thankfully, it pulled a piece of skull off the back of his head. A piece that burst like a dirty bacteria."

He lowered his head, as if ashamed by the embarrassing admission of pleasure.

"I relished seeing his brain splashed on the wall, seeing the blood splattered all over like a powerful cleanser washing the walls of his ignoble club, leaving an indelible mark screaming aloud that people die for a reason, and that ugly executions are the due reward of despicable parasites. I relished looking at his ugly face—the face of an expressionless moron, wiped of its arrogant smirk, smug no more."

Carmina and Sig were both shocked—yet, felt that a sort of primal justice had been served and that a threatening predator had been executed. As abhorrent the crime, the murder was a misdemeanor compared to the hideous rape of childhood.

They remained a minute in silence, not knowing what to say. A much needed pause to overcome the surreality.

"What does all this have to do with Keene?" asked Carmina. The mere fact they were both in the same wrestling club didn't by itself make a significant connection.

Spike pulled a flattened piece of metal from the bag and held it in his open palm.

Still made no sense.

"The wrestling studio was in a desolate warehouse district, without any commercial activity within striking distance; on a dark evening on a cold day, the surroundings were deserted. Yet, Keene saw it all; he had forgotten his watch at the studio, and was running back hoping to make it before the coach locked things up. From a distance, he witnessed the extermination," he said, using words as if cockroaches had been sprayed with DDT. "Far enough not to be seen but close enough to recognize me.

"A few hours later, he came to my house. Once my parents were beyond eavesdropping distance, he dropped in my hand the flattened bullet he had dislodged from the masonry wall where it had buried itself after exiting the coach's head. He didn't judge me. He didn't say anything. He just looked at me, puzzled as to what could possibly have been my motive.

"I had to tell. Tell it all. I did. That wasn't an easy thing to do, but he deserved that much for his discretion.

"He nodded, and left. He never told anybody for as long as he lived. At least, as far as I know—otherwise I probably would have been arrested and jailed for life given the incontestable evidence," he said, slightly raising his hand holding the bullet. "That was our secret, never to be told."

"Until now?" asked Carmina, presuming about the letter Spike received from Keene.

"No. He never asked me to say anything. All he requested in his letter was that I give you what you came here to get—a bullet. I don't know anything more than that. But Keene was a good man—a trustworthy and honorable man. Just like he wrote that you are a trustworthy and honorable woman and that he entrusted you to collect this burden. It is honor and dignity that compelled me to tell you the whole story."

Spike put the flattened bullet in her hand. She closed her fist.

He looked her in the eyes. Was she outraged? Understanding? Compassionate? He couldn't tell. She didn't know either.

"For ten years after, I tried to forget my dark secret—without success. A decade of guilt. Not for my acts, but for my naivety; for having been had, for having fallen prey, for having been so stupid allowing myself to become a victim. Sadly, killing the moron—which I never regretted and never will regret—didn't heal the deep wounds. These wounds were like tall prison walls around me. It was a long tedious process to climb these walls to escape the prison. It took a long time.

"A long, long time.

"Until I found my calling. I became a mechanic."

Carmina was relieved that Spike rediscovered a peaceful footing and balance in work. Glad he was passionate about it too, as shouted by the excessive decorations that burdened the apartment.

"It's such a peaceful job to be a mechanic. Machines make so much more sense; they're logical and predictable. With due maintenance and love, they never deviate from their chosen path.

"Yeah. A mechanic.

"Officially.

"The stable 40-hour job left me with enough time to pursue my calling. My real calling: A labor of love that takes lots of time, and lots of detective work. Long hours of detective work. See, I became a garbage collector, dedicated to clean the scum from this world. Dedicated to take out the worse rotten garbage that's lying around—that nauseating trash whose disgusting stink is carefully hidden behind rosy fences or artfully camouflaged by sweet folding screens."

This was becoming creepy, Carmina thought.

"This world is so full of disgusting scum posing as distinguished members of society. Horrible people who do horrible things to vulnerable preys and never get caught, leaving behind them a trail of powerless victims, unable to denounce—too ashamed to denounce, or too powerless to do so. Monsters lurking in the shadows of glitzy offices and temples built of lies, cathedrals of ego and power erected to camouflage the cesspools of inequity and vile created in their underworld, where dark secrets hide. And for those victims who find the courage to recognize that they haven't done something wrong and find the strength to proclaim that it is not their fault? Nothing! After all, who would believe any accusation against the pillars of society without ironclad proofs of wrongdoing, without undeniable evidence—the kind of evidence that simply can't be garnered given the nature of the crimes, or the kind of evidence that our sacred institutions deny release.

"Horrible pieces of garbage. Everywhere. Look around you. If you pay attention, what will you see?

"Sleazebags that destroy the lives of little girls, pretending to be loving uncles sharing little secrets with all of their favorite nieces; loving neighbors showering candies and more secrets with naive kids; loving relatives destroying innocence without punishment."

He pulled a second bullet from the bag. He tried to drop it in her hand, but slapped it on the table because of her closed fist.

"Policemen who perpetually violate the trust of citizens, so corrupt that no disinfectant-based aftershave lotion could be powerful enough to hide their putrid smell; so wretched that robbing houses, stealing drugs, and abusing whores at gunpoint is routine; so abject that hardened criminals serving lifetime sentences in the most hellish jails are angels in comparison.

"Number three," he said, depositing another bullet on the table.

"Chief Executive Officers who plunder corporations' coffers, paying themselves multi-million dollar performance bonuses for shuffling plants to third-world countries hospitable to pollution where widgets can be manufactured for nothing by little kids working 16 hour shifts; pink-slipping thousands of co-patriots while pulling retirement and health benefits from under their feet; breaking employees and their families without an ounce of scruples—all while cheating their wives on superyachts."

He dropped a bullet on Carmina's lap—her hands were still fists.

"Cream of the crop, top of the top: the grand guardians of morality, custodians of the gods, pontificates of all denominations, self-serving gurus who preach genocide, ethnic cleansing, religious wars, discrimination of all types, while robbing and raping their blind servants, abusing kids, despising women, justifying their heinous crimes by tortuous mind-games. Crooks! Crooks paying lip service to the higher principles they have sworn to uphold, dispensing clichés like tidbits of wisdom to attract naive souls who need solace into a treacherous sanctuary where predators await. All these holy places, so infested by vermin..."

Spike flipped the brown bag upside down, dropping dozens of bullets on Carmina's lap and throwing the bag in the air, in a grand theatrical gesture.

She jumped up.

The bullets fell on the floor.

"You're sick." She couldn't take anymore of that vigilante's self-righteous gospel.

"Of course."

"You need help," she clarified, less firmly, realizing she had forgotten about the gun.

"I'm not going to shoot you," he said, realizing for the first time the emotions of his guests. He almost said, "I'm not crazy," but realized that this was a self-defeating prophecy.

Carmina didn't trust Spike's reassurances. She started to slowly navigate sideways towards the door, as Spike had to be circumvented to exit the room.

"Where is the line between rightful justice and blind vigilantism? Who gives you the right to decide for the world what is right or wrong?

"Every one of these bullets went through a person so inhumanly repulsive that it hit no soul. They traveled through total emptiness, only crushing... E. coli."

"How do you know? How can you judge people like that?"

"They weren't random targets. They were awful criminals. Hours of detective work. Trust me"—as if she could—"the wrestling coach was a cherub next to them. I could show you all the evidence—"

"I didn't need to know all of this. Why did you tell me all that?"

"You were sent here."

"I just needed to pick up a piece of Keene's stupid puzzle."

"That's just what I gave you."

"I didn't want the bullets."

"I gave you more than that. I gave you their stories."

"I don't want that either."

"I probably gave you a key."

"What key?"

"I don't know. Maybe something for your puzzle?"

"Sig. Come on," she said, extending a protective arm without looking back, hoping he was following close.

"Whatever it is that Keene wanted me to tell you—"

"What did he tell you?"

"Nothing. He just wrote."

"What did he write to you?"

"That I had to give you the bullet. One bullet. I mean, just the first one. It's the only one he knows about. That's the secret he probably needed to have released so that he could die peacefully. I guess. Whatever it is that Keene wanted me to tell you—"

"What did he tell you?"

"Nothing. I told you already. He only wrote."

"What else did he write to you?" she said, impatiently.

"Nothing more."

"Nothing?"

"Nothing."

"I don't believe it."

"As I'm trying to say, whatever it is that Keene wanted me to tell you, I don't know. He wrote he was dying; he wrote a bunch of weird stuff about strawberries and wine; and he wrote that he wanted you to pick up the bullet. The one bullet. The rest—the story, my story—is my gift to you."

"A gift?"

"The bullet can't leave alone; it is bound to its history."

"I don't need your bullet. Or the other ones. And I don't need... your stories" She almost said bull, but judged it prudent not to provoke an unhinged mind.

"Fine. Whatever. You're the one who came here to pick them up."

"I only came here to collect what Keene wanted. No more."

"When a body is riddled with bullets, taking just one out won't do any good."

"When a body is full of lead, it is dead! Dead, dead, dead!" she shouted nervously. "Pulling bullets out of a dead body won't bring it back to life!"

"You'd be surprised."

She finally reached the doorknob. She caught a glimpse of Sig over her shoulder, just behind her.

"Come on Sig," she said, making sure the gun was far enough on the table that they could outrun any sudden insane reaction from the deranged man.

Spike just leaned on the wall next to the door, still, inexpressive, not an obstacle as they rushed out.

"Thanks for the visit. Hope you'll come back. You're welcome anytime. It's always good to see nice people."

With her hand in a tight grip around Sig's wrist, she ran down the corridor to the nearest exit. She nearly tripped up the stairs and along the sidewalk when looking back to make sure Spike's apartment window wasn't visible. Unable to free his hand, Sig was annoyed by Carmina's nervous zig-zagging—as if a sniper could possibly hit them from a basement window without a view on the street. Fortunately, she let go and slowed down after a few blocks when her adrenalin level dropped a notch.

As they walked away at a nervous pace, Carmina heard a maracas-like sound. She first feared Spike had caught up to them, but figured that serial killers rarely use maracas to spook their future victims. The noise came from the brown bag that Sig had in his hand—swaying as he walked. The "damn kid" had picked up the bullets in her back while she confronted Spike.

She tried to swipe the bag away, but Sig jumped out of range.

"We're on a mission," he said, making it unequivocal that the bullets were coming home to Keene—at least, whatever he could pick before the rushed exit, hoping the symbolic first one was in the bag. "How do you expect to solve the puzzle if we leave clues behind?"

Seven

This time, there had been no miscommunication, no blunder. Sig was invited first, and Carmina was asked if she could join them.

They had accepted.

Justin had spent the day frantically preparing his house—not so much cleaning it, as a cleaning lady took care of the dusting and scrubbing once a week, but rather attempting to turn a dull place of residence into a welcoming abode, a bland domicile into a warm home. A warmer one at least.

Throwing in storage boxes anything that lay dormant on the top of desks, counters, tables, appliances, and chairs; swapping stacks of books for bunches of flowers (again); leaving the windows wide open to refresh the air; selecting fine wines; debating how much to dim the lights; and exterminating any evidence of a bored bachelor's life.

Also, most importantly, planning a strategy. A stressful task for the worst strategist on earth.

Time was running short; they were at minus a few days because Keene was at minus a few days. Keene would soon be dead again—definitively this time—and Carmina would not return.

Justin almost became the first man on earth to die from a heart attack triggered by a doorbell.

There she was—with the cute kid. There was Sig with his cute mom. Cute guardian. Whatever.

"Wow," said Sig, looking at the enormous bumblebee flying through the room—an uninvited guest that had zoomed through the wide open windows.

Justin thought he was looking at the acoustic guitar hanging from the wall.

"You can play with it if you want."

Sig gave him a strange look. He was way past the age of running after bugs.

"You play?" asked Carmina.

"I wish."

Sig gave him an even stranger look.

"There's something mesmerizing about music. Making music, that is. You pluck a string, a sound is created, it is sustained for a while, and then it slowly fades away. Something out of nothing, and then nothing again."

He almost added "just like life itself," but feared it might sound like a reference to Keene.

Sig, finally seeing the musical instrument and understanding the invitation, rushed to take it off the wall. Guitar in hand, he bowed to the audience, and attacked the strings by swinging his arms like a windmill, complete with the occasional heavy metal scream. A one-chord song—all open strings, free of bothersome fretting.

"That's just about my repertoire too," said Justin.

Whoever had invented the guitar had forgotten to make sure that it creates a pleasant sound when the right hand is vigorously strumming but the left one is too shy to touch the frets along the neck. The open chord might have had a name—E minor 7th Sharp 9th Suspended 4th, like some of the ugliest things in life have pretty names—but harmonious, it was not. Its repetition ad nauseam didn't help, although the auditory pain inflicted by that chord would likely subside over time, as those within range of the assault would get accustomed to its scorching attributes.

"We'll go read Keene's letter in the other room, while you just go ahead with your concert," said Carmina, hoping this would incite him to stop the acoustic massacre.

Sig continued to fool around, certain he'd have time to complete his opus before they'd even get started reading.

The kitchen a few walls away wasn't totally soundproof, but Sig's ruckus was sufficiently muffled by those partitions to make a normal conversation possible.

"Do you want to have dinner before or after Keene's letter?"

"After."

Justin seemed disappointed.

"But I'd take a glass of wine."

"Perfect. I went to the liquor store and found one of those fancy bottles that Keene raved about in his letters."

"Justin. I've been thinking about adopting Sig," she said, out of the blue.

He stopped, an expensive Chardonnay bottle in his left hand, the cheap refrigerator door handle in the other. Where did that thought come from? They were talking about wine!

Was it a feminine impulse inspired by the poetry of the moment, or a long repressed emotion suddenly freed because they were finally alone? Either way, Sig's clanging provided the confidentiality she needed for that confession—the same open chord kept being banged, although possibly to a different screaming tune.

"I've been thinking about it a lot in the past few days."

"Yes."

"He's a great kid. He would be about the age of my son, if we had had a son before our separation."

"Yes."

"Don't get me wrong. I know he's his own person. I would never try to pretend he'd be that other son that never was. That would be too much of a burden to carry—for him to carry."

"Yes."

"But he's a great kid. A really great kid. I know he has problems to work out."

"Yes."

"But he's past the age of adoption. It will never happen, you know. He'll just bounce from foster home to foster home, one after another. It's so unfair."

"Yes."

"Don't think it's about pity! It's not. It would be cruel and unfair to be adopted without being loved, and a profound humiliation and unbearable shame to any poor kid who'd discover that his adoption was nothing more than a humanitarian deed. No. I'm thinking about adoption because I really love that kid."

Justin prayed she would someday soon repeat that last sentence substituting "Justin" instead of "that kid"—or maybe "my sweet and tender Justin" in his wildest dreams.

"Yes."

"I can't tell you how much I value that you're so sympathetic just now. You're such a good listener."

"Yes."

Justin had mechanically repeated the word to conceal his partial mental absence, as his brain raced to figure out what to do, sorting through possible scenarios and ensuing outcomes. On one hand, the kid had pyromaniac inclinations and had threatened to express his flaming art on his belongings—maybe as passionately as he was now destroying his guitar. On the other hand, he seemed stable in Carmina's presence—with respect to fire at least. Whether or not this stability would remain, or for how long, was unclear. Yet, if it were Carmina's desire, Sig would become like an irrevocable clause in a contract, like the little bonus prize in a package deal bundle, like a binding appendix. Nothing could be done to change her decision. Carmina would become Carmina-plus, Carmina-enhanced, Carmina-Sig's mom.

"Do you think I'm crazy?"

"Yes."

She stopped talking. The sudden silence—not counting the slamming open-chord noise in the other room—brought him back to reality.

"I mean no, no. This makes perfect sense."

"Really?"

There were so many words to say that remained jumbled up in this mind, like a pushing and shoving crowd waiting for the gates of a rock concert to open. Words dying to reveal the solemn truth but that remained hidden in silence. He had to break the silence. This travesty of his true feelings had to cease. All confusion had to cease. He had to man-up.

"Carmina, I love you."

"What?"

Justin's romantic intrepidity lasted a grand three seconds. He was already embarrassed to death by her surprised response to his heartfelt revelation. Or was it fear? He had violated the canons with an abrupt slip that had to have made him look like a maniac, and her like a prey lured into his lair. Four silly words tantamount to the prerequisite deranged admission that usually precedes a chainsaw massacre.

"I mean, in a professional way. You're a dear client. My best client."

"Ah."

Coward, coward, coward. Scared like a lawyer who accidentally told the truth. Scolded for four truthful words that had escaped from his lips.

"That's why I will help you."

"You will?"

"Absolutely. As soon as we're done with this Keene business, I'll help you. Adoption is not my direct expertise—I work closer to recently dead people than recently born ones, you know—but it's just lawyer's paperwork after all, so I'm sure we'll figure it out."

"So you think it is the right thing to do?"

"If that's where your heart leads you to, yes. Absolutely. One must always follow his heart."

He could hear all the vegetables in the fridge, some yelling "Tell her, tell her," others screaming, "Coward. Coward. We'd kick you in the butt if we had legs." Just realizing that, in his stupefaction, he had held it open all that time, he slammed the refrigerator door—carrots and celery had no right to lecture him.

Maybe the veggies were right though. He should have listened to his own heart, and declared his love to Carmina. Didn't he just say one must always follow his heart? She was right. No more "should have" and "would have." He had to do it now.

Unfortunately, Sig Presley ended his concert at that very moment, and Justin wasn't about to undertake a second open courtship attempt in presence of such a critical audience.

"I want some too," shouted Sig, as he burst in the kitchen and saw the wine bottle.

Carmina grabbed him like a desperate wrestler and hugged him so hard, he would have been convinced she was trying to choke him to death if not for the fact that she kept saying: "You're adorable! You're so adorable!"

Sig was impressed. This rock 'n' roll stuff really worked with chicks—and, yet, he only knew one chord. He could only imagine the possibilities with two or more chords and some practice.

"You're just in time, Sig. We're about to read Keene's letter."

"Mmm hmm wmmf," answered Sig, still deprived of air.

Carmina released her grip, and kissed him on both cheeks.

"Hey, I'm not a kid," he complained, wiping the kiss off with his sleeve.

"That has nothing to do with it. I kiss men too you know."

Justin wished.

"I'm not a kid, I'm a rock musician."

"Already?" replied Carmina.

"I'll tell you what," said Justin. "If you promise to take lessons, I'll give you the guitar."

"Cool."

"You have to promise to take guitar lessons."

If Carmina was to be his sweetheart, the ambient noise that was likely to surround them had to be cleansed of that dreadful E minor 7th Sharp 9th Suspended 4th.

"Deal."

"If you make a deal with Sig, I want to make a deal too."

Justin's heart jumped.

"Yes."

He was back in "perfect listener mode," but hanging to her every word this time.

"I'm the one reading Keene's letters from now on."

"No, I want to know what's in the letters too," snapped Sig.

"I'll read them aloud."

"So what's the other part of the deal?" asked Justin. "What do I get in return?"

"I don't know."

"A legal contract involves at least two parties."

"Stop being a lawyer. I'll think of something."

Justin could hear the muffled screams of the vegetables in the fridge. "Coward!"

"You know what? You're right. I can't stop being a lawyer," said Justin, thinking out loud. "Contracts are just crutches to make sure there is no ambiguity, to kill any possible misunderstanding."

"But you can't live without them."

"I can't. I'm just like Keene," he replied. "He can't stop being an engineer; it's not just a job, it's a reflection of who he is—just like being a lawyer is part of who I am.

"So you're going to quit your job and start drinking wine full time now," said Sig.

"No. Keene's ahead of me on that. I'm still chained to my crutches. But, Carmina, here's the deal: Effective immediately, you get to read all of Keene's letters, and at our next meeting, I'll bring a draft contract spelling the terms of what you can do in return. Non-binding. Just for your consideration."

"You're silly," laughed Carmina.

"If you don't like the terms, I'll just resume the reading of the letters from that point onward. No penalties assessed for today's freebie."

"You'd have fun doing this?"

"It would give me immense pleasure."

"You're crazy."

"Deal?"

"Deal."

Justin finally had found a way to express his true emotions to her. He would be able to deliberate his every word to her, to craft unambiguous statements, to advocate, to provide all the evidence and deliver a winning closing statement, all in a document binding his heart to his words. This would not be a boilerplate contract full of insipidities intended to confuse. No. There would be no legalese, no contractual nonsense, no obstructions to clarity. Just facts. Just truth. Straight from the heart. A love letter without the poetical clutter. A letter that, once given, could not be rescinded by second thoughts driven by a humiliating cowardice. A bold move that would be applauded by his leguminous acquaintances in the fridge.

"Here's Keene's letter."

She took it, slowly unsealed it, and unfolded it ceremoniously, looking Justin straight in the eye, almost reading his mind. As if he was channeling Keene's warmth.

Somehow, Keene felt closer at that very moment—she felt closer. As if some sacred bonds were being renewed.

"Here we go."

"Day Minus 3.

"It is strange to go to sleep every evening without knowing if there will be the opportunity to wake up the next morning. It is even stranger to wake up that next morning realizing that the gift of another day to live has been granted.

"I'm clearly beyond the six month limit and working on borrowed time.

"Three days ago was the date I had circled on the calendar 182.6213 days before then. I stayed up until 11:25 p.m., which I had penned in that square of the calendar to be the official time of my death—as declared by omniscient medical doctors.

"Nothing.

"Then came 11:26 p.m.

"Still nothing.

"11:27 p.m., 11:28 p.m., 11:30 p.m., 11:45 p.m., midnight.

"Still nothing."

Although Keene had determined never to reveal the cause of his death, the severity of his illness transpired throughout the letter. Uncorrected typographical errors, missing punctuation, formatting problems, and other blemishes hinted that pain was fought at each keystroke. Keene may have hidden much by avoiding the treason of calligraphy, aware that his block letters molded by the rigors of technical drawings could have degenerated into streaks and tears, but hiding behind a computer wasn't foolproof. Keene had not anticipated that she could wrestle from Justin the guarded privilege of entering the privacy of his editorial failures. She could not unmask the nature of the illness, but she could witness some of its ravages.

From letter to letter, noticing the progressive degradation of Keene's perfectionism, Justin had polished the flaws, smoothen the edges, filled-in the missing bits, for sake of clarity in communication. She understood it. Now. She also understood it to be her obligation to do the same.

Yet, at the same time, she wondered what kind of disease could make the enjoyment of wine a glorious panacea and the task of writing an agonizing chore. It had to be painful. Otherwise, why wait three whole days to talk about the night when he had expected to die?

"My expiration date came and went.

"And another day started.

"What a bummer.

"What to do when waking up the morning after the night one is supposed to die? No plans had been made to fill that bugger of a new day.

"What would the world come to if engineers worked like medical doctors? The mean time to failure of every part in a system would become 'about six months' without any implicit warranties provided—an absolutely meaningless rating. Nice brand new car, but who knows how long it's going to work. Warranties? Nope, no such thing. Planes would fall out of the sky every now and then, water might not always be safe to drink, toasters would set houses on fire, and porous latex would increase the nation's birth rate.

"Although, in fairness, if medical doctors stated plain truths with bland engineering frankness, their prestige might not survive. 'The 95% confidence assessment is that this unrepairable body has a 43% chance of working for six more months, no more. This is because of a grossly deficient initial design, faulty operation procedures, critical deferred maintenance, total ignorance of the mechanisms that led to the discovered system fault, and consequently absence of knowledge on economically viable repair strategies.' Bad marketing when clients expect miracles.

"So, as a victim of medical ignorance, I find myself facing another day, with nothing planned to do. I was supposed to be dead and now I'm not. Almost a disappointment!

"Of course, I'm kidding. Like a prisoner on death row, I sure can enjoy a reprieve—for lack of a pardon.

"Maybe I could spend part of the day pondering what mysterious force is keeping me alive so long. One could speculate that the curative value of red wine by far exceeds its known cardiovascular benefits and can regenerate heath and youth like the fable spring waters discovered in the new world by multiple Spanish explorers—who incidentally all died eventually. Or is it the cathartic process of breaking all ties to engineering that is paying unexpected dividends? How about the theory that passionate writing, keyboard wired directly to the soul, can extend longevity? I am one data point corroborating that postulate. If so, the letter I wrote yesterday to someone dear might buy me enough living energy to last a few more weeks."

Carmina wondered which letter that might be. She hadn't received any "dear Carmina" letters. She hoped the "someone dear" wasn't a reference to Hannelore. An important missing milestone in the chronology of Keene's countdown to his death was the point when he actually decided to plan the whole crazy treasure hunt business, but for sure his plans had to have been completed long before because Keene was now writing on borrowed time.

"The part of the day devoted to probing the nature of the mysterious forces keeping me alive is over. Time to go wine shopping. Today, I'll buy seven bottles, as a contribution to my assiduous numerology studies—because I've reached seven now, just as I'm entering the seventh month of my new life.

"Problem though is that the world has gone bananas with seven.

"All those lucky sevens fanatically pursued.

"Just like all these spiritual sevens that entrap us.

"The seven deadly sins and seven levels of purgatory. Just like the seven paths to heaven and seven heavenly cows of ancient Egypt—and Osiris' seven halls of the underworld.

"The multitude of sevens in Jewish tradition—from the seven days of the creation to the seven candles of the menorah.

"The seven everything of old superstitions.

"It's an endless list!

"No wonder seven is a number of riddles, questions, magic, mystery—that there are seven chakras on the human body, and that one gets seven years of bad luck for breaking a mirror.

"So a bunch of gods each get seven wives, mothers, or sisters, or ride chariots pulled by seven horses—just as casually as Snow White gets seven sex slaves—and we get the seven days of the week. Days incidentally named after the seven planets of ancient astronomy, or their corresponding ancient gods and planets: Sunday, Moon-day, Tiw's-day (Norse Mars), Woden's-day (Germanic Mercury), Thor's-day (Norse Jupiter), Frigg's-day (Norse Venus), and Saturn-day.

"The metaphysical world gets its irrational sevens, and we get seven white notes on a piano scale. Or we get confused in our rationality and get the seven subjects of liberal arts—defined in medieval times as the sum of the trivium (grammar, rhetoric, and logic) and the quadrivium (music, arithmetic, geometry, and astronomy).

"But in the end, how does seven really talk to me?

"Some say it is shaped like a bent old man, other say it is a man carrying a lantern at the end of an extended arm, holding an insignificant light in a dark world of unknown. A small inquisitive mind burning in a cold universe, like the soul of a mystic, praying for enlightening visions.

"It is inquisitive, meditative, introspective, and esoteric. It is the recruiting agency for all those seeking silence and peaceful solitude.

"Seven is definitely not a party animal.

"Seven has no friends."

Carmina paused in front of the obvious, before reading the next line, realizing at that instant that she could have said just the same talking about herself.

"I am Seven."

Sig, who had not interrupted once, understood too. He was Seven. He had no friends. There was Carmina, but "mothers" are an exception.

"So what?

"What's wrong in being a loner? I have no friends and I'm not 'incomplete.' I'm not about to buy a pet or a fish tank to compensate, because there's nothing that needs compensating for.

"Besides, what's so wonderful about friends? I've been robbed by friends. I've been tricked by friends. I've been back-stabbed by friends.

"Is friendship great or what? I need friendship like a nail in the head.

"So what about longevity? If the theory that passionate writing extends longevity is true, is this why I'm dying so young—days later than recently predicted, but still decades youn-ger than the national average? Because I have nobody to write to?

"An engineer can get absorbed by the task of building a bridge for the benefit of society. The bridge must safely carry, in addition to its own weigh, the worse traffic loads expected over its lifetime; it must be detailed to accommodate thermal expansion of its materials; it must withstand the onslaught of floods, hurricanes, and earthquakes; it must resist millions of cycles of loads without developing fatal cracks. Although a complex problem, when starting with a blank page, all kinds of solutions are possible, and achievable at reasonable societal costs.

"However, the engineer can get so engrossed by that stupid project, that the more important bridge that exists with the love of his life suffers. Without the constant maintenance it de-serves—and requires—it deteriorates, weakens, and rusts, until the day when the accumulated problems have irremediably jeopardized it. When its deficiencies are revealed—the rotten structure screaming in pain—the bridge is closed, labeled as unsafe. From that point onward, professional and non-professional opinions will abound, as it becomes more a political problem than a technical one. Some will call for a new bridge, advocating demolition of the eyesore that the obsolete span has become. Others refuse to abandon the old structure, confident that rehabilitation can return it to service, enhanced to perform even better than before. Calls of misplaced nostalgia and technocratic bullying fly, emotions run high, and compromises aren't possible.

"The engineer may attest that everything is fixable, and that repairing the older bridge might even be the more economical solution, but the arguments may not be about costs anymore. It's about rekindling the old flame versus embracing the future. It's about rehabilitating versus destroying. It's about retying the knot versus divorcing. It's about letting go of the ring, or not.

"Longevity can't be taken for granted, but when it has been jeopardized, not all is hopeless.

"While my late words to you may have lengthen my stay on this earth by mere milliseconds, more importantly, they have made it possible to stroll anew across an old previously closed bridge, one last time.

"I sincerely thank you for helping me fulfill my last wishes, for having stayed with me this far—if you did indeed condone my final fantasy."

This was the first time that a part of Keene's letters was explicitly addressed to Carmina—directly talking to her. If anything, it confirmed her assumptions about the chronology of his last decisions.

"However, I believe the next item on my list may be the hardest one to collect, so I've included a bottle of exquisite champagne to keep you company and bolster your spirits through this hardship.

"Please enjoy the letter a swan sang yesterday."

Reading aloud Keene's letter, as opposed to hearing it, left Carmina in a haze. It has been an unexpected communion.

"Sounds like we are flying out real far to somewhere real special," said Sig.

"Not really," corrected Justin.

The End

"I'm not going."

"You can pick any treat you want—something for both of us."

"You want junk, you go get it. I'm not stupid."

Of course he wasn't.

"You're just trying to get rid of me."

Of course, she was.

"Please, Sig."

"I want to know what's in Keene's letter."

"And that's what I want for you too."

"Oh yeah? Are you going to hold the letter on the window for me to read from across the road?"

"Don't be silly."

"Do you prefer that I use my X-ray vision to read it through the walls?"

"Sig!"

She looked at him in a way he wasn't sure how to decode. Was she mad? Had he pressed the wrong buttons? One thing for sure, all the whining didn't score points.

"Sig. You're not a kid. You are certainly old enough to understand that this letter might be a bit more personal. More intimate."

This time, Keene's instructions on the index card had just stated, "make yourself comfortable." The card was stapled to a fancier stationery envelope addressed to "My Carmina." Justin had not read it either. However, contrary to Sig, he was old enough to understand. Mature enough to recognize when privacy was in order.

Whatever needed to be fetched at this crucial stage of the treasure hunt was spelled out in that mysterious letter, and Sig wasn't about to miss it for the sake of an unnecessary errand to a miserable convenience store five infinitely long blocks away from the hotel.

"There's no reason why I should go."

"There is."

"No there isn't. Give me one reason."

"Because the SOMUNOM says so," thought Carmina, wondering why she was negotiating with a twelve-year-old kid. But she felt she could do better—an education rather than a negotiation. Her pedagogical skills couldn't be any worse than that of the average parent.

"Do you like Justin?"

"What does this have to do with anything?"

"Just answer me."

"He's OK I guess."

"Like what?"

"Like what, what?"

"He's OK like what? Like a friend?"

"Like a lawyer, I guess."

Carmina had higher hopes. Surely Sig wouldn't have said "like a father" since he had no concept of what real fathers are supposed to be, but "lawyer" was a letdown, undermining her central argument.

"Come on, he's more than that. Be honest."

"He's OK like a buddy?" he said looking at Carmina as if this was a quiz, waiting to see if he got the right answer.

"Don't try to please me, be honest."

"I don't know," he said, genuinely wondering. "He's honest," he conceded, reusing Carmina's word to tease.

"That's it?"

"That a lot considering that he's a lawyer."

"That's it?"

"I don't know. Why all those questions?"

"Would you set fire to his office, like you told him the other day?"

"Of course not." Then, to qualify the limits of this verbal contract, he clarified: "Unless he starts to be a jerk."

"OK. So let's assume that he didn't start to be a jerk, and that he remained an honest lawyer. Maybe even a very friendly honest lawyer. And let's say that for some reason, you set fire to his office."

"I just said I wouldn't."

"Say you do."

"But I wouldn't."

"Assume that Justin said something stupid that he regrets, but before he gets a chance to apologize, you set fire to his office. He made a mistake, you made a mistake. People make mistakes. That's life."

"Hrm."

"Also assume that Justin and you stopped talking to each other for a while after that incident because you were both upset. Now, imagine that one day, you feel bad about the whole think and wish to write a letter to him."

"Why?"

"I don't know. Just to explain yourself. Maybe to apologize, maybe not. Who knows."

"Just to see if we can still be friends?"

"Yes! Exactly!" she shouted, delighted that he picked the word "friends."

"Now, imagine that this letter, addressed to me, is a letter just like that."

"Keene set your office on fire?" he said laughing.

"Maybe he did. Or maybe I did his."

"That's going to be a good letter. No way that I'm going to miss this one out."

"No. You're missing the point altogether. This is a very personal letter."

"I thought we were a team."

Carmina didn't know how to convince Sig anymore. Or did she have to? The "because the SOMUNOM says so" explanation seemed more appealing than ever.

She left to start filling the bathtub with hot water, for lack of a private boudoir. No bubble bath—the door would have to be closed and locked for privacy.

Coming back while the tub was filling, she said, "Yes we are a team. But team members are allowed some private time too."

Sig's sad puppy face said it all.

"Sig. I love you. I really do. But this may be a difficult letter for me to read."

"If you let me stay, I'll tell you what SOMUNOM means."

That's as much as Sig could bid. What else could a twelve-year-old kid offer?

Carmina paused for a good minute, admiring the cute kid who might soon be her son—aware that she shouldn't ask him the big question before getting more information from Justin about the legal adoption process, restrictions, and procedures—and felt that at one point or another, he would become privy to all parts of her life. Even the harder and painful parts. In some ways, their shared journey of the past few weeks had revealed a lot more than she would have ever willingly disclosed. Yet, Keene was unpredictable, particularly in his weirdest reincarnation, and nobody likes an audience when crying.

"I'll tell you what. Give me a chance to read the letter first, to digest it a bit. When you come back from the convenience store, I'll read it to you. It will be a pleasure to read it a second time, just for you. Besides, if Keene makes me cry the first time I read, it will give me a chance to brace myself for the tough parts the second time around."

At heart, Sig wanted the live feed, not some sort of delayed broadcast. However, not seeing Carmina cry was an enormous benefit given that he acutely felt her pain each time it happened—not enjoyable. Part of him wanted to concede, but another part was determined to whine some more to underscore the immensity of his sacrifice and possibly wring more concessions.

"It's so far. Five blocks! I might get lost. I might never come back."

"Five blocks. Square city grid. Safe neighborhood. Come on, Sig. You're not a kid."

He pouted, making it clear than one more bone had to be thrown on the negotiation table if she wanted to close the deal.

"I'll even wait for you to open the champagne bottle, and I'll let you taste."

"Ew! Wine with bubbles. Yurk." Not much of a bone.

"Trust me, it's much better than wine. It's really sweet, bubbly, and delicious. The bottle Keene gave me is real champagne too, from France."

That wasn't much of a selling point to Sig as his only French wine reference was the "goat piss" served by Didier. He concluded that if violating the country's drinking laws was all she could think of, there wasn't much to gain by further extending the negotiations.

"You promise you'll read me the letter?"

"You promise you'll first tell me what SOMUNOM means?"

"Deal."

He offered a handshake, but she buried him gasping for air into the flesh of a crunching hug.

Freed from her claws, Sig thought Carmina was getting weirder everyday. That Keene guy had a strange effect on her—despite being inconveniently dead.

She handed him a few bills—enough to indulge in the available junk food offerings.

"I'll be back in no time," he snapped, running off the door.

"Don't put the change in the same pocket as the room key card; the coins can demagnetize it," she shouted as Sig escaped, for lack of a better maternal admonition.

Alone at last.

A hard-won privacy to which she was fully entitled, at the price of some guilty feelings. A privacy of unknown length, as Sig sprinted out to run the five long blocks, and might not take much time to decide which candies to buy for the pairing with champagne. Nonetheless, the minutes to come were hers, and hers alone.

Alone.

She hadn't been alone for weeks now. Such a difference.

She surrendered to the steaming hot bath. No time to fine tune the water temperature, but no complaints—lobsters had it harder than her anyhow, if only by a few degrees.

Settled comfortably, spirits propped by symbolic buoyancy, she opened Keene's letter.

"My dear and beloved Carmina."

She was afraid it would start like that. Afraid, yet pleased.

"I will never forget the instant I fell in love with you. Experts claim that 'love at first sight' is just an overused trope littering the artistic landscape, like a contagious disease concocted by antique gods, spread by troubadours through medieval times, infecting Romeo and Juliet, Marius and Cosette, the Little Mermaid and her prince, and myriad others exposed to the virus at the hands of far less talented novelists who lack the patience or craftsmanship to better develop characters, or—worse—at the mercy of screenwriters who must cram a love story into 90 minutes. Experts testify that the sting of Cupid's darts may be inebriating, but that lasting love isn't founded on impulsive first impressions that can be sociologically, psychologically, and scientifically explained. Experts dismiss the romantic lighting bolt as a trite hormonal-driven infatuation that distracts from the stronger bonds of true love.

"Fortunately, I'm no expert.

"Thus, I will always remember your hair floating in the wind while your mind was immersed in the dystopia of Huxley's *Brave New World*, possibly drowning in the satirical warnings against a frightening future that is already here, or soon to be. I will always remember the powerful attraction of intellect and beauty in an era where cracking open a book is an aberration and where well-rounded sentences are endangered species. I will always remember your sparkling eyes drenched in sunlight, when I sat next to you on that bench, wondering if it would be fatally clumsy to introduce myself by commenting that one shouldn't be allowed to be born in a capitalistic society before having read this novel, as Cupid's arrow pierced my heart.

"To an eternity of heaven, hell, or nothingness, I will always cherish that love-at-first-sight."

"I remember that day. Those days," thought Carmina. "I remember that handsome guy who silently sat at the other end of the same bench without saying a word, reading a book full of equations, and who showed up the next day with *After Many a Summer Dies the Swan* by Aldous Huxley. I remember laughing, waiting for the obvious pick-up line, and breaking the silence first when it didn't come. I remember closing my book, turning my head and asking with a smile 'and who are you exactly, shy neighbor?' and you responding, 'I'm a failed one man circus!' "

"A one man circus?"

"A failed one. Very much so."

"And how is that?"

"Well, first, I am a failed magician. I make ribbons of steel and concrete fly across wide rivers and canyons, or jump across wide highways, opening new pathways for vehicles and pedestrians of all shapes and sizes."

"What's the failure in that?"

"Nobody claps."

"Of course not. Building a bridge is not magic."

"What is magic if not an illusion supported by science?"

"But a magician doesn't a circus make, as Shakespeare might say."

"And he would be very right, but I'm also a failed acrobat."

"Let me guess. You defy gravity by... by stacking piles of steel and concrete up to dizzying heights."

"Yep."

"But nobody claps."

"Correct."

"That's because it's not a new trick. It's been done many times before."

"People clap for jugglers, and I have yet to see a juggler do something I haven't seen before."

"But a magician and an acrobat doesn't a circus make. A circus needs clowns. I mean, a failed circus needs failed clowns."

"I am that too."

"Failed?"

"Sure. I can't control the laughs. Girls laugh at me all the time because I'm not an athlete, or an artist, or mysterious, yet that's not the joke I want them to laugh at."

She had laughed.

"See."

She had responded by clapping.

"Stop. You are making my failed circus fail at being a failure."

She remembered it all too well. All the tiny seconds that had conspired together to push that unique moment back in time never could erase it. The words on Keene's letter were as vivid as the present.

She could have savored the moment more, but had to finish the letter before Sig's return.

"I will never forget our wedding day. Its deliberate and exquisite simplicity," wrote Keene. "Just the two of us—and the mandatory official to fill the unavoidable paperwork. No family, no friends—easy for me, harder for you. No open bar for guests to drown in, no extravagant buffet to burst waists, no wailing big band to shake booties. Just a sacred and private moment between those for whom it mattered most, in a symbolic place forever etched in my mind.

"A special place carefully chosen to reflect the pregnancy of our engagement. Not a goofy stunt, like exchanging vows while skydiving or immersed in a giant aquarium surrounded by sharks; not a fake setting, like a medieval theme, or Star Trek fest, or other amusement-park concepts; not a pre-packaged romantic rip-off, like sunset on a Hawaii beach with a dozen hula dancers, half-a-dozen fire jugglers, and a ukulele band, showered in rose petals and premium champagne. No illusions. It had to be something real. Something inspiring, true, beautiful, and sound.

"I'm sure you remember our brainstorming sessions."

"You bet I remember," thought Carmina. "We considered a desert beach in New Zealand, with its crystal clear waters of purity and undisturbed peace, but felt it was too far from our roots. We envisioned a cliff-edge union at the Grand Canyon, with its awesome grandeur and indebtedness to time, but feared the symbolism of nearby free-fall, or of the canyon as a divider, standing someday on different edges across. We fancied mountain tops, to be rejuvenated by fresh breezes and closer to the sun, but could just as well have been blown away by summit gales and sunburnt though thin air."

"So many options we considered," wrote Keene.

"So many, indeed."

"Never giving up."

"Never."

"Until it became clear that our marriage was a bridge, linking two unique beings together. An essential linkage more important than a lifeline, distinct from all other bridges. An entirely human creation of our building, whose strength and careful design would determine its longevity. Unequivocally, a signature span. The perfect idea—especially in those days when I still believed engineering to be of some meaningful significance."

"I remember your passion for all the bridges we discussed," replied Carmina, "the basic engineering principles you described in simple terms to explain how they defy the forces of nature, the history behind their construction and their place in the Parthenon of engineering. I remember how you fancied the Québec bridge, the longest of its type in the world, reaching cliff to cliff, across the majestic Saint Lawrence River, and how I rejected this option on the grounds that it collapsed twice during its construction and that it was rusted beyond belief, in urgent need of paint and tender loving care—enough bad omens to scare the bravest. I remember how we both liked the Brooklyn bridge, an engineering achievement that became the longest suspension bridge in the world when it opened, dramatically longer than any previous record-holder, and one of the most aesthetically pleasing landmark of a world-city; until you told me that its chief engineer suffered a debilitating injury during its construction, leaving him paralyzed and relying on his wife for eleven years to supervise all work to its completion. So many options you proposed that I rejected. I was hard to please."

"You were a bit hard to please, but we found our perfect location. A bridge than many said could not be built, spanning turbulent currents of eddies and whirlpools, that became the longest suspension bridge in the world when completed. An international engineering landmark of outstanding appeal and symbolism, combining intelligence and beauty, as a reminder of the first day I meet you. A bridge exceptionally well maintained under the supervision of an engineering colleague and co-conspirator who allowed us to sneak up to the top of a tower before dawn, to get married during sunrise, high above a carpet of fog that hid the rest of the world, except a few soaring mountain tops.

"To an eternity of heaven, hell, or nothingness, I will always cherish our union atop the Golden Gate Bridge."

A tear left Carmina's eye, unable to defy gravity.

"I will never forget our wonderful years, our daily complicity in facing the world, jumping hurdles together, ducking under hazards together, dodging the often cruel blows of life. You were my best friend—my only friend. You were my lover—my only lover. These were the best days of my life—my lost life. Floating on clouds, I blindly assumed you were armored against the often-insane demands of engineering, against the slave-driving inhumanity of unrealistic timetables and all that fast-tracking nonsense. That our love was immune to erosion from the constant pounding of hours slipping out of our hands. That it was impervious and that it could never rot."

"It was dinged, but not lost, not rotten," confessed Carmina. "I had my own career, with its own inhumane demands, because our world has forgotten the importance of enjoying life, and I also fell into that nasty trap, Keene. You can't blame yourself for it. That's not why we broke up and you know it."

"I know that it isn't what shattered our dream. It had weakened our daily communion, but not diminished our passionate love, not shaken our unwavering trust, not broken our relationship. What did wasn't my blindness, but my stupidity. My absolute belief that making it relatively sane into adulthood is nothing short of a miracle given the total insanity of our cruel and dangerous world, and my uncompromising conviction that bringing new lives into this mess was akin to madness. You didn't understand me then, and I didn't understand you. My insistence in frustrating your wishes of motherhood is what pushed you away.

"To an eternity of heaven, hell, or nothingness, I will always curse my stupidity."

"You are too harsh on yourself, Keene. I didn't know your first steps along the path of life; you didn't know the last steps you would walk. The user's manual was never written."

"You hated me for it."

"I've hated you for it. For a long time. But not anymore, knowing what I now know."

"You wanted to divorce me."

"You never signed the divorce papers."

"I never signed the divorce papers. I was incapable of not loving you. Unable to erase from my life the only human being in this world that mattered to me."

"I never brought you to trial for it."

"You never brought me to trial for it."

"I never could. This was private pain."

"I'll never know why."

"Idiot. What do you think?"

"Maybe you didn't hate me so much."

"Maybe."

"I long caressed the hope that we'd be back together someday. Maybe if I only could have forgotten all the pain, all the madness, all the cruelty of this world and convinced myself that our love wasn't an aberration, that it wasn't a lost island of idealism in a dog-eat-dog world of lies and deception. If only I could have forgiven the whole masquerade that was intended to give a semblance of respectability to a twisted and dark reality. If only I could have. How things could have been different. Maybe. But I couldn't."

"Now I know why."

"Now you know why. It was hard to change."

"Until six months ago."

"Of course, until six months ago. Now, awed by the beauty of life, the flavor and complexity of a strawberry, the caress of mellifluous music, the inspiring majesty of a pastel sunset, the soothing breeze of an infinite ocean, the divine perfection of wine, I want to have a child with you."

Carmina broke down in tears.

"Stupid, Keene! Idiot. Why did you wait so long?"

"I know. Terrible timing. They're keeping a spot for me in the book of records under the entry 'world's biggest dumdum,' although I think the specific name of that category is a bit more blunt."

"Moron," she said, a burst of laugh through the tears. "Don't make me laugh when I'm crying."

"I apologize if this made you laugh when crying. I know you hate that, but you know what they say."

"Better to laugh than cry."

"There must be a reason for it."

"Keene, Keene, Keene. Why didn't you call me before dying?"

"As they say, there's always a reason for everything. I'm just too dumb to figure out what it might be in this particular case. I should have called you, instead of sending you stupid letters from the otherworld. I should have. But I couldn't. I couldn't find a way to say all that needed to be said in just a few seconds, afraid that you would have rapidly hung the phone that fast if I had called. I couldn't imagine how you could have understood, how you could have trusted the sincerity of my feelings. There's no upside to dying, and there comes a time when it's too late for regrets."

"You should have tried."

"Even then, one doesn't bring a child into this world out of pity for a dying love. Not in this cruel world. That isn't the right way."

"Fool. You should have tried."

"There's nothing I desired more before dying than making love to you one more time, passionately, tenderly, in pure communion, in total ecstasy. But it was an impossible desire. Impossible because of the dying card—that most inconvenient card trumping all hopes for clarity of feeling."

The text ended in the middle of a page, like a long pause. It resumed on the back.

"It would help greatly if you could make me laugh a bit here," wrote Keene, crushed under the weight of lost opportunities. Carmina understood what had happened. She also needed a moment, contributing some drops of her own to fill the bathtub.

She resumed reading as soon as she could see the text in focus through all the water.

"Now, I need to be pragmatic. Clearly, we will never conceive a child together. Time has run out, and freezing my genes in a test-tube is undignified of the renewed romance we deserved but never consumed. Doing so would violate the sacred souvenir of our love story, sad as the end may be."

"Thanks. That would have been weird."

"So what to do?"

"I can't believe you'd say this."

"The only way forward is for you to adopt a kid on our behalf."

"You're amazing."

"Pick a nice kid. Someone who had a hard life, a bit like me maybe. A cute kid who needs the amazing you. One that touches you. One on whom you could shower unbounded love each and everyday of his life. One whom you could teach to be less stupid than his adoptive father."

"I love you Keene. I love the new Keene even more than the old Keene. More than ever."

"Give the kid all the love you could have given me. In return, all I ask is permission to hold your wedding ring in my hands during my final journey, to bring it along with all my other important mementoes that you collected in the past few days."

That would be easy; it was in a crystal bowl on her nightstand. She had kept it there, as a reminder that Keene had to sign the divorce papers. The thought of returning her ring made her realize that both their separation and their union were now complete—as if she had just pulled it from her finger.

"To an eternity of heaven, hell, or nothingness, I will always cherish our union. I will never forget."

"I will never forget you either, Keene."

"Take care of the kid. Cherish every second with him. Don't waste that precious time. We never know when life will be stolen from us."

"I will. Promised."

Carmina closed the letter.

She would have pressed it on her heart, if she hadn't been all wet in the bathtub. She had to keep the ink from smearing and the paper dry to be able to read it over and over again, for the rest of her remaining life, as a reminder of the sanctity of her contract with Keene.

She also had to read it to Sig, as she had promised. It then occurred to her that this could be a problem.

She had already resolved to adopt him. However, if Sig saw the last part of the letter, he could imagine that she adopted him only to fulfill the last wishes of a dying man. That would be very wrong—a terrible way to establish a lasting parenting relationship. In spite of his objections to the contrary, Sig was just a kid. How does one make a kid understand such complexities? As much as she loved Sig, her parenting skills were null. She would start being a mother twelve years late in their relationship. Any doubts as to whether her love for him was genuine could throw him in such a turmoil of emotions. Back on the pyromaniac and suicidal path—maybe fatally this time.

Before she could rationalize all those emotions and figure out what to do, there was a loud knock on the door.

She had lost track of time. She had run out of time. She jumped out of the tub and grabbed a bathrobe.

"I had told you not to put coins in the same pocket as the magnetic room key," she shouted putting on the robe, leaving puddles under every footstep.

She swung the door open, ready to give him another hug, but her enthusiasm died abruptly, as Sig wasn't there.

"Are you Sigfried Hope's mother?" asked the older of the two police officers facing the door, holding in his hands Sig's wallet and the room key card she had given him.

General Hospital

Silence.

An oppressing silence surrounded Carmina like an abyss. Like a morbid chasm in time that numbed all her senses.

It's all that was there.

Silence.

The waiting room was full of silence. So crowded with it that the air was heavy and deprived of its oxygen. A silence pregnant with anxiety, sadness, distress, fear. A negative silence, begging for positive forces that could cancel all that negative energy.

Silence.

A silence sometimes violated by whispers. Whispered prayers to saints, gods, lucky charms, or whatever else hopes could cling to. Whispered kisses to loved ones that shared the choking silence. Whispered sobs.

Silence.

A slow silence. A silence where both the seconds and heartbeats are at a standstill, waiting for good or bad news.

Silence.

Just silence.

A silence broken every now and then by the opening and closing of the door that separated the waiting room from the rest of the hospital. The ripping buzz validating a scanned magnetic card, the low clank of the electronically disengaged dead bolt, the whooshing lament of dampers that had long ceased to dampen anything, the sweeping of the door seal on the floor, the final banging closure—each time capturing the attention of all in the room, desperate for news, crushed with disappointment when the threshold was only crossed by nurses going to the coffee machine.

Insignificant noises triggering false hopes, shooting Carmina's blood pressure to critical levels, only to be tortured anew by silence after the deception.

Justin had answered Carmina's distressed call, dropped everything, and rushed to the hospital. He could only imagine the noise—the screeching tires, the impact, the screaming bystanders, the ambulance. He could only imagine the commotion—the paramedics yelling orders, the frantic rushing of the stretcher, the dizzying weaving of a maze of wires and tubes. He could only imagine. All he experienced was silence.

A heavy silence, sharing Carmina's vigil, waiting for better news. Any news. Anything that could sustain hope. Longing for a recovery that was late to arrive.

An intern had showed up to dispense well-rehearsed banalities as part of his training to learn how to manage stressed relatives.

"He is in critical condition," just restated the obvious. It didn't help.

"We are doing everything we can to save him," didn't provide much encouragement either.

Although the intern had been pleased with his empathetic performance, to Carmina it sounded like the trite nonsense rehashed by unimaginative athletes "giving it their 110%" and "trying to capitalize on their chances."

How about some truths instead? Keene could have suggested some options. How about, "Our evening shift operating room staff screws up only 10% of the time for patients who arrive in such bad shape" or "We won't tell you anything meaningful because, even though our professional liability insurance is good, lawsuits are a pain in the ass for which there is no cure"?

No. Only silence.

Justin didn't know if he should hold her hand or put his arm around her, to console her. He didn't, afraid it would just stress her more, but he stood ready to lend arms, hands, or shoulders at any hint that it would be welcome. Besides, Sig was alive, so Carmina wasn't bereaved, just stressed like crazy.

One thing for sure, the example of adoption papers he had dug up would remain in his pockets, along with the other "contract" he had promised her—the one spelling out the terms of conditions by which she was allowed to read Keene's letters.

Contracts that might never be signed. As soon as Carmina had left his office, he had started working on the clauses.

"Whereas, Ms. Carmina Jewel (hereinafter referred to as 'the Client') has from her own will and initiative approached Mr. Justin Lawson (hereinafter referred to as 'the Provider') with regards to execution of legal services." He deliberately did not mention Keene's name, to keep her mind off her past love interest.

"Whereas, the Client expressed a desire to take responsibility for reading documents related to execution of a will and that the Provider has agreed to transfer this right and privilege in exchange of other considerations, spelled out herein," which he included to remind her of their verbal deal.

"Whereas, both the Client and Provider enter this agreement with clarity of vision and certainty of purpose," as it should be.

"Whereas, the Provider prepared this document in good faith for the Client's review and possible approval, with the best of intentions and sincere hope that it will be received with an open heart and mind," which departed a bit from contractual language, for good intent.

"Whereas, the current offer goes beyond a mere exchange of services and pertains to deliverables of a scope beyond what can be captured by any legal document," as a first hint that she should read between the lines.

"Therefore, the Provider requests an undetermined block of time in company of the Client, free of all constraints pertaining to professional services, for the sole purpose of providing an opportunity for each of the parties to learn more of the other party's background and interests, to discover possible shared priorities and aspirations, to deepen their knowledge and understanding of their differences, to appreciate and value their respective views of the world, and to allow their embryonic relationship to grow and possibly blossom someday into a special, committed and nurturing relationship"—which was as much legal language he could wrap around his feelings without actually saying "I love you."

To lighten the mood, he had closed the contract with added boilerplate sentences, such as "each party has the capacity to execute this agreement, and neither is in any way impaired from doing so by reason of immaturity of age, character or judgment, physical or mental limitation, or any impairment of reasoning or perception arising from the consumption of intoxicating substances or use of medication, however recognizing that reasonable consumption of good wines may have provided some inspiration, bits of courage, and due enjoyment of life in a way that does not in any way invalidate this contract."

However, he could not have foreseen what had happened. Exhilarated by the words that at last disclosed his true feelings, blinded by his dream of an embracing response, he had forgotten the standard Force Majeure clause that can kill contracts—the standard escape clause that states that "neither party shall be liable for any failure to perform obligations under this agreement where such non-performance arises from unanticipated catastrophic circumstances beyond reasonable control including, but not limited to, acts of God, war, riot or civil commotion, fire, flood, terrorism, drought or act of government." In this case, the Force Majeure was the suspension of hope by an imbecile that had struck an innocent kid.

Hence, instead of sharing his lovingly crafted contract as part of what should have been a delightful evening full of revelations, he was bound to silence.

Silence.

Just like Carmina, in her abyss. She was prisoner of an unwelcome silence that couldn't be broken—even if she screamed—because it wasn't a rational silence that noise alone could erase. It wasn't just silence.

It was silence and the nonsense of it all.

The burden of an unjust life. Sig was only a kid. He didn't deserve the harsh life bestowed on him by fate—or by cruel and cynical gods to whom human pain and suffering is merely an entertaining circus act. He didn't deserve the rocky road laid ahead of him. How could such a nice kid get such a raw deal and keep his sanity? No wonder he had tried to check out of life so often.

And it struck her there.

Did Sig try to commit suicide?

Was it her fault?

She tried to replay their last conversation, but her memory failed her. She couldn't cheat, like in a book, and go back to verify the exact words said, spot the disastrous confusion, rectify a possible misunderstanding. The mere thought that she might have accidentally pushed him over the brink terrified her.

Had she said an unfortunate word that had alone pushed Sig into a sudden depression? A guilty slip, fatally misconstrued against her best intentions, which became powerful enough to destroy a beautiful life. What could such a word have been? Could a single word really be so powerful, so tragic, so calamitous? It seemed impossible, but what if it wasn't? The mere possibility that such an inadvertent miscommunication could have turned her into a killer—committing an accidental homicide—was unbearable. An excruciatingly painful torture. She was guilty.

Or was it her insistence to be alone for a moment? Wasn't she allowed an intimate moment, like legitimate parents deserve from time to time? But she wasn't a parent. She was a guardian. She had a legal responsibility to watch over him, to ensure his safety, to protect him from others and from himself—and she failed. She miserably failed to protect him. Like a bad mother, she had pushed him away, rejected his pleas for an embrace, cut him off in her pursuit of a selfish love. She had emotionally strangled a son begging for acceptance. She was guilty.

Guilty of something she had said or done. Guilty of something she had not said or not done.

She was building around herself a prison from which she could never evade—a dungeon to die in. Guilty of her thoughts.

No.

Wait.

Sig wasn't dead.

Keene maybe, but not Sig.

She was not going to succumb to despair. She wasn't going to be crushed by dark thoughts.

He wasn't dead.

She decided things would not end like this.

He wouldn't die. He would fight with all his might to live.

He would.

He would fight to live, because he had started to enjoy a real life. He was strong; he had been stronger than she in those past days. He was brilliant; he had more sparkles than any twelve-year-old human alive. He was on a mission; not a word she could have said, not a thing she could have done could have broken his resolve to complete Keene's silly treasure hunt—for whatever purpose he could see into it, the whole enterprise was not just a challenge, but an emancipating revelation. Sig was at the forefront of a revolution and he would not purposely have done anything to miss seeing its outcome. She could tell, without any doubt—and a wall of the dungeon collapsed.

He would fight to live because she was ready to adopt him. Even though she hadn't said a word about it, he had felt that force. That powerful love had transcended the words and infused him with a certain will to live. An inescapable passion for life built by love. She could tell, without any doubt—and a second dungeon wall overturned.

He would fight to live because she had already lost Keene, and wasn't ready to part with anyone else that she loved. She wasn't about to relive another decade of crushing loneliness, with melancholy and sadness as her only friends. Her depleted batteries had been revived by a mysterious energy since Sig had tagged along, and that powerful force was strong enough to drive the future to its right destination, to choose one's destiny. She could tell, without any doubt—and the dungeon was now an open field surrounded by scattered stones.

Sig would fight to live. Because she said so. The SUMONOM said so.

This wasn't hope anymore. It was a certainty. She was going to fight with him. Together, they'd survive. They had a life to live and no time to waste.

Keene had inspired a young mind, reignited his will to live, given him the strength to free himself from the throes of death. He had freed him—and her—from lonely lives of despair. Boring lives. Turbid lives.

They had been changed completely. Like new buds blooming.

They had already beaten death. They had won.

The only thing ahead was an amazing brightness. Not hope, but a certainty. That's all that could be. A brilliant future ahead for Sig and her.

And plans. Tons of them. Plans to build a paradise on earth, to become beach bums on a sandy beach, to throw snowballs from the top of a mountain, to feast in the middle of a strawberry field, to dance like fools at a wedding, to snorkel around coral-covered shipwrecks, to roast marshmallows over a fire pit, to blow soap bubbles using a real tuba, to hide behind a tropical waterfall, to sleep outdoor on a starry night, to enjoy a book in bed wrapped in

flannel pajamas, to sail into the sunset on a northern lake, to carve
eternal messages on the bark of a white birch, to sing along with
Beatles tunes to the echo of bathroom tiles, to visit blind crickets
in deep caves, to watch fireworks with a melting ice cream cone,
to run across a mile-long lavender field, to count the seconds
between lightning and thunder, to skate halfway around the world
on an endless frozen river, to build a birdhouse with almost
straight nails, and—in due time—to sample all of the earth's wines
in the ultimate tasting jamboree in memory of Keene.

And to find love in the eyes of a soul mate.

That's it.

The future was waiting and there was no time to waste, no
one to stop them.

She wanted to talk to a doctor.

No. She didn't want to. She needed to.

It wasn't an impulse. It was a conviction.

It was an order.

Enough of the heavy silence.

She needed to appraise every second of Sig's combat, to see
his struggle, his punches, his uppercut to the jaw of death. She
was not going to wait passively when the greatest battle of Sig's
life—of her life—was going on in another room.

She needed him.

Sig needed her.

He was just a kid.

He couldn't be left alone to face death—to beat death—without his coach.

He needed to hear her loving voice and encouragements to
give him strength in his struggle.

He needed to hear that she was going to adopt him. Right
now. That she needed him. That she loved him—even more than
he loved her. She needed to seal that sacred bond to right all the
wrongs and pump his heart with the will to live—a fleeting will for
all his life, but so urgently needed at this very moment.

"We're adopting Sig. We are," she told Justin—shattering the
silence.

We? Justin couldn't believe she had said that word. He
prayed she meant "we" as "loving couple," not as client and lawyer
filling paperwork. He had to look her in the eye, to try to decipher
her true sentiments, but before he could figure out how to do that,

she grabbed him by the lapel and locked her embracing eyes into his.

"We're adopting Sig," she repeated half a dozen times, shaking him to extract his approval.

"Yes, yes, yes," he replied, hoping to calm her down. He was afraid she was losing it. It was bad enough that he struggled to figure out how to cope with romantic love; he had no clue how to deal with a loved one who was freaking out.

Carmina jumped to the nurse's counter. Justin, stunned by her impulse, met her there, by reflex.

"I want to see Sig. Now!"

"Ma'am, please remain seated. We will call you as soon as we know—"

"No, I need to see him now."

Justin tried to hold her arm for comfort, but she shook him off.

"Ma'am—"

"Now!"

"He is in operating room, ma'am. There are no observation bay windows to the operating rooms—"

"I don't want to watch him like a fish in an aquarium. I want to hold his hand through it all."

"Family members aren't allowed—"

"I don't want your stupid rules. He needs me there to survive. He needs the love, the energy. He's just a kid."

The nurse wasn't about to unlock the door that accessed the treatment rooms.

"I don't have the authority—"

"Then get someone who has authority. Don't they teach in med school that love is the best medication? That a kid needs to hold his mother's hand to find the strength to fight to survive? Who's the arrogant genius that runs this place?"

The nurse was trained to handle nutcases from behind her glass window. A discrete alarm to security was also at her fingertip under her counter. Yet, she didn't think Carmina dangerous. She, too, was a mother.

"Please wait. I'm going to ask the doctors," she said.

She left. Just for show, as she went to chat with a colleague, out of view, to escape the abuse and give Carmina a chance to cool off.

Silence.

For a long time.

Silence.

Carmina could hear Keene whisper to her: "She just left to go to the bathroom. She's not about to open the door to a hysterical woman. For all she knows, you could have been the one who ran over Sig with your car."

At that moment, a couple of fat doctors on their way to the coffee machine opened the locked door.

She rushed in, barely squeezing through between the two men in light green-blue garments. Stunned, realizing that the triage nurse wasn't at her post, the doctors understood something was askew and ran after her. Justin looked both ways, more by a shyness reflex, as if it was at all possible to be unnoticed after all that ruckus, and slipped through before the door closed, trying to keep pace far behind.

Driven by a desperate rush of adrenaline, oblivious to the absurdity of the situation, Carmina zoomed through the corridors in panic, the out-of-shape doctors puffing in pursuit like incompetent Keystone Kops re-enacting a Mack Sennett wild chase. Bouncing from one small window to the other, randomly hitting doors with a few bangs, she frantically searched for her son-to-be.

She had expected a long corridor flanked by rooms on both sides, as is typical in institutional buildings, but instead found herself caught in a maze of illogical divisions and intersections, like a starved albino mouse rushing around, desperate to find the cheese. She should have known. Messed-up floor plans in hospitals weren't the work of architects on drugs; she remembered Keene's story of how, to the delight of contractors ready to execute the extra work at a premium, doctors walking in a hospital for the first time after construction completion always drafted a long list of changes necessary to accommodate their professional practice—room sizes to be altered, walls to be torn down, access doors added or widened, as well as some purely ego-driven remodeling adjustments, all attesting of their inability to read architectural plans. That was now the labyrinth in which Sig was imprisoned.

She was bouncing from doors to windows to open rooms, pushing curtains, banging her fist on glass panes, staying ahead of being caught, calling "Sig," shouting, yelling, telling him to hold on to dear life, that she was here for him, that she was coming to him, that she was going to find him. She knew she'd find him. No hospital is too big; no stupid building can keep a son from his mother's love.

The near-hysteric fit of her motherly instincts gone amok caused quite a stir, alarming other staff members to join the Kops in trying to slow her down. The two pursuers became three, then four, and five—some much fitter that the two butterballs that had failed to catch her.

Inevitably, she ended up surrounded, like a trapped beast, and helplessly collapsed on the floor in broken spirits, weeping.

"Sig. Sig," she whispered in sobs.

Two male nurses each grabbed an arm and pulled her up.

Like an awaken lioness, she struggled to free herself from the their grasp, possessed by an urge of love, burned by the inextinguishable fire of love, craving to hold Sig in her arm.

Then she saw him in the corridor. Out of the operating room, at last. She had found him—or he had found her. Her eyes needed to hear his voice. They were begging—begging for any words to break the oppressing silence that had returned. She couldn't wait any longer. She had to ask.

She shook off the Kops and threw herself into his arms, her face crushed into his chest, her voice trembling.

"Is he going to make it? Please tell me. Please, doctor, tell me, now. Now!"

In refusing to break his silence, he answered her.

Her fears had taken root and sucked all hope out of her.

She fainted.

The worse had happened.

Pointless Ranch

There was no point in continuing.

One may fight, and fight, and fight, but in the end it will come to naught, just the same. There are battles one is destined to lose, being nothing more than a peon—a mere peon—tossed to hell to be slaughtered. There are lives out of control—like all lives for that matter. So Carmina thought.

She felt like one more faceless passenger caught in an airplane, sitting for hours at the gate or on the runway, going nowhere, denied a satisfactory explanation. As if blaming mechanical problems, the bad weather, the lack of crew, or other causes presumably beyond control, would make one say: "of course, it's all so logical" with a smile, instead of being disgruntled for having missed a flight, a connection, an important event, a friend, a life. Evading accountability, confusing excuses for execution.

Like a greedy airline, life messes one's plans, disrespects schedules, and refuses to compensate for it. It doles setbacks, troubles, futility, and refers you to the service counter for complaints—where the line is so long that shoes take root and where a hapless customer representative recites the standard company policy blurb that explains why they are not responsible for any of the inconveniences because flying, after all, is a game of chance. A plane ticket, like a glorified lottery ticket, is at best a probability—not a promise—that one will be brought to destination, on time or not. There is no escaping the annoying turbulence, the rude flight attendants who throw peanut bags like feeding time at the zoo, the incoherent delays for all kinds of reasons, the crowded uncomfortable seats, the insulting extra fees and surcharges—for food, for basic luggage, for fuel, and for using the lavatory. There is no escaping cancelled flights—the ultimate insult.

Cancellations. The abortion of a trip that barely got started. Promises that failed to materialize.

Like a bumped passenger on an overbooked flight, Carmina felt tricked.

A ticket had been cancelled. There was no possible refund to compensate for the missed opportunity. The ultimate sanctity of the trip had been defiled. It was a terrorist attack on life—no less.

In spite of all the gadgets and devices deployed to give the illusion of security, imbeciles had taken the plane down. They had crashed Sig.

The beautiful vessel that had departed towards a wide-open horizon, that had just deployed sails to cruise on a fascinating journey, that had finally seemed to escape turbulence to find a smooth peacefulness, had been sunk. A senseless act, without rime or reason, without a purpose, without justice—and all the unfitting clichés that miserably fail to capture the simple truth.

Sig was dead.

There was no other word, no other reality.

She had lost a son, no less.

She had lost a part of herself.

The silence had never left.

It had stuck to her, like static.

The cops called it an accident. Death by accident. Hit by the proverbial bus. A delivery truck to be exact.

Cops didn't know Sig. It wouldn't have crossed their mind that it could have been suicide.

The shaken truck driver told them that Sig crossed the street without looking. A simple mistake. The almost "hit and run" he committed, speeding up after impact, but slamming the brakes 500 feet away was also just a simple mistake. Was he afraid that a witness would be found, that his "TRUCK YOU" vanity license plate was too easy to remember? The police called it shock. A slight misjudgment in an instant of sheer panic, they assumed. It would remain an "almost hit and run."

Would it remain an accident?

The driver had sworn that Sig emerged from a side street and that the imposing bank building on the corner hid all incoming motorized or pedestrian traffic. He had claimed that he was caught by surprise when the kid ran into the street without looking on both sides before crossing—as foolish kids are prone to do. He had insisted that, had an adult done the same, jumping under the wheel of a truck so suddenly could only have been a deliberate and desperate act.

But why would Sig commit suicide now? It made no sense. Things were going so well. The pyromaniac tendencies seemed dormant—maybe cured. The suicidal tendencies too—he had a golden opportunity at *Col-de-l'Enfer*, but had chosen life. Besides, he was "on a mission," enjoying every minute of the treasure hunt.

Yet, those final last words. Was it "I'll be back in no time" or "I'll never come back"? Her memory failed her like a miscreant.

The guilt. Had she been so blinded by what she wished Sig to be that she missed flagrant distress signals?

The silence.

Mostly the guilt.

And the burden of the silence.

Always.

There was no point to it all.

So she stayed home. Curtains drawn. Not to be disturbed. Never to be disturbed.

Yet, someone knocked at the door.

Had she known, she would not have looked through the peephole. It was Dick and Dick. The two clowns.

She would not open.

"Come on, I've seen the shadow in the peephole."

Maybe he bluffed.

"Carmina, I know you are there."

Impossible.

"We are here to offer you our most sincere condolences."

Clearly, they felt it was her loss, not theirs. In the grand spreadsheet that drove decisions at the Ranch, Sig must have been expendable.

"Just send a card," she shouted through the door. A moment of weakness. Now they knew for sure she was there.

"Carmina. You're a friend. We won't send you an impersonal card."

A friend. Sure. What's a friend anyhow? Keene was so right.

"Go away."

"Just give us a minute. We drove long hours to come here. Everybody's worried about you at the Ranch."

The pointless Ranch.

"We loved Sig too, Carmina. It's our loss too."

She didn't believe them. In another moment of weakness, she opened the door ajar—just enough to see their faces, not distorted by a lying lens, looking for evidence of sorrow.

The psycholo-chick was also there. She must have been beyond the range of the peephole.

Without a word, she let them slip into her apartment—not due to a goaltending error, but because they seemed to be grieving. She had given their sad faces the benefit of the doubt. They each hugged her—disingenuously, it seemed. Hugging the Dicks felt like hugging punching bags—leathery, cold, stiff, fake.

"I quit," she said, barely leaving them time to rest on their seats. They jumped back up.

"You are under a lot of stress right now," said the psycholo-chick. "Don't make hasty decisions. Take some time to rest and recover. You don't have to make any decision right now."

"Your place with us is secure," added Dick. "You're part of the family. Always will be."

Bogus affection.

"This is all about the money, isn't it?"

The two clowns looked at each other, shocked.

"Absolutely not. This is about you, and our caring thoughts for you."

"Good then. It's all perfect. I'll be in your thoughts, and for my own good, you'll never see me again."

The two clowns, without looking at each other this time, but still in unison, looked more shocked.

"Carmina, we will respect your decision, one way or the other. We share your grief, you know. Sig was one beautiful member of the Ranch's family. We know you had a special, privileged relationship with the kid, but we loved him too. He will be most sincerely missed."

Their sympathy seemed so genuine for a moment that it caught her off-guard. She felt a bit ashamed of her cruel judgment.

"It's certain that the money would help the Ranch—"

The smidgen of shame vanished.

"You are just two greedy bastards. It takes guts—"

"Don't misunderstand us—"

"Oh, I understand very well."

"Don't judge our intentions. You don't know us—"

"I don't? You think people don't understand what you're all about? You're so fake, even the kids hate you. You're just a PODWO to them."

"Ah, come on, Carmina, that's just kid's stuff, just like she's psycho-chick, and you're SOMUNOM."

They knew!

"Do you really think you're a Sweet Old Maid in Urgent Need of a Man?" said the other Dick, to make a point—echoing his boss.

SOMUNOM. That's what it meant. How come everybody knew, but her?

"Kids will be kids. But overall, they have a really good rapport with us. They love the staff. All the staff. Because we care, Carmina. We care for them."

Sweet old maid?

In need of a man?

Urgently?

"Deep down, the kids love us, respect us all. You too, Carmina. They would really miss you if you were to quit."

"They call you a pair of dicks without one, and you find that impressively respectful. Great rapport indeed."

"It's just typical kid's defense mechanisms, trying to escape the authority structure. It doesn't really mean anything."

That ignited her. That psycho-babble nonsense was insulting.

"OK. Thanks for your sincere wishes," she said, ushering them to the door, pushing. "I quit just the same. You won't hit the jackpot. Keene's money will burn with him."

"But, but—"

"Goodbye. It was nice working with you," she said slamming the door.

SONUMOM. She couldn't believe it. Why would the kids call her that? It was hurtful.

Where did that come from? Weren't kids supposed to be instinctively insightful? Is it really how they saw her? How could they condemn her to such an afflicting nickname? Was it what she really was?

Of course, her life after Keene hadn't been particularly joyful, and in fairness, she did behave a bit like a loner—or at least like an oddball adult who preferred sitting at the kids' table during lunch.

Maybe she radiated a terrible sadness, like a call of distress so powerful that even kids couldn't help notice.

But an old maid? She wasn't an old maid. At least, not literally. She had been married. To that crazy Keene, no less. It had to be just silly kids stuff. Kids exaggerate. They magnify small adult imperfections to protect themselves from their own insecurities. Psycholo-chick was at least correct in that regard. Yet, any exaggeration needs a kernel of truth to be funny. For sure, that truth was an unmistakable sadness, maybe deeply buried subconsciously, but not deep enough to fool others—not even kids.

Renewed knocking broke the silence.

They're insisting?

"I said goodbye," she screamed as she yanked the door open.

Justin stood there stunned.

"To me or to the grumpy folks I crossed in the stairs?"

"Did you know I'm a SOMUNOM?"

"Uh, what's that?"

"I'll let you guess. Come in."

She still couldn't believe that everybody at the Ranch knew what it meant, but never told her. Some colleagues. One should never misplace workplace colleagues for friends. Or never believe there is such a thing as friends, Keene would have warned. Her resolve to quit her job at the Ranch was unfaltering. She was also quitting the treasure hunt. Justin's timing was good. She would tell him at once.

"Can I hug you?"

"Why?" asked Carmina.

"To offer you my most deeply felt sympathy, I guess," replied Justin, disappointed that she wouldn't have just embraced him unconditionally.

She relented.

He held her with all the warmth he could muster, feeling her cheek against his, the lovely smell of her hair, the comfortable embrace.

She was surprised at Justin's warm, tender, long-lasting hug that was honestly companionate. She didn't think lawyers could be so... human—as opposed to caring professionally for their clients.

"I miss Sig too, you know. I didn't get to know him for long, but he was a really nice kid."

She burst into tears, collapsing in his arms. Justin wished she stayed there forever, convalescing in his embrace, waiting for the return of her will to enjoy life, maybe together with him. She would recover. Had to. Eventually. He vaguely remembered a theory that described grief as a five-stage process—crying and depression just being one step of that process—so it was inescapable that she would recover. In time.

She eventually pulled away, trying to regain her composure, drying her tears on her sleeve.

"I'm sorry."

"Please don't be."

And it was back to silence, as neither of them knew words that could take the pain away.

After long minutes of silence, Justin, as if prompted by a cue that all missed, out of a sense of duty, pulled an envelope from his jacket.

"Oh no. No, no. I'm not continuing to partake in Keene's folly. That's a very bad timing, Justin. I'll have to ask you to leave if you open that envelope."

"It's not what you think, Carmina."

He froze under her questioning look. All the possible explanations and justifications that crossed his mind sounded terribly weird, so he couldn't expand beyond that last sentence. Thankfully, it wasn't his job to explain.

He held the envelope at arm's length, staring at her beautiful eyes, hoping she wouldn't shout at him. The envelope dangled at the tip of his fingers, like a ripe bunch of grapes in the wind, until curiosity got the best of her.

"It's not what you think," he repeated as she grabbed it.

She slowly opened the envelope, while fixing Justin's irises.

"A money order? Over three million dollars?"

"Yes. $3,108,330.13 to be exact. That also includes your travel expenses for the past two weeks."

She was puzzled.

"My fees have already been covered by Mr. Mason. This the total net payment to you."

Mr. Mason? She recalled that Justin had called him Keene before. Was this formality to underscore that he was purely conducting a business transaction on behalf of a client? Or was it because the insane amount on the check called for some reverence?

"What's that for?"

"For what you called the treasure hunt."

"No, no, no. Keene can't buy me. I said I'm not continuing, and I'm not. I stop. Now."

"And that's OK. Mr. Mason had instructed me to give you that envelope if you bailed out of this crazy endeavor, no matter when that would be."

Justin had expected a reaction—maybe an explosion of outrage, maybe some shrill insults, or at least some chastising—but she just stood there, with a blank stare. If she was incensed, he couldn't tell. Unsure what to do, he searched for other words to reiterate the message more clearly.

"Given that you had quit—"

"Quit?"

"Well, decided to—"

"Whether I did or not, either way, I don't recall telling you anything about that before you pulled the envelope."

"I figured you would," he said, hesitating. "Or maybe that you should."

He didn't have the courage to add, "Even if the thought that I might never see you again crushed me."

Although there was no a priori reason to distrust Justin, she wondered if these were really Keene's wishes. It seemed magnanimous to the extreme.

Justin read her doubts, and wondered if his hidden affection had been unmasked—at last—or if she just thought he was lying to her because burning millions of dollars in a bonfire wasn't a pragmatic lawyer-thing to do.

"He left a little note too on the back of the envelope," said Justin, flipping it to show the undeniable evidence of his allegiances to the wishes of his client.

Carmina read it aloud, as if to confide in Sig.

"I hope you had a good time meeting me anew. I hope our new promenade patched up a bit our first bumpy ride together. If you didn't make it too far down the list, I hope you'll at least consider reading letter number seven."

"The seventh letter is the one I gave you during our last session," clarified Justin.

She knew number seven. She'd never forget the letter she read in her bath, before Sig died. The one she had promised to read to him when he'd be back from the errand. The letter that Sig would never see, because she sent him to his death—guilty. Who's the idiot who invented the "Lucky seven" nonsense?

"You made it pretty far, you know. There were only eight 'treasure hunt' envelopes."

She broke into tears again, pressed against Justin's already soaked shoulder. He was pleased to oblige, unsure if the tears were for Sig, or Keene—or both. Or him? Had she been touched by his friendship—was it still just a friendship to her? He would have traded his shelves of law books for one user's manual with some tips to understand women—like a bible of established jurisprudence for matters of the heart, to untangle all those knots of ambiguity.

She hugged Justin, gave him back the envelope, turned him on his heels, and gently pushed him through the doorframe.

He turned around.

"I must—"

She put a finger on his lips to dam the upcoming flood of objections—legal or otherwise.

"I need to think."

"But—"

"I need to sleep."

She rose on her toes to kiss him on the cheek.

That was infinitely more effective that the finger on the lips.

As Justin left speechless, she sighed. Keene claimed he had engineered his death, but the scope of work of that project had significantly expanded, far beyond its original budget. This "engineering nouveau"—like its "art nouveau" counterpart—rejected straight lines.

However, what mattered now was that she could stop. Quit. End it all here.

It was in her power to write "The End," putting the final dot on a bad story right here.

∞ - *Eight*

"I'm doing it for Sig," answered Carmina.

That excuse was good enough for Justin. All that mattered was that she was here. He had been afraid that she'd never come back. For lack of a better strategy, he had been racking his brain in search of an excuse to visit her, to deliver an altered version of his love letter clumsily disguised as a contract—improved to account for the sensitive circumstances. Since he hadn't found any satisfactory excuse, her presence was a blessing.

At first, he thought her surprise visit was only to pick up the envelope she had refused the day before when despair clouded her better judgment—three million dollars could do a lot of good, and she was the only heir entitled to decide how this bonanza could be spent to support a deserving charity. But she didn't want the check.

"And Keene," she added. "I'm also doing it for Keene."

"Of course."

She didn't have to explain anything. He understood.

"And you," she clarified.

"Me?"

"Yes."

"Why—"

"Don't ask."

User's manual. Badly needed.

Justin didn't dare pressure her to expand on the two words that had just thrown fuel on the embers. It was premature to panic: he would see her again at the funeral. There would be time. For now, this was a business meeting.

She had decided that Sig was to be cremated together with Keene, in four days. She had made all the arrangements, confident that nobody at the Ranch would dare challenge her authority as guardian of the defunct.

Unknown to her, the adoption contract drafted by Justin had already been incinerated—as a fitting ceremonial to a young pyromaniac. That would remain his secret. Telling Carmina that he had a draft adoption contract ready the night Sig died would have just killed her. Her surviving four days until the dual funeral would be painful enough already.

Four more days were all she could bear.

Since there was only one more letter, and thus only one more trinket to collect to fulfill Keene's final wishes, four days was plenty. It was pointless to delay the ceremony further. The time to end this sad story had come, with Sig and Keene departing together for the unknown.

Except that Sig wouldn't be embalmed in Saint-Émilion. Just a regular funeral for a regular kid.

Justin and Carmina might be the only ones at the service, but she would be there for Sig, her whole heart and soul accompanying him throughout the ceremony—and forever after. Justin and her; two lone pallbearers by his side for his last journey.

A regular funeral that would also risk being Justin's last chance to be with Carmina, alone. Of course, someday, when his racked brain would at last discover the credible excuse that wouldn't make him look pathetic, he would invite himself to her place, but until then, the funeral would be his last guaranteed opportunity for a few hours alone with Carmina. Unless she invited Sig's friends from the Ranch, in spite of the SOMUNOM incident, in which case he'd have to think of a strategy to pry her away from the crowd, although he hadn't figured out yet what he would do after that. His desire was to hand her the "love-letter contract" that he had promised her, aware that it would have to be cast in a different light given the changed context, but he knew that this would be far from a sensible thing to do at a funeral. Reading a love declaration during a funeral might be no more enjoyable than watching a drunk clown on a high wire set himself on fire and jump to his death.

"You don't have to go through another one of those, you know," he nonetheless cautioned while digging through his folders for the eighth letter.

"I know."

"Keene will understand the circumstances," he added, as if he could object from his coffin.

"Are you going to read this letter or not? You have a contract to fulfill."

"Ha! Here it is."

He put it on his desk, with a letter opener, next to one of the dried rose bouquets.

"You read it," he said, unconditionally. "In hindsight, that's the way it should have been from the very beginning."

Justin, expecting she would read silently, was touched that she read it aloud, as if Sig was sitting in the oversized chair, eyes wide open, awaiting his mission instructions.

"Day -31.

"I am way past my expiration date. If I were a loaf of bread, one month beyond the date printed on the bag, I'd be tattooed green. A quart of milk, I'd be worse than sour. A peach, I'd be a stinky blob of shrunken mold invaded by worms. A cheese, I'd reek. A banana, I'd have grown legs and be walking away from the fruit bowl, followed by clouds of flies.

"Instead, I'm sipping champagne, celebrating one drop at the time each additional heartbeat extending my brief stay on earth.

"But I'm not fooling myself. My train has reached the last station. Incidentally, this is also where I get off the numerology wagon—I have not just run out of time, I have run out of numbers. It the terminus, but it doesn't matter because it's the journey that was the destination.

"So I've reached number eight. Not very far considering it took six months, but it obviously wasn't a race. Appropriately, numerology tells me that eight is a red flag, indicating that incredibly hard work will be required to repay my karmic debt. The Karma Credit Bureau—which tallies my growing karmic debt as the sum of all the negativity I have created—informs me that they are about to send their repo man; my karma history, plagued by bad actions and failed relationships, has rendered me insolvent, bankrupt, unable to ever repay my debt to enjoy life fully in this or future lives. I am ruined."

Sig's flippant editorial comments were badly missed. Justin and Carmina expected to hear an impromptu remark, an oddball objection, a deliberate provocation, a spontaneous insult—but none came. The anomalous silence was heavy.

"So much for the positive aspects of eight, like the fact that there are eight Muslim paradises, and eight lucky petals on a Buddhist lotus flower; so much for the fact that eight is an auspicious number, underscoring sound judgment, success, wealth, business acumen, ambition, political skills, commanding decisiveness, executive perks, and frequent flyer miles.

"It doesn't change a thing. The snowball has rolled down the hill to become a crushing avalanche that has killed the workaholic. The stress, the impatience, the repressed pleasures, the materialistic priorities, the failure to live, have killed the boring engineer. I am no more.

"All in all, that's not a big loss. Who cares about engineers in the end? Nobody—conveniently forgetting where the comfort taken for granted comes from. Engineers are just a commodity, a convenient fact of life, a human oddity. Just like the formally provable mathematic oddity that the square of any odd number, minus one, always equals a multiple of eight ($3 \times 3 - 1 = 8$; likewise, $5 \times 5 - 1 = 24 = 3 \times 8$, and $7 \times 7 - 1 = 49 - 1 = 8 \times 6$; etc.), or about the fact that there are eight bits to a byte. Really. Who cares? It's not a big deal.

"The real significant thing for me about eight is that lying on its side, the numeral symbol 8 becomes ∞, which mathematically commonly represents infinity. Hence, as I am about to lie on my side and find some path to an infinity I don't understand, it is most appropriate to end here my travels into the world of numerology in which I pretended to seek a humble quest for significance. I can't tell if it has enlightened me or not in the end, but it has rekindled a fire that urgently needed care and provided excellent wine-filled readings and reflections that led to the firm conclusion that there is more to enjoy in life and in the beauty of wine than in any promised reward after death. It is all the simple things in this world that make up the paradise promised by all and missed by so many—a heresy that has been forever crushed by more marketable spiritual ideas on which empires can be built.

"So as I'm about to lose this paradise, for what it's worth, I've taken stock of my life to reach peaceful closure.

"In the end, I am grateful for only two things in life.

"First, to have had the chance to deeply love a woman. It would have been better if she had loved me too, but a half broken heart is not as bad as a fully broken one."

Carmina read those words with a different perspective. She knew that this letter had been written before her bathtub conversation with Keene just before Sig died—a communion between reunited lovers that was real. It could only be real. Not surreal. Real. There was no arguing about it. Nobody could prove otherwise. Besides, what's reality if not what one tangibly perceives?

"Second, the unique pleasure of having had six month to live before I died. Or, maybe I should say six months to live after I died, because, as far as I can tell, that emancipating death blessed me with a second life. A good one. It would have been bliss if I could have shared it with the love of my life, but these are dreams better left untouched. All in all, it was the better of my two lives.

"It all ended with a dream.

"The dream that I lived, and it was good. The dream that I was blessed with a few seconds of paradise, and it was good. The dream that while no one will miss me, I will miss everyone. The dream that I resurrected before dying. And it was all good.

"And those dreams healed me. I am healed!

"Healed, as far as healing is reprogramming our thoughts. My mind's my hospital."

Carmina could just hear Sig reply, "Your wacko friend thinks he's healed. Seriously! He needs to talk to the psycholo-chick big time."

Justin could just hear Sig reply, "That wine thing really works in strange ways—too bad it tastes like liquid rubber." Without saying a word, he felt their shared vibrations, like harmonics on the same guitar string.

Carmina didn't quite know if her tears were for Sig, Keene, or both—or for herself—but she continued to read, discreetly wiping them out with a sleeve that was progressively becoming damper.

"Yet, the end is here. The senseless time to leave. I am about to dive into the unknown.

"Like a lost soul standing alone on the Great Wall of China, where all is foggy and elusive, trying to believe—maybe to make it easier—that life and death are illusions, but convinced otherwise by the alarm of pain and pleasures that insist that the arbitrary is real."

"What was the point of it all?

"Still is a mystery—points are, after all, mathematical abstractions.

"The original point—as an analog signal of finite duration or digitally discretized to arbitrary units of time that may itself not exist. A point that itself may just be an energy, or something that can only be subjectively defined by what the senses can perceive, and is otherwise intangible. The birth point of an idea, a concept. The last resort going into the past—where one can find further roots. A small intangible infinitely small ignition point to all that followed. A bang, no more, no less. As big as it might have been, it remained a point, spawning more points.

"Infinitely more points, of which I was but one. What was the point of it all?

"Being. Being one.

"A point. About to be erased."

In spite of Carmina's correcting errors and grammatical inconsistencies, she felt that Keene's flow of thoughts had become disjointed, as if he was fighting death with all his remaining strength, but definitively losing the battle. This ultimate letter felt as if it had been written over days, lacking a final proofreading. Carmina couldn't fill in the blanks in Keene's thoughts, the incongruences, the incoherence of his discourse, flipping from one idea to the next, but she could still provide dignity to his sentences.

"If my life followed the tired but always effective formula of sappy fiction, it couldn't end here.

"We would just have reached the fall. The point where the protagonist stands to lose everything. The big crisis near the end of the story.

"I wished.

"My life could have started like a movie, recounting a horrible hardship intended to make me (the protagonist) likeable—but it has not. Something really sad, to make me sympathetic—but I'm not.

"Then, I would have faced a clear conflict, something major that needed resolution for my life to move forward—but it will not.

"I would have then been confronted to challenges, problems, foes, brutal confrontations, all more difficult than the previous one—but I've been a boring engineer, pushing paper day in, day out.

"Then, the crescendo of challenges would have built-up to the crisis—the 'now' moment needed to resolve the fundamental conflict.

"Well, this is now. This is the crisis.

"This is the point when 15 minutes is left before the end of the movie—ten minutes before the closing credits.

"Set your DVD-player's clock to display 'time-remaining' instead of 'time-elapsed,' and you'll see it flash 15:00. The hero stands to lose everything (the crisis), just before the uplifting finale that saves the day. That's what Hollywood needs to do to make the audience go down the roller coaster of sorrow before the final uplifting high.

"Now, like a bad magician, I've revealed the most important trick of the trade. It would appear that I've destroyed the magic, reducing the rabbit-out-of-a-hat into its basic ingredients: a mere formula. The magic is gone. The rabbit is just a rodent with long ears, and it is hatless.

"But it doesn't matter because it's a fireproof formula. Time proven. Works all the time. Even full knowledge of the magic recipe cannot kill the ultimate enjoyment of an uplifting finale. Our DNA needs it. It's the result of evolution. It's a hope interwoven into our soul to ensure our survival.

"Isn't it an amazing formula? I just wish I could have used it for my life's novel.

"Because, without a doubt, we're at the crisis, now.

"Right now.

"The bummer is that I die. Bloody hell!

"I'm the protagonist, and I lose everything.

"My dumb life is not following the proven formula. The end is here and it is not uplifting.

"I just die. Period.

"There is no high, no uplifting finale, no saving of the day. Just the boring fact that I die. This is where reality takes over fiction.

"Turn off the lights..."

Keene's letter ended there, as abrupt and unpredictable as a last breath.

Carmina folded the paper. The last part of his letter had been surprisingly coherent—and characteristically cynical. He had not lost his marbles in his last few breaths, as she had feared. His mind had remained lucid up to the not-so-grand finale.

"They found him alone, a bottle of champagne in hand, the letter in the printer bin, the room littered with empty wine bottles," said Justin.

The soul mate she had discovered in the past few days was now dead, just like the stranger who was once her husband. Had she found him earlier—had she found her own self earlier—maybe their former union wouldn't have been doomed. Maybe they would have had a chance to truly love each other.

Maybe.

Surely.

If they had not been ignorant of their respective and common humanity, their journey would not have been interrupted by accident, be it an accidental blindness, or an accidental misunderstanding.

The journey!

"The 'treasure hunt' instructions?"

"They must have been written before that," he inferred, handing her the letter. "Do you want me to join you on that last one?" he offered, overcoming his fear of rejection, knowing with an unwavering conviction that he wanted to participate in her journey—a proposition for which he had gathered all of his courage.

"No. Sig will be with me. All the time. That's how it should be. Like for the others. Just the two of us."

He had been rejected. His courage sunk like a rock. He wanted to scream his love for her, but ran out of ideas to make the obvious obvious. He kept a straight face, deeply hurt without showing it. A tear collected in his left eye—the one closest to his heart—but he erased it discreetly, rubbing his eyes as if he was just tired.

"I need to do this last one with Sig, in spirit. I owe it to him."

"Of course," he said, thinking he was a coward, afraid of revealing his true emotions, afraid of rejection, afraid to scare her by revealing his true feelings.

"But promise me you'll come back to tell me all about it."

The Temple

The last visit. A visit without Sig. It felt empty. Like a car out of gas, cruising downhill on neutral, aware that there is no gas station at the bottom.

For what?

The HPS temple? She couldn't believe it. She checked the address. Twice. Thrice. A temple?

It had to be a transcription error. Or the slip of a mind on its last flicker. If Keene had found religion in his last days, it was in wine, not in a brick-and-mortar temple. Keene was an atheist; a hardened heretic; an infidel—the kind suicidal bombers would die for.

The door opened itself. She had been noticed. An old maid motionless on the porch, stuck like a leafless tree on a windless December day, frozen and lifeless.

"You must be Mrs. Mason."

"Jewell."

"Oops. Sorry for the misunderstanding. As you may guess, I was expecting someone else—"

"Carmina Jewell."

"Carmina! It is you then. Pleased to meet you. Keene has told me so much about you."

Obviously not everything.

The man talked a lot. She didn't listen a lot.

Hundreds of words flew by, like bullets around the hero in a bad spy movie, never hitting their intended target, and before she knew it, she was standing in the middle of a temple.

Sort of.

No cross bearing a bloody crucified man. No statue of an obese meditating man. No carpets on which to prostrate.

Just a giant screen hung from the ceiling, facing randomly arranged couches, sofa, recliners—and a popcorn machine. Large stainless steel doors of fridges behind a fully stocked bar, and a fancy outdoor barbecue grill visible through a series of French doors.

"Where's the temple?" she asked, interrupting the senseless flow of words.

"The temple? It's here."

"Here? What do you mean here?"

"I mean here. You're right in the middle of it."

Carmina had the puzzled look of a three-year-old trying to fit a square peg into a round hole.

"Keene didn't tell you?"

"There's a lot of things he didn't quite get to tell me before he died, you know."

"It's the HPS Temple," he said, as if it was self-evident, spreading his arms as if to embrace the decor, with pride. He had to be the priest, assumed Carmina.

"HPS being what? Humane Pentecostal Saints?" she ventured, refraining from sharing that Hysterical Praying Swindlers also crossed her mind.

"Oh my god. There *are* a lot of things Keene didn't tell you."

"You wouldn't believe," she said, taunting his faith.

"Holy Pigskin."

"You can say that," she replied, thinking this was his choice expletive.

"That's what HPS stands for," he clarified. "Holy PigSkin."

"Holy Pigskin Temple? What the hell is that?" She was still taunting—almost hoping to provoke him.

"Keene didn't tell you at all about this? About me?"

"And you are?" asked Carmina.

"I am Father Angelino Santos," he said, realizing that he must have talked to himself for the past fifteen minutes. "But everybody calls me Coach."

Carmina dropped into the closest La-Z-Boy, sighing "Holy pigskin." She wasn't ready for another of Keene's practical jokes. Coach leaned onto the armrest of the adjacent recliner, wondering if his visitor was about to faint.

"Pig skin, like a football?"

"Exactly!" he shouted, exuberantly as a kid having pulled a mischief without being caught.

"This isn't a temple. It's a sports bar!"

"The highest authorities beg to disagree with you," he said, pointing to the official certificate framed on the wall. "We are officially recognized as a church: The HPS Temple. Fully tax-exempt."

Her blank stare called for further explanations, which Coach was delighted to provide.

"Our country's constitution, supreme courts and tax codes are exquisite in their inability to vet theological verity or religious orthodoxy. Jurisprudence establishes that religious belief is personal, and need not be bound by reason and logic. Isn't it amazing? It enshrines the right to any beliefs and unproven theories on the origins and purpose of life and the hereafter, recognizing that holy truths for some are mere heresy to others."

"So?"

"In short, our government doesn't have a clue and, contrary to totalitarian states, is afraid to offend. So our entire public decision making process—from courts to tax collectors—uses the term 'church' but does not define it. Rather, it spells out what is needed to be recognized as a church."

He sprung up from the recliner's arm, with the energy of a preacher, pacing left and right as if walking through the Ten Commandments.

"Item one: A distinct legal existence!" he said, pointing to a framed incorporation certificate next to the tax-exemption one.

"Item two: An established place of worship!" he added, slowly spinning, arms extended at the grandeur of his temple.

"Item three: Regular congregations and religious services! We never miss a Sunday's game, and we congregate non-stop, from pre-season to playoffs.

"Item four: Distinct religious history! It doesn't get more distinct than that."

"You're not unique," snapped Carmina, stunned by the absurdity of it all. "There are tons of other people watching football games every week."

"So what? Tons of civilizations believe in God and they're not all in the same church. Besides, you're thinking about distinct as a synonym of being unique, but it can actually also just mean recognizable and unequivocal. And that, we sure are."

"No doubt—and a bit crazy too," thought Carmina.

"Item five—that's a good one: Literature of our own! What do you think? What authoritative book of sacred writings contains our dogma?"

"The official rule book?"

"Spot on!"

"Wait a minute. Don't you need to have some sort of recognized creed and form of worship, some doctrine, something serious, to be called a church."

"Aha! Item six! Yes, yes, yes, indeed."

He sat back on the armrest.

"You want to know about the serious business."

"That's what religion is all about, isn't it?"

"You're right, Carmina. Who cares about all those rules that require a definite and distinct ecclesiastical government, a formal code of discipline, a membership not associated with any other church or denomination, an organization of ordained ministers selected after completing prescribed courses of study, a Sunday school to indoctrinate the young—"

"So what do you really believe in?" she interrupted, almost annoyed.

"You just said it."

"What?"

"The magic word."

"What word?"

"Believe! It's about beliefs. Unprovable beliefs about unprovable facts. It's the Big Faith! The ultimate answer to the three Big Questions: Where do we come from, why are we here, where do we go after death?"

She didn't know if he was being genuine or facetious. Either Coach shared some DNA with Keene, or they had conspired in mischief.

"And the best part is, you can believe anything you want! Nobody can ever prove you wrong. You are right as long as you believe you are. Isn't it grand?"

He stood up again.

"That, my friend, is the true power of religion," he added, euphoric, like a kid on a cola boost.

"So what's your theory?" enquired Carmina. "Is there football after death? Do you get to meet the grand Jock who created the game, lick his cleats, and listen to his grand plans for eternity?"

"No, no, no. Simpler than that. Invisible to us, in a parallel universe, is an infinite jelly bean bowl from which we all come. We take human form to worship football because that's the only war we tolerate. Hopefully, between games, we do some good. After death, those of us who didn't screw up too badly will ascent to the ultimate status of red jelly bean for eternal beatitude—and a free pass to come back to earth anytime they wish, for another go at the fun ride—while the others have to rot at the bottom of the bowl in penitence, waiting longer for their turn back."

"It's ludicrous! It's an absolutely asinine gospel of no redeeming value. It's an insult to human intelligence. And you got a tax exempt certificate for that?"

She didn't have the energy anymore to jump around, or stand up and leave. She just slumped further into the La-Z-Boy.

"Woman of little faith. You are so lucky that we are a peaceful religion that doesn't burn heretics and infidels, like others casually do."

"You call that faith? You call that the meaning of life and death?"

"What else do you propose? Life is suffering? Deny all pleasures? Spend your every free moments to fast and pray? Deprivation, self-flagellation, abstinence from all that life has to offer? Be my guest. But I think we have it better. At least, we enjoy life while it lasts. And we serve drinks."

"You expect people to flock around that kind of gospel?"

"Flock? No. What for? Growth? We don't need that. For that matter, we don't ban contraceptives for sake of growing our membership ten-fold from generation to generation and achieve world domination, we don't send missionaries to convert people who are quite happy without us, and we don't deride or massacre those too stupid to see the plain holy truth that we have discovered. That by itself is worthy of a tax-exempt status, for lack of a Nobel Peace Prize."

"So is this what it's about? Is Keene dipping in red wine to become a red jelly bean in the hereafter?"

Coach paused for a moment, trying to get the joke, to no avail.

"I have no clue what you're talking about. All I know is that it's better to not wait until one is about to die to ask the three fundamental questions of life, and better to not fall under the spell of an international racket whose sole purpose is to sell you a package of answers while brainwashing you with a social code intended to serve its own twisted agenda."

"An international racket?"

"Exactly. They're easy to recognize as they usually consider themselves to hold the truth and want to tell you how to live your life. Your very own life! They are dangerous criminals who will suck you dry, ready to set up crusades to impose their belief system and peddle their full line of hardware and folk symbols."

Coach paused for a moment, almost as if he felt a disclaimer was in order.

"By the way, the HPS Temple also has a store selling official team merchandise and apparel, but we won't throw an atomic bomb on you if you are not interested and prefer to stick to a rosary or whatever pagan amulet you fancy."

Coach looked at Carmina in her recliner. He did not try to guess why she was silent. Her thoughts were hers and hers alone. He was not in the business of thought control, consistently with his latitudinarian and undogmatic philosophy, unlike others. He trusted that she would find whatever she was looking for in the end, as any quest in itself—with its questioning, hypothesizing, reflection, and rummaging through old and new ideas—is always a discovery. Free will in its purest form, unrestrained.

"We must be one of the rare religions on earth that honestly doesn't care if you join us or not."

Carmina started to laugh.

Nonstop.

A wild and loud uncontrollable laugh of pure release.

The kind of genuine connection with one's inner self that, as therapeutic as a massage, cleanses the mind.

A wholesome laugh that kills the stress and clears the fog.

An insane laugh.

Her first in a long, long time.

This whole church was so much like the new Keene. A masterful engineering construct, wacky to the hilt in its convictions, astute in its unbreachable logic, and endearing in its absolute determination to enjoy life.

"Looks like you've being touched by the holy grace," said Coach.

"It's a miracle, Coach!" she tried to reply between laughs.

"I'll get you a drink. Scotch, whiskey?"

"Holy wine if you have any," she replied, drying her tears.

Coach took his time and came back with two glasses.

"I'm so conventional. Red wine in a church," said Coach, offering a toast.

"Are you going to ask me for a donation now?"

"I hate to say that because we could use a new flat screen television, but no. You're not an official congregation member. You're just a tourist."

A tourist. With all that nonsense, Carmina had forgotten the purpose of her visit.

"So Coach, you seem to know why I'm here."

"Don't you?"

"Not exactly."

Keene's index card only contained an address and the instructions: "Bring back the most important stuff."

"It's a shame. All I knew was that you were coming."

They remained silent for a moment.

Silence can be good.

Sometimes.

Inspiring.

Sometimes.

She wondered what would Sig have done in this temple? For sure, Coach would have been in no danger of seeing his temple set ablaze. She imagined them like two kids in the giant playground temple. With an unquenchable thirst to live, to the fullest.

"If he didn't give you any specific clues as to what you were supposed to do here, maybe he wanted you to buy us that flat screen after all."

"No. As I said, he told me to bring back the most important stuff."

"It can't be the television then, I can tell that much."

"What is it then? You're the priest, you should know."

"I'm the Coach. Not the same thing. I hold no truths. Just beliefs."

"What do you believe then?"

"I believe that what I believe is irrelevant. It's what you believe that matters, isn't it?"

Carmina paused for a while, thinking about the HPS dogma, the jelly bean madness, Coach and his temple, churches and religions. What could be most important in all that nonsense? None of that seemed to matter much. Then, a light flicked.

"You're right," she exclaimed.

"I'm right?"

"You just said that it's what one believes that matters."

"Yeeeeees?" he wondered, unsure of where this was leading.

"So it's me. I'm the most important stuff. To me, I'm the most important thing. I could lose everything else, but if I lose myself, then I might as well be dead. If not actually really dead."

"Oh that. Sure. I'll drink to that."

"Wait a minute," she objected before Coach could take another sip of red wine. "That sounds so selfish."

"Why?"

"The world will self-destruct if everybody only thinks about themselves."

"And why would they have to do that?"

"It's completely egoistic to only think about oneself."

"You didn't say that. You just said that you are the most important thing to yourself."

"Isn't it the same thing?"

"No, no, no."

He started pacing again. Carmina wondered if it was a preacher's habit, as if stimulating the feet did the same for the brain.

"I think you are confusing self and selfishness. Selfishness is driven by the ego, greed, and unbridled ambition. Taken to an extreme, for example, it's easy to imagine what would happen after an earthquake if all those in positions of leadership only acted in ways that served their career ambitions above anything else. It would be like living in a world gone askew—almost absurd—where rampant egos would create multifaceted existential messes when cooler heads should prevail. It would be a disaster in full bloom created by individualism, worse than the earthquake itself. What an ugly mess it would be. Immensely entertaining for sure—the kind of cynical stuff that would make for a fun novel. But that kind of disturbingly narcissistic society certainly would not be an enjoyable world. Selfishness is the domain of ambitious, rapacious, self-righteous, conceited, moronic, and flawed individuals driven by their inescapable human folly.

"Recognizing the self, on the other hand, is recognizing that you have been given a precious life to cherish. A life to cherish, honor, and value—never to be controlled, abused, or stolen by others. Self is acknowledging that life is the most important thing, and taking time to savor it and be dazzled by its simple beauty."

"So what do I bring back to Keene?"

"Just you I guess."

There was a disconnect here. She wasn't about to jump in a coffin with all the other trinkets she had collected for Keene to enjoy his cremation.

"You know Keene's dead, right?"

"Of course."

There had been no such thing as "of course" in the crazy days she had passed, so she had to ask.

"So what does this all mean?"

"I don't know. That's for you to figure out. Maybe Keene wants to make sure that if you are there when he is buried, you'll be there for yourself, not for him."

"He won't be buried. He'll be cremated."

There was no "of course" this time. Obviously, he didn't know the full story.

"Makes perfect sense. It's all about keeping the fire going as long as possible."

"Keeping the fire burning," thought Carmina.

That was the missing connection. It made so much sense. The doubts vanished, the weight of guilt lifted. If Sig had been there, she would have locked him into another choking bear hug.

Sig had attempted multiple times to commit suicide, never succeeding. Yet, how could one consistently fail to kill himself when life is so easy to extinguish? Nobody can be so unskilled, not even a twelve-year-old kid—particularly, a kid like Sig who knew too much about life. Dying is so easy, and living is so hard, that one cannot make a complete botch of all his suicide attempts. Failure in repetition is just a cry for help. She had understood that a long time ago. However, it had just become clear that Sig's pyromaniac tendencies were so intricately connected—not as a separate behavior problem stemming from the same sadness and frustrations, but rather as a desire to keep the fire burning.

Keeping the fire burning.

Setting up fires was like making smoke signals, communicating his will to live. The fire of life that burned in him was one flame that the pyromaniac kid couldn't bear to extinguish. Never. There would always be a flame burning, and he would put it in your face.

Literally.

She had hoped and prayed that Sig had not attempted suicide while away from her that night. That terrible night. She now knew he hadn't. He couldn't. He might have thought about it one more time, seeing the truck coming—too late to escape, it would just have been a mind game to change an inevitable outcome into a deliberate one, but nonetheless a thought. It was an ideal opportunity. Nobody watching. Nobody to stop him. But, by his own reckoning, he didn't see the point. By his own volition, he did not want to commit suicide. He wanted to keep the flame alive. He chose to live—up to the instant he accidentally died.

Keene too wanted to keep the flame burning. Filling his coffin with wine was symbolic in many ways, but it also provided enough fuel for a pool fire to burn for many more hours than the usual expeditious cremation. To Carmina whom he hoped present on that day, it would have been a final testimony of his love for life, his will to live, and his love for her—of his desire to keep the flame burning.

"Keene was a very pragmatic man," added Coach, thinking about his last remark almost like a priest enjoying the symbolic value of fire—but lacking Carmina's deeper understanding of the situation.

Carmina looked at him with an intent gaze. A thought flashed back. A "religious" man might be of assistance with one unanswered question.

"What do you think I should do with the cremains?"

"Depends. Did you love Keene?"

"Yes."

Coach thought for a moment. Carmina saw that as a good sign. At least he wouldn't suggest burying them in the middle of a football field or some other HPS fantasy.

"A lot?"

"Very much so."

"I can't tell you what to do, but if it was me, I'd rub the cremains of my lost love all over myself everyday, for as long as there's enough ashes to do so, and I wouldn't wash for five years. But that's just me."

Imaginary Numbers

Keene was dead.

Again.

After the death of their marriage, and his physical death, this one was the hardest. There would be no more letters, no more divagations, no more odes to the beauty of life, no more treasure hunt—no more of anything that was purely Keene-esque in its beautiful insanity.

The last death was a drought. The flow of letters had dried up and desertification was inevitable.

Within the span of a few days, she had forever lost the only two people who had ever loved her. First, a loner without friends, who, it turned out, was tied to a motley bunch of hidden acquaintances, and second, an unadoptable dejected kid, who turned out to be a sweet soul in bloom. Two beautiful human beings that she thought she knew, only to see their transcendent inner beauty revealed.

Two discovered loves. Two lost soul mates.

Now she was alone.

Alone.

It struck her.

She was just like Keene. Without any friends or family.

Worse, her work had been everything; it had been her entire life. Keene had just been ahead of her by six months on that count.

It couldn't be. She was a personable, outspoken, amiable professional valued by her colleagues and dedicated to her work.

Her work.

That's where it stopped.

At work.

She had to admit; colleagues aren't friends. The psycholo-chick wasn't a friend. The PODWO either. The kids were kids. She had no friends.

She was just like Keene.

Yet, this revelation didn't sadden her. She had a life ahead—more than six months of it—and it was an amazing gift. One she shouldn't squander.

That thought alone gave her strength. It gave her the will to live. Not just to survive, but to revive. Better yet, to relive. Not rhyming those words like some sort of love guru mantra, but embracing them as the only logical path forward, like some sort of engineering logic stripped of equations and scientific basis, down to its core of common sense and engineering judgment. Con-strained to make reasonable decisions in a world of uncertainties, full of perils, in hope of a desirable outcome, at best probable, possibly reliable, never absolute, her engineered choice was clear.

All she had was herself. Eternally indebted to Keene and Sig, but alive and herself. The grieving and mourning wouldn't vanish overnight—the burning pain being too intense—but it wouldn't last, for she knew Keene and Sig were with her. For sure, her two lost loves would live in her heart and soul every remaining day of her life. But far from being enchaining her in a prison of pain and despair, she would soar with them to the higher peaks, souls fused as one. That was to be her destiny, their legacy.

She held those thoughts as inescapable truths, with an unwa-vering certitude.

What remained unresolved, sadly, was Keene's final message. She had collected all the pieces of the puzzle—in large part, thanks to Sig's diligence—but couldn't fathom their collective meaning. The father's day cards, the photo, the shoes, the comic postcard, the genius plaque, the bullets, the ring—and her. Sure, each was a milestone in Keene's life, but she believed there had to be more. It had to be some clever riddle engineered by a wine-soaked sphinx. Some devious game Keene played to give her his last hidden message—to wish her farewell.

Maybe he had intended to give her the key to unravel the code, but died too soon—unlikely as this seemed. Maybe he pur-posely wanted to leave an unsolved mystery to tease those he left behind—like a hieroglyphic enigma that may never be decoded. In truth, she'd never know, which was bothersome. Death has a bad habit of keeping secrets. Of course, maybe there was no enigma, no grand plan, and no logic to it all; maybe this was a garbage collection of dubious sentimental value devoid of any higher meaning. This certainly was a credible hypothesis, but one she couldn't accept. Somehow, there had to be a meaning. An engineer like Keene couldn't vanish without one last practical joke, without perpetrating some final mischief.

She tried it as a rebus, but nothing made sense. The first two items could spell "wish me" or "wish you," depending on perspective, but "shoe card gold bullet ring" or "walk comic sign bang diamond" was total gibberish—even when considering all possible permutations. Sig surely would have stretched it to say, "I wish you walk into a comic bookstore and buy Sig gangster graphic novels—ring them up!" like a little sugar-boosted Robin tackling one of the Riddler's twisted enigmas.

She felt like a poor Robin-deprived Batman.

Taking a different tack, she stuffed all those "treasures" in a box and visited a Numerologist, hoping to uncover a numerology link of some sort between all those items. Given Keene's near conversion to that esoteric creed, it seemed like a worthwhile thing to attempt. Although internet search engines had a tendency to provide the address of "neurologists" to the query "numerologists," she managed to locate one only a few hours' drive away: a nice man who accepted to see her on the same day, in spite of his busy schedule—which Carmina took as a bluff, as she refused to believe that numerologists were in huge demand.

Unfortunately, the nice numerologist looked at the old worn-out shoes, the meaningless postcard, and wasn't inspired. Although he was usually good at figuring out how to make money from any client, the oddity of the request made him question her mental health. There was a law against exploiting the mentally ill, and, as much as he would have like to keep the engraved gold plate for "further study," he feared Carmina might have been a reporter with a hidden camera.

"If these are things that your husband gave you, why don't you just ask him what it all means?" he said, stopping short of saying that her husband would have better luck in bed if he offered her flowers instead of garage sale junk.

She was too embarrassed to tell him that Keene was dead—that she was playing a dead man's stupid game. She didn't want to have to explain the numerology connection, the treasure hunt, the wine, and so came back empty handed.

So she asked Justin.

He was delighted. It was a breakthrough: she had asked him to do something of major significance to her. There was his chance to make an impression on Carmina. But if she was a poor Batman, he was an even worse Robin. The practice of law is about rules, and rules are in books, expertly crafted, factual, direct, and intended to minimize guesswork. He was a lawyer, not Sherlock Holmes. Yet, the potential payoff was incentive enough and he tried with all his might, like a five-year-old spinning a Rubik cube in the hands of luck.

As it became clear after hours of mind twisting that engineers and lawyers lived in different galaxies, and that betting on a lucky break to win Carmina's heart was a tenuous gamble, Justin thought that a good referral might be a more effective way to solve the problem, while still being esteemed for having thought of a solution that might yield positive results. Just like finding a Rubik cube repair shop is just as good—and faster—than hopelessly spinning in place if all one cares about is the result, and not the way to get there.

With Carmina's permission, Justin called Irma Ether, a former client who used to be a psychic, asking if she could, as a special favor, do a reading of some prize possessions for a friend, without asking questions about the origin of the objects.

Irma had closed her business long ago. There had been better times. A few lucky guesses, followed by a steady flow of clients convinced that her psychic powers were above the norm—whatever the norm might be in such matters. Then, as lucky guesses never strike steady, the solid stream of customers dried up day by day, until the psychic business stalled and became a sideline while other occupations took precedence to pay the bills. When her husband died, the insurance payments allowed her to retire, and she closed her psychic shop to the general public.

Yet, some former customers still regarded her talent highly—or at least high enough to recommend her services to friends, for lack of frequent visits themselves. Justin had never been a customer—it was more the other way around, in this case, when her husband died—but she was the only psychic he knew. He insisted on paying for the consultation, even if it was a legitimate business expense that could have been charged to Keene's special last-wishes account. If a psychic couldn't read the subliminal messages left by a dead man, he had no chance himself, so there was nothing to lose.

Irma, thrilled by the referral, had spent the hours before the appointment rehearsing her best stories and refreshing her memory of the tricks of the trade by reading cue cards that she had developed to accelerate her readings and fight the dulling wait between clients. Like a paunchy former body-builder cramming push ups in hope of instantly regaining the muscle tone and bulk of a glorious past, she sharpened her mind flipping through all her tarot cards, prepared some tea leaves, and polished her crystal ball, just in case, not knowing in advance if the nature of the consultation would call for all that paraphernalia. She also downed half a bottle of wine, as part of the sacred ritual—and because she was a bit of a drunk.

The psychic's excitement toward one more thrilling séance of supernatural gamesmanship deflated a bit when Carmina dumped her box on her table. There was not much that was inspiring in it. What was she supposed to do with a bunch of father's day greeting cards, an old photo of what appeared to be a younger version of her customer, and other bottom-of-drawer crud.

She reminded herself that she was a professional. The show must go on. Always. She would need to find the inspiration in Carmina herself instead.

"I see that these are important treasures," said Irma to break the ice.

Carmina was stunned. Treasures. From the treasure hunt, obviously. That psychic was good.

"They are special to my husband."

Treacherous waters. Irma had to establish if the foundations were sound.

"Is he special to you?"

"Very much so."

"And you are special to him."

"Even more so."

"I sense that this is a great love that will be stronger than death," she said, sticking her neck out a bit to see how this resonated with her client.

Carmina smiled. That psychic was not good; she was amazing.

Irma saw that she had scored points. She had also established that the items in the box were genuinely from her husband,
and not from some suspected mistress or other negative source.

"I believe that all these items are extremely meaningful on
their own, but it is their global meaning that is sought, correct?"
she said, not telling her that these words were Justin's specific
instructions when he contacted her.

"Exactly."

"May I touch them?"

"Be my guest."

One by one, Irma took the items out of the box, reverentially,
as if they were objects of a cult in pristine condition.

She had no clue what these old dusty bits and pieces meant,
but it was her special talent to weave a coherent and believable
story from just about anything—stories sometimes so good that
they even convinced her that she was getting her inspiration from
another world, that the words had been whispered to her by spirits
of the ethereal kind, with a little help by those of the liquid kind.

"I must get a glass of wine. This ritual calls for it. Would
you like one?"

Carmina was stunned. It was as if Irma had sensed Keene
floating in Saint-Émilion.

"Do you have Saint-Émilion?"

"You're reading my mind!" replied Irma while getting a second glass. "You're a bit of a psychic yourself, you know."

She didn't have any "saint amoulions" but gambled that
Carmina wouldn't know the difference with a coarse California
red—at least that was wine in a bottle, not in a box. To make sure
she wouldn't see the label, she emptied the bottle into an exotic
crystal container that she normally used as a flower vase. Carmina
assumed it was a decanter fitting for the mysterious decor.

The time it took to pour the glasses and gulp it down proved
valuable to find some meaning to those items she had pulled out
of the dustbin, but it wasn't enough. The junk Carmina had
brought was far from inspiring.

Irma randomly shuffled the items on the table, just like seven
tiles on a Scrabble rack, hoping for words to appear.

More time, she needed more time. More hints.

"That's not just your regular kind of love. It's very powerful. I feel intense vibrations. Your husband and you have an unusually unique relationship."

"It's one of a kind," answered Carmina.

"He likes to build things," she guessed, as most men do—from garden sheds to pyramids, depending on tastes, patience, and means.

"He's an engineer."

She surprised herself for not saying, "was."

"A damn boring engineering," thought Irma. "I need inspiration and I hit an engineer. Damn it."

Irma took the gold plaque. "Wynn Gold - Genius and Fame Manager." Plenty of letters there to do something. She threw out the "Wynn" as this was no real scrabble game—there were no points to be gained by using letters assigned a higher value and she didn't need the aggravation. She kept "Gold Genius Fame Manager." What kind of anagram could she make out of that? Anagrams always impress clients.

Take some words, permute the letters, and get new words with new meanings. It's baffling. No wonder it's so effective to win over clients. It works almost every time.

Fame. Frame. Flame. Male. Female. Female was good, but it didn't leave much else to work with. All she could find was "Female Dangerous Gaming" and "Female Guarding Mangoes." Utterly useless. Did she have too much wine or not enough? She refilled her glass and added the missing drop of "sante meleyon" in Carmina's glass, being a good host.

"I'm feeling amazing vibrations. It's out of this world. He must be quite something that husband of yours."

"He's an angel," said Carmina, not letting Irma on the joke.

At last, something to build on.

Angel. It was there. That's a start.

Angel Madman Fries Gouge.

Angel Demons Gaga Fumier.

Angel Gaga Founders Mime.

Angel Amused Among Grief.

All nonsense, except the last one if Irma had known Keene's story.

Angel Orgasm Enigma Feud. Nonsense too, but orgasm was interesting.

If Angel Nude Orgasm A Gem. Whoa, that was interesting. The wine was definitely working. A few more sips couldn't hurt. What if she dropped the angel and kept orgasm?

Orgasm Genuine Flag Dame. Weak.

"How many children do you have, if I may ask?"

"None," she replied, with a barely noticeable inflection that betrayed her secret. Irma latched on that revealed disappointment.

Orgasm Manage Fluid Gene. Close but a bit too graphic.

Aging Nude Female Orgasm. Sounded like masturbation. But close, she felt it.

Then she saw it. Like a revelation.

"Carmina, Carmina! I see something. It's amazing. You won't believe it. You know what an anagram is, right?"

"Yes."

"Look. When I take 'Gold Genius Fame Manager,' I immediately see two powerful anagrams in it. They're so powerful, they're jumping at me—they're aggressors."

"You do?"

"I warn you they are a bit graphic. Sexual that is."

"In my job, trust me, I've heard it all."

"But they're sexual about you."

"Uh, fine. No problem."

She almost said, "I haven't had sex in so long, what have I got to lose?" but that would have revealed too much.

Irma wrote on a piece of paper "If Angel Nude Orgasm A Gem."

Carmina was amazed. She counted the letter, cross-checking with the gold plaque. All the letters were there, shifted to reveal new truths.

"Wow."

Irma knew she had a special talent with anagrams, but always enjoyed to see her clients' mouths agape. It was like her special standing ovation.

"It's not all."

Immediately under it, she jotted down "Engage Orgasm Fluid Amen." There it was. Graphic lovemaking, ecstasy, ejaculation, conception. Irma downed the rest of the glass, like a due reward while Carmina was still checking all the letters.

"You didn't use the letters in Wynn."

"Never, never, never include the letters from a first name in an anagram," she chastised. "That would corrupt the entire process. That would be throwing all kind of genetic stuff into the mix, like trying to impregnate spirits. No, no. One must always eliminate any person-specific words from the working material of an original host for an anagram to be truthful to another host."

Carmina seemed to swallow it, hook, line, and sinker.

After that tour de force, Irma felt it was "anything goes" with the rest of the objects. She'd get away with it, no matter what—which was convenient as she was getting way too drunk to continue for long.

She lined up left to right the father's day cards, her photo, the shoes, the comic postcard, the ring and the bullets, and pronounced her psychic vision with a solemn assurance.

"The wishing cards, shoes, photo of you, and cartoon postcard are your husband's way to tell you he wishes to walk with you through life as a joyous celebration of your love. The bullet and ring mean that you'll be his wife until death do you part." Ad-libbing under the influence, she added, "and for long after that," because it sounded more romantic.

"Mission accomplished," thought Irma. After all these years, she hadn't lost the magic touch. She gave Carmina her money's worth—actually a lot more given that it didn't cost her a dime, as Justin was footing the bill. Afraid that she couldn't walk straight anymore, aware that a stumble on the furniture or other evidence that she had long lost her balance could ruin her credibility, she remained glued to the table's edge, and let Carmina find her way out.

Carmina was impressed, for sure. The powerful images swirled in her mind, dizzying her as she drove back to her hotel, yet soothing her through a long hot bath, and pampering her as she was laying on top of the bed, wrapped in a towel, motionless in a pensive mood.

Of course it was a fairy tale. Of course she had been played. She knew it full well. The engineering had rubbed off on her, and she didn't believe in psychics. But the wild treasure hunt needed a resolution. Just dumping Keene's prized possession in a coffin would have been wholly unsatisfactory—like a jelly bean without its sugar coating. Her journey couldn't end in a dead end, with two senseless losses and half a life left to live alone. Irma had provided a good story to tie the loose ends, and like a kid who knows from experience that kissed frogs don't turn into princes, that godmothers can't transform pumpkins into carriages, and that going through a looking glass only leads to a hospital, and yet remain entranced by the fantasy, Carmina was enthralled by the beautiful connections that Irma had provided. She was impressed. She was touched.

There were obvious errors. The whole whoopee thing, complete with fluid and baby, was never going to happen—with Keene pickled as he was, he would be quite challenged to impregnate her—but given that she hadn't told her that he was dead, she could be forgiven. One shouldn't expect psychics to guess these things.

Less than forthright, Carmina had also failed to disclose that she was the eight piece of the puzzle. The infinite piece. Not the youthful and naive Carmina whose only wrinkles were those of the old repatriated photo, but today's Carmina: engineering savvy—if only by osmosis—and determined to enjoy life, like Keene did, hopefully longer, no less intensely. An emancipated Carmina.

"Don't belittle the past. I saw all those qualities of Carmina in the gleeful eyes that graced that photo and that I loved."

"Oh, stop it."

"The infinite flavors of Carmina. Some within reach, some escaping me then, but all marvelous."

"Seducer!"

"No, just seduced. You know I've always been spellbound by you."

"Aren't you supposed to be a red jelly bean by now?"

"Of course I am. Engineers are automatically granted that special status upon arrival, apparently in recognition of their contributions to the common good—except for those engineers who served the needs of the military."

"Then why aren't you back here for real, silly. The red ones get to come back I was told."

"Well I'm here, aren't I?"

"Not in the flesh."

"Nobody said in what form the red jelly beans came back."

"This is ludicrous."

"What? Two grown ups talking about jelly beans?"

"No, ludicrous that I've lost you when I've finally found you. Life's so unfair."

"It's not. It's what it is, we're who we are. There's no instruction manual in this package deal, so we can only improvise, trying to put a million-piece puzzle together by trial-and-error. Mostly errors. We get real busy, tying ourselves in chains, building our prisons, oblivious to the nonsense of it all. We just forget to enjoy it while it last. We forgot to enjoy ourselves, Carmina. We gulped it down and choked on it as if it was a race, instead of tasting it to the fullest, slowly, like a good wine."

Carmina chuckled.

"What?"

"I was just thinking. Considering how long you've been soaking in a coffin full of wine, there's no doubt your jelly bean is red by now."

"Yeah," said Keene with a large smile. "Ain't that romantic."

They both laughed.

"I've gone insane. I'm talking to my hallucinations. Just dress me in rags and let me push a grocery cart that carries my possessions, and I fit the bill."

"I'm the one who's gone insane, Carmina. Do you realize I'm talking to a non-jelly bean! I'm illegally crossing a closed border. That's a serious breach of protocol."

"So what? What's the big deal? You'll get punished? You'll get the death penalty?"

"The true penalty is that it's unfair to you. I'm jeopardizing your chance to enjoy the rest of your life. It's dishonest of me. You have to let go of me and find yourself, again. You have to love again. Love yourself, love life, and love others."

"I will Keene. I will. After. After I tell you that you too have been my true friend, my true love, my true lover. I never told you enough. I have been so harsh with you..."

"I broke your heart with my foolishness, my blindness."

"I missed you, Keene. And I miss you now more than ever and I'll miss you forever."

He took her in his arms. She melted.

They didn't need to talk anymore. Their embrace was sweet as a poem, in harmony with the mellifluous music of their hearts. It was a brazing embrace beyond the meek power of words. Souls intertwined, she felt his delicate caresses, his warm breath on her neck, his passionate hug. A long lost declaration of love reborn, touching all her senses, sending shivers down her spine.

Fused together, they shared the pleasure of being one for a brief moment of infinity. An ecstatic moment of infinity. Drugged of each other, they loved each other as if they were discovering how to love life, every breath, every heartbeat, every instant. Their eternal embrace gracefully gliding above the finite world, they harvested energy from the dawn of times to create a divine love.

Caught in perfect harmony, vibrations amplified, in pure resonance, building up exponentially, unbounded, free, unstoppable.

Then, as the crescendo of excitations reached its ultimate climax, where no higher heights exist, like a flame blown by a gust, Keene vanished.

Carmina, on top of the bed, motionless, soaked in sweat, had kissed her lover goodbye. His final embrace would remain with her forever.

Their love never felt so real.

Nothing ever did.

Some would say it was a dream, a vision, an illusion. Wishful thinking gone astray. Foolish sadness harassing a distraught soul. Bruised senses brushing with madness.

Others would dismiss it as nonsense, pure and simple. An improbable story—no, an impossible one. A terrible ending to an unredeemable bad movie. The kind of stupid plot twist only found in cheap literature—not even literature, just cheap fiction from the naive brain of a fledgling author.

But all these gossips and calumnies would be stillborn, as her blessed private moments would remain secret. Her secret. What others thought—could think, would think, might think—was irrelevant. Her life was hers now, forever and ever. It was untouchable.

She knew that every moment of her life, up to their shared orgasmic climax, without any possible doubt, had been real. Pure unalterable reality.

It felt real. It was real.

To all her senses, to all her self.

That's as real as love needed to be.

Pi (Epilogue)

"My dear and beloved Keene. The story doesn't end here as life goes on, as it always has and always will. Even as I stay with you and without you, since you are with me now, more than you ever were, your comforting and everlasting presence is all embracing. And because your story did not end 27 months ago with the most bizarre and combustible cremation ever witnessed on this planet—one that will be fueling entertaining conversations at funeral directors' conventions for years to come—I am compelled to write the last chapter of your saga."

It had taken Carmina more than two years to realize that she had to write the letter that had become engraved in her mind. The one that wrote itself every night, in the dark, a few words at the time, effortlessly, like ghostly apparitions out of nothing but pregnant with meaning, to the point where, after months, each paragraph was clearly formed and memorized. A virtual letter she would read to herself, always reaching the end before falling asleep, sometimes repeating it like a mantra. Like an elegy delivered too late, for she had lacked strength at the funeral and remained silent then. Until it struck her that, if she was to die, which never happens on one's terms and schedule, a fragment of eternity would be again lost. So it had to be written. With resolve, unwavering, she did just that.

"You already know what I'm going to tell you. Your soothing breath on my neck in the wind, the warm caresses of your body through the sun, and the Cartesian humor of your engineering ways in all the gadgets that fail, disclose your presence everyday, like a timeless confession. But it must be put in writing for closure, to be bundled with the letters that documented your journey in the last six months of your life—that extended slightly beyond the decreed 182.5 days, although I'll never know with engineering precision by how much—to leave a record of how you changed my life in unexpected ways, in an emancipating way, for all of us, as we will be forever joined in spirit for lack of sharing the earthly pleasures of life together."

She never cried when reciting the letter alone at night—not even close to a single tear—even though she felt the piercing intensity of each word. But seeing the words on paper, feeling them through another sense, forged an acute connection that had been missing—like completing a circuit to finally bring current to the light bulb—and pushed tears to her eyes.

"This last chapter has both good news and bad news. Knowing you now more than ever, and being thus aware of your preferences in this regard, I'll start with the bad news and serve the good ones later, as a redeeming panacea.

"Sig died, hit by a truck. There. The proverbial bus, but bigger.

"You always told me that the direct approach to deliver bad news is the best one—less unpleasant, less traumatic, less dramatic. It's the engineering way. Just the facts. No softening of the shock, no apologizing introduction, no meandering narrative to create anticipation of the dreaded foreseeable conclusion, no crescendo building up to the terrible outcome; just a straight blow to the face. It doesn't make it any easier, to say, to hear, to write, to read; to realize that, he too, will never come back, and that things will never be the same."

The engineer in her, awoken, was embracing the facts, and not withholding emotions as she knew that behind all those numbers, equations, sketches, and logic, hides the humanity that can be hurt, suffering from the same pain, with the same feelings.

"So he died, and again, I have lost someone I loved.

"Like a freshly bloomed flower swept away by a wind storm, he was robbed of his time in the sun, deprived of the rewards of a warm summer, having only survived a harsh and bitter winter to face a cold and unjust death—as it is always unjust for kids to die and he was still just a kid. He had grown from ugly ducking into a gorgeous white swan, with your unsuspecting fatherly help, but never got his wings. He has been clipped by a careless driver with the audacity to claim for his defense that he couldn't avoid him—as if Sig would have jumped in front of the truck on purpose."

Carmina paused writing, in a natural moment of silence. Staring at the pen on the desk, she was grateful that all the possible doubts had never returned since that day they had vanished. Years ago, Sig could have done that, to show that in absence of freedom and love, there was ultimately one thing he had the power to control in his life; committing suicide for the luxury of deciding when and how to end one's time on earth. Despair masquerading as strength. Or is it the reverse?

On the day he died though, it was crystal clear that he had lost that power, that life now had a grip on him. Besides, a Sig intent on committing suicide would not have purposely left without a warning, or at least a small note—even if only just some hints alluding to his plans, hidden in witty remarks or Daliesque sketches. None of that happened. It was only a cruel and unfair accident. It was true after all—as she now knew with a visceral certainty—that "life's a bitch, that's all there is, and one has to make the most of it."

Keene had said it; Sig had lived it. The brutality of it was raw. Yet life wasn't any less beautiful for it. Just like the most poisonous flower can be appreciated for its intoxicating beauty. Just like the law of the jungle does not invalidate the beauty of nature. Just like the awareness of conflagration and forest fires cannot prevent being enthralled by the mysterious dance of a single flame.

Sig burned like a candle lit at both ends, emanating a hypnotic soothing glow but burning too fast. Like a meteor in a starry sky, he lived only a moment but stole the show from all the other stars. At least, to the eyes of one person, which is all that matters in the end.

She wiped a few tears with the back of her hand before taking back the pen.

"Beyond the indestructible bonds that Sig created in a short time, his physical legacy is a joint one. His webpage 'Keene's Five Stages of Grief' is a big sensation on the internet, with millions of hits every week. Either there are too many engineer-like souls killing time on the internet, or you are having an unmeasurable impact—be it for pure entertainment value or for helping others forced to walk in your last steps recognize that six months can be an emancipating lifetime."

Maybe Sig had found his balance, achieved his plenitude, and just departed because he was ready to do so, or maybe she was just idealizing the situation trying to rationalize the senseless loss. Either way, it offered peace. One that she had to find, as there was no escape from living in the present, the now. There was nowhere else to live. She would have added a sixth level to Keene's stages of grief—an extension of "Verify—never trust a single M.D.," "Quit non-essential activities," "Don't annoy anyone with your booboos," "Survey your options to fill the remaining time," and "Scope out your last project." A sixth stage that should have said "Love, live, and don't look back, as life is now." As adverse to engineering such a statement might appear to the busy bees building the future, forgetting the present as a wager for a speculative future wasn't a gamble worth taking. The present was to be lived—embracing the past as a treasure chest of souvenirs and experiences that contained some unique jewels to forever cherish.

"I will miss Sig every day of my life, for the beautiful and glowing humanity he so briefly rediscovered and revealed. His contagious smile was one more reason to live and will remain etched in my heart forever."

It was pointless to further expand on the bad news. The death of a child was already horrible enough and beyond logic—something that nobody should ever be forced to accept—that continuing piling words together was futile. No eulogy could compensate for Sig's sudden fall from the tree of life. This was her intimate letter to Keene, not a grand drama to play out. The world is already saturated with millennia of literature and theater, as well as decades of cinema and television, that have played out the drama of such a loss, spreading it over pages and hours, expounding on the pain and suffering of those who remained, milking that cow dry of all the emotions it contained. Thousands of writers, directors, and producers have perversely prospered by expertly bringing audiences to the scene, to witness the blood and broken glass everywhere, to be repulsed by the bones protruding out of the flesh and other gory details, to ride in the ambulance together with the sobbing relatives, to watch the futile attempts at reviving the victim in the emergency room or patching it together in the operating room, and to learn the bad news at the same time as the family left without their beloved one, so cruelly cheated by fate.

She had lived all of that nonsense and had no intentions of sharing those details in writing. As much as it might have been highly rewarding drama for some, it was just too painful for her.

As if a part of Keene in her had just awaken, it struck her that if her life was to become a movie, in some strange twisted way, part of the story would be struck out. The Hollywood executives, adamant that Sig's death distracted from the main plot, would order a rewrite to ensure an appropriately uplifting ending full of wonderful clichés. A new ending in which Carmina would have adopted Sig, followed by a string of cute short video clips showing them bonding as a wonderful family, gardening together, harvesting tomatoes and flowers, building up to the final scene in which they would hug together at sunset in front of Keene's tombstone—ashes being not visual enough for the big screen—zooming far out into the sky while the end credits rolled. As dictated by the box-office, all movies must have an uplifting ending; that's the rule. But this was real life, and she had been reminded by Keene that life does not care about happy endings—nor does it care whether an audience leaves the theater uplifted by a love story, or upset for having wasted 25 dollars on a downer without redeeming value that even a giant popcorn bucket could not make enjoyable. If it did, Sig would still be here.

"Fortunately, I also have a few good news items for you.

"First, your three million dollars have been blown in one huge spending spree, approved by your will executor: I have purchased Springwell Ranch, renamed it Keen Hope Manor, fired the entire management team, and replaced those idiots with professionals who love kids as much as—if not more than—the boss does. The new ownership is not sheltered from the vagaries of the economy, but at least, it's no longer subjected to the fickle whims of an uncaring Board of Directors. Caring is all around now. Always. In fact, it so happens that the entire staff always sits with the kids in the cafeteria—spontaneously, not out of requirement or policy, because that's how it should be.

"The second piece of good news is that your well-engineered funeral went smoothly, exactly as planned. To top it all off—something the engineer in you had definitely not anticipated—it was a smashing success with the gathered crowd in attendance. Yes, I took liberty of inviting all your friends.

"Interestingly, even though Frederick had only received greeting cards from you over the years, he cried throughout the entire ceremony, as if his very own son had died. He shed more tears than a little girl would at the funeral of her teen idol. I'm not sure if it has anything to do with it, but since then, he has served as a foster parent for both anorectic Aymee and autistic Austin, who have now each beaten their own record for number of consecutive days in a given placement. Frederick has even approached me to discuss their possible adoption. Of course, he is still a bit pompous, but he has a good heart, and neither Aymee nor Austin would feel compelled to set his office on fire at the first ruffle.

"Didier would have loved to fly over an ocean to attend, but like most dead people, he didn't have a valid passport—it seems that there are some aggravations to holding an 'officially dead' status, and this is one of them. Instead, bartering a truckload of goat cheese, he acquired a laptop and video-conferencing software and I provided a similar set up on our side so that he could at least virtually participate in the funeral. When he saw your burning coffin on his screen, he apologized for having shipped by overnight courier ten bags of marshmallows 'to roast over the bonfire'—as something had obviously become lost in translation during our earlier communication. Half visible on the video screen, sitting next to Didier, was the travel agent who had brought to his attention the fact that his old passport had long ago expired. I was afraid that the whole antics of the funeral would have scared the poor woman away, but last week, I received a wedding invitation from Didier. Whether Didier is resurrecting for the occasion or it will just be a paperless wedding is unclear, but I most certainly will attend.

"Dalton spent the whole event sitting, but he couldn't stop telling everyone about how he had has lost 30 pounds in a few days—which was hardly impressive to those around him, given that he had a remaining 470 pounds to go. He kept saying how the whole process was like preventing a suicide in slow motion and getting a new lease on life, and how even though he had likely melted a bit all around, he felt as if all the weight had been taken off his shoulders. Since then, he has lost another 250 pounds— not all from his shoulders, obviously.

"Hannelore, most elegantly dressed, was accompanied by a slightly older man she presented as a colleague. As I later learned, he was the president of a large skeptics organization courting her, both professionally and romantically. Within a few months, the Flat Earthers and other conspiracy theory believers were evicted from the Conviction Fortress, and the Skeptics Fortress was established. One of the new tenants is the National Interpersonal Communication Association, an organization devoted to the promotion of timely and clear communications between individuals, who has a capable and devoted chair in Hannelore.

"Wynn was quite impressed by the spectacular funeral show you put on. He called it a stroke of genius. Engineers rose a few notches in his esteem. He has also started to hire kids from the Keen Hope Manor as interns. I always send him a few with Sig-like personalities, which can fight for their points of view and remain grounded in reality when facing surreal conditions. The kids have so far come back enlightened—tickled pink to have discovered that there is room for all kinds of people in this world, and dysfunctionality is all relative and not necessarily a fatal condition. Wynn must like the constant whooping they give him, because he keeps renewing his contract.

"Spike came to the funeral with a psycholo-chick of his own, whom he had contacted after Sig and I left his house. Somehow, the fear he saw in our eyes, in spite of his best intentions, convinced him to consult a professional—under a confidentiality agreement, as justice is unkind to vigilantes. Strangely, Dalton and he got along extremely well on that day—I even heard Dalton promise to play a round of golf with Spike the day his weight hit the 200 pound mark—which should be within a few months if extrapolating Dalton's immense progress. Spike's psycholo-chick (whose name is Yumi) encouraged him to release a few primal screams during the ceremony, provided he warned everybody and explained ahead of time that this was solely for therapeutic purposes and done without anger. Didier was convinced he heard one of those screams from his home, even when the sound on his computer was muted—but it likely was just a goat's scream.

"Coach brought the entire HPS Temple choir to the event, and they spent an hour singing various sports anthems—most likely, another innovation as far as funerals are concerned. Nowadays, he serves as the Manor's non-denominational chaplain, helping kids learn to love themselves—and to develop some fondness for jelly beans, together with a little bit of football for good measure. His program is wildly successful, and Coach often brings a bunch of kids along to visit retirement homes; the kids' job is to provide a fresh supply of energy and vitality while his is to explain Keene's Five Stages of Grief, which has become a hit with that crowd too.

"Keene, my dear, you have had a bigger impact than you could even have imagined.

"As for more good news, I would like to introduce you to Angela, a pretty blue-eyed blond that calls you daddy every time I show her your picture. She is an eighteen-month-old perpetual-motion machine, who spends days jumping for the sun, exhausting squirrels and cats by chasing them at warp speed, wearing the stairs down to their undercarpet in imaginary bobsleds, rock climbing the highest bookcases, competing with Ringo on the kitchen pans, and racing her tricycle on the Indy 500 track that circles the house. In her rare quiet spells, she uses all her crayons to draw angels that compete with butterflies for richness and number of colors.

"When her big deep blue eyes look at me, I see the purest love and the deepest and most peaceful eternity unfold in ways that words cannot capture; I see billion-year-old stars pushing a breath of life into a few cells; I see the water sustaining them for-ever returning to sustain us today; I see the cosmic scale shrunk into a blue puddle and life at the sub-particle scale colliding with it; I see the pillars of civilizations that have since long disappeared propping a blank slate asking for wisdom to be engraved; I see Velcro-coated atoms that will cling without release to those kind and open hearts that come too close; I see your eyes; I see you and I."

She had to put the pen down a moment. The same water had returned to her eyes, but they were different tears sprung from a different well. This time, gushing. She shook for a few minutes, giving outlet to all that water that had been dammed for so long. A cleansing flood. She felt submerged waist-deep in the tears filling her office.

The evidence was flagrant. She didn't need any test. There was no doubt in her mind and there would never be. It defeated engineering and scientific logic, but who needs logic. Centuries of enlightenment were constantly flouted by religious beliefs, and scoffed at by the half of the planet still caught in the middle ages by a total absence of reason, so she felt entitled to her very own lack of logic. Besides, what she had in hand was more than circumstantial evidence; it was a living and breathing proof that the universal machine had gone haywire for a moment and created a most welcome anomaly. It didn't matter if it was true or not, if it was an undeniable fact or a figment of her imagination that wished to believe in its desires. It didn't matter if nobody ever figured out how the impossible happened, or if it even did, because she was accountable to no one but herself, and the beauty of it was that she knew it with an invincible certainty.

She took a few minutes to recompose herself, to realign her emotions with her thoughts instead of the opposite. She found the inner peace needed to push the pen further.

"Wynn said that a tsunami of blue and an avalanche of green assault him when he hears Angela's voice, and that he fears she might nonetheless become an engineer, something I don't fear as she wouldn't be one of the boring kind. Just to be safe, Wynn keeps sending her games that claim to develop geniuses, and she truly enjoys putting all those puzzle pieces in her mouth or stacking them to build high-rises for her dolls and teddy bears to destroy.

"Uncle Justin, your friend as you know, has also been spoiling her irremediably, juggling to balance his unbounded love for her with my requests for moderation. Beyond being himself a gift for Angela, and beyond the professional relationship that you imposed on us, the kind but boring lawyer has become a kind and dear friend. Hard as it may be for him, he accepts that friendship as a good start, and recognizes that if it ever was to grow beyond that, he could only be fourth in line after my love for Angela, Sig, and you.

"A few weeks after your funeral, lawyer-like, he presented a most interesting contract which I enjoyed very much, but didn't sign. I told him instead that the best relationships are those free of any impositions or requirements, and that while I welcomed his friendship, only time could tell where it would lead. I'm living the present fully, and we'll see what the future brings."

Carmina no longer wondered if she would ever be ready for another relationship, but rather when. Confident in the strength of her maturity, she felt that Prince Charmings with glass slippers in hand were best left in fairy tales for the naive, and that love was best grown from the inside out. If she was to start kissing frogs, that would be for the love of frogs rather than for other ill-advised purposes—feeling some remorse for having morphed Justin with a prince-less frog in her mind, albeit just for an instant and with the noblest purposes.

"Justin is clueless as to who is Angela's father, and courteous enough to pretend to have no curiosity in this regard, but he has nicknamed Angela the 'little miracle'—leaving it hanging as to whether he diplomatically refers to my age or to the mystery of her conception. Although I'm not the only single mother in the park, he not so tactfully reminds me that I am the oldest one—but cutest one—that he has ever met. That, however, represents a fairly limited sample size, given that my close friends never have a very broad social circle. Yet, with respect to age or time remaining to enjoy life, I'm not sensitive; I'm rather grateful to be still a few years away from menopause—just in case.

"More often than not though, I'm in the park alone with Angela. I've noticed that, for whatever reasons, people are attracted to her. Either cute kids have an irresistible natural charisma, or there is a powerful attraction to the embodiment of a newly started life and of all the opportunities that it offers, maybe because it reminds us of the paradise at the dawn of our own life before that gift became messed up, corrupted, or highjacked, for whatever reasons. Inevitably, past the original attraction and a few minutes seeking interaction with that pure world, people ask me about her father. While the question is presented as small talk, maybe it hides a more serious investigation prompted unknowingly by a response to an instinctive reflex encrypted in human DNA and intended to ensure that the young lives in our predatory world are adequately protected.

"I always answer that Angela's father is a constant traveler, almost like an astronaut reaching for the farthest galaxies, busy working with endless numbers and passions.

" 'Oh, he is an engineer?' they reply.

" 'Yeah, I married a boring engineer,' I always respond laughing, all the while thinking about your wine-filled coffin, your weird friends all over the world, and the other nonsensical fun things I discovered about you—and I. It's a shame that we both found each other a bit too late, but as someone whom I dearly love once said, 'I'm certainly not going to sleep until I die—I've missed enough of life as it is.'

"That is why, everyday, I rub a little bit of your ashes on my arm as a symbol of our communion. I don't know how long you'll last before you're completely exhausted from this intercourse, but to sustain my hope of being able to do that forever, I only rub a speck of dust or two after my morning shower, and never wash my arm thereafter while you're with me.

"Finally, as it should be, every night before falling into a slumber, eternally grateful for another day of awesome pleasure from enjoying the beauties and blessings of this world, I share a glass of fine wine with you, my love."

That final dot in her letter, like a pivot point for the denouement, like a crater left by a lifted anchor, like a long lost landmark finally posted, eternized the letter that had incrusted itself in her heart and soul. Her reborn love to Keene had been sealed and consecrated.

She transcribed the letter on a scroll of rice paper purchased specially for the occasion, with an almost calligraphic penmanship, added a postscript, wrapped the whole thing in a padded wooden box, and mailed it with instructions.

The directions were clear. The box had to be filled with wine—a case of Saint-Émilion was on its way in a separate shipment—and cremated, as a fitting memorial to Keene and his crazy emancipating death.

Like a fitting candle to their love.

Incredible, yet possible.

Forlorn, yet blissful.

Doomed, yet blessed.

Lost, yet eternal.

"More stuff from the wackos," thought the funeral director after reading Carmina's request. It was bad enough that the previous flambé—which nobody was supposed to attend but that attracted a dozen crackpots nonetheless—almost damaged his equipment. He wasn't about to repeat the experiment, no matter the compensation. Sure, he would cash the check, but he wouldn't waste a single BTU of natural gas for some hippie ceremony to honor a goofball.

The scroll was too large to fit in his shredder but would be most suitable for his fireplace where it would burn well along its padded wooden box.

"My dear and beloved Keene," whispered the first line of the scroll, accidentally revealed, like a silky thigh escaping from the slipping edge of a dress. The first few words of a secret, like the tip of an iceberg, cajoling a perverse curiosity.

Might as well snoop a bit, if only to kill time a bit, and be entertained by the batty divagations of his crazy clients.

It was a quick read anyhow, up to the postscript. That last paragraph, in red ink and slanted like an annotation, was unmistakably addressed to a different audience.

"And dear funeral director," it said. "I hope you enjoyed my letter to Keene. Just to let you know, you will also forever remain in our thoughts, not because this whole saga started with your scorn, but because of what you unknowingly represent. In a small way, just like the perennial butterfly leads to a hurricane, just like all of us are butterflies, you are an icon."

"Nutcases! All nutcases," he said as he crumpled the scroll into its box, reminding himself that he much preferred to deal with normal people who died normally and were cremated normally. Although dealing with nutcases had its perks too, he thought, opening another bottle of exceptional Saint-Émilion. Thanks to Keene's conservativeness in accounting for engineering tolerances, his stash will last quite a few years. Or maybe it was all planned that way...

The End

Supplementary Material from
Keene Mason's Day 182.5 Letter

Appendix A

The Kübler-Ross Five Stages of Grief (Denial, Anger, Bargaining, Depression, Acceptance), proposed as a logical and reasonable path along the grief process, to create order out of the chaos of emotions one likely encounters in such circumstances.

It goes a little bit like this.

In the first stage of the cycle, with respect to death, the grieving individual denies the obvious, refuses to accept that an end-date has been irremediably stamped on his forehead like on a grocery item about to turn stale, or like a T-bone about to turn brown, and then green, in spite of all the carbon monoxides sprayed on it to give it an artificial red glow and illusion of freshness. "I can't die; it has to be a mistake; it's the promiscuous drunk-driver next door who never uses a condom and smokes two packs a day who should die first," says the poor mortal in denial.

Then, anger arises. Because an injustice has been committed, because it is unfair that everybody else gets to live, because nothing can be done to change fate, because good money was wasted on a fancy calendar that will only go half used, and because the entire world is to blame for being a hazardous mess of coronary-clogging fast foods, cirrhosis-prone national drinking habits, AIDS-blind peer pressure, emphysema-inducing second hand smoke, myeloma-friendly global warming, and carcinogenic everything else. Anger nurtured by a debilitating resentment for the absurdity of death over life, coupled with a bitter deception for years of foolish privations—never splurging on a convertible roadster or a sailboat to cruise around the world, stupidly saving for retirement instead of maxing out all the credit cards to keep up with the Jones. Anger for loss of control over life and death.

A third stage, of intensity proportional to faith—particularly faiths suddenly rediscovered to hedge bets—is to negotiate with whomever one believes has the power to change the inescapable outcome. Negotiating, bartering, haggling, for a little bit of time in exchange for a reformed lifestyle, a bit less pain against a burst of philanthropy, a little bit of repentance for one more chance to find love. It's "Let's make a deal!" time, and anything goes. But bargaining is grueling when one has nothing to offer, and no receptive ear is listening.

Which leads to the fourth stage, depression. Tears after tears to drown the realization that there is no point after all—the dreadful conclusion that a stolen prized possession will never be returned. The desire to accelerate the process, to end it all sooner, since there's nothing to gain but more pain and sorrows.

Finally, fifth, the slow waiting game, boring as the re-run of a sports event whose final score is known. Taking the time to clean the house one last time, pack suitcases, give the house plants to neighbors, leave money for the bills, draw the curtains, turn off the lights, lock the door, and depart. Alone.

Appendix B

Going wild and crazy, going faster, going charitable, going down, or going spiritual: Conventional things that can be done to fill six months to live, and why they aren't appealing to me. Disclaimer: this list may be incomplete since I didn't buy a book on the topic.

The going wild and crazy option provides a great outlet to release a lifetime of frustrations. Best suited for those who have felt oppressed all their lives, going completely nuts can be expressed by being daring or being a jerk.

Being daring means going extreme, as in bungee jumping, or bodysurfing down rapids (riverboarding), or BASE jumping off a cliff, or wingsuit flying. The advantages of bungee jumping over the other options is that it usually starts at the top of a masterpiece of engineering, like a fine steel bridge crossing a deep ravine. But it's downhill from there. Indeed, why jump in the first place? For what? The thrill of free falling, screaming like an idiot in sheer terror, relying on the saving grace of a big rubber band tied around the ankles by a teenager (who is more attentive to the heavy metal banging on his eardrums through earphones powerful enough to be reference speakers, than to safety measures learned in an intensive half-hour training session), waiting too long for the pull on the ankles to dislocate all vertebras, enjoying the pleasure of bouncing at the end of a rope, upside down, hanging two hundred vertical miles below the bridge, like a worm at the end of a hook, delighted to have forked out an extravagant fee for a souvenir photo to provide incontestable evidence that one has indeed gone completely mad, pleased to still be alive and wondering if it is a worm or a mullet that is dangling at the end of that line?

Being a jerk means, well, being a jerk. Doing things that could taint one's reputation in normal circumstances, but that suddenly seem acceptable to the individual who has no future, based on the conviction that a tainted reputation beyond the grave is immune to the societal backlash that once might have made one think twice before revealing the inner jerk. Some will try to ride a bull naked, or cram as much sex as possible in the time available, or try to have sex while riding a bull, or with the bull; others will gorge on chocolate, candy, ice cream, pastries, fried cholesterol, alcohol—rarely on Brussels sprouts and cauliflower.

For some reason, I do not feel oppressed or repressed with regards to any of those and indulging in extreme sports, sugar, sex—and especially cauliflower—wouldn't be a fulfilling way to spend my remaining time.

The going faster option is for those who keep a list of things they dream to do in life, and now realize that time is running out while most items on the list remain unchecked. Be it a vaporous mental list, or a precise one outlined on fancy paper, life becomes a stampede to fulfill every unfulfilled dream, with activities crammed to pack every idle minute, to turn it into a summer camp on steroids—this being of course the perfect time to max out all credit cards and lines of credit to finance whatever imaginable orgy of extravagant spending, and leave the unpaid bills to the banks. While it can be exhilarating to burn money at warp speed to indulge in the world's oyster, as far as I'm concerned, I can't think of any items to put on such a list at this time.

Traveling? My professional work has afforded me plenty of chances already to witness how people eat, dress, think, behave, misbehave, build, demolish, love and hate differently all over the globe. I do not feel compelled to spend six months in airports, airplanes, taxis, rental cars, and hotel rooms to see more of the same. I have my own photos of the world wonders already. The rest is just more people everywhere, as always.

Things I didn't do for fear of death? None that I can think of. It might be therapeutic for some individuals to skydive or BASE jump, for the sake of confronting their fear of death, but, personally, knowing that death is already in the waiting room, I feel no need to do something just to confront fear—I'd rather confront death itself, in my own terms.

Things I've always wanted to do? I'm afraid my list is anemic. Always wanted to be an engineer—check. Then what? Time, money and health? Had two checked, but un-checking one right now. A loving wife I could grow old with? That didn't go so well up to now, and even though I'm not looking, short of a Russian bride scam, it wouldn't happen in six months. Fancy toys and gadgets? As any good engineer, I already have had all those I ever desired. Fantasy camps and trips? What's the point of paying thousands of dollars on a rock 'n' roll make-believe weekend to shred "Smoke on the Water" with famous musicians-for-hire, pretending to be a rock star—instead of a boring engineer—even if it comes with its own hotel room to trash and TV set to throw out the window?

Going charitable provides an opportunity for all kinds of altruistic endeavors, from volunteering a few hours at the local retirement home to full time missionary work in the third world. To many, such emotional outlets, accompanied or not by large cash donations, can help find a purpose to a desperate situation. However, having already spent half a lifetime in the anonymous service of society, treated as a commodity for most of it, the thought of investing my last chips into doing more service doesn't leave me emotionally charged.

Going down is just to speed up the process—to shrink an agonizing six months wait into an expedient six hours or six minutes one. Techniques abound to achieve this goal, as not-living is substantially easier than living. Engineers have even helped, providing many exciting options to those who desire to end it all in style rather that step out unnoticed. Sometimes with the help of architects, as is the case with the sidewalk railings of the Golden Gate bridge in San Francisco, which were originally engineered to be 5.5 feet tall, but shrunk to 4 feet at the last minute by the bridge's architect—a short man who presumably wanted an uncluttered view of the formidable landscape—turning the bridge into a golden gate to heaven, crossed by one satisfied customer every other week since its opening, in spite of counseling center hotline phones located along the span.

Yet, what's the point of committing suiciding when you know exactly when you are going to die—in 182.6213 days in my case, or a little bit less since time flies as I'm writing this.

That leaves going spiritual. Not exactly a practical engineering project. Humanity hasn't reached a consensus on that topic in more than 182 millennia, so what can I realistically figure out in 182 days?

www.ingramcontent.com/pod-product-compliance
Lightning Source LLC
Chambersburg PA
CBHW060402260626
47160CB00006B/2411